THE CORPS JUSTICE OMNIBUS VOL. 1

Books 1-3

C. G. COOPER

CORPS JUSTICE

"CORPS JUSTICE"

Book 1 of the Corps Justice Series
(originally titled BACK TO WAR)
By C. G. Cooper

Copyright © 2012-2014, 2018, 2019, 2021 JBD Entertainment, LLC. All Rights Reserved

This is a work of fiction. Characters, names, locations and events are all products of the author's imagination. Any similarities to actual events or real persons are completely coincidental.

This novel contains violence and profanity. Readers beware.

A portion of all profits from the sale of my novels goes to fund OPERATION C4, our nonprofit initiative serving young military officers. For more information visit OperationC4.com.

REFORMATTED AND REMASTERED VERSION April 2018

Want to stay in the loop?
Sign Up to be the FIRST to learn about new releases.
Plus get newsletter only bonus content for FREE.
Click here to sign up or visit cg-cooper.com.

DEDICATIONS

To my wife Katie for listening to all my crazy ideas. I love you.

In Memory of Lieutenant General Charles G. Cooper, USMC (Ret)

PART ONE

SECOND AVENUE, DOWNTOWN NASHVILLE, TENNESSEE

The gang members stayed hidden as they watched the young couple from the third story window of the parking garage a block away. The couple was blissfully unaware of the five observers. Why should they worry? They were in the middle of the busy downtown nightlife. Police were present as usual and the crowd flowed smoothly along the packed sidewalks.

The tallest of the gang was a thirty-something Black man named Dante. He had a short Mohawk cut and a pencil-thin goatee looked down at his latest recruit.

"You ready to do this thing?"

The young recruit looked no more than fifteen. His hazel green eyes starkly contrasted with his three-inch afro. He wore an oversized t-shirt with the New Orleans Saints logo plastered from front to back. His huge jeans were sagging and obviously way too big for his skinny frame. He looked like the prototype wannabe gangster. They called him Shorty.

"Yeah. I'm ready."

He was visibly nervous but vibrating with excitement. His drug-induced adrenaline kick was in full effect and he was ready to go. This would be his final step prior to being inducted into the small yet growing gang whose roots began in the hoods of New Orleans but were transplanted during Hurricane Katrina to the confines of Nashville.

The young couple they continued to track was chosen for one simple reason: they were white.

Most other gangs chose a less public criminal act for their young recruits. N.O.N. (New Orleans Nashville) had a special reason for choosing the outwardly normal pair. Although typically a subtle crew, their leader, Dante West, believed that the root of all the suffering he and his extended family had endured during the aftermath of Katrina was the fault of the white majority. Sure, there had been decent white folks who had helped with food and transportation, but his resentment was bred through the constant bombardment of the race-filled preaching of fellow gang leaders. *Shit, hadn't that badass rapper even said that the President hated black people?*

He believed his own gang now thrived because of two things: profitability and hate. Yes, Dante thought, that anger and emotion would help him grow N.O.N. to the size of some of the local Hispanic gangs. Also, Dante's cunning and expertise would further his expansion of N.O.N. The initiation ritual was the one deviation from his otherwise underground organization.

Dante looked down at his group of four brothers. "Now remember what I told you, Shorty takes the first hits. We only jump in if he starts getting his ass kicked."

The other members laughed out loud as Shorty spit out a nervous chuckle. "I ain't gonna get my ass whooped, Dante. That white boy is gonna get his ass whooped."

"I know, I know. You just do this thing right and tonight we'll get you some pussy and champagne."

Shorty nodded and pulled out the slim tools he'd brought for the night's work: an eight-inch buck knife and a metal mallet he'd picked up at a local hardware store. He took an awkward swing with the mallet and a quick stab with the knife. He was ready.

"Shorty, remember what we told you. You're not gonna kill 'em. Just hurt 'em both real good so they remember never to fuck with us."

Shorty made a disgusted face like he hated being talked down to.

"Shit, Dante, I ain't stupid. Just let me do this thing so I can go get me some."

With that Dante nodded and waved his newest recruit toward the stairwell. They let Shorty get a decent lead and then hit street level themselves. Always within sight, he was easy to spot in his black and gold clothing.

They continued to follow as Shorty closed the distance between himself and the young couple. He could now make out their features. The young man wore a pair of faded but stylish jeans and one of those cowboy plaid-looking shirts that were popular. The man looked to be in his twenties, just shy of six feet, and walked with a casual air. He had a medium build. Nothing special. His light brown hair was short and slightly spiked in the front. He looked like a ton of other white boys Shorty saw every day at school. The young man smiled as he talked to the girl whose hand he was holding.

The girl also had light brown hair that she wore straight and that hung just past her shoulders. She was attractive and looked athletic. She wore jeans and form-fitting pink t-shirt. Again, nothing over the top amazing, just normal.

Shorty gauged the distance between himself, the couple, and the alley Dante had appointed as the jump spot. He was twenty feet from the couple. The man and woman were fifty feet from alley. The time was almost right.

As the couple nearly reached the small alley Shorty quickly closed the distance to the couple. The plan was to quickly grab the girl and pull her into the alley. The boyfriend would, of course, follow and try to get her back. Meanwhile, the rest of Dante's crew would close in and seal off the end of the alley and shield the scene from potential onlookers. It would sound and look like a normal post-bar brawl that were common on any night in downtown Nashville.

He could see his soon to be gang brothers swiftly approaching. It was time to act.

Shorty closed the remaining distance from the couple, wrapped his right arm around the waist of the young woman and pulled her into the small alley. She screamed to her fiancé.

"Cal!"

Shorty kept a wary eye on the boyfriend and was surprised to see the young man already following.

Not a problem. His boys would take care of him.

Shorty pulled the now struggling girl farther into the alley and threw her down roughly while simultaneously turning, extracting his weapons, and prepared for the approaching boyfriend.

The young man was five feet away and had a look on his face that Shorty wasn't expecting. Shorty thought the young man would be scared shitless. Instead, his pursuer looked stone cold determined without the smallest trace of fear. *What the fuck?* Shorty thought.

As the final foot between them closed Shorty swung at the man with an overhand chop. The young man ignored the mallet and rushed full steam into Shorty. Both men fell to the ground with the new recruit exposed on the bottom.

Shorty quickly felt the man's hands gripping his head and the man's thumbs found his eyes. *This motherfucker is gonna take out my eyes!* thought a now frantic Shorty.

What Shorty couldn't know was that the young man had realized the trap, although too late, when he glimpsed the remaining gang members block the opening to the alley. His one chance was a full-on frontal assault. Take out the first man, and then see if he could deal with the rest. In the meantime, hopefully his new fiancée could get away and find help.

The man continued to apply pressure as Shorty dropped both weapons and scrambled to free himself. Too late. The would-be victim ripped out both eyeballs as Shorty wailed and clawed at his now empty eye sockets.

The young man grabbed both weapons and hopped back up to his feet.

One down. Thought Cal. He had seen and done worse on the battlefields of Afghanistan. Then it was for his country and the survival of his Marines, now it was for the wellbeing of his new fiancé. *Fuck,* he thought.

As he turned to the alley entrance the remaining gang members closed within striking distance. Two moved towards Jessica and Dante and another slowly approached the young man.

"You shouldn't have done that to Shorty, boy. Now you're gonna get something from me." Dante withdrew a shiny silver handgun from his coat pocket and pointed it at Jessica.

Cal stiffened. "You point that thing at me, mother fucker. You wanna fuck with someone, fuck with me."

"OK, boy." Dante swiveled the weapon back to the young man. "I'll fuck with you now."

Dante leveled the gun back to his fiancé and fired four shots into her body.

"No!" Cal screamed in defiance and with knife leading ran the five feet and jumped on the gang banger closest to his now immobile fiancé. The knife plunged into the chest of his target just as Cal simultaneously brought the heavy mallet down on top of the man's head.

As the man fell to the ground Cal planted his feet, pivoted right and backhanded the third gang member with the mallet in the side of the face. He followed the third crew member's descent and followed the initial mallet blow with a deep knife slash across the man's neck. Blood shot up like a geyser and immediately coated Cal's face and chest as he bent over the now dying man.

He turned back towards Dante with a look of total bloodlust and charged. In his mind he knew that unless he took out these last two men, his fiancé would die. That could not happen. How had he survived multiple tours and numerous wounds in the war-torn lands of Afghanistan only to fall prey to these men?

Although his mind raged with bloodlust, his mission remained clear: Kill the enemy.

Closing the short distance to his assailant Dante fired his remaining rounds at the battle raged young man. Six of the eight shots missed wide because Dante was suddenly unnerved by the skill of this supposedly 'normal' white boy. The last two shots hit their target only because the final distance was a mere two feet. One round hit the young man in the chest and one in the shoulder.

Still the young man managed to grab hold of Dante and take him to the ground. A blood-soaked Cal head-butted Dante two times in the nose before the only other remaining gang member pulled him off.

As he was being pulled back Cal tried to turn and face his newest attacker. Instead he fumbled with the blood drenched weapons and staggered back. With his strength fading and the pain from his two bullet wounds increasing, the young man's mind started to fog. *Focus dammit!* he yelled in his head.

He shook his head and turned to see the fourth gang member. What he wouldn't give to have his pistol right now. *Gotta make do*, he thought.

Instead, he hefted the now excruciatingly heavy mallet and heaved it at the fourth man. Instead of watching whether the mallet hit its target, Cal followed right behind, knife blade once again leading, and bowled over his target while plunging the blade into the man's gut.

The man squirmed, screamed and struggled to get away from his attacker. Cal left the gutted gang member and turned to look for Dante. The fearless leader was now half-staggering and half-running towards the opposite end of the alley, glancing over his shoulder as he ran.

Cal suddenly noticed the presence of a quickly growing crowd at the entrance of the alley. He stumbled for a step and fell to his hands and knees.

"Jessica!" he screamed as he crawled towards his fiancé, who was now lying in a large pool of blood. "Jess!"

He reached her side and painfully pulled himself so that his face was next to hers. Her eyes were strangely clear as she looked at him. He'd seen people die in war and by the look of her wounds he was sure Jessica was on her way.

"Hey, baby," Cal whispered. "It's gonna be OK."

Jess smiled. Her voice was weak. "Don't you lie to me, Cal. You know I always know when you lie."

"OK, Jess, but I'm here with you."

"I love you, Cal. I love…"

"Jess? Jess!"

Her breathing stopped and her eyes lost their spark. Cal's world caved in. Nothing mattered anymore. As he faded to blackness, his thoughts were of Jessica and war. Two things he needed and could never seem to avoid.

VANDERBILT UNIVERSITY HOSPITAL, INTENSIVE CARE UNIT, NASHVILLE, TN

I mages swirled in his mind. The dry air of the open desert. Bloody comrades screaming for help. Friends, family, enemies.

Jessica in a blue gown at the Marine Corps Ball. Jessica walking down the Lawn at the University of Virginia. Jessica crying as he slipped the sparkling engagement ring on her finger. Jessica breathing her last breath.

Jessica, Jessica, Jess…

―――

CAL STOKES slowly opened his swollen eyes. His body felt completely immobilized. *What the hell?* he wondered. Slowly and with no small difficulty, he tried to focus on his surroundings. He was obviously in a hospital. The writing on the door still looked like a grayish blob so he decided he'd figure out the particulars later.

He remembered the attack in the alley. He remembered Jess dying. The pain in his heart returned.

When he thought about that last moment with his dead fiancé, he tried to focus on her beautiful face and her tranquil eyes. He'd always felt that her eyes were what really did him in that first night they'd met six years before. Those beautiful eyes would always haunt him.

As he pondered his misery, the door swung open and a young Hispanic looking hospital staff member walked in.

"I see you're awake," he said. "How you feeling Staff Sergeant?"

Ignoring the question and the comment about his prior military rank, Cal answered with a croak. "Where am I?"

"They brought you over here to Vandy after the attack. You were pretty damn beat up. Haven't seen anything like that since I was in Iraq."

As he talked, the nurse busied himself by taking notes from the machines Cal was hooked up to.

"How long have I been here?" Cal asked.

"About a week. You were full of holes and in critical condition. You got lucky though. The bullets missed anything vital. No permanent damage, mostly blood loss. By the looks of your other scars, this isn't the first time you've spent in a hospital. The docs wanted to keep you sedated for a bit so your body could heal."

"When can I leave?"

The man chuckled. "Just like a Marine. Staff Sergeant, you're not going anywhere for a few days. Why don't you kick back and let us pamper you a bit?"

As the nurse continued around the room in what looked like a practiced habit of checks and rechecks, Cal wondered how he'd found out about his military service. *I guess you can find pretty much anything on the Internet these days. I've gotta get out of here and talk to Jess's parents.*

The man circled around again. "Can I get you anything, Staff Sergeant?"

"Call me Cal. I left that Marine stuff behind. What do I call you?"

"My name is Brian Ramirez. Or you can call me nurse-man."

"You said you were in Iraq. Who were you with?"

"I was with you jarheads. I was a corpsman with 1/2. You were with 3/8, right?"

"Yeah." Cal groaned as he readjusted. "How about I just call you Doc."

"No problem. Takes me back to the days with my platoon. You

dumb grunts can never remember anyone's real name. You need anything?"

"I'm good. Thanks, Doc."

Brian nodded and left the room.

Cal was surprised to have a corpsman taking care of him. Maybe he'd been paired with Brian once they found out he'd been in the Marine Corps. Whatever. He just wanted to get out of the hospital.

OUTSKIRTS OF NASHVILLE, TN

Dante was screaming into his cellphone. "What do you mean that motherfucker's still alive?! I pumped that boy full of lead!" He listened intently as the speaker on the other end of the conversation relayed more information. "Well you tell that bitch she better keep her eye on things and tell me as soon as that fucker gets released!"

Dante stared down at his phone seething with rage. How the hell had everything gone so wrong? A week ago, he'd had a crew of promising members and a highly profitable business. Now he was left with a crew full of worthless bitches.

To make matters worse, the media and the police had picked up on the bloody attack and now Dante was on the run. Never in the same place two nights in a row. He'd done it before down in Louisiana, but this was different. He felt like the whole world was looking for him.

Maybe it was time to head back to New Orleans? No. He had to stay in Nashville and finish what he'd started. Besides, if he went back south he'd be laughed at as he ran back into town hiding from the authorities. He'd worked too hard to let everything go bad. He had too much raw talent.

No. He had to finish things with this damn Marine.

Damn Marine! How the hell could they have known that Shorty was about to attack a Marine hero?!

It was plastered all over the news about how the returning Navy Cross winner and his fiancé had been brutally attacked in the middle of busy downtown Nashville. Local authorities and veterans' groups were in an uproar. Roving bands of retired military and their supporters walked the downtown streets just waiting for provocation.

The Marine veteran had turned into a folk legend in a matter of days. Stories varied as to the exact chain of events from that night (the police were being unusually tight-lipped), but what no one could deny was that somehow this one former Staff Sergeant, in self-defense, had killed three men, blinded a fourth and wounded the only one to escape: Dante West.

What seemed like a simple initiation at one point had now turned into a complete nightmare for Dante and his crew. Just over a week prior his hookers could peddle their wares, his pushers could sell their drugs, and his boys could walk the streets sporting their colors. Now the police had identified the once silent gang. Shorty had helped their efforts by squealing like a pig and unloading anything and everything he knew about Dante and N.O.N.

Other than Dante, the blinded Shorty was the only other gang member to survive Cal Stokes' wrath. Shorty had been taken to the hospital, where he'd been pronounced healthy save the loss of two eyes, and remained under the supervision of the police and hospital staff.

Under very basic interrogation, a scared and defenseless Shorty had divulged the entire plan for the night's attack, including why the couple was picked and who N.O.N. and its members were.

Shorty had outed Dante and his entire crew. It was a complete and total disaster for Dante who'd spent the time since his move to Nashville carefully choosing new recruits and keeping his base of operations under the radar of the local police and other rival gangs.

Now N.O.N. was national news and he'd already felt the pressure from his rivals. Hell, the media had even taken to making fun of the gang's name. Enough was enough. It was time for Dante to take back control. He hadn't worked so hard to let it fall so fast.

He would push the envelope and show that damn Marine how bad things could really get.

VANDERBILT UNIVERSITY HOSPITAL, NASHVILLE, TN

It had been two days since Cal had regained consciousness. His mind's sharpness returned, he focused on exceeding his doctor's expectations of recovery so he could get out of the hospital sooner.

His only companion and now friend was the nurse, Brian Ramirez. Over the preceding two days Brian filled Cal in on what was being televised about the investigation into the attack that killed Jessica.

"So, you're telling me they know who led the attack and they still don't have him in jail?" Cal asked.

"Yep, this guy Dante West is supposedly the leader of this little transplanted gang. They say he's a pretty mean sonofabitch." Brian took a minute to write something down on his clipboard, then continued. "Came up here from New Orleans after Katrina. They interviewed some of his extended family down south and they were all pretty tight-lipped. I think they're afraid of him coming after them. Cops say he was apparently into drugs and running with local gangs by the time he was twelve. Has a long record including attempted murder and battery."

"If they know who he is why can't they find him?"

"The cops I've seen on TV say he's hit the streets. They've got a huge manhunt out for him. Word is the military vets on the police force can't wait to find him and hope he'll go down fighting. Nobody likes the way things went down with your girl."

"Yeah." Cal's voice sounded absent.

Part of him hoped and prayed he would be the one to find that piece of shit. To put a couple rounds into his gut and watch him die might make his despair a little more palatable.

"So, what do you wanna do today?" Brian asked.

"What are you—my nanny now?"

"Let's just say the hospital staff has decided no one else has the patience to deal with a grumpy grunt."

In fact, Cal knew the real reason Brian seemed to be his now constant companion. He had a feeling Brian had requested the crap duty of babysitting him. He'd even heard a heated conversation between Brian and one of the head nurses the previous night. Apparently, it was the end of Brian's shift and the head nurse had pushed him to go home.

Brian had been half yelling, apparently not too worried about who heard him. "If you're so worried about me why don't you go get me a cup of coffee and let me do my job?"

The calming tone of the head nurse's voice was probably a good indication of why she had the job. "Brian, you know we can't pay you for the overtime. Hospital policy is pretty strict on that these days."

"I don't give a shit about the pay," Brian had said. "I'll clock out, but don't tell Staff Sergeant Stokes about it. He's one of my Marines and I'll be damned if he sits here all alone after losing his fiancé. Hell, didn't you hear that even his parents are already dead?"

The head nurse had relented and Brian strolled into Cal's room as if the altercation had never occurred. Cal decided to play along and didn't mention overhearing. Sometimes it was good to have even a swabby corpsman on your side.

"So, what do you wanna do today?" Brian repeated.

"Let's get some of this rehab out of the way. I've gotta get the hell out of this place."

"Alright, Cal, but don't forget what your doctor said. You've gotta take it easy for a while."

"Yeah, yeah." Cal looked up at his nurse. "Look, I've been through this shit before and I'm really getting sick of the crappy hospital food. I'd rather be eating MREs right now."

Brian chuckled. "My ass. All right, Marine. Let me go get a wheelchair and we'll head down to physical therapy."

As Brian left to retrieve the wheelchair Cal started to pull himself up and out from under the covers. He was still in intense pain. Hell, taking a couple shots was never a vacation. Luckily that dumbshit gang-banger had missed anything too vital. Apparently the EMT's and ER staff had patched him up pretty quickly. It also hadn't hurt that he had been shot at point blank range. Better than taking a round at 100 yards.

By the time Brian returned Cal had managed to work up a sweat but had slipped his legs over the side of the bed and was in the process of putting on his hospital slippers.

Shit, rehab was going to be a real bitch.

HEADQUARTERS MARINE CORPS, NAVY ANNEX, WASHINGTON, DC

The Marine Captain had some time between phone calls so he decided to peruse the day's news on the internet. *"The Drudge Report"* was set at his homepage and he did a quick scan of the day's top stories. Capt. Andrews – Andy to his friends – was trying to kill time in an otherwise boring day. He paused a quarter of the way down:

Navy Cross Marine Loses Fiancé in Bloody Gang Attack, Hero Kills Four with Bare Hands

Despite the recent conflicts overseas there still weren't many living Marines wearing the nation's second highest award for gallantry in battle. He knew two personally.

The Captain clicked on the article link and started reading:

In a rare act of restraint, Nashville police have somehow kept a recent bloody attack out of the local and national spotlight. What was initially reported as a mugging gone wrong now seems to be much more.

This publication initially reported that an unidentified man and woman were mugged on Second Avenue in downtown Nashville. The man has been identified as former Marine Staff Sergeant Calvin Stokes. Through our contacts in the military establishment it has been confirmed that SSgt Stokes was honor-

ably discharged from the Marine Corps earlier this year. Even more interesting is that SSgt Stokes is a bonified hero having received the Navy Cross for gallantry on the battlefield in Afghanistan.

Our next segment will have the award citation in its entirety. Our sources have been able to tell us that SSgt Stokes was awarded the Navy Cross for saving the majority of his platoon after being ambushed. Still unconfirmed is whether SSgt Stokes also killed twenty enemy combatants during the firefight.

What we can tell you about this most recent attack in Downtown Nashville is that SSgt Stokes's fiancé, Jessica Warren of Franklin, TN, was killed along with four members of the local gang N.O.N. Still unconfirmed is the status of a fifth man who was apparently blinded during the downtown battle.

Police confirmed that SSgt Stokes is the man responsible for killing the four men, blinding the fifth and wounded a sixth. The method of wounding is still unconfirmed but initial reports from eye witnesses point toward SSgt Stokes using his hands and a knife for the majority of the attack.

SSgt Stokes is currently being held in the intensive care ward of Vanderbilt University Hospital. He is said to be in stable condition.

We do know that local police and the Tennessee Bureau of Investigation (TBI) are searching for Dante West, the alleged leader and founder of N.O.N.

All this raises the question: What happened in that alley?

This publication is still sifting through various eye witness accounts and speculation. If you have any additional information on the attack please contact us through our website or 24-hour hotline.

"Shit," Andy muttered.

He picked up the phone on his desk and dialed information.

"Vanderbilt University Hospital in Nashville, Tennessee, please."

VANDERBILT UNIVERSITY HOSPITAL, NASHVILLE, TN

The phone next to his bed rang. Cal picked it up and answered by habit. "Stokes."

Brian was on the other end. "Hey, Cal. You've got a call from Headquarters Marine Corps. Some Captain says he knows you. You want me to tell him you're out for a stroll?"

"He mention what his name was?"

"Yeah. Captain Andrews."

Cal took a deep breath. "You can patch him through."

Capt. Andrews had been Cal's platoon commander on his last two tours in Afghanistan. Capt. Andrews had then been First Lieutenant Andrews and one of the Marines Cal had saved in that damned ambush. Andrews had reciprocated on their next tour by carrying a badly wounded Stokes, then a Sergeant, out of another firefight. For that action, and for saving a bunch of Marines and Afghan soldiers, Capt. Andrews had later also been awarded a Navy Cross.

The phone clicked through and Cal heard the voice of his former platoon commander. "You there, Stokes?"

"Hey, Captain," Cal answered. "Didn't know they had you riding a desk at Headquarters. You playing butler for the Commandant?"

"Very funny, Stokes. No, they've got me sitting here waiting to take a platoon at Eighth and I. And didn't I tell you not to call me Sir or Captain? We've been through too much for that, brother. Call me Andy."

Capt. Andrews's real name was Bartholomew G. Andrews. For obvious reason he didn't want to be called Bartholomew or the even more heinous Bart. As a result, all his friends shortened his last name and just called him Andy.

"Hard for me to turn that switch off, *Andy*."

Andy paused for a beat. "Just heard about what happened to Jess. I can't tell you how sorry I am, Cal. If I'd known sooner I would've flown out. Anything I can do?"

"You think you can get the Commandant to get me out of this hospital?"

"What kinda shape you in?"

Cal looked down at his body, which was propped up in the hospital bed. "Not too bad. Up and walking. Don't really need to be here."

"If you're still anything like you were a couple years ago that probably means you're pretty beat up," Andy said. "Weren't you the dumbass that snuck out of that hospital in Germany and tried to stowaway in that C-130 on its way back to Afghanistan dressed like a Navy nurse?"

"You know why I did that, Andy. I had to get back to my Marines."

"I know, I know." Andy sighed. "I just want to make sure you take care of yourself. According to the papers, you got into some real shit."

"Thanks, Sir. I just want to get as far away from this place as I can."

"You talk to the police yet?"

"Yeah, they sent in some former Army guy. He was all right. Asked me some basic questions and didn't press too much. If anything, it looks like the cops here in Nashville take care of the military."

"Yeah, that's what I'd heard too. Anybody giving you a hard time?"

Cal thought back to earlier in the week. "Had some random calls from reporters but I've got a pretty good former corpsman that screens the calls for me."

"He the guy I just talked to?"

"Yeah. Pretty good guy. Speaking of which, could you do me a favor and do a little digging on him?"

"I thought you said he was a good guy."

"It's not that. But you know me. Never hurts to have a little extra intel."

"No problem," Andy said. "One of the perks of being close to the puzzle palace is that I can get the scoop on almost anyone. What's the doc's name?"

Cal told him what he knew about Brian, which wasn't much.

"Give me a few minutes and I'll call you back."

The line went dead and Cal hung up as well. Cal mulled over the conversation.

So, Capt. Andrews was at Headquarters Marine Corps. Large probability that they got him to make that move kicking and screaming. The good Captain might not look like much, around five feet nine inches, but he was a helluva shot and knew how to take care of his Marines. Most people thought he was a candyass when they first met him because he looked barely twenty-one, but the man was a natural leader. Under the surface lurked a coldly calculating mind not unlike Cal's. Maybe that's why they'd gotten along.

His mind ticked back the seconds, then the minutes, then hours and days and years, back to when he first met then Second Lieutenant Andrews...

ANDY

Corporal Stokes sat at the duty desk counting down the minutes to midnight. This was the much-loved twenty-four-hour duty on a prime Friday night in July. He had a list of junior officers that were supposed to report in to the battalion from the Infantry Officers Course by 23:59. All of the four reported in at various times during the day except one: a 2ndLt. Bartholomew Andrews.

Bartholomew, huh? Probably some Naval Academy weenie.

The Gunnery Sergeant assigned as the duty officer was a real prick and wanted to be woken up as soon as each officer reported in. It didn't have to be that way, but this particular Gunny, a GySgt. Remer, got a kick out of giving young officers grief when they reported in.

Cal knew why too. The prick had been dumped by two Company Commanders for doing a shitty job as Company Gunny. Now he was assigned to the S-3 shop as some assistant to the assistant's assistant. Basically, the Battalion staff was biding its time until they could dump the waste of space onto another Battalion or get him kicked out of the Corps altogether. Remer loved to abuse any power granted to him by the Marine Corps, even the limited power of the Officer of the Day. Guys like that tend to relish OOD duty as their time to shine.

He'd seen the guy earlier that week, pacing before two unfortunate new arrivals like a rooster with a hard-on. He shoved his pecking beak into one poor officer's face.

"Lieutenant, where are your written orders?"

He liked to say 'Lieutenant' like it was some obscenity he'd been whipped for in Catholic school.

"In my car." The poor guy was shaking.

"In your car?" screamed the Gunny. "Is your car pulling duty now, Lieutenant?"

"No, Gunnery Sergeant!" The young officer was bubbling with unease now.

"You are to carry your written orders at all times like they're nailed to your chest, you understand, Lieutenant?"

"Yes, Gunnery Sergeant!" There was a slight whine in the officer's tone now, like a banshee who'd lost its voice.

"Yes? So, you agree with me?"

"Yes, Gunnery Sergeant!"

"Then why don't you have them with you?"

The officer's jaw jittered for a moment. "I—"

"I what? You gonna start giving me a bunch of excuses, Lieutenant?"

"No, Gunnery Sergeant!"

"Here's what I need, what the Marine Corps needs. I need you to sprint back to your car right now, you understand, Lieutenant?"

"Yes, Gunnery Sergeant!"

"I want you to run like the devil himself is about to rape your mama, and bring me back those written orders, Lieutenant."

"Yes, Gunnery Sergeant!"

"You think you're special, Lieutenant, cuz the Corps doesn't have room for special cases."

"No, Gunnery Sergeant!"

"You think you don't need written orders?"

"No, Gunnery Sergeant!"

"I want you back here in under two minutes or I *will* call the Battalion Commander and let him deal with you." It was said conversationally, like Remer didn't care, but the threat was as plain as the grass is green.

After this lovely exchange, the officer turned and ran. Cal saw the smirk appear on the Remer's smug, self-satisfied face. Then the prick actually laughed out loud.

Cal wasn't looking forward to the last guy, Andrews, getting there. The second lieutenant had ten more minutes. It was also obvious that the Gunny was saving the best for last.

"Bartholomew," the Gunny sneered to Cal. "Anyone with a name like that is just begging to be messed with."

No, Bartholomew wasn't Cal's first choice to name a kid, but at least he had the decency to keep that fact to himself, and not make it the justification for some petty abuse to make himself feel like he had a pair.

At five minutes before midnight, 2ndLt Andrews walked into the duty shack with his orders ready. He looked squared away and fairly at ease. Most new Marines Cal had seen checking in to their first unit tended to be more than a little nervous. This young officer didn't seem to have that problem.

"Checkin' in, Corporal."

Cal looked up at him. "Roger that, sir. If I can just get your orders. I've gotta go get the duty officer to get you logged in."

"No problem."

Cpl. Stokes got up and walked smartly into the next room, which was used for the duty officer and his clerks as a sleeping area.

"Hey, Gunny. That last Lieutenant just walked in."

Remer opened his eyes with what looked like a mixture of disdain and excitement. Yep, he was gonna give the new guy some kinda shit alright.

Cal waited as the Gunny took his time putting his utility blouse back on and donning his web belt with pistol. Cpl. Stokes was surprised the guy could even fit into any issued gear. The Gunny's belly gave his buttons a workout.

Finally ready, Cal followed Remer back into the duty shack. Not two steps through the door, the Gunny started in.

"You Lieutenant Andrews?"

"That's me, Gunny," Andy said. "Just checkin' in."

"I'd appreciate it if you called me 'Gunnery Sergeant,' Sir."

That was one of Remer's favorite lines. Get the young officers off-balance from the get-go.

"Sorry, Gunnery Sergeant. Didn't mean any disrespect." Lt. Andrews responded without the obligatory flush of embarrassment. Cal couldn't yet put his finger on it, but he didn't think this baby-faced butter bar was even close to being a candyass.

"Says here you were supposed to report in by 2359, Lieutenant. It's now 0002."

Andy nodded toward Cal. "As I'm sure Cpl. Stokes will tell you, I stepped in and reported at 2355."

The Gunny smirked. "Well, sir, that's not really my concern. The point is when I put you in the logbook, you'll be reporting in late. Helluva way to start your tour with this fine battalion."

Just then Cal caught the look of cold anger flash across the eyes of the young officer. Then just like that, it was gone. This guy was no candyass.

From the look on the Remer's face, it was obvious he'd missed the warning sign. Cal decided to step in. "Hey, Gunny, the Lieutenant's right. He checked in right at 2355. I wrote it right here in my own log."

"You shut your mouth, Corporal," Remer snapped. "Looks like you'll have to come back tomorrow morning to meet with the Battalion XO, sir. He likes to come in Saturday morning and check-in with the OOD to see who fucked up the night before."

Surprisingly, Lt. Andrews still stood in front of the duty desk with a look of complete calm. "OK, Gunnery Sergeant. Why don't you just pick up that phone and call the XO right now. If I'm gonna get my ass chewed, I'd rather not wait until tomorrow."

Visibly confused, Remer paused to think about that most unexpected request. Calling the Executive Officer would put *his* ass in a crack, and he was all about keeping his ass out of cracks no matter whom he had to blame to take the fall for him.

Remer's voice became condescendingly soothing. "Well, Lieutenant, I don't think it's appropriate to call the XO at this hour. Why don't you just come back in the morning and I'm sure everything will be fine."

"I think I'll take my chances, Gunnery Sergeant. Why don't you give me his number and I'll call him right now on my handy-dandy cellphone."

The corner of Remer's mouth twitched, barely imperceptibly. He was starting to lose his patience. "Now, Sir, that's really not how things are done around here."

Andy's voice was suddenly commanding. "Well then how are they done around here, *Gunnery Sergeant*? It's obvious you get your rocks off shitting on us new guys. Get the damn XO on the phone and we'll get this done. *Now*."

The placid demeanor had evaporated and a look of calm fury now radiated from the young officer's face. And by the look on Remer's face, the shitbird Gunny was finally getting the point: He'd messed with the wrong guy. He could either back down or push forward. Cal hoped he'd pick the first option.

The Gunny sneered in Andy's direction. "Now look here, *Lieutenant* I don't appreciate—"

"Get on your feet, Marine!" Andy bellowed. "You stand at attention when you talk to me, *Gunnery Sergeant*."

It therefore came as a complete surprise to Cal when the Gunny jumped out of his seat and popped to attention. *Holy shit!* What was going on?

"Now as I see it," said Andy, "you have two choices. Number One, you log me as reporting in at 23:55. Number Two, you get the Battalion XO on the phone right now and he can resolve the issue. What's it gonna be, Gunnery Sergeant?"

Remer stammered as he answered the other man. "I'm just trying to do things by the book, but I think we can trust your word that you reported in at that time."

"Sir."

"Excuse me?"

"I said you call me '*Sir*'," Andy said. "I'm only asking for the same respect you so kindly asked of me."

"Yes, Sir," the Gunny said.

"Alright, let's get this done so Cpl. Stokes can get some rack time. He's looking a little sickly."

As Remer leaned over to begin his entry in the duty logbook, Lt.

Andrews gave Cal a quick wink and a mischievous half smile. It was the same smile he'd see years later on the side of some God-forsaken mountain in Afghanistan as he and Lt. Andrews prepared to rush an enemy position by themselves.

And it was that first meeting, and the look in that young officer's eyes, that made Cpl. Stokes think he never wanted to get on the officer's bad side.

VANDERBILT UNIVERSITY HOSPITAL, NASHVILLE, TN

The bedside phone rang again a couple minutes later. Cal picked it up on the first ring. "Stokes."

It was Brian. "Cal, I've got Capt. Andrews on the phone again."

"Put him through."

"You there, Stokes?" Andy asked.

"Yes, sir."

"I got some info on your corpsman."

Cal shifted into a more comfortable position. "What'd you find?"

"Says here that he served with 1/2 during the initial invasion of Iraq. He got to be part of that big mess in An'Nasiriyah. Hold on a minute."

Cal heard mouse clicks on the other end.

"Well, well," said Andy, "looks like you've got yourself a brother there, Marine."

"What do you mean?"

"This record says that Hospital Corpsman First Class Brian Ramirez is a multiple award winner. Won a Bronze Star in Iraq then a Silver Star in Afghanistan. Hmmm... the first was for dragging some of his Marines out of a burning AAV. Says he got some pretty bad burns himself. The Silver Star citation says that this kid not only saved ten of his Marines' lives, but that he also took up a couple M-16s and killed a few bad guys."

"No shit?"

"No shit."

"Impressive. Well, at least I know now."

"Need anything else?" Andy asked.

"Unless you can get me out of here, I'm good."

"Wish I could, buddy. I'll be in touch."

The line went dead. Cal replaced the receiver and laid back in his bed.

So, Brian was a warrior. *Interesting.*

A FEW MINUTES later Doc Ramirez came in to check on Cal.

"What do you want for dinner tonight?" Brian asked.

"You didn't tell me about your Bronze and Silver Stars."

Brian quirked an eyebrow. "You didn't tell me about your Navy Cross."

"Fair enough. I'd give that thing back just to have my guys alive right now."

"Me too. Now, what do you want for dinner? Chicken or mystery meat?"

Cal snorted. "I'll take the chicken."

As Brian nodded and left the room Cal thought about the quick conversation. It was rare to find a medal recipient who bragged about their award. Most just wanted to be left alone. He'd seen guys give their medals away as soon as they'd been received rather than once again re-live the memory of their dying comrades. Funny that heroes come in all shapes and sizes, but the true heroes are almost always silent about their accolades.

Brian returned balancing a cafeteria tray with a domed cover. The faint smell of roasted chicken wafted toward Cal.

"Hey, Doc, wondering if you could do me a favor."

Brian set the meal down on the table next to Cal. "What's that?"

"I was wondering if you could swing by my place on your way home and pick up a couple things for me."

"You have a place here in Nashville?"

"Yeah. I've got a little condo down in the Gulch."

"Sure, no problem. You got your keys?"

"You actually won't need any. There are two keypads: one at the building entrance and one at my unit. I'll just give you the codes."

"Ew, fancy. What are you some rich kid?" A brief look of anger passed across Cal's eyes and Brian backtracked. "Did I say something wrong?"

Cal shook his head. "Don't worry about it. Can you run by there tonight?"

"No problem. I get off at seven. I'll run by after that. What do you need me to pick up?"

"Call me when you get there and I'll walk you through it. Won't be easy to find without me telling you."

Brian's eyebrow rose. What was this Marine having him deliver? He'd find out soon enough. He was *pretty sure* he could trust Cal Stokes.

GULCH DISTRICT, NASHVILLE, TENNESSEE

Compared to Brian's tiny apartment, Cal's building was the Taj Mahal. He pulled up to the side of the high-rise condo. *What the hell does this guy do for a living now that he's out of the Corps?*

He got out of his car and walked to the building's entrance. A collection of mixed citizenry walked the sidewalks on either side of the street. Brian could see at least two high-end restaurants within a block of Cal's building. Looked like the area was really taking off. He'd heard that there'd been a lot of redevelopment in the Gulch in recent years. Not a bad place to live.

The passcode Cal gave him got him in the glassed front door. A few steps inside he could see what appeared to be a receptionist glancing over at him. As he got closer, she perked up.

"Can I help you, sir?"

"I'm good. Just picking up some things for my buddy in the hospital."

She looked startled and came out of her seat.

"Is that Cal you're talking about?"

"It is."

"Oh my God, is he OK? We heard all about it on the news! He's such a nice guy. When is he coming home?"

"I can't say for sure, but he's doing a lot better. I'll tell him you asked about him..."

"Irene."

"I'll tell him you asked about him, Irene."

Brian exited the elevator on the 23rd floor. There were only two doors visible along the hallway. Cal's was almost directly across from the elevator.

He quickly punched in Cal's code and entered the condo. Despite its opening smoothly, he could feel the weight of the door. Standard issue or an upgrade Cal had installed? *Curious.* The thing reminded him of some of the armored vehicles in the Corps.

By habit he turned around swiftly to lock the door and deadbolt it. No deadbolt. There were, however, two buttons; one about two feet above the door handle and one two feet below. He pressed the button above the handle and heard a mechanical scrape as the deadbolt engaged. He did the same with the lower button then turned to get his bearings.

Even the lobby downstairs hadn't prepared him for this.

What was visible of the unit was almost completely open. You could see the living and dining area from the kitchen. It looked like there was another hallway leading to the bedroom.

The furniture looked new and modern in a Spartan way. Color accents here and there but mostly clean lines and polished stainless steel.

He hadn't met many enlisted guys with a place like this. Once again, he wondered what Cal's whole story was.

What really took his breath away was the view. One whole wall consisted of windows that faced the Nashville skyline. At this time of night, he could see the city clearly.

He pulled out his phone and dialed the hospital switchboard. Seconds later he was connected to Cal's room.

"You get in OK?" Cal asked.

"Yeah. You said you had a little condo in the Gulch. I wasn't expecting Superman's Fortress of Solitude."

"Where are you standing right now?"

"I'm in your living room."

"OK. Head down the hallway toward my bedroom in the back."

"Got it." Brian made his way toward the hallway. Walking into the bedroom he noticed the pictures on the wall. Cal and his fiancée in every shot. *Poor bastard.* "Alright. I'm in your bedroom."

"Go over to my closet and open the doors."

Brian pulled open the two doors, peered inside the huge walk-in, and switched on the light. The closet felt as big as his apartment.

After a couple seconds' pause, Cal continued. "Go to the back of the closet and open the panels of the built-in armoire."

"Done."

"Now take out the bottom right drawer."

Brian put a hand on the handle but didn't pull on it. "You mean open it?"

"No. Take the whole thing out and put it on the floor."

"Now feel along the right side of where you took the drawer out," Cal said. You should feel a button about the size of a dime. Press it and step back."

He suddenly had the nagging sense that he wasn't going to like what was coming next. This was obviously a compartment for some kind of secret stash. Drugs, or something worse.

With some trepidation, he pressed the button and heard a mechanical click. He could now see that the interior of the wardrobe had moved forward a bit. There appeared to be a seam in the middle.

"All right, now open the panels. Once you get that open there's a separate light switch inside."

Brian pulled the two heavy panels apart and stepped back. Well, it was definitely a secret stash. Just not the kind Brian had imagined.

Neatly held in racks, and now lit by the interior light, was a bottom row of an assorted number of rifles. The top row was half pistols of varying calibers and half full of other gear like knives, GPS, compass and survival gear.

What the hell? thought Brian. *This Marine is ready for war.*

"Grab the first pistol on the top left," Cal said. "Should be my Beretta nine mil. Grab the one next to that too: the forty-five caliber Springfield XD."

Brian shook his head but didn't move. "Hey, man, I can't bring these things back to the hospital. Administration tends to frown on personal arsenals."

"Look, Doc. I know I'm asking a lot on this one but I need your help. You should know me well enough by now to understand that I don't like asking for help."

Brian laughed. "Saw a small glimpse of that the other day when you refused my help getting up to take a piss and landed flat on your face."

Cal sighed, like the memory was a sharp pain in his side. "Yeah, I know. But look, I just have this funny feeling and I want to be prepared. You ever get that feeling in your gut while in the field that something bad was gonna happen?"

"Of course, but, Cal, this is different. You're not in the field and you're surrounded by trained hospital security staff. Not to mention the local cops are always stopping by to see how you're doing."

"You're right," Cal said slowly, "but I thought the same thing about taking Jess out to dinner at a seemingly safe downtown restaurant." Cal let that sink in for a couple seconds and continued. "You know I wouldn't let you take the heat for this. If anyone finds it on me I'll blame it on myself. Thing is, the minute I walk out of that hospital I'll need to have some protection of my own."

Brian's stomach was uneasy. He trusted Cal, but the thought of bringing loaded weapons into the hospital still did not sit well with him. Worst case, he could get fired *and* thrown in jail. He liked his job at Vanderbilt and wasn't planning on leaving anytime soon.

On the other hand, whether a new friend or not, Cal Stokes was his brother-in-arms, a fellow warrior that upheld the highest standards of the military establishment. He knew deep down that Cal would never let him take the fall.

In for a penny, in for a pound.

"OK," he conceded. "You said the Beretta and the Springfield. Anything else?"

Cal went on to ask for a couple boxes of ammunition and one of his knives from the top row. Then he instructed Brian to grab one of his gym bags from the front of the closet, fill it with some random clothing and hide the weapons inside.

Brian put the phone down and grabbed the first pistol, reflexively ejecting the full magazine and checking the chamber. *Fully loaded. Just like a Marine.*

The next pistol was the same. With both magazines reinserted he stuffed each into a separate pair of boxer briefs. Next, he grabbed two boxes of ammunition: one of 9mm and one of 45 cal. He finished by hiding the knife in a pair of socks and loading some workout pants, shirts and sweatshirts on top.

Mission completed, he picked the phone back up. "Anything else you need?"

"Yeah. Grab my cell phone. I think it's either on the kitchen counter or on my nightstand. Thanks again for doing this, Doc."

"Yeah, yeah. You just make sure that if we get sent to jail you're the one that gets to bunk with Bubba."

Cal chuckled. "You got it. I'll see you in the morning."

Brian put his phone back in his coat pocket, picked up the gym bag, now laden with a small arsenal, and took it out into the bedroom and laid it on the bed. He went back into the closet, closed the hidden panels, replaced the drawer, and re-sealed the armoire.

He found Cal's cell phone on the night stand. The thought occurred to him that it was strange how Cal didn't have it with him that night. Didn't most people carry their cell phones everywhere?

He did one final sweep of the condo. Pausing by the nightstand, he grabbed the photograph of Cal and Jessica. It was a portrait of the couple sitting on the edge of a dock at some lake. They looked happy.

With the small picture frame now wrapped in a t-shirt and safely packed in the full gym bag, he headed for the door.

BRIAN DECIDED on the way back down to the lobby not to wait until the next morning to get the weapons back to Cal. The night staff at the hospital was lighter and going in through the staff entrance would attract less scrutiny.

He waved to Irene as he went by.

"You tell Cal that we want to know as soon as he's getting out," she said, her voice obnoxiously bubbly. "Maybe we can throw him a little party when he gets back."

"Hope I'm invited," he replied.

It was small talk. The last thing Cal would want coming home was a cocktail party. Guys like Cal didn't want or need that kind of attention. Better to be among close friends or, even better, with a couple Marine buddies drinking beer and swapping sea stories.

He'd tell Cal that the girl had said hello but also warn him about the possibility of a homecoming fiesta. The idea triggered an uncomfortable memory lodged in the back of his brain.

His parents had thrown him a surprise welcome home party once, when he'd returned from overseas. By then, unbeknownst to him, the Navy had already informed the Ramirez family of Brian's valor in battle. His parents decided the best way to convey their pride was to show off their son to a bunch of friends and a few neighbors Brian didn't even know.

He still remembered the look of devastation on his mother's face as he'd screamed at her for throwing the party. She'd left the room crying. Somehow, his father diplomatically ushered the guests out of the house.

Looking back now, his soul ached at the memory of his behavior. It wasn't their fault. His parents were not raised in a military family. They had no idea what it was like to serve in the armed forces. To them it was all parades and a clean-shaven son returning home with apple cheeks and great posture. They just wanted to celebrate their son the hero, to honor Brian in the only way they knew how.

The last thing he wanted was public recognition for acts of gallantry. He didn't even want the awards they'd given him. He just wanted his Marines back.

In time, he'd managed to explain this to his parents. His mother and father loved their only son, evidenced by how hard they worked to understand what he'd been through, realizing that there might never be a right time for him to tell them the whole story.

He'd seen other friends return to similar homecomings, families that had not understood their need for privacy. It was never a good thing. Such breaches of personal space tended to wear out familial bonds, as if no one in the family spoke the same language, causing resentments over a small matter of communication.

That was a problem with serving in the military. The only ones who understand what you've gone through are those who've served as well.

FIFTEEN MINUTES LATER, he pulled into the staff parking lot and headed through the staff entrance carrying Cal's things. Security presence was scarce, mainly because most of the doors were locked, only accessible by key-card at this time of night.

He was back in Cal's room in five minutes.

"Hey, doc, I wasn't expecting you back until tomorrow morning."

"Yeah, well, I didn't really want to be lugging around your arsenal for the next twelve hours."

"Thanks again for going. I won't forget it." Cal's eyes were sincere.

"Yeah, yeah. Just don't let anybody see it. It's my ass if the Marine I've been assigned to gets caught with all that gear. Just be careful, OK, Cal?"

Cal nodded and struggled out of bed to grab the gym bag. "Hey, Doc, you wanna do me a favor and go watch the door for me?"

"Sure."

Brian walked over to the door and leaned against it, keeping an eye at the window slit while Cal unpacked the bag.

The first item he pulled out was the framed picture of him and Jess. He stared down at the picture and touched Jess's face.

Maybe bringing the photo wasn't the best idea. There was something terrible in the Marine's eyes. They watered, as if the pent-up grief was about to overwhelm his resolve.

Something in the man's face changed. His jaw stiffened. Brian heard the sharp intake of breath through the nose. Cal's body straightened as he reverently placed the picture frame on the side table. The whole series of bodily motions, which took all of eight seconds, conveyed a single, powerful decision: *I'm not gonna do this now dammit.*

Next, Cal checked the weapons to make sure they were loaded and ready. Then he took both guns, loaded each into one of his white socks, and stuffed them back into the bag along with the knife.

The Marine had a conspiratorial grin on his face. "The dangerous stuff is back in the bag, Doc. Have a seat if you want to stick around."

Brian narrowed his eyes at him. "Stick around for what?"

"You'll see. I've just got a feeling."

Cal grabbed his cell phone, sat on the edge of the bed and started scrolling through the phone's touch screen. He shook his head and mumbled, "A shit-ton of voicemails."

Brian moved up next to Cal and looked down at the phone. Cal clicked a small camera icon on the home screen and entered a nine-digit pass code. Video footage appeared in a series of scrollable files.

He couldn't believe it. Cal was scrolling through videos taken at his condo.

"Hey, is that me?"

"Yep. I'm starting with the most recent and moving back. I've got these things rigged so that they're motion sensitive. Got 'em hidden pretty well in each room. Bet you didn't see them, did you?"

Brian shook his head. "Why do you have all that surveillance gear up? Speaking of which, what's with the armor-plated door and access code add-on?"

"I thought you might pick up on that. You're not as dumb as you look, swabby." Brian rolled his eyes as Cal continued. "The video surveillance gear is actually through a local security company. Nothing too fancy. I had it installed just as a precaution. I've found you can never be too safe. I usually turn it off while I'm there so I don't waste space filming myself in underwear."

He turned the phone so Brian could get a better picture. "See, here's you getting to my front door. The next camera picks you up coming into the foyer, et cetera."

"Pretty cool."

"Yeah, my dad was in the security business. I guess I picked up on some of his habits."

Brian added that tidbit about Cal's dad to the back of his brain for inquiry at a later date. A family security business would definitely explain the vault and arsenal at Cal's place.

"So, what are you looking for?" Brian asked. "Just want to make sure I wasn't rifling through your panty drawer?"

"Just want to see if anyone else made a visit." Cal sounded distracted.

As Brian watched, Cal fast-forwarded through the footage. He saw the front door's exterior camera pickup residents walking by Cal's unit. After a couple minutes of forwarding Cal stopped. "Hmmm. Looks like Irene stopped by."

"Hey, isn't that the girl from the front desk?"

"Yeah, her name's Irene. Nice enough girl, but kind of nosy."

"She said to say hello by the way."

Cal ignored the comment and kept his eyes on the small screen. At first, Irene looked like she was knocking on the door. Then she pulled out her cell phone and made a phone call while standing right in front of Cal's door. She looked nervous. The video didn't have sound but Brian got the impression that Irene didn't like what she was hearing from the other end.

Finally, she hung up the phone and put it back in her pocket. She approached the door again and it looked like she was entering a pass code to get in.

The next frame showed Irene stepping into Cal's foyer just as they'd seen a few minutes before with Brian's visit to the condo.

Cal sat up. "What the hell is she doing?"

"Maybe checking to make sure you hadn't left the stove on or something."

"Doubt it. The building staff isn't supposed to enter the private residences unless there's an emergency. Plus, she doesn't know I have cameras installed."

As they both watched, Irene made her way through the living area and kitchen. She seemed to be looking for something. She paused to open random drawers and peer inside. Nothing she saw seemed to be of much interest.

"What the hell is she looking for?" Cal said.

Irene moved from the living area to Cal's bedroom. She opened the drawers on the bedside table and picked up Cal's cell phone out of the charging cradle. It looked like she'd pressed the unlock button on the phone but without the unlock code she quickly grew frustrated and put the phone back down in its charger.

She moved to the other side of the bed and picked up a small package that appeared to have already been opened.

Cal clenched his teeth. "Tell me that package was there when you went by, Doc."

"Yeah it was there, I think. What is it?"

"Just a little engagement gift from Jess's parents."

Peering back down at the phone, they watched as Irene set the package down and advanced her search.

The woman did a quick scan of the bedroom closet then headed back towards the main living area. She looked around one more time then left through the front door.

"Irene's gonna have a little explaining to do."

Brian crossed his arms. "You wanna tell me what's going on?"

"The less you know the better, Doc. I already exposed you by having you go by my place. Don't worry about it. I'll take care of it."

Brian scoffed. "Look, brother, I don't know what the hell's going on but I do know that you're in no condition to be doing much of anything. So, if you need help, I'm here."

Cal stared at Brian for a moment and nodded. "If this goes to shit in a couple days don't say I didn't warn you."

"Sounds like what my platoon sergeant said to me after I volunteered for that ambushed patrol."

"Didn't you learn never to volunteer for anything in the military, Doc?"

"Yeah." Brian smiled. "I guess I'm just a slow learner."

"OK. Here's what I think." Cal looked back down at the video. "That guy that attacked me, Dante West, isn't done with me yet. I'll bet he's not happy about what I did to his crew. He's also pissed that I messed up his face."

"You think he's coming after you?"

"Yeah."

"Why not your family?"

"All my family's dead. I'm all that's left."

Brian's eyebrows knit together. "What about all those phone calls you've been getting? The ones you don't want to take?"

"They're guys with my dad's company. I'll deal with them later."

"Hey, man, I know this whole situation sucks but you've gotta talk to someone. You can't just hole up here and pretend the outside world doesn't exist. I'll bet those guys are worried about you."

Cal stared at Brian for a minute then nodded. "I'll call them in a minute. Can you do me another favor?"

"What now? You want me to go break someone out of jail?"

"No, smartass. Can you go get me some coffee? I think this is gonna be a long night."

Brian agreed and left the room. As he made his way to the cafeteria, he thought about what Cal had said about his family. He was sure Jess's family had tried to see Cal, only the stubborn Marine had refused any and all visitors.

He also had a stack of messages from various callers all waiting to check on Cal's condition. Brian had kept tight-lipped until now, but he knew that would have to change. In order for Cal to make a full physical and, more importantly, mental recovery after losing Jess, he'd have to let his friends help. As a nurse and corpsman, Brian had seen a lot of troops clam up and refuse treatment. Some never made it back to reality. Others drowned their demons in booze and drugs.

Cal Stokes didn't seem like the type to go off the deep end, but having a strong support system would still be crucial in getting back to full form. If Cal didn't make the calls himself, Brian would make some for him.

There's no other decision to make when your brother falls. You pick him up. That's that.

VANDERBILT UNIVERSITY HOSPITAL, NASHVILLE, TN

Cal Stokes stared at the ceiling. He had the urge to chuck pencils at it. A moment later, Brian entered clutching a stack of papers in one hand and a cheap Styrofoam cup in the other. At least it was hot.

"Forgot I'd stashed this back at the nurse's station. Phone messages."

Cal grabbed the coffee and the inch-thick stack of messages. "This many people called for me?"

"Yeah. You must be famous or something." Brian chuckled. "I put what sounded like friends and family on the top and left the reporters and weirdos on the bottom."

Brian left the room and Cal looked down at the top message. It was from Jess's dad, Frank, earlier that morning. He thumbed through the rest and saw that Frank had called at least three times a day. Under those messages, was a bunch from his dad's company: old friends checking to make sure he was OK. *Sorry guys but you'll have to wait a little bit longer.*

He took a deep breath, picked up his cell phone and dialed Jess's parents' number by memory. Frank picked up after the first ring.

"Cal?"

"Hey, Frank... I... I..."

All his experience in tactical maneuvers, and yet nothing prepared him for this moment.

"I know, son..."

Suddenly, Jess's old man was real. He wasn't just some piece of collateral damage to be figured into the equation after the fact. He saw the man's kind eyes in his head. Remembered the plainspoken way he had about him. The way he called him 'son'.

Cal could hear the muted crying on the other end, and that's when he lost it. "Frank, I am so sorry... so sorry... tried... sorry..."

Something had crawled inside the hole in his life and poked at its walls with a dagger. It began with a soft sob, and a feeble attempt to suppress it. All decorum went out the window and he broke, dropping the phone into his lap.

The tears and the sobs continued for a few minutes.

This was grief. This was every loss magnified, replayed. This was the dagger poking, sticking and twisting in his gut. He'd run this conversation over and over before it happened, but all his preparation was for nothing. The depth of his grief and despair lay open.

He'd lost the love of his life. The one woman who'd understood him. The woman who could help him make sense of all the madness in the world. She'd filled in all the empty spaces. Now that beautiful woman was gone. He hated that the only picture he could remember of her was the final moment in the blood-soaked alley. No one should die in a place like that. Especially his wonderful Jess. *I'm so sorry, Jess.*

To his surprise, Jess's father was still on the line when he picked it up.

"Son, are you OK?"

How can he ask me something like that right now? Shouldn't he be yelling and screaming at the man that got his daughter killed?

"Yeah, I'm OK. Frank, I just want to say I'm sorry..."

"It wasn't your fault, son. You did your best. Jess wouldn't want you to blame yourself."

Cal could barely keep his voice above a whisper. "I know."

"When can we come see you?"

"I'd really rather come to you guys," Cal said. "When's Jess's funeral?"

"We were waiting to hear from you. When are they releasing you?"

"I'm not sure. I've got a couple other phone calls to make. Can I call you back when I know more?"

"Sure." Frank paused for a beat. "And, Cal?"

"Yeah."

"I love you, son."

Unable to respond, the tear-soaked Marine hung up the call. He couldn't bring himself to turn his head and see the picture of his beloved, captured in one of their happiest moments. He understood now why some cultures erase all physical traces of a deceased family member. We are finite vessels, after all, and some grief is just too much to bear. He realized that not even a lifetime in battle could prepare you for the death of a loved one. The pit of emptiness he felt in his stomach threatened to overwhelm him. He tried to push it away.

Work, dammit. I have to work.

He took a cleansing breath, followed it with a healthy swig of tepid hospital coffee, and turned to the stack of handwritten phone messages.

The next calls were from his cousin, Travis Haden, a former Navy SEAL who ran Cal's father's company.

He speed-dialed Travis and waited for his cousin to answer.

"Cal?"

Cal took a deep breath before answering. "Hey, Trav."

"Shit, man." Cal could hear the relief in his voice. "What the hell is going on? Why didn't you return my calls? Me and some of the boys were about to raid the hospital!"

"I've had a lot on my mind, Trav."

Trav's voice grew softer. "Yeah, I know. I can't tell you how sorry I am about Jess, cuz."

"Thanks, but I really don't wanna talk about it."

"OK. How about you? How are you feeling?"

"It's never fun to be shot, but I'm doing OK."

"What are the doctors saying?"

"They say I need some physical therapy and want me to stay here for a couple weeks. Is there anything you can do about that?"

Travis always seemed to know someone that could pull a few strings. "I've already looked into it. How about we get you a ride in an ambulance back to the compound and have a doctor check on you a couple times a day?"

Cal thought about the two-thousand-acre campus south of Nashville that housed Stokes Security International (SSI). It would be good to see it again. "I'd love it. I can even put up with any doctor if I can come home."

"You got it, Cal. Let me make some calls. You sit tight and I'll call you back within the hour."

With that, the phone went dead and Cal put it back on the nightstand.

The rest of the messages were from friends/employees within SSI. He'd wait until he got back to the compound before talking to them.

True to his word, Travis called back within the hour.

"So, I talked to the hospital staff and they weren't too happy about the situation, but I explained that we'd have a doc to escort you back to the compound and that he'd be on-call twenty-four-seven."

Relief flooded Cal's body. "Cool. Thanks for doing that."

"They only had one request. I guess they've got some male nurse taking care of you?"

"Yeah. Former corpsman. Good guy."

"Perfect. Can you get him on the phone?"

"Yeah, hang on while I press the call button."

Thirty seconds later, Brian walked into the room. "What's up, Marine?"

"I need you to do me a favor. My cousin's on the phone and he's helping me get out of here. He needs to talk to you about some request the hospital's made."

Brian tilted his head in confusion but nodded and grabbed the phone. "This is Brian Ramirez."

Cal watched as Brian nodded his head and grunted "yes" a couple times. Then he said, "Yeah, I can take some time off."

Cal couldn't hear the conversation but he had a feeling about what was coming.

"OK," Brian said. "I'll see you soon."

Brian handed the phone back to Cal.

"You wanna tell me what's going on, Trav?" Cal asked.

"Brian will fill you in on the details. We're working to get the ball rolling and get you out of there today."

"Awesome. Thanks again."

"No worries. I'll see you soon."

Cal replaced the phone on the nightstand and looked at Brian. "What was that all about?"

"Your cousin just hired me for a couple weeks."

"*He what?!*"

"I guess the hospital would only let you out of here if one of their staff went along with you," Brian explained. "Since I've been your wet nurse they figured I was a perfect fit. That way the hospital minimizes its legal exposure and you get good care. I've got some time off I can take anyway AND your cousin said he'd put me up in that compound place and pay me double what I make here. Any chicks in the compound?"

Cal laughed. "Only one and you don't want to mess with her."

"OK, then let me get some things together and I'll pack up your stuff. Anything you need?"

"Any way I can avoid you being my babysitter?"

"Not if you want to get out of this hospital. Just suck it up, Marine, and let me get paid."

Cal reclined again and turned his eyes back up to the ceiling. It wouldn't be so bad having Brian around. Walking was still a chore. Having someone he knew pushing him around in a wheelchair might be OK. Plus, the compound was a big place and he'd have way more to do there than he would sitting around the hospital. Hell, SSI was technically *his* company after all.

The future brimmed with possibilities.

Chucking pencils at the ceiling wasn't one of them.

CAMP SPARTAN, ARRINGTON, TN

"OK, Cal, we're pulling into the compound. How are you feeling?" The voice belonged to Dr. Rich Hadley, the physician Travis had hired.

"I'm good," Cal said, coming to after a quick doze in the ambulance. "Here already? I was just getting used to your stories."

Dr. Hadley chuckled. He did not have what you would call a 'normal' medical practice. After successfully completing his double residency and fellowship in internal medicine and general surgery, Dr. Hadley had decided to take a left turn, becoming a concierge doctor for the country music stars in the Nashville area. It was "Music City" after all.

It was a great conversation starter, which had paved the way for a sort of interview session Cal conducted to pass the time on the car ride.

Dr. Hadley had struggled for the first couple years after school, until he'd met Cal's cousin Travis. Travis, being the social butterfly that he was, quickly became friends with outgoing and adventurous Dr. Hadley. Both were in their late thirties and had the luck of being endowed with rugged good looks. Both shared a love of two things: outdoors and women.

Between the pair, they'd cut a wide swath within the ranks of the southern belles in Nashville.

Over time, Travis had introduced Dr. Hadley to his country music friends. In the past five years his private concierge practice had grown to include most of the respected country singer/songwriters in the area. Why go to a crowded clinic when you can call your own doctor?

Dr. Hadley had also been more than happy to help Travis and SSI on occasion. This was one of those times.

"Once we stop I'll have some of the guys lower your stretcher down and roll you into the VIP quarters."

"Travis is putting me in VIP?" Cal asked.

"You'd rather he put you in one of the Quonset huts?"

"Not really."

"Good. Now make sure you don't move around while they cart you in. Travis would be pissed if I delivered his favorite cousin in a bloody mess."

"Whatever you say, doc."

The ambulance pulled to a stop and Cal could hear the driver getting out of the cab and closing the door. The back doors were opened and Cal saw a couple of the roving security guards moving in to help lift the gurney out of the ambulance.

Cal looked around and felt the pull of home. He'd spent plenty of time in the compound that his father had christened "Camp Spartan" due to his fascination with the ancient warriors of Sparta, but also due to the fact that it was a fairly accurate description of the spartan facilities.

Much of the compound was modeled after Marine Corps bases. You had headquarters and then separate buildings for each division. Battalions were located on the lower levels of their respective division.

Cal's father had put a lot of time into hiring former military. He understood that these warriors craved the familiar look and feel of military surroundings. That's not to say that the grounds weren't state of the art. Cal Sr. had insisted on having a top-notch facility while at the same time maintaining a Marine Corps look and feel.

The compound was actually more of a campus. The mess hall was located behind the headquarters building, and the living quarters just behind that. One of the things the company found was that many of the families of employees also enjoyed living in close proximity, just as they had on military bases around the world. As a result, a portion of the campus was devoted to single-family homes for the families of SSI employees. There was even a condominium compound for non-married employees.

It was easy for spouses to come home for lunch or meet their families to eat in the mess hall. Needless to say, morale was high as was retention within SSI.

The exception to the spartan décor was the VIP quarters. Housed on the highest point of the property, the structure looked like a huge hunting lodge resplendent with a carved log exterior and large paneled windows. There were even rocking chairs on the huge front deck for visitors to enjoy.

The entire structure stood at right around 30,000 square feet with ten large guest suites. It was, therefore, no wonder that the employees had taken to calling it the Lodge.

Soon after SSI experienced its enormous growth, Cal Sr. realized the benefit of having the ability to house VIPs on site. It allowed visitors to see firsthand the inner workings of Stokes Security International. If potential clients weren't sold after the initial presentation, they certainly were after being wined and dined by the staff at the Lodge.

Dr. Hadley directed the paramedics to take Cal up through the ramped entrance. Cal noticed Brian standing next to his car parked in front. The former corpsman walked over and followed the crew into the building.

Brian leaned over and whispered in Cal's ear. "Do I get to stay in here too?"

They moved into the inner sanctum of the Lodge. An old-fashioned bar, fully stocked, stood in the corner facing a variety of comfortable looking leather chairs.

"I'm sure they're gonna put you in one of the suites next to where they've got me."

"Suite?"

"Yeah." Cal laughed. "They've each got a couple bedrooms and a nice living area. This is where the company houses visitors, prospective employees and VIPs."

Brian continued to stare wide-eyed as they passed through each enormous room. "Are they looking to have an old corpsman turned nurse on staff?"

"I don't know. I'll ask."

Cal smiled at his friend, glad to have some levity in an otherwise degrading experience of being wheeled in on a gurney.

They arrived at a bank of elevators. Dr. Hadley pressed the button for the second floor. "Travis has you in the corner suite."

Cal nodded. He thought that's where they'd keep him. The corner suite was more like a Presidential Penthouse. 4,000 square feet of living area, way more than he needed, but at least he could take advantage of the view. The floor to ceiling windows overlooked the majority of Camp Spartan. It would be good to see it again.

The team moved into the oversized elevator and it rose to the second level. Exiting the elevator, they turned to the right and headed to the end of the hall. One of the staff members withdrew a card key, inserted it in the lock and held the door open for the stretcher.

Brian, who'd been following behind, let out a small, impressed gasp.

The place was huge. Furnished with the same décor as the rest of the Lodge.

"What do you think?" Cal called back to him.

"I think the corner suite is bigger than any house I've ever lived in."

Dr. Hadley was all business as he instructed the crew to move Cal to the oversized sofa that faced the glassed wall. With some effort Cal scooted to the edge of the gurney, maneuvered over to the sofa, and sat back.

"I'll call Travis and let him know you're settled," said Dr. Hadley. "I'm sure he already knows you're here, but he wanted me to give him a heads-up once you were safely in your room."

"Great. Now I'm gonna have to check in with Trav before I take a piss."

Dr. Hadley pursed his lips. "You know he's only looking out for you, Cal."

"I know, Doc."

"Here's my card. If you need anything call me. For the rest, Brian will take care of you. I'll stop by a couple times a day to check in. I'm right down the hall."

"You're staying here too?"

Dr. Hadley grinned. "Are you kidding? Have you had the bread pudding here? If your cousin is going to employ me I will be happy to take full advantage. Besides, my place is thirty minutes away and Travis' instructions were for me to be immediately available."

"Thanks for doing that, Doc."

"Don't thank me. Thank Travis for paying my enormous bill."

The good-looking doctor smiled and left the room.

Cal turned to Brian. "I'll bet he's not even charging us. The good doctor tries to play the part of the money-hungry surgeon but it's obvious he enjoys this cloak and dagger stuff."

"Yeah, I got the same vibe. Seems like a pretty good guy. You know, for a doctor."

"Yeah."

"All right. So now you're gonna tell me what the hell this place is. What does your dad's company do? They must be making millions."

Cal laughed. "You want the long or the short version?"

"Where do I have to go? I'm your babysitter, remember?"

"Don't remind me. OK, I'll start at the beginning…"

CALVIN STOKES SR.

Cal's father was a rising star in the Marine Corps during the first Gulf War in the early nineties. He'd been commissioned in 1971 just as the Vietnam War was in full swing. After attending The Basic School, he'd been shipped first to Okinawa, Japan, and then to Vietnam.

He'd commanded a platoon and earned a Purple Heart and a Silver Star during his two tours. Cal remembered how his father had described those times patrolling the paddies and jungles of Vietnam. It was also where he'd learned the importance of two things: completing the mission and taking care of your Marines. It was a lesson he carried on in all aspects of his life up until the day he died.

Throughout the seventies and eighties, Cal Sr. moved up through the ranks while at the same time moving his small family all over the world. There were stints in Camp Pendleton, Monterey, Okinawa, Camp Lejeune, Nashville for recruiting duty, and more. Along the way he and Cal's mother, Denise, bore a healthy and rambunctious little boy.

Cal had enjoyed his early days on Marine Corps bases. Living on a military base had its perks: a high level of security for family, a large number of young children to play with, good prices for food and a solid school system. It was a life you could get used to.

Needless to say, over the years Cal Sr. did more deploying than fathering. That wasn't to say that he was a bad father. Actually, the opposite was the case. He cherished his time at home with his wife and son and took full advantage of being on leave.

As Cal closed in on his teenage years, tensions increased in the Middle East culminating in Iraq's invasion of neighboring Kuwait. He remembered watching the footage with his mother, both knowing that it was only a matter of time before Col. Stokes would lead his Marines into battle.

Sure enough, orders were quickly passed down through the ranks and Cal Sr. headed to war commanding his regiment of Marines.

Left at home, Cal's behavior took a nose dive. In retrospect, Cal understood that the way he'd acted was his method of dealing with the possibility that his father could die. First it was talking back in school. Then it was a fight with one of his classmates. Finally, Cal was arrested by the Camp Lejeune military police when he got caught breaking into the PX at two in the morning trying to steal cigarettes.

Cal's mother was devastated. Not only was her husband at war, her only son was now a criminal.

Word travels fast on Marine bases and this was no exception. Mrs. Stokes soon received a request by the base commanding general to come for lunch. The wives of Marine colonels do not get invited to lunch with generals. If anything, it would have been the general's wife doing the inviting.

Again, not so in this case. Mrs. Stokes arrived at the commanding general's quarters the next day. She was ushered in by the general's aide.

General Willard met her at the entrance to the dining room. "Nice to see you again, Denise."

"Thank you for having me," she said demurely.

"Why don't we have a seat. Gunny Fred is about to bring out some club sandwiches. Does that sound OK?"

"That would be fine."

The two moved to the dining room table. The leaves had all been taken out and what could at times seat twenty officers and wives now could only seat six diners total.

They both sat down and the food followed shortly. The general made small talk as they ate. Ten minutes later they were both finished and Gen. Willard began.

"Denise, I just wanted to have you by so I could make sure everything's going OK at home. I know how trying it is to have Colonel Stokes overseas. Add to that the mischief Cal Jr's been getting in and I know you have your hands full."

More than anything at that minute Denise Stokes, a proud southern woman and wife of a Marine colonel, was embarrassed and frightened. She'd always enjoyed the evenings at the Officer's Club mingling with the other wives. This was something entirely different. To be summoned to the throne room was unbearable.

"General, I know there's nothing that can fix what my son has done. I only ask that he be given the punishment he deserves and maybe he'll learn his lesson. I will say that I have tried my best but sometimes teenage boys don't want to listen to their mothers."

"I appreciate you saying that, Denise," said General Willard. "You do, however, realize that Cal Jr. is part of the Marine family and as a Marine I have a duty to help."

"I understand."

"How about I have a little talk with the boy? Maybe even give him a tour of the local juvenile detention facility. I know the warden pretty well and he's always happy to help me keep our kids on the straight and narrow."

"If you think that would help, I'd be much obliged."

General Willard nodded sharply. "Consider it done." He turned to the door and yelled for his aide. "Captain Nelson!"

Capt. Nelson walked into the room. "Yes, General?"

"Please schedule to have my driver pick up young Calvin from the Stokes residence tomorrow morning at 06:00. Bring him to the PT field and then I'll ride back with him to the office."

"Yes, sir."

General Willard turned back to Mrs. Stokes. "Well then, Denise, please don't hesitate to call if you need anything. Anything at all."

"Thank you, Sir."

She sincerely hoped she would never have to call the General. She picked up her pocketbook and made her way to the door.

The next morning, right at 06:00, Calvin Stokes Jr. was waiting with his mother on the front step of their two-story home. He wore his best Sunday khaki slacks with a white button-down shirt. His hair was buzz cut as he'd worn it during the past year and the look of anger and dejection was evident on his face.

The night before when his mother had arrived at home, she'd delivered the news. A screaming match ensued ending with Cal slamming his bedroom door in her face. Temper tantrum or not, he was ready for the General's driver at 05:30. He knew the alternative.

Without an appetite, he waited quietly, glaring at his mother as she'd casually eaten her own breakfast.

A government vehicle pulled up at 06:00 and what looked to be a six-foot five Marine sergeant stepped out of the driver's seat. He was dressed in firmly creased utilities and marched smartly to the door.

The sergeant had a baritone voice. "Mrs. Stokes?"

"Yes, Sergeant, I'm Mrs. Stokes."

"Is the young Mr. Stokes ready to go?"

"He sure is, Sergeant. I appreciate you coming out here to get him."

"Not at all, ma' am. You ready to go son?"

Cal sounded nervous when he answered. "Yes, Sir."

"Don't call me Sir, son. You can call me Sergeant Kraus."

"Yes, Sergeant Kraus."

"Well let's get going. The General's waiting."

He walked back to the car and held the back door open for Cal. Cal slid into the back seat and fastened his seat belt. Sgt. Kraus waved goodbye to Cal's mother and walked around the car into the driver's seat.

Kraus started the car and they began their trek. Cal looked back to see his mother still standing on the front step. Too mad and embarrassed to move, he didn't even wave back.

The next eight hours were torture for Cal. Sgt. Kraus picked up the general at the PT field and then took the pair back to the Headquarters building. The whole way not a word was spoken to Cal who sat sullen in the back. All his bluster from the night before had evaporated.

After a stern talking to while standing at attention in front of the general's huge desk, he was taken by the ever-present Sgt. Kraus to the juvenile detention facility just off base in Jacksonville, NC.

There the warden, stone-faced but cordial, instructed his staff to get Cal dressed in a prison jumpsuit. He'd changed into the oversized outfit under the disapproving glare of two male and one female guard.

Then the warden, followed closely by Sgt. Kraus and the three prison guards, gave Cal a careful tour of the entire facility.

Cal saw the looks on the faces of the kids serving time. Some looked scared. Some looked resigned. Others just looked like career criminals. By the end of the two-hour tour, Cal knew he never wanted to return.

Although the shock of the prison tour seemed effective for the short term, Cal soon fell into his old routines. This go-around, however, he did a better job covering his tracks. He no longer committed outright mischief; instead he skirted the rules and bent them to his will.

Even at a young age, Cal excelled in academics. He'd enjoyed a challenge and far outpaced his classmates. He now used his mind to mold the rules as he saw fit. He was never again caught for any overt acts of fighting or stealing, but he would return home with smoke and beer on his breath. His mother could never prove it.

His behavior remained poor until Cal's father returned from war. The homecoming was more of a relief to Mrs. Stokes than to Cal. He waited with a mixture of fear and anger as his parents discussed his fate.

Looking back, Cal knew his disruptive attitude was a kid's way of coping with an absent father, but even in the midst of the turmoil, deep down he knew he'd crossed the line. That did not, however, mean he would beg for forgiveness. It wasn't HIS fault that his father had gone off to war.

Col. Stokes received the news with a strange calm. He'd already been tipped off by a friend on the Commanding General's staff so he knew the majority of Cal's infractions. Coming home from his second war, Cal Sr. understood the actions of young men. When given the chance, they could excel beyond anyone's imagination. Left alone without proper guidance, young boys could just as easily fall on the wrong side of the tracks.

Col. Stokes understood why Cal had misbehaved. It didn't make it right, but it was what it was. So, although his star shined bright within the Marine Corps, Col. Stokes personally delivered his retirement papers to the commander of Second Marine Division the next day. The general did his best to set Cal Sr. against his chosen path, but the Marine and more importantly, the father would not be dissuaded.

Col. Stokes knew it was time to spend more time with his family.

THE STOKES FAMILY packed up and relocated back to Nashville, Tennessee, a few weeks later. Through teary goodbyes with lifelong friends and an emotional change of command ceremony where Col. Stokes was awarded the Legion of Merit and a Bronze Star, the Stokes clan moved on, uncertain of the future.

Cal Sr. used his considerable accrued leave time to reach out to his numerous contacts in the civilian world. Throughout his time in the Corps, he'd come in contact with various influential individuals both on the national and local scene. Although his skills from the Marine Corps didn't equate to one particular job in the civilian world (not many regiments to command on Main Street U.S.A.), his Marine determination knew he would find something.

He spent his days making phone calls and his nights and weekends with the family. Most time devoted to the family found Cal and his father bonding and figuring out each other. There were camping and fishing trips. All the while, Cal's father treated his son like a man and started to relay life's lessons.

Cal's spirits and attitude improved. He'd needed his father and once again things felt right in the world.

Not long after settling in the Nashville suburb of Franklin, TN, Cal Sr. was hired by a local government facility as a consultant to evaluate the facility's security and operations. The contact had been arranged by an old friend now serving at the Pentagon who had sung Cal Sr.'s praises to regional director in charge of all of Tennessee state's federal facilities.

Although he'd never done anything like what he'd been hired for, the money was right and like a true Marine, he'd figure it out as he went.

Long story short, after evaluating the facility, interviewing employees, cataloging procedures, and simply observing for six weeks, Col. Stokes delivered his thirty-page summary to the regional director. The director was very pleased with the recommendations and asked Cal Sr. to stay on-board to help implement his suggestions.

Cal's father didn't want to be employed by the government, so instead he asked if a new consulting contract could be drafted for the follow-up work. The director agreed and Cal Sr. spent the good part of the next six months retraining the facility staff and implementing the upgraded security protocol.

During the entire process he made it absolutely clear that the job would not interfere with his home life. He insisted on leaving no later than four thirty each day in order to spend time with Cal. It was a habit that he'd continue until the day he died.

Throughout his first consulting gig, Cal Sr. began to see the possibilities in the world of national and international security. He'd recognized the rise of international terrorist cells during his time in the Marine Corps. He's lost friends in the Beirut bombing. Col. Stokes knew it wouldn't be long before those attacks hit American soil.

Over the next couple years, he formalized the structure of Stokes Security International. He leveraged his abundant contacts within state and federal agencies to help win jobs that included law enforcement training, security analysis, VIP protection, etc. Over time, his staff grew as did his reputation for being absolutely dependable.

He refused jobs that would take him away for long periods of time. He refused offers from certain Middle East governments with reported ties to developing terrorist organizations. While no longer an active duty Marine, Col. Stokes still felt an intense desire to protect and defend the United States.

Along the way, he hired former military officers and enlisted men to be part of the growing SSI. He soon became known within certain circles as the man who gave second chances. Col. Stokes knew from experience that everyone has at least one bad day and sometimes good troops fall by the wayside.

His first "second chance" hire, strangely enough, was Cal's cousin Travis. At the time Travis was a Navy Lieutenant serving as a platoon commander with the SEALs. A highly intelligent young man (Rhodes Scholar in college), and an impressive athlete who'd started at defensive back on Ole Miss football team for four years, Travis seemed to be on the fast track to Navy stardom.

That all changed when he found out that one of his SEALs was beating his wife. A deeply honorable man, Travis confronted the enlisted man. During the short conversation the SEAL admitted to abusing his wife and told Travis it wasn't any of his business.

Although the sailor outweighed Travis by almost fifty pounds, he still found himself waking up inside a San Diego hospital with a broken arm, a dislocated shoulder, a cracked jaw, four broken ribs, a broken leg and one helluva headache.

Travis, after calling the ambulance, turned himself in to the Shore Patrol and was confined at the brig until the unconscious SEAL could wake up and testify against his platoon commander.

The man decided not to press charges but the damage had already been done. By turning himself in, Travis had admitted his guilt. There was nothing the Special Operations community could do except let him leave the Navy quietly. At least it was better than spending more time in the brig.

Cal Sr. found out about the incident from his brother, Travis' father. He invited Travis to fly out to Nashville to spend a little time with family. During the two-week stay, Cal's father introduced Travis to the inner workings of SSI. He never made it seem like he was courting a new employee; instead, he quizzed Travis on how SSI could improve its operations.

By the end of the visit, without prompting, Travis made up his mind. He asked his uncle if he could join the company. He explained that he would rather sweep floors for his uncle's company than to beg for work elsewhere.

Needless to say, Cal Sr. took him up on his offer. Instead of starting Travis as he'd requested on the bottom of the totem pole, the CEO of SSI took Travis under his wing. For the first year he rarely left Cal Sr.'s side. Some people called Travis "The Bodyguard" but he served as more of an aide and apprentice. Travis would later admit that the time spent with his uncle and his family probably saved him from a depressive fate.

Never a word was said by the rest of the company staff other than to give the new man a friendly ribbing. Many within SSI came from similar backgrounds and circumstances. It was the former Marine turned CEO who had helped many of his staff over the years. They respected their leader's decisions and believed in his vision.

The second and probably more important reason, was that the entire company harbored a deep and open respect for the Stokes family. Col. Stokes was a tough man but a fair man. He always made time for his family and was known for walking the halls and kicking his employees out so they could spend time with their own loved ones.

Every person up and down the chain felt like they had earned the title of SSI employee. The feeling was very similar to the young man crossing the parade deck and finally being called a Marine. It was an atmosphere that Cal Sr. worked hard to foster from the beginning.

Other key players in the SSI family also came from employment similar to Cal's cousin. There was the logistics chief, Martin Farmer, a former Marine Master Sergeant who'd been relieved of duty after falling deep into alcoholism and depression upon coming home from deployment to find his wife sleeping with the Marine next door. There had been no violence, only the swift decline of a man once revered by his peers and now hindered by the bottle.

Farmer's crusty old Sergeant Major was the one to give Col. Stokes the heads-up. The Sergeant Major and Colonel had served together on two separate occasions and held each other in high regard. So, when the phone call came from his former Marine, he was glad to help.

He'd reviewed the Master Sergeant's record that, minus the present problem, was exemplary including two meritorious promotions. Next, he hopped a flight to Camp Lejeune and was formally introduced by the Sergeant Major.

Col. Stokes recognized the pain in the man's eyes and made a deal with him. He would pay for the man's rehabilitation and counseling. At the end of the program if Farmer came out clean, he would be hired at SSI. Like most Marines, MSgt Farmer was a proud man and fully appreciated the helping hand he'd received. He flew through recovery and reported in to work ninety days later, right after a brief stop in North Carolina to finalize his divorce.

MSgt Farmer became one of Cal Sr.'s brightest stars and totally revamped SSI's logistics division. It seemed early on that Col. Stokes had an eye for talent.

All along the way, Cal Jr. became a welcome aide to the SSI CEO. He'd often sit in on high level meetings and interviews. Sometimes he was in the room; other times he was next door listening through the conference intercom system. Cal learned that his father was a special man that invested in his fellow man first in order to better himself and others. Cal learned that his father had a special place in his heart for those in need of a second chance, but that second chances always came with stipulations. Cal Sr.'s sense of morality was strong when it came down to the activity that caused any potential employee to get into trouble.

He remembered the time an old friend had gone out on a limb for a certain Navy Master Chief. Apparently the two didn't quite know each other but somehow the Master Chief knew enough people to get referred to Col. Stokes. The story Cal Sr. received from his old friend differed drastically from the story that finally came out of the ill-fated Master Chief's mouth. Apparently, the sailor believed that *any* first infraction warranted a second chance in the mind of the founder of SSI. He soon found out otherwise.

It quickly surfaced that the man had twisted his story in order to gain sympathy with his former commander. The commander, an old friend of Col. Stokes, took the man for his word and was more than happy to pass along a supposedly trust-worthy sailor to his buddy.

It turned out that the man had severely beaten two young sailors who'd just reported into his unit. Apparently, alcohol was involved, and what started as an innocent hazing ritual soon turned violent.

Sitting in front of Col. Stokes, it was obvious the sailor still held no remorse for the situation. He actually had the audacity to blame the Navy for accusing him unjustly. Little did the man know that Col. Stokes held no room in his world for bullies and liars. The man was swiftly escorted out by Travis and two other former SEALs, and a report was submitted to Col. Stokes' friend which he in turn filed with the Navy.

It was during this altercation that Cal finally understood his father's true sense of right and wrong. He believed that any abuse or offense against a lesser human being was morally wrong. At the same time, Cal Sr. did believe that there are times when a man must take the law into his own hands as long as it was the right thing to do.

Cal asked his father about this supposed duplicity and he'd listened as Cal Sr. calmly explained that although America was the best country in the world, even America's laws were not always fair to all and oftentimes sheltered criminals for the sake of due process.

His son knew his father approved certain covert missions for various government agencies that, if seen by the liberal media, would be criticized as being barbaric and unconstitutional. Each of these undertakings was always scrutinized for its ethical basis by the headquarters team at SSI. A mission was never green-lighted if the outcome and the methods did not live up to SSI's high moral standard.

Col. Stokes would later solidify his belief with a motto he would dub Corps Justice.

CAMP SPARTAN, ARRINGTON, TN

"So, let me get this right," Brian said. "This company is gonna be yours?"

"Well, I guess technically it is mine," Cal admitted.

"Holy shit! You're like a billionaire!"

Cal felt sheepish. "Not really. I guess you'd call me a multi-millionaire. Don't spread that around."

"Are you kidding me?! No one would believe that a dumb grunt like you is a billionaire anyway."

"Millionaire!"

Brian waved him off. "Whatever. It's all the same."

"Do you even know the difference? Anyway, do you want to hear the rest of the story or not?"

"All right, go on Mr. Billionaire."

Cal ignored the comment and continued. "So, my Dad taught me that many worlds exist within the law. He learned early on in the security business that he would have access to certain intel that could benefit others for good and bad. His deep sense of moral duty kept him from profiting from the bad side. At the same time, he knew there was a huge gray area left for him to interpret."

"I'm not following you."

"OK." Cal took a deep breath before continuing. "I remember Dad telling me the story of the first instance when he hit a real gray area. On a certain job a few years back, one of his SSI passive surveillance teams found out that a neighbor of the target was running an illegal prostitution and drug ring and that both the women and drugs were being supplied from Taiwan."

"All right. So, he just gave that intel to the cops, right?"

Cal shook his head. "Nope. Think about it. Every American citizen has a certain right to privacy. Technically, the intel was gathered because one of the team members was curious about the girls coming in and out of the house. So, the team shifted a couple of listening devices over to the other house along with a camera and just monitored it for a couple days. Well, they found out pretty quickly what was going on but the dilemma was the legality of the source of information. Any two-bit lawyer could've had the case thrown out of court."

"There's gotta be something the authorities could've done."

"Their hands are tied, man. They would've loved nothing more than to bust that whole thing down. Our company has a lot of contacts in local law enforcement so one of our guys cautiously asked what they would do with the situation without giving away the details like location, etcetera. The cops basically said that unless they were allowed to build the case from the ground up or catch the ring red-handed, there's not much they could do."

"But that's bullshit! They're here to protect us from that kind of stuff."

"I know. But remember that in order to live in a democracy like we have in this country, certain laws must be in place to protect individual freedom and avoid abuse of that freedom."

"Alright, so you're telling me that your dad just sat on the intel and did nothing?"

Cal smiled. "That's the opposite of what he did."

"You gonna tell me or just sit there with that cheesy grin on your face?"

"I know I don't have to say this to you but I will anyways: you can't say anything about what you see around here to anyone outside SSI. Oh, and don't go telling Travis what I've told you. I don't think he'd care, considering who you are, but I don't want him to think I've been running my mouth."

"Who do you think I am? I know how to keep my mouth shut."

"OK. So, my Dad ordered the team to wait until the original mission was over. He didn't want to tip off the ring leaders. Once the first job was finished, the team covertly rounded up all the ringleaders and made them get caught."

"Hold on. What do you mean *made* them get caught?"

"Some of our top snoopers caught the guys, tranquilized them and set them all up in one of their vans in a park down the street." Cal laughed at the memory. "The team loaded the criminals with some booze and their own dope so it looked like they'd passed out after a little partying. They loaded all the drugs and weapon stash in the back of the van so when the cops were anonymously tipped off, the drug dealers and pimps woke up to a slew of cops yelling at them to come out with their hands up and get on the ground. I heard the whole thing was pretty funny."

"What about the slaves they had in the house?"

"For their own safety, they were knocked out too and a minor fire was set. Just enough for the alarm system to alert the fire department. When the fire department busted in and searched the house, they found the girls locked in a back room."

"I still don't see why the cops couldn't have just knocked down the door and swept the place."

"That sounds easy but think about those raids you did with your Marines over in Iraq. Did you ever like going into a situation not knowing what you were gonna get? Who knew what those guys would've done to the local cops busting down the door? The way our team did it, no one was hurt and the criminals were dealt with." Brian still didn't look totally convinced. "Are you really so naïve to think that the police can do anything they want? Come on, doc. You've seen the shitty things people do in this world."

"I know." Brian sounded resigned. "I guess I never really thought about it that much until now. It's like the cops are handcuffed from doing their duty. Reminds me of those times in Iraq when the Rules of Engagement kept my Marines from killing bad guys."

Cal nodded. "Exactly. If they don't do things by the book, these good cops that don't get paid squat could lose their jobs. The law's made it to where police hesitate because they're worried about getting in trouble."

"Yeah. Last week I saw that some cop was getting sued by a guy who got shot while robbing a bank. The cop shot him *after* the guy shot one of the tellers and refused to give up. It's bullshit."

"Yep. That's where Corps Justice comes in."

"Explain that," Brian said.

"Well, like I told you before, my Dad lived and breathed the Marine Corps way. It was my fault he got out of the Corps, but you could never take the Corps out of him. That, mixed with his moral sense of right and wrong, made him adopt his motto about Corps Justice."

"So, is this *Corps Justice* like a company credo or something?"

"Kind of. It's more of an overarching guidance for SSI employees for when they encounter gray areas. Hang on a sec."

Cal grabbed his wallet and pulled out what looked like a business card on tattered paper. He handed it to Brian. "I got that from my Dad when I went off to college."

Brian looked down at the card:

CAMP SPARTAN, ARRINGTON, TN

- CORPS JUSTICE -
1. We will protect and defend the Constitution of the United States.
2. We will protect the weak and punish the wicked.
3. When the laws of this nation hinder the completion of these duties, our moral compass will guide us to see the mission through.

Brian looked up at Cal. "This looks like you can do whatever you want as long as you think it's right."

"I know that's how it seems, but you have to remember that my Dad's moral compass wouldn't allow us to conduct acts of undue aggression. Besides, only the top management within SSI can green light those kinds of jobs. Dad handpicked that leadership."

"Does this come up a lot?"

Cal shrugged. "I don't think so. Keep in mind that most of the work SSI does is consulting and training. Yes, we do have security teams and quick reaction forces, but most of the missions they undertake are cut and dry. There's typically a clear bad guy and that's who we're sent in to take care of."

"It sounds more like the gigs you take on are government sanctioned."

"Keep in mind that I don't know everything. I don't work here. But you're right. The federal government is our biggest customer, but we have a lot of divisions that trump even that big account."

Brian scratched his chin. "Like what?"

"We do a lot of R&D work and either sell the final product or retain the rights. There's a lot of money in that kind of stuff."

"I'll bet. Are you gonna run the company?"

"Nope. Trav is better at it than I would be. I'll probably be involved somehow but he's a much better schmoozer than I am. Plus, I've still got some things to take care of."

Cal gazed out the expansive windows, trying to stop the intrusion of memory.

"So," said Brian, "tell me how the hell you went into the Marine Corps instead of working here?"

Cal maintained his gaze for a moment, then turned to Brian. "I started my first year of college at the University of Virginia in 1998. My parents were excited about the high caliber of the university, but they still wanted me close. By that time, the company was doing a lot more work with the feds. Dad had anticipated the rise of terrorism and built the company to combat those threats with the ability to augment the American military. He was even doing some work for our allies like the U.K. and Germany."

He paused and shifted his weight trying to find the right words. "Like I said, my parents were really happy about me going to UVA but still wanted to see me. I wanted the same thing. We'd been through a lot together. The great thing about money is that there's not much you can't do when you have it. At that point, SSI was probably a tenth of what it is now but Mom and Dad had more money than they could ever spend. Well, on one of their trips to Charlottesville to watch a UVA football game and visit me, Dad went house shopping. I thought he was just looking for a condo or something they could stay in for weekend trips in. Dad didn't come from much money but always loved the idea of owning land. He always told me that land was one thing you could never reproduce or take away from a man. In Albemarle County, Virginia there's a lot of land. You know Monticello, right?"

"Yeah, that was Thomas Jefferson, right?"

"Yep. Founded UVA too. Anyways, there are a lot of estates like that out there. So, Dad goes out and finds a spread a lot like this one here. Around two thousand acres. He called it his little getaway. What he ended up doing was turning that into our second headquarters. He called it Camp Cavalier because I was at UVA. It turned out great because he built an almost identical campus there that we have here in Nashville. That gave the SSI the ability to be really close to Washington, D.C."

"I'll bet your parents spent more time there too."

"Yeah. It was great to have them close by and they understood that I needed my space too. They'd come over for football games and sometime take me out to dinner. That was a great three years."

Cal paused and returned his gaze to the window and continued. "In the fall of 2001, I was starting my last year in school. My parents had just been by to visit, then headed up to D.C. to visit new clients and old friends. They were going to jump on a plane out to Los Angeles for a quick vacation then head down to Camp Pendleton to see some more friends and fit a little work in too. My parents boarded American Airlines Flight 77 the morning of September 11th. They tried to call me from the flight when it became clear to my Dad that the flight was hijacked. I was in class and didn't get the call. Both calmly told me that they loved me in hushed voices and my Dad told me they'd always be with me."

Tears were now streaming down Cal's face, but he continued. "I could hear my Mom try to choke back her gasps. My Dad was all business, but he still sounded scared. More than anything, I think he was worried for my Mom and for me. That's the way he always was. He finished the message by telling me how proud he was, and that I'd been his greatest accomplishment on earth."

Cal stopped again. His breath now coming in gasps. "I never got to say goodbye. Those fucking terrorist thugs took the most important people out of my life. I sat there playing that message over and over again as I sat with my classmates watching the attacks on TV. I was just numb. Before I knew it, a couple guys from our Charlottesville headquarters barged into the room and found me. Apparently, Travis had sent them to come get me and secure me somewhere."

He reached down and grabbed the bottom of his shirt and wiped his eyes. Then, anger iced his veins. "They tried to take me out of there but I shook them off. One of the guys tried to get me on the phone but I wouldn't do it. I ran out of there and went straight to the ROTC building at Maury Hall. I wasn't part of ROTC, but I knew some of the guys. The MOI was a mustang and had served with Dad. I found him and asked him how I could get into the Corps. He was sympathetic but said it wasn't that easy. There were a lot more hurdles going the officer route. Before he could finish, I bolted. I knew where the Marine recruiter's office was and ran all the way there. There were a bunch of other kids there apparently doing the same thing as me. I pushed my way to the front. No one wanted to mess with the sweat-soaked kid with the tears running down his face. The Gunny sitting at the desk glanced up, annoyed that I'd broken his routine. I asked him how I could get to go overseas the fastest. I told him I wanted to kill the people that had killed my parents. His face changed and he softened up. He stood up and took me to the back of the room where we could talk in private. The Gunny told me that he was getting flooded with similar requests and that he only had one slot left to ship kids to boot camp later that week."

Cal took a deep breath. "I asked him how I could get that one spot. He told me I'd have to compete for it and volunteer to be a grunt. Well, being a pretty smart college kid, I aced the enlistment-screening exam and maxed out the physical fitness test that day. I got the slot and left for boot camp two days later."

Cal looked back at Brian and continued. "I know you're thinking that by the time I got on that bus I regretted my decision. Nope. It was the opposite. Every moment I grieved for my parents, I also felt like I was doing *something*. Hell, even if I wound up cleaning latrines, at least I would've been serving. Enlisting in the Marines was the best thing I could've done. The rest is history."

Brian let the words sink in for a minute. "Holy shit, Cal," he said, his voice softened, "I'm really sorry about your parents. I had no idea."

"Yeah, well, it's not something I advertise. Look, Doc, I don't regret what I did then and I definitely don't regret what I did to those gang bangers. If you're not cool with that, maybe you should leave."

Brian's face became indignant. "Who do you think I am? I'm not some pussy that gets sick over a little bit of blood. I don't give a shit that you killed those guys. They deserved it. I wish you'd finished off the other two." He stopped and took a deep calming breath. "Look, I'm here to help, OK? You've gone through some really shitty situations. I'm more concerned about you mentally than some dead criminal."

"I'm fine. I know how to take care of myself."

"Yeah, right. I know you didn't learn *that* in The Corps. We're brothers, remember? You've gotta be straight with me, man!"

Cal snapped his glare back at Brian. "You want me to tell you that my body aches all day because Jess is dead? You want me to tell you that half the day I wish I'd died with her? You want me to tell you that I want to *kill* those motherfuckers over and over again?"

"Yes, as a matter of cold fact! You can't keep that shit inside, man! You've gotta let it out or it'll eat you alive. You've seen some of those boys that come back from the desert and just clam up. Most turn into drunks or druggies. I don't want that to happen to you!"

Cal stared at Brian. The guy was panting from the exertion.

Then it happened.

It was like a door had been opened. He sure as hell didn't open it himself. In walked Jess.

She looked as she had always looked to him. Beautiful, with her thousand-year-old soul staring out through her eyes. And she did all the little things, like stick her tongue out at him when they met eyes across some crowded room; or purse her lips when she was in deep thought, not realizing he was watching. A wordless gesture here and there; her small yet firm hands stirring milk into tea; the clinking of the spoon and the cup. The rolling of her eyes when he made a dumb joke. Her laugh. Her tears. Her smile.

Her smile.

He laid back and threw his hands to his face and sobbed uncontrollably. The bottled-up pain surfaced in full force. He felt Brian's comforting hand on his shoulder.

Maybe it was like this for five, ten minutes. Maybe it was half the night.

He fell away into deep, dreamless sleep.

Brian expertly checked his friend, making sure Cal was OK. It was time for the Marine to get some well-deserved rest. He stood up and walked across the room, sat down in a leather recliner, and began his vigil.

PART TWO

N.O.N. SAFE HOUSE, NASHVILLE, TN

"What do you mean he *left?*" Dante listened to his cell phone as anger raged on his face. "You told me they had to tell you if they were gonna release him. *Fuck*. Did you at least find out where they took him?"

The answer he got was not what he wanted.

"Well then, I guess you're about to have a bad night. And don't even think about not showing up. You've got some explaining to do."

He shut off the call and sat back on the dirty couch. Dante was sick and tired of being on the run. The only good news was that he'd somehow managed to recruit a couple more boys to join his crew. He only got that done by offering way more of a cut than he usually did. It really was his only choice. Everyone knew Dante couldn't show his face on the streets.

Once this thing blows over, I'll take my money back anyway.

Dante's plan of taking out the hero Marine as he was leaving the hospital was now scrapped. He'd have to find another way to get to the guy. The gang leader was still confused about how the dude had managed to be released without having to go through normal hospital protocol. Maybe there was more to this guy than he knew. He'd have to do some digging.

As he sat thinking in the dingy hideout, a plan began to formulate. If he couldn't get to the Marine himself, he'd somehow have to get him out in the open.

Think, Dante, think.

CAMP SPARTAN, ARRINGTON, TN

Cal awoke to the thin stream of light coming from the curtain-covered bay windows. His eyes focused on Brian asleep in the leather chair across the room. *I'll bet he's been sitting there all night.*

He tested his balance as he slowly rose into a sitting position. His wounds still throbbed but they'd be muted a bit after a couple pain killers. Cal quietly shuffled to the bathroom to relieve himself. After he was done, he brushed his teeth, washed his face, and threw down two pain pills. *Time for breakfast.*

As he walked back into the main room, Brian got up from his chair and did a quick stretch while yawning. "How you feeling, Cal?"

"All right. Listen, about my bawlin' last night, I—"

"Don't worry about it. I'm glad you got it out. Now we can work on getting you better."

Cal nodded, allowing himself this tiny bit of humility. "So, what's on the schedule for today's torture?"

Brian chuckled. "Travis stopped by while you were passed out and he said you guys have a nice gym on campus."

"That we do."

"I thought I'd wheel you over there and we could do some stretches and PT. You up for it?"

"Yeah. I need some fresh air."

"Me too. Let me go take a leak and then I'll help you get changed. You wanna eat before or after?"

"Let's do after. I don't want to puke up everything at the gym. My gut's still not right."

"Cool. Give me a minute and we'll head out."

Fifteen minutes later, the pair emerged from the suite. Cal rested comfortably in an off-road looking wheelchair. *Probably some super upgrade Trav hooked up for me.* At least they could take it on some of the trails if they wanted.

After leaving the Lodge, Cal directed Brian to take a left and head down three blocks. As they traveled Cal described some of the surrounding buildings. "That one over there is the mess hall and the one behind that is the HQ."

At a brisk pace, they reached the gym in only a couple minutes. Although sparsely decorated, it looked to Brian like all the newest equipment was housed within the facility.

"This is the main area with free weights and machines," Cal said. "We've got a cardio room around the corner that has flat screens. Where should we start?"

Brian looked around. "Let's head over to that spot with the mats. We'll kill some stretches first."

Thirty minutes later, Cal was drenched in sweat and panting with exertion. The stretching alone had been excruciating for the wounded warrior. Moving on to the treadmill felt like death. Nevertheless, he finished the tortuous physical therapy session with a determined smile on his face. It felt good to move again.

Brian stood up and surveyed his patient. "All right, that's good for today, Cal."

Cal nodded and rolled over. "Let's go get some food and then I want to introduce you to some people."

Brian looked at his friend quizzically but kept his mouth shut and helped Cal into the wheelchair.

The duo left the gym facility and headed toward the chow hall. As they entered the smell of scrambled eggs and pancakes greeted them. They found a booth in a corner and Cal took a seat.

"What do you want me to get for you?" Brian asked.

"Two eggs over-easy, country ham, a stack of pancakes and some orange juice."

"Got it. I'll be right back."

The companions finished breakfast with the occasional greeting from company employees who stopped by to say hello to Cal. Brian noticed that rather than be embarrassed or standoffish, Cal spoke openly with the visitors and knew most by their first names. It wasn't something he'd expected and mentioned this on the way out of the dining facility.

"Yeah, I've spent a lot of time on both campuses over the years," Cal explained. "I've even been in on some of the hiring interviews. Dad really wanted me to see the inner workings at SSI and included me whenever he could. I even had a hand in hiring some employees. That reminds me, take a left up here. I want to introduce you to somebody."

Brian took the next left. They walked down four blocks, finally reaching a low structure. Brian pointed at the front door and Cal nodded. As they passed through the double doors, the former corpsman noticed the pressurized feel as the heavy glass door sucked back into place.

"What is this place?" Brian asked.

"We call it the Bat Cave."

"Guess that makes you Batman," said Brian.

The two strolled up to the front desk. The two security guards, heavily armed, greeted Cal by his first name, coming around the desk to shake his hand. It was obvious to Brian that both men – each the size of an NFL linebacker – liked and respected Cal. These weren't some employees attempting to suck up to the future boss. These guys really admired Cal, and it seemed that they held him on some sort of pedestal. *Interesting.*

They waved goodbye, Cal promising to meet the two guards at the gym soon and headed to the bank of elevators.

They boarded the first to arrive and Brian shifted around to select a floor. There was only a second floor and nine buttons below the first floor. *A bunch of subfloors.* He looked at Cal questioningly.

"Press B9," Cal said.

Brian pressed the very bottom button. *Nine levels down?*

It took less than a minute for the elevator to descend and open its doors. As they opened, Brian smelled the incoming air. It smelled like the air wing hangers he remembered from his time with the Marines. That unique smell of oil, grease and metal. The smell brought back a flood of memories from his time spent at Cherry Point and his cruises on the gator freighters.

Cal took a deep breath. "OK, before we head down to see Neil, I want to give you a little background. Neil was one of my finds for the company. We went to school together at UVA. He was two years ahead of me. He'd been my resident advisor my first year. Neil was a brilliant triple major who hardly studied. He was a funny mix of hip social butterfly and technological genius. I won't tell you what his IQ is, because you won't believe me. So anyways, his family came over from India when Neil was a little kid. They didn't have a lot of money and really worked hard to make ends meet. Fortunately, his father was almost as smart as he is. Mr. Patel started a cell phone company out of his garage, if you can believe it. He grew it into this booming business that he exported back to India. Made a helluva lot of cash. Neil grew up tinkering with the surplus cell phones his dad had lying around. Pretty soon he was doing all the repairs for the company. He just had this knack for fixing and building stuff. There was this little joke around town that he could fix phones by looking at them."

"How'd he wind up in a dump like this?" Brian joked.

Cal smiled. "Well, going into his fifth year at school his mom and dad went on a trip to India then over to Pakistan. Business trip. They were there to meet with contacts who were going to open a new headquarters for Mr. Patel's company. While they were in Pakistan, both of Neil's parents were kidnapped and later killed."

Brian shook his head. "Holy crap."

"Some tiny terrorist outfit claimed responsibility. No one was ever caught."

"I can't imagine how the son must've taken that," Brian said.

"Neil went into a real tailspin. He and his father were really close and Neil didn't know how to cope. He went off the deep end; started drinking all the time, screwing anyone he could get his hands on, and started dabbling in drugs. Let's just say he really didn't give a shit anymore."

Cal looked up at the ceiling. "So I bump into him one night at some party and I notice he's a little crazier than I remember. I somehow convince him to stick around and hang out with me. Over way too many drinks, he finally broke down and told me the story about his parents. Up to that point I'd had no idea. It was obvious that he'd given up and didn't want to deal with life let alone school. Then the poor dude passed out on my couch."

"What'd you do?"

"At the time I didn't know exactly what to do but I knew I had to help the guy. We were little more than casual acquaintances but he'd always been a great friend. I called my Dad the next morning and explained the situation. Luckily Dad was at the Charlottesville headquarters and asked that I set up a meeting with Neil. I agreed and somehow got a very hungover Neil into my car and out to Camp Cavalier."

Cal chuckled. "The coffee on the way seemed to revive him a bit, but pulling into the main gate really woke him up. Long story short, my Dad instantly liked him and outlined his plan for Neil. He wanted Neil to lay off the partying and finish up school. Then he'd bring him on in the company's brand new R&D department. I think this might've done the trick, but Dad threw in a kicker. He promised Neil that if he came onboard, SSI would do anything within its power to find the men responsible for the Patels' murder and bring them to justice."

"No shit?"

"Yeah. By that time, Dad had some pretty serious contacts internationally and within most of our government agencies. Not to mention SSI's intelligence gathering capabilities were really ramping up. Neil jumped at the chance and didn't let my Dad down. Six months after Neil graduated, the terrorist cell that took credit for Neil's parents death were killed in a raid by Pakistani special forces. Justice was done."

"So, Neil's been here ever since?" Brian asked.

"Yeah. He and my Dad really hit it off. Plus, in no time Neil was leading the R&D department with some pretty heavy technological advances. My Dad kept trying to get him to take a new title like Head of R&D or Vice President for R&D but Neil always refused. He always said he's just a developer."

"Developer, huh? What kind of things does he develop?"

"You name it," Cal said. "It started with little tech gadgets for the military: small cameras, light weaponry, tactical gear. The guy was a triple engineering major. He'll tell you which ones but I'll tell you they're all way over my head. Anyways, he and Dad figured out pretty quickly that rather than develop stuff for individual jobs, Neil could instead develop technology that SSI could license out to other entities. Call it the Microsoft model. *That's* when the company really starting making a ton of money. Dad made an agreement with Neil that Neil would keep fifty percent of the sale or ongoing licensing fee from any of the stuff he researched and developed. Neil didn't want the deal, but Dad felt it was only fair. Let's just say that Neil will never have to worry about money ever again."

"So, the guy knows his stuff, huh?"

"He does, but he still tries to play the part of dumb gigolo. I never know how many girlfriends the guy has. Let's go introduce you to Neil."

NEIL

The men headed straight ahead towards a long corridor lit by fluorescent track lighting. As they neared the room at the opposite end of the hallway, Brian inhaled sharply at the size of the place. It looked like a huge cavern.

"What the hell is this place?"

"I told you, it's the Bat Cave. Head over to the left and that bunch of tables."

At their approach, a slim man in glasses looked up from his work. He stood about six feet tall, slim, like he could've been an actor in Bollywood. Curiously, he wore a pair of black shades around his neck.

Neil took off his reading glasses and walked over to Cal. He bent down to wheelchair level and hugged his friend. "I'm so sorry Cal."

"Thanks."

"Is there anything I can do?"

"We'll get to that in a minute. First, I want you to meet my new friend."

Neil nodded and stood back up. He looked over at Brian and extended his hand. "Hey, Doc. I'm Neil Patel." He extended both arms. "Welcome to the Bat Cave."

Brian took the man's hand with some trepidation. "Good to meet you, Neil."

Neil smiled conspiratorially and explained. "Don't look so shocked, Doc. Travis sent over your file before you got here. I know all about you."

Brian looked a bit uncomfortable with the lopsided conversation but kept his mouth shut.

Cal stepped in before Neil could make Brian feel even more awkward. "What are you working on?"

Neil gestured grandly to the nearest table and spoke in a mock British accent. "My new toys are waiting for your inspection, good sir."

Cal shook his head and rolled himself over to the table. "What is that? One of those remote-control helicopters from Brookstone?"

Neil made a face of mock indignation and continued in his English accent. "Sir, how dare you accuse me of such a thing! What you see is the latest in nano-drone technology. Courtesy of yours truly." He waved his arms before him and bowed slightly.

Cal picked up the small helicopter-looking device. The thing fit in the palm of his hand and couldn't have been more than the size of a silver dollar in diameter. "Where's the remote?"

Neil pulled off the pair of sunglasses from around his neck. "Right here." He handed the black shades to Cal.

"If this was someone else I'd think they were pulling my leg. But with you I'm pretty sure you're not bullshitting me."

Neil grinned. "Nope. Those sunglasses control the drone. Put 'em on."

Cal did as he was told and put the glasses on. They looked and felt like a normal pair of sunglasses. "You gonna tell me how this thing works?"

"Push the emblem on the right side of the frame."

Cal did so and immediately the left-hand lens lit up.

It looked like a freaking video game.

He jumped back as the tiny blades on the drone kicked on and set it into a hover. "You could've warned me about that!"

"But then I couldn't have seen the silly look on your face."

"OK. So, what do I do now?"

"You see the screen on the left?" Neil asked.

"Yeah."

"Use your eye and tell the drone where to go."

"Dude. I have no idea what you're talking about."

Neil sounded exasperated, but excited. "Just turn your head and look at something you want the drone to go to."

Cal turned his head and could feel the drone lifting higher. That's when he noticed that the view in the left lens had changed. He was now seeing from the point of view of the drone.

"Holy shit!"

Neil beamed. "I know, right?"

Cal directed the drone to a nearby set of cabinets. He realized that as he focused on an object, the drone would move closer. "How do I keep this thing from running into stuff?"

"You don't. It does. It has a proximity detector. With stationary objects, it's flawless. I'm still working out the kinks on non-stationary objects within the drone's environment. You know, like people running around on the battlefield, cars, animals – anything that moves."

"You can do that?" said Brian, sounding incredulous.

"Pretty easy actually. Hey, Cal, just so you know, the technology in this thing is probably gonna make us all a lot more money. We're thinking we can equip cars with it. Imagine, no more traffic accidents!"

Cal could do nothing but smile with childish bewilderment. This little toy was too much fun. "How do I get it to fly back?"

"Just click that button on the side again and it'll go back to its charging dock over there on that desk."

Cal pressed the button on the sunglasses again. Sure enough, the little drone found its way home, without guidance, to what looked like a miniature landing pad on one of the desks. He removed the shades and handed them back to Neil. "How the hell did you come up with that?"

"Actually, some of the technology's already been around for a while. Apache pilots have been able to control some of their weapons systems with monocles for years. I just made the system better."

"Who are you building it for?" Brian asked.

"No one yet. All the small spy drones right now are way bigger than this little guy. I know there are some other companies in the hunt, but I think ours will be the best. Pretty sure it'll be an easy sell."

"I would've loved one of these over in the desert. Would've made fighting house to house a lot safer if I could send this guy in first."

"That's our target market for this thing," Neil said. "I want to give the troops something that's cost effective and easy to use. A whole freakin' platoon could have one of these things. Trav is talking to a couple of commanders out in the field right now that are gonna try it out for us free of charge."

"You got one that I can borrow?" Cal asked.

Neil cocked his head, making sure his friend wasn't messing with him. "We've got a few almost ready. You can take that one if you want."

"Don't mind if I do. What are you doing for lunch?"

Neil pointed to a nearby fridge. "What I always do. Work."

"How about you join Brian and me over at the Lodge around noon?"

"Sounds good. Should I wear my drinking boots?"

"In a word, yes."

CAMP SPARTAN, ARRINGTON, TN

Cal took a long hot shower methodically washing all his wounds. The damned things still hurt like a champ, but the hot water helped to soothe the pain. He had to stay out of that fucking wheelchair. His whole body was stiff. It'd be good to move around more. Plus, he had work to do.

Travis called out from the other room. "You in there, Cal?"

"Give me a minute."

Cal shut off the water and wrapped himself in a big towel. He walked into the master bedroom and found Travis, scotch glass in hand, standing next to Andy.

"The front gate guards found this guy begging like a starving dog to come in," Travis said.

Andy rolled his eyes. "Very funny. How you doing, Cal?"

"Better now. It's great to see you, brother."

Andy walked over and gave Cal a hug. "I had over sixty days of leave time stocked up so I thought I'd come visit the Music City, maybe hit a couple honky tonks."

"Seriously, man," Cal said. "What are you doing here?"

Andy looked Cal dead in the eye. "If I know you at all, I know that you're planning something."

Cal looked away. "I don't know what you're talking about."

"You're planning to go after this Dante guy."

"Why the fuck do you care?"

"Do you even have to ask?"

"So what? Are you here to stop me?" Cal balled his hands into fists.

"Do you not know me at all, Cal? I'm here to help, you idiot."

Cal looked from his former platoon commander over to Travis. "You don't look too surprised."

"I *am* your cousin, Cal." Travis held out his hands. "Plus, you know how we take care of family around here. Your dad started that."

Cal's voice was soft now. "Yeah."

"So, what's the plan, cuz? What do you need from the company?"

"Trav, I really don't want to involve the company. Could you imagine what would happen simply if the media finds out that I'm involved? There'll be a real shitstorm."

"You think this is our first rodeo, cowboy? Look, I'll give you the benefit of the doubt because you've been off serving in the Corps for a while, but SSI has evolved. We've taken what your dad started to a whole new level."

"What are you talking about?"

"Corps Justice."

Now Cal was really confused. He knew the company had gone off the reservation at select times in the past, but now it sounded like there'd been a lot more happening than he'd known.

"You wanna explain or do I have to pry it out of you?"

"We've been doing a lot more work under the radar in recent years," Travis explained. "Mostly domestic stuff against terrorist cells and organized crime, but the calls keep coming. The shitheads are coming out of the woodwork."

"You said the calls keep coming? From who?"

"You name it. Your Dad had a whole network of contacts that I didn't even know about until they started calling me after your parents were killed."

"I'm still confused. Who are these people?"

"Everyone from former presidents and CIA officials right on down to local law enforcement. Shit, I had to have Neil build me a whole new secure database so I could somehow track them all. And the list just keeps growing."

Andy was suddenly intrigued. "Wait, so these contacts hire you to do wet work or something?"

"They don't hire us, per se. It's more like they inform us of something they've caught wind of, you know, just sort of casually mention it, then look the other way."

"How the hell haven't you been caught?"

Travis laughed. "Are you shitting me? I may be a SEAL but I'm not an idiot. The team Cal's dad built around here is more like family. Haven't you noticed that most of us are second-chancers? I don't know of any other corporation in the world that has employees that would literally lay down their lives for the team."

"Sounds like the Marine Corps," Andy said.

"Exactly. Uncle Calvin took an interest in people and treated them right. He was always tough but always fair. The people he brought onboard knew he would give his own life for them. We've lived by the same rules since he left us. This company is tighter than a clam's ass, and that's watertight."

"So, who pays for this secret work?" Cal asked.

"It's a complicated combination of systems," Travis said. "We pay for most of it, but we have other sources."

Cal quirked an eyebrow. "*We* pay for it?"

"Cuz, your dad setup a whole other division within the company to do this stuff. With money coming in from our patents and fees, there's more than enough."

"So, the company is still financially sound?"

"Listen to you. You sound like you're thinking about taking over."

"I'm just curious, is all. Now that I'm officially out of the Corps, I'm gonna need something to do."

Travis thought about it for a minute. "What did you have in mind?"

"Well, I sure as hell don't want *your* job. You can keep that. I was thinking more along the lines of R&D but this other stuff sounds like I could make a difference."

"Funny you should mention Research and Development," Travis said. "I was talking with Neil the other day and we thought that's what you might like. In fact, it works out perfectly. Our new division actually does a lot of the initial trial work for R&D's creations. Neil's even been known to get dressed up in black and join the teams."

"You've gotta be shittin' me!" Cal said. "We can't afford to lose him!"

"Relax, Cal." Travis waved away the concern. "Neil's always hunkered down out of reach from the bad guys. We get him just close enough so he can monitor the use of the new gadgets and feel like he's part of the crew. The field teams love him."

"I'll bet they do."

"So back to the original question: what do you need from the company?"

Cal took a minute to think about it. Hell, before this enlightening conversation, he thought he'd have to "borrow" the tools he'd need. "I'd like access to some of Neil's toys. Mainly surveillance stuff to start. This Dante guy is probably hunkered down somewhere and I've gotta dig him out."

"I think we can help with that," Travis said. "Neil has some hacking software we've used in the past. One program can infiltrate a cell phone and track all calls. The fool even figured out a way to listen to the calls remotely. The damned thing is almost flawless."

"Is it something you have to load onto the cell phone?"

"Not like you'd think. He actually accesses it with some kind of laser. You can sit on a rooftop a mile away with this thing, paint the targeted cell phone, and it's yours."

"It doesn't sound like you're kidding," Cal said.

"I'm not. Don't ask me how the damn thing works. I just know it does."

"OK. I'll take one of those please."

"Alright. What else do you need?"

DANTE'S CALLS to New Orleans had finally paid off. Earlier in the day, a car arrived with four mean-looking bangers from down south. It was the first shipment of what would eventually be nine new men. These were some of his cousin's top enforcers. He'd owe his cousin some serious cash after all was said and done, but it would be worth it to take care of SSgt Cal Stokes.

CAMP SPARTAN, ARRINGTON, TN

Cal and the boys were holding rocks glasses with two fingers of scotch in each when Brian entered and made his way over to Cal.

"How you feeling?"

"A little sore, but better after that shower. Why didn't you tell me I smelled that bad?"

"I didn't want to make you cry."

"Hey, Doc," said Cal, "you know Travis and Neil, but let me introduce you to the rest of this motley crew. This is Captain Bartholomew Andrews. We served together in the fleet and I consider him one of my closest friends."

Andy leaned over and shook Brian's hand. "How are you, Doc?"

"I'm good, Sir. We talked over the phone at the hospital, right?"

"That was me. And you can cut the 'Sir' crap. Just call me Andy."

"Got it."

"Now" said Cal, "this other fine fellow here is the amazing former Marine Master Sergeant Willy Trent."

Brian looked up at the huge black man. "Didn't we see you at the chow hall?"

Cal laughed. "See, Trav? I told you he was sharp for a squid. Willy runs the mess hall when he's not kicking the crap out of the troops in the gym. Not only is he a professionally-trained chef from Johnson and Wales, he's also one of our martial arts and urban raid instructors."

Trent bent his hulking frame over and shook Brian's hand. "Good to meet you, Doc."

"You too, Top."

"We were just discussing our upcoming mission," Cal said.

Brian looked between Cal and the others in the room. "I'm sorry, what?"

"Let's just say I'm about to start playing out of bounds and you need to tell me right now whether you want out. You can still stick around but we'll politely ask you to leave whenever we're talking operationally."

"What you're talking about?"

Cal fixed a stare at the nurse. "It has to do with finishing the job I started in that downtown alley."

"You're talking about going after that West guy."

Cal smiled. "Well, I'm not talking about sending him a nasty letter."

"In that case, I'm thinking you're about to go *way* out of bounds."

"Listen, Doc, if you're not up to this, just say so and we'll come get you in an hour or so."

Brian stared at Cal like he was trying to make up his mind. "Can I ask a couple questions?"

"Shoot."

He pointed at Cal's glass. "First, can I have one of whatever you guys are drinking?"

"The Famous Grouse," Cal said.

"Never heard of it."

"My dad's favorite scotch and pretty much all I drink around here. We've got pallets of it."

"Sounds good."

Travis walked to the bar to get the drink for Brian.

"Next question?" Cal asked.

"Why not find the guy then alert the cops?" Brian asked.

"I'll answer that one," Travis said from the bar. "We've already been monitoring the situation through discrete channels. Believe it or not, even with the eyewitnesses, they don't have enough evidence to pin it all on West."

"Really?"

Travis raised his glass. "Welcome to our world, brother."

"How are you planning on getting away with this?"

Cal glanced at the other members of the party. Each held a loyal and conspiratorial look. "Well, apparently there's a lot that this company can do that I had no idea about until about an hour ago. Before we got here, I thought I was going to borrow some of Neil's toys and go do some snoopin' and poopin' by myself. Thanks to these guys, it looks like I won't have to do that alone anymore."

Brian's face changed to a look of disbelief. "Cal, you can't go waging some kind of private war on the streets of Nashville!"

Cal scrutinized his new friend. How well did he know this guy anyway? "Look, Doc, I can't promise things won't get dirty, but the initial plan is that we find this little shit and dump him in the laps of the local cops. I've gotta say, part of me hopes he'll fight back."

"Can I ask another question?"

"Sorry, Doc, unless it's about the scotch, that's it. Either you trust me and you're in, or you can go take a break in your room. I've made my decision and so have these guys. You're either part of the family or you're not."

Brian's eyes flashed with reserved anger as he continued. "I'll give you the benefit of the doubt that you weren't trying to be a total prick with that last statement, and that maybe the booze is talking a bit. I was going to ask you how *I* would fit into this little operation."

Cal flashed a conspiratorial smile and nodded to the team. "I told you he wouldn't puss out, guys. He belongs here."

"Tell me you didn't just put me through some kind of test, Cal."

"What can I say, Doc? Once a Marine, always a Marine. Didn't your company gunny give you shit until he knew you weren't just another swabby?"

Brian chuckled. "Yeah. That guy rode my ass for months. Good guy though. He's one of the guys I saved."

MSgt Trent stepped forward. "Look, Doc, you might as well get it through your head that this place is a lot like the Marine Corps, including Cal's smart-ass comments. We all give each other a hard time, but in the end, we take care of one another. You've probably already heard some of the stories of some of us second-chancers."

Brian's eyes went wide as he stared at the six-foot seven mass of muscles. "You're a second-chancer too?"

MSgt Trent's chuckle sounded more like the rumble of a mountain landslide. "A former screw-up just like the rest of these boys. I had the misfortune of getting on the wrong side of a prick Major. I was working in the chow hall with Fifth Marines at the time. Long story short, turned out this guy was not only looking at kiddie porn on our government computers, he also made some inappropriate passes at my young female Marines. The guy had the balls to do it right in front of me. He was a terminal Major with close to twenty years in, so I guess he thought he could do whatever he wanted. Well, as soon as one of my Marines told me what was going on, I confronted him. He denied it in one breath, and in the next told me that even if he was doing anything, it wasn't any of my business. I told him the next time I heard about him messing with any of my Marines, he'd end up in the hospital."

MSgt Trent continued. "I hoped that would be the end of it. He wasn't that smart or lucky. A week later, I went into the walk-in freezer to get some supplies. I open the door and find this Major with his hand up the shirt of one of my female Marines pushed up against a produce rack. It was pretty obvious she'd been struggling. The prick had the nerve to tell me to leave. Instead I picked the scrawny fuck up by the front of his cammies and threw him through the door."

There was a pause before the story continued. "I'm not proud of what I did next, but he'd had his chance. Let's just say he won't ever have the option of getting a woman pregnant. The MPs showed up five minutes later and I told them the whole story. While the regimental commander was sympathetic, he couldn't ignore the fact that I assaulted a Marine officer – and robbed him of his chance to make little future Marines."

MSgt Trent gestured over to Cal's cousin. "Next thing I know, I'm getting a visit from Travis over there. He tells me who he is without getting into details, then offers me a tryout here at SSI. Needless to say, I jumped at the chance."

"And the rest, as they say, is history," Travis said grandly.

Trent nodded thoughtfully and continued. "Listen, Doc, nobody's forcing you, but if you walk away with anything today I want it to be this: This company and these guys will become your family. They're fair and will fight to the death for you once you're here. Besides that, the pay's pretty damned good too."

He smiled as he finished and took a long pull from his glass.

Travis, now visibly in the cups, picked up where Trent left off. "I guess what we're saying Doc is that this'll be the last job you'll ever have."

Brian seemed close to reddening with embarrassment as the small group of men smiled knowingly. "Wait, are you offering me a job?"

"You're technically *not* a second-chancer, but I think your record and Cal vouching for you pretty much makes you a shoe-in," Travis said. "Plus, Neil told me he'd love to have some input from a medical combat vet on some of the life-saving gear he's developing."

The young nurse was completely floored. "No shit?"

"Well, you'd have to split the royalties from any new patents with Neil and the company, but I don't think that will be a problem. That would be on top of your salary."

Brian looked between Travis and Cal. "But you guys don't even know me!"

Travis chuckled. "Look, Doc, we've been doing this for a while. We've obviously got an eye for talent. Cal aside, everybody else around here is in the top one percent of their peer group."

"Screw you, Trav," Cal said, smiling. "What my cousin's trying to say is that we've done our homework on you. We know about your awards. We know about your perfect PFT and shooting scores. We know you're like us. I know this is a big decision, but we're all in agreement."

"What would I do about my other job?"

"Up to you," said Cal. "Would you rather be working there?"

"That's not what I'm saying," Brian said, slowly. "They've been good to me and the pay's not bad."

"Come on, Doc, nursing is a good service for humanity, but your talents are being wasted there. Besides, you really want to go back to changing bed pans after what you've seen around here?" Cal grinned. "Plus, I'll twist Trav's arm to take care of you on the salary side."

"It does look like you guys have a pretty good thing going around here," Brian said. "I guess I'm in."

Travis walked up to Brian and put his non-drinking arm around his new employee. "Then welcome to the family, my boy. I just have one more question for you. You're obviously a smart guy, super fit, a warrior. How come you didn't go to B.U.D.S and become a SEAL?"

Without pause, Brian innocently answered. "Because it only took me one time to pass the ASVAB."

The whole room exploded in laughter as Travis shook his head. "Looks like you'll fit right in around here, Doc."

DANTE CUT the connection on his cell phone and looked around at his newly assembled forces. "I just got the address. Be ready to go tomorrow night after I do a drive-by."

The hired guns all nodded and continued preparing their gear for the impending mission. Dante looked around the room appraising his beefed-up crew. Bullet proof vests and automatic weapons weren't cheap, but they were effective. Things were about to change. A war was coming.

That Marine's about to feel some pain.

CAMP SPARTAN, ARRINGTON, TN

The newly formed team spent the following days going over "borrowed" police reports, courtesy of Neil.

"Someday you're gonna have to show me how the hell you find this stuff, Neil," Travis said.

"It's called plausible deniability, Mr. CEO. If I don't tell you, you can honestly tell your interrogators that you had no idea how I got my hands on this stuff. Besides, I can't show you all my secrets."

"Fair enough. How about you give us a quick rundown of what we're looking at. My eyes are starting to hurt."

"OK, here's the gist." Neil waved a hand at the reports. "The local authorities haven't come up with much. I will give them credit though; they've put a lot of resources into this investigation. Based on what Cal has told us, it looks like their rendition of what happened in the alley is pretty spot on. On the other hand, their search for West is lacking. They just don't have the resources. They've beaten the bushes and interrogated this Shorty guy but haven't come up with much. This kid was a new recruit and didn't have much knowledge of West's hideouts and operations. What they have gotten from him, they've exploited pretty efficiently."

"So, what you're saying is that we don't have much to go on," Cal said.

"Right," Neil said. "I've gone over everything they have and it really doesn't give us much help on finding West."

Cal turned to MSgt Trent, who was carefully studying a map of the Nashville area. "What do you think, Top?"

Without turning away from the map, Trent answered. "I think we need to start beating some bushes too. I'll volunteer to start on the north side of town."

"No offense, Top, but you're not the most inconspicuous of detectives," Cal said.

"Don't worry about me, Cal. What my size lacks in subtlety it more than makes up for in intimidation. I figure West is probably not only in deep shit with the cops, but also with some of his customers and rivals. The way these guys work, they're all thinly connected by financial obligations and past favors. I'll just pretend I'm looking for Mr. West to pay back the money he owes me. I can be pretty convincing when I want to be."

Cal relented. "OK. Can't say I have anything better. Neil, what do you think?"

"I'm with Top. We need to get some boots on the ground. He'll blend in best in that area anyway. I can give him some help with some gadgets if he wants. Just let me know what you need, Top."

Cal turned to his cousin. "Trav, I know you're busy but can you spare some time to talk with some of your contacts within the Metro Nashville Police Department?"

"No problem. I'll see if I can swing a lunch with a couple of my buddies. We've made some good friends on the force around here. They've even spent some time in our simulators and on our live fire ranges."

"Good. See what you can find out about on-going operations to find West and make sure they don't think we're jumping into this thing."

Cal turned to Brian next. "That leaves me, Doc, and Andy."

"OK," said Brian. "What are we doing?"

"Now that I'm getting around on my own power, I want to go have a little talk with Irene."

"The girl at your condo?"

Cal nodded. "I have a bad feeling that her walk through my condo wasn't just casual curiosity. Anybody have any other questions, comments, or concerns?"

Travis raised his hand. "Yeah, we may have one small issue. Just got a text from our legal department. Seems as though we've gotten a couple of inquiries from some local reporter. He was trying to find you and was looking for a comment on the investigation."

"Just tell them to blow him off," Cal said.

"I did but I've heard about this guy," Travis said. "He's a tenacious fucker. Young and ambitious. Gave the local police hell earlier this year over some alleged abuse scandal. Turned out to be nothing, but it really gave the police a black eye. This guy smells a story."

"What's his name?" Cal asked.

"Henry Bellinger."

"Why do I know that name?"

Travis shrugged. "You've probably seen his name on any story condemning conservatives, the military, or the police. He loves conspiracies and is smart as hell."

"So how do we deal with this guy?"

"Let me think about it. I may just put the Hammer on it."

Brian looked at Travis. "The Hammer?"

"Otherwise known as Marjorie Haines. She's our lead attorney. Don't call her Hammer or she'll kick your ass."

Cal thought about the problem for a minute. "What if I give him an interview over the phone? What could that hurt?"

Travis shook his head. "No way, Cal. This prick will find some way to twist your words. He's already suggesting that you should be arrested for the murder of those guys in the alley."

Cal's anger boiled over. "Any idiot can see that my actions were in self-defense. What's he trying to prove?"

His cousin answered by pointing his finger at Cal. "That's what he's trying to prove: you're some kind of animal that should be caged. He hates the military and would love to get a juicy story on the Killer Marine. I'm saying that if you get on the hook with this guy he'll make that famous short fuse of yours to burn out really quick."

Taking a labored, calming breath, Cal nodded to his cousin. "Touché. Guess it's pretty easy to hit my hot spot sometimes."

"Yeah, well, even your dad wasn't perfect there either," Travis said. "He had a killer temper on that rare occasion he got riled."

"Tell me about it. Alright, I'll stay away from this reporter and let you handle him. You guys ready to go?"

Everybody nodded and headed for the door.

―――――

DANTE DROVE by the home without turning his head, but instead used his peripheral vision to take in the details. The property was probably a couple of acres and far removed from any neighbors. It was situated in the Leipers Fork area in the city of Franklin, TN. The area was known for the mansions of some of country's oldest and brightest stars.

This home was nothing like the homes of the stars. It was a modest one level with a three-car garage. No frills. The driveway was lined with neatly spaced trees and the lawn was well maintained. Basic.

Dante drove a little way past the property and looked back. There didn't seem to be any activity outside. He decided to take a chance and pull into the vacant land adjacent to the target property. A densely wooded entryway gave him a perfect opportunity to conceal the late model Honda Civic he was driving.

Carefully slipping out of the car, he pulled down his ball cap and checked his aviator sunglasses to make sure his face was properly hidden.

He didn't have to go far to find a decent spot behind a tree that afforded him a clear view of the whole property. From the distance he couldn't see any movement. He pulled out a pair of small sport binoculars he'd purchased for cash at a nearby gas station. His eyes adjusted and focused onto the side window that seemed to be part of the living area. All he wanted at this point was to confirm that the owners still lived at the location and were alone. The last thing he wanted this go-around was more surprises.

He waited ten, twenty, thirty minutes. Nothing. Just about the time he'd decided to leave and come back, Dante caught a flicker of activity in the back of the house. *Please don't have a big fucking dog.* Dante thought.

A middle-aged man walked out the back door onto a wooden deck trailed by a tiny Chihuahua. Dante watched as the man waited for the dog to relieve itself. Finished, the small dog ran happily back into the house and man followed. *One here. Now I've gotta make sure Mama's home too.*

He shifted his gaze and, minutes later, saw what he'd waited for. The man's wife walked into view after opening the garage door. Dante focused on the two modest vehicles and didn't find the telltale signs of a family trip or impending visitors. It looked like the couple would be at home tomorrow, alone.

He took his time walking back to the car. He ran the details of the upcoming assault through his head. This time he'd be the one leading the way just like the old days. Things wouldn't go wrong this time.

GULCH DISTRICT, NASHVILLE, TN

The three companions exited and headed for the front door of Cal's condo building. Through the glass, Cal could see Irene sitting at the welcome desk. A deep breath, and he passed through the doorway.

Irene looked up with her courtesy smile and yelped in surprise as she recognized Cal. "Well, well, look here! Cal! How are you?"

Cal noticed that the look of shock mingled with a hint of guilt on Irene's face. This girl was hiding something. Years of learning when junior Marines were lying to his face had honed his bullshit detector. He put on the nicest smile he could muster and pushed forward.

"Hey, Irene. How are things around here?"

"You know, occasionally busy, boring the rest of the time. You look great! How are you feeling?"

"A lot better, thanks. Just wanted to stop by and get some of my stuff. Oh, my fault. You've met my buddy Brian here and this is my friend Andy. Andy's a buddy of mine from the Marine Corps. They do all the heavy lifting while I just point to things."

Irene laughed dutifully, as did the others. The strain on the woman's face intensified as she processed the trio. "Are you... moving out or something?"

"Nope. Just gonna stay with some friends for a few days. Anybody been in my place since the last time I was here?"

Irene shook her head. "No, just your friend Brian the other day. I've got a bunch of mail for you. I can go get it for you and you can pick it up on your way out."

Cal looked over his shoulder. "Andy, can you go with Irene and get my mail? We'll be back down in five minutes."

"No problem," Andy said.

As Irene turned to head to the mailroom, Cal touched his right temple and glanced at Irene's desk. Andy followed his gaze, saw the cell phone, and nodded back to Cal. It would be Andy's job to use Neil's laser gadget to tap Irene's phone. Not a problem.

Cal and Brian headed to the bank of elevators and boarded the first to appear. As the doors closed, Brian turned to Cal. "You think it'll be as easy to do as Neil said?"

"Probably easier," Cal said. "By the time we get the mail, Neil should have her whole system tapped."

They were both anxious to hear from Neil and continued the rest of the way up to Cal's floor in silence, each wondering quietly what the cell phone hack would lead to.

As Cal was entering his pass code, his cell phone buzzed. He answered it on the second ring. "Yeah."

"Hey, we just got a positive connection and we're starting to download all her recent activity."

"OK. Call me back when you have a better idea of what we're dealing with."

"You got it."

Cal slipped his phone back in his pocket and walked toward the master bedroom. He came back a minute later with a small rolling suitcase. "You ready?"

"Do you need to get anything else?" Brian asked.

"Nope. Just got some extra pieces from the locker and some clothes. The rest I can borrow from the company."

Brian grabbed the suitcase and followed Cal back to the elevator. As they exited on the ground level, they found Andy waiting with a thin stack of junk mail. Irene was once again sitting behind the welcome desk, texting. She looked up as they walked toward Andy.

"Did you get everything you needed, Cal?" Her voice was still a little too bubbly.

"I did. Hey, Irene, has anyone been here recently looking for me?"

She did her best to keep the fake smile plastered on her face, but Cal noticed her face drop slightly at his questioning.

"Just the police. They came by the day after your... incident."

"Anybody else that you can remember?"

"No. I see everyone that comes in during the day. You know that the doors are locked after-hours and on the weekend."

"Yeah. I was just curious. Thanks again for keeping an eye on things, Irene."

"No problem," Irene said. "Let me know if we can do anything for you."

He started to leave, then paused and turned back. "Oh, forgot to mention one thing. Give the staff a heads-up that I installed a video surveillance system a few weeks ago. Nothing to worry about. I haven't had a chance to review any footage since getting out of the hospital yet. Just thought you guys should know."

Without waiting for a response from the open-mouthed Irene, he exited through the front door trailed by his two friends.

Andy waited until they'd reached the car before saying anything. "Real discreet, Cal. I wouldn't be surprised if she has a heart attack."

"Serves her right. I'm tired of sitting back and doing nothing. I guarantee she'll be on the phone with whoever she's been talking to as soon as we take off. In ten minutes, we'll know where West is hiding."

Without a good response, the other two climbed into the car and they were soon back on the road to Camp Spartan.

DANTE STROLLED into the dark room, shedding his layers of disguise as he went. The twelve men waiting were in various states of relaxation. Some were slumped on one of the couches smoking; others were playing video games or snacking on a huge bag of Popeyes takeout.

"All right, listen up," Dante said. "I just took a look at the house we're hitting tomorrow. I figure we can get in and out pretty quickly. I don't want to be there more than five minutes in case some hillbilly decides to stop by with his shotgun. No shooting unless we can help it. Everybody got that?"

A chorus of mumbled agreements answered.

"Good. Now, I want all of you to get some good rest tonight. I don't want anybody draggin' ass tomorrow night. That means go easy on the booze and weed."

One of the huge men from New Orleans raised his head and spoke up in a bored southern drawl. "This ain't our first rodeo, Dante."

"I know, I know. I just don't want any fuckups this time."

Someone else called from the back. "You mean not like the way Shorty went down?"

The comment was followed by snickers from the rest of the hired crew.

Dante growled his response. "You trying to challenge me? If you've got a problem, I'll take care of it right now."

The guy from the back was still smiling. "Relax, boss, I was just messin' with you."

Dante turned and headed for the back room. The sooner he could send the New Orleans bangers back home, the better. The walls of the small house were starting to close in on everyone. Just the day before, one of his original crew had gotten into it with one of the newcomers. It would've come to blows if Dante hadn't happened to walk in. He was tired of babysitting.

No matter. Tomorrow would be the night it would all end.

CAMP SPARTAN, ARRINGTON, TN

Cal, Andy and Brian arrived back at Camp Spartan to find Neil helping himself to the liquor in Cal's suite. On the bar, he'd arrayed an assortment of laptops, high tech headphones and speakers, and half-eaten room service. As Cal walked in the door, he saw Neil listening intently into one side of the set of headphones perched on his head. His concentration was so deep that he didn't even acknowledge the trio's entrance. Neil remained this way for another minute, then his eyes shot open and he ran his fingers deftly over the keyboard, apparently making notes from what he'd just listened to.

"Well?" Cal asked.

"Hold on a sec," Neil said in a flat tone, typing furiously.

Cal walked around the bar and pulled a beer out of the fridge. He motioned to the other two with the beer and both nodded. He pulled two more bottles out of the fridge, expertly popped off the tops on the side of the bar, and brought them around to Andy and Brian.

Andy waited patiently with a look of quiet amusement as Neil wrapped up his note-taking. Brian walked to the large bay window and took in the beautiful day. Cal tried to look over Neil's shoulder just for a glimpse of what he was doing, but Neil shooed him away.

Finally, Neil finished and swiveled his bar stool around to face the others. "OK," he said with a sigh, "I've got bad news and good news."

Cal was impatient. "Would you just tell us what you found out, dammit?"

"Patience is a virtue, my boy. Anyway, the good news first. Your girl Irene has not been tipping off Dante West or any of his crew."

"And the bad news?"

"She's been doing spy work for that reporter, Bellinger."

"What?"

"Looks like little innocent Irene is a little short on cash and this guy Bellinger loves good contacts within the ranks of hotel and condo concierge," Neil said. "They've usually got the most access, so he targets them pretty heavily."

"What was she rooting around my place for?"

"Any little tidbits he could use to write a story. Your Navy Cross citation to start. He wanted her to see if you were maybe a druggy, closet gay, or something like that. Anything to make his story juicier."

Cal growled. "I'd love to pay that guy a little visit."

Andy shook his head. "You know you can't do that, Cal. It'd just make things worse. Besides, you said that from the surveillance video you watched, she couldn't find anything."

"It still pisses me off."

"I know but listen to this." Neil's gestures became more animated. "So, it looks like this Bellinger guy is desperate for intel. By the tone of his voice over the phone, it's pretty obvious he's grasping at straws. Who knows, maybe he'll give up soon."

"I doubt it," Cal said. "He'll keep digging until he finds something. I'll just have to be careful about being seen in public doing something stupid."

Brian couldn't resist. "When you say stupid, do you mean like hunting down a fugitive and leaving him hog-tied for the cops?"

"Yeah. I guess we just need to make sure we don't get caught."

Brian groaned. "You can say that again."

It was obvious Brian still wasn't convinced the operation could be pulled off without the authorities or this reporter finding out. He took a pull from his beer.

Cal could see the apparent discomfort on Brian's face. "Have a little faith, Doc. You haven't seen any of us in action yet. I think you may be pleasantly surprised."

"That's what I'm afraid of," Brian said wryly, "actually enjoying this shit."

THE TEAM of four spent the next couple hours running through Irene's cell phone logs and recent text, email, and phone conversations. Other than the dialogue with the reporter, she seemed like any other twenty-something working girl.

Cal yawned as he looked at his watch. "Alright guys, why don't we break until tomorrow morning? By then, Top should be back and we may have a little more insight into the location of our beloved bad guy."

"Sounds good to me. I'm beat." Andy stretched and headed for the door. "I'll see you ladies in the morning. Anyone wanna join me for a little motivating PT run at the crack of dawn?"

Brian perked up at the mention of physical activity. "I'll go with you."

Cal laughed. "I don't think you know what you're getting into, Doc. Good ol' Andy is a marathon runner. I remember how he used to take our whole platoon on these God-awful runs. You look at the man and he doesn't look like a runner, but I've never seen anyone beat him in distances over five miles."

"I think I'll take my chances," Brian said. "I could use a solid ass-kicking after eating all this good food you guys have around here."

Andy feigned innocence. "Don't worry, Doc, I'll *try* to be nice. I'll come get you in the morning."

The rest of the team packed up and headed to their respective rooms. Cal took a minute to gaze out the window and imagine what the next day would hold. *We've gotta find that guy, dammit.* And with that, he walked to the master bedroom and fell into a fitful sleep.

TOP

MSgt Willy Trent was no stranger to the dark streets. Growing up in Atlanta, he'd quickly found that his premature growth spurt elicited a certain amount of respect among the neighborhood kids. Even the teenagers five years older than young Willy often deferred to his ever-growing stature.

He'd found a love for weight lifting and sports at a young age. His size was an obvious advantage on the football field and the basketball court. Unlike a lot of kids that grow quickly and have a hard time dealing with the awkwardness of clumsy long limbs, young Willy seemed gifted with natural balance and athleticism.

His size and talent quickly led him to lord over most of the young toughs in the neighborhood. Typical of adolescent mischief, fights were common. Nothing too violent, just a couple of boys punching each other, one usually walking away with nothing more than a bloody nose or soon-to-be black eye.

Because of his size and quickness, Willy never lost a fight before the age of fifteen. Up until then, he could do no wrong. The only thing he didn't succeed in – and it wasn't because he couldn't – was school work. His mind was focused only on playing sports and running his neighborhood crew. Later in life, his mental ability would be tested, and Willy wasn't too surprised to find out that his IQ was in the ninety-fifth percentile. It was this ability that made him a natural leader and crafty athlete. Brains plus brawn were a mighty combination.

At the time, Willy made it a habit to sneak out at night (and infuriate his poor mother to no end) to hang out with his friends. They'd never do any real damage, just roam the streets hooting and hollering like kids do.

It was on one of these occasions that Willy's young crew encountered one of the local punks and his small gang of hoods. Typical of Atlanta summer nights, the air was thick with humidity and a lot of kids would hang around the local 7-Eleven, sipping ice-cold Slurpees and trying to stay cool.

On this particular night Willy's crew got to the 7-Eleven after the older and larger gang led by Leshon Braxton. Leshon was in his early twenties and ran the gang with an iron fist. No one in the local neighborhood wanted to get on Leshon's bad side.

As was typical when walking the streets, Willy led the way. He recognized Leshon and nodded in acknowledgement. Leshon's eyebrows rose as he appraised the towering teen.

"Hey there, Willy!" Leshon said. "I saw you on the football field last week. Helluva game, brother."

Willy stayed quiet, nodded his thanks and continued on his path toward the front door of the store. "Hey, Willy, what's wrong? Don't you want to talk to me?"

A couple of the older boys snickered as they watched their leader egg Willy on. The tall young man turned to face Leshon. "It's all good, Leshon. Me and my boys just wanted to go get something to drink."

"OK, but that can wait a minute. Why don't you boys head on in there and get your drinks? Give me a minute to talk with Willy."

The younger boys looked to Willy for guidance. He nodded his consent and moved aside as they filed into the store.

Leshon waited until they were out of earshot to start talking again. "So how come you've never come to hang out with me and my boys, Willy?"

"You know how it is, man. These guys have been my friends since I was little."

Leshon nodded paternally. "I get it. I get it. But you know what, you're not getting any younger. Maybe it's time for you to upgrade to the big boy crew. What do you think, Willy?"

Willy knew this day would come. One of the problems with his size and ability he'd been gifted with was that he'd become a target. Some older kids searched him out because they thought he would be a good conquest. Others, like Leshon, seemed to prize Willy because they saw the strength and intelligence in the young man.

Young Willy recognized the look in Leshon's eyes. He wanted a new recruit. It'd happened before with less capable crews, but Willy got a bad feeling staring back at Leshon. He didn't seem like the type of dude that would take no for an answer.

"I don't know, man. My mama wouldn't really want me hangin' out with older guys."

At his comment about his mother, the older boys laughed out loud. One of the problems with being the target was that you just had to stand there and take it sometimes. There's no way he could match the six guys either in an argument or a fistfight. He'd just have to sit there and accept it.

"Don't you worry about your mama, Willy," Leshon said. "I'll take care of her. I'll take *good* care of her."

Leshon punctuated the lewd comment by licking his lips lasciviously.

Willy took a calming breath trying to stave off the inevitable boiling over of his anger. He wasn't the best at listening to his mother's lectures, but he was very protective of the widow. His father had died in a factory accident when Willy was three and the boy had made it his mission to protect his mother ever since. *Calm down, Willy. Getting mad will only make things worse.*

"Come on, Leshon. Can I just go inside now?"

Leshon's eyes grew wide. "You telling me what to do now, Wee Willy?"

Willy was desperate now. "No, man. I just need to get back home before my mama notices I'm gone."

"I told you, Willy, I'll take care of that fine mama of yours."

He smirked as he looked around at the matching grins on his crew. Leshon wasn't going to let him out of this.

"What do I need to do so I can go, Leshon?"

"You can start by not being a little bitch," Leshon said. "Is that what you are, Wee Willy? A little bitch?"

Willy's head snapped up. Even his tolerance for mockery had its bounds. Later in life, friends would comment that he was like a friendly giant; kind to a fault and slow to anger, but once riled he could not be stopped.

Leshon smiled at the incensed youth. "Now I see that fire, boy. How about we see how that fire burns? What do you say you and me go a couple of rounds?"

A stirring began in Willy's gut. Leshon was famous for his street brawls. He'd sent a couple of kids to the hospital, and it was rumored he'd once been a semi-pro boxer in his old hometown. Leshon was definitely built like a heavyweight fighter: standing six foot three and well into the middle two hundreds. He was an imposing figure to most other kids.

But Willy wasn't as easily deterred. Even at fifteen, he was already close to six foot four and just over two hundred pounds. Added to his formidable size were the countless hours of honing his body to athletic perfection on the football field and in the weight room. Willy was confident in his abilities one-on-one.

But not six-on-one.

"I don't wanna fight you, Leshon." His voice was a whisper.

"I didn't ask what *you* wanted, boy! Now get your ass around the back of this building and let's see who the big dog is around here!"

Leshon's companions whooped a cry of delight and pushed the reluctant Willy toward the other side of the building. Their leader led the way as he pulled off his shirt showing off an impressive array of tattoos.

Willy glanced back to the store and noticed his friends peering out of the window; wide-eyed and realizing he was in big trouble.

As the small gang reached the back of the building, Leshon turned suddenly and landed a wide right hook into Willy's left cheek. He'd seen it at the last possible second and was able to minimize the hit by turning his head to the right, but holy hell did it hurt. The blow spun Willy to the right and down to his knees. He couldn't help it.

Leshon kept taunting him. "Come on, you little bitch! Get up and show me what you got!"

Well, there's no way out of this now. Willy thought. He shook his head once and stood up to his full height. In that second, something in his demeanor changed. Leshon noticed it and so did the others. Willy's look of supreme confidence and cold anger caused a hush in the small crowd and made Leshon think twice about charging.

Willy used the pause to make his move. He bum-rushed Leshon and swung a right-handed haymaker. Only it was a calculated ruse, for just as he was about to connect with his attacker's blocking arm, however, he used his momentum to hug Leshon into the path of his forehead. There was the sound of cracking shells as Willy's forehead connected with Leshon's exposed nose. Blood splattered from the flattened nostrils as the two young men fell to the ground.

Willy knew he had him. One of the things he'd learned in his early fights was that despite the rage he mustered to take out an opponent, his mind stayed serenely calm. It was yet another gift that would serve him well later in life.

He used that talent to quickly weigh his options. If he incapacitated Leshon now, he'd most likely have to turn and take on the other five. Not the best opportunity for getting out of the mess relatively unscathed. Just as Willy cocked back to headbutt him again, Leshon screamed in fear.

"Get this motherfucker off me!"

The next three minutes were a complete blur as the remaining crew members jumped into the fray. Fists flew and boots stomped as the gang pounded away at the defenseless Willy. He balled up in a fetal position to protect himself.

At some point, between blows to the head and torso, Willy heard his mother's voice. She was screeching at the other young men. He looked up through bloody eyes to see his mother holding his father's old shotgun. He didn't even realize his mother knew how to use the weapon.

She leveled the shotgun at Leshon. "I'm giving you boys two seconds to get the hell out of here or I'm gonna shoot."

"This ain't over, bitch!" Leshon yelled back as he quickly fled the scene. His crew followed close behind. No one turned a head back.

"You OK, son?"

Willy raised his bloody face and looked up at his mother. In the limited light, she reminded him of a guardian angel. A shotgun-wielding guardian angel. He tried to answer, but the words came out as a slur. It was now obvious that his jaw was broken and he'd sustained other injuries to his whole body. He felt like his entire high school football team had literally run him over. Twice.

"Come on, son," his mother said. "Let's get you to the hospital. Don't try to talk."

It wasn't easy for Willy's mother to help her son off the ground, but they somehow made it vertical and around the side of the building to her idling car.

Willy later found out that one of his friends had called Mrs. Trent as soon as Leshon had provoked the fight. Luckily, the Trent household was right around the corner.

He remembered the look on his mother's face as she nursed the beaten and bruised Willy. There was a sadness there that he couldn't place. At the same time, he saw a deep determination in her eyes. He didn't know what it was until days later when his mother came in and announced that they were moving across town to live with his grandmother.

"I should've seen it a while ago, Willy," she said. "In this neighborhood, you're gonna get nothing but trouble. I've already talked to the private school across town and they say that, with a partial scholarship for football, they can put us on a payment plan. I've already talked to my cousins over there and they're gonna help me get extra work."

"I don't want you to do that, Mama. I can handle things around here."

"It's not in your control, son. You don't get nowhere fast with a target on your back. If it's not those boys that attacked you the other night, it'll be someone else. We've outgrown this town. We need to start a new life in a better place."

It was obvious to Willy that there was no use arguing. Her mind was made up and he'd have to go along with her decision. Deep down, he knew she was right. He would always be a target.

The move proved to be surprisingly easy. It was good to be close to family and Willy quickly excelled at school. The mostly-white high school was amazed at his talent on the football field. With the help of some very diligent teachers, Willy soon caught up to, or surpassed his peers in the classroom. He learned to love his studies and eventually became not only captain of the football and basketball team but also senior class president and valedictorian.

Not a bad rise for a walking target.

MSGT TRENT THOUGHT back to those days as he strolled the streets of North Nashville. It'd been a while, but most inner city neighborhoods had a similar smell and feel. Dressed in dark clothing with a long leather trench coat, he was glad he'd never have to live in such a place ever again. *Thanks to Mama,* he thought as he said a silent prayer to his now-deceased guardian angel.

His mission was clear: infiltrate the area and get intel on the location of Dante West. He and Cal had agreed that it would be highly unlikely that Trent would stumble on West. They just needed some better information so they could hopefully triangulate the guy's whereabouts.

So far, he'd questioned a couple of winos and hookers. They'd all said the same thing: Dante hadn't shown his face in a while. He changed tactics and started pushing the fact that West owed him some big money and he was going get paid tonight or heads would roll. It was time to light a fire and see what came running out of the woods.

He finally hit pay dirt around two in the morning. One of the hookers, obviously high on something, had led him to one of Dante's supposed drug houses. Trent snuck around the side of the dilapidated duplex trying to get a better feel for what he was up against. He pulled his Beretta out of his coat pocket just in case.

Making his way to the back of the house, he heard a television through the open window. Obviously, the inhabitant wasn't trying too hard to keep the space secure. He glanced in through the corner of the window and saw two black men sitting on a dirty couch watching television and enjoying some weed. Bottle-shaped brown paper bags sat pinned between them. Both men had pistols within arm's reach on the couch. Clearly, they weren't completely stupid.

Keeping a low profile, Trent shifted his gaze around the room and saw two women sprawled naked on the floor on top of soiled blankets. Both women were passed out and probably high by the looks of their slack jaws. He didn't see any other visitors and wondered what was upstairs.

He squatted down next to the house and reached into his other coat pocket. He pulled out the small box Neil had given him. Opening the box, he extracted the pair of sunglasses and then gently handled the tiny flying spy camera. *Better safe than sorry.*

He put on the sunglasses and pressed the side arm. The tiny drone went airborne and the left lens mirrored the camera's point of view. He directed the camera to fly up to the second story window. The slight buzzing was completely muffled by the sound of the television and nighttime noises. As it came up to the second level, the drone slowed and hovered. Trent peered into the darkened room and looked through night vision eyes at the empty floor.

The device moved into the room and rotated to give Trent a full view of the contents. Lots of trashed furniture but no people. He completed the scan of the upstairs by directing the drone into the bathroom and a second bedroom. Empty. *Good.*

Next, he directed the spy camera down the stairs and into the kitchen. Other than a sink and table full of used to-go cartons, the place was empty. That left the two pushers and their girlfriends in the living room.

He brought the drone back outside and stowed it and the glasses in his pocket. After a second to think, he knew the easiest way to find out what he needed was to just knock down the back door. He was pretty sure he could take care of the two men.

He stashed his pistol back in its holster, then withdrew two more of Neil's presents. They were specially modified tasers. They were a lot smaller than the commercial version used by police and private citizens, but just as powerful. In Trent's hands, they each looked like matching Pez dispensers, roughly the same size as their candy counterparts.

Out of habit, he checked to make sure the laser sights worked. Before leaving, Neil had suggested taking two just in case. Trent would have to remember to thank the techie for the forethought. If he was lucky, he could incapacitate both men without much noise. The last thing he wanted to do was burst into the house with guns blazing.

He stayed in a crouch as he moved around to the back of the little house. The keys to what he was about to do was overwhelming force and surprise. Having the two idiots shooting at him wouldn't do any good. MSgt Trent was hoping he'd catch the men with drug- and alcohol-slowed reflexes. He took two more settling breaths, squared himself to the back door and pictured the two men ten feet from the rear entrance. Holding the Pez tasers loosely in each hand, he took one big step back then exploded through the door with his size fourteen boot leading the way.

The door shattered the locking mechanism and Trent followed the door into the room. He looked down at the surprised expressions of the two drug dealers and didn't hesitate to aim each taser at their chests and depress the triggers.

Before the guys could reach for their guns, the taser wires reached out. The probes penetrated their thin shirts and instantly started pouring voltage into their nervous systems. Trent held down the switches for five seconds then released. The shocked duo slumped back down on the couch.

Without hesitation, the former Master Sergeant started the interrogation. "Where's Dante?"

The first man cried out shakily. "What?"

"I said, where's Dante? You don't start answering my questions and I'm gonna keep shocking."

"No, *please...*"

Trent switched on the electricity and watched as the men writhed in agony. Turning the juice off, he started again.

"Like I told you," Trent said, "answer my questions. Now, one more time: Where's Dante?"

The first man spoke again. "I don't know, man!"

The next shock threw the man's head back, hitting the wooden frame of the couch with a sharp crack. Turning off the power again, Trent explained calmly, "I'm gonna tell you this one last time. Dante owes me some money and I mean to get it tonight. The only thing I want you boys to tell me is how I can find the motherfucker."

The second man finally spoke. "OK, OK!"

Despite the screams and grunts, neither of the passed-out women on the floor had yet to stir.

"You ready to tell me where he is?" Trent asked.

"We don't know exactly where he is," the second man said. "He's been moving around a lot."

"You mean since he killed that girl?"

"I don't know anything about that, man. All I know is that the cops are after him and we haven't seen him for a while."

"So how do you know he's still around?" Trent asked.

"He calls us a couple of times a day. Dante wants to make sure we're still making money for him."

"Does he call you on your cell phone?"

"Yeah." The man motioned with his head at the end table where two new mobile phones sat in chargers. "Usually calls once in the morning and once at night. Wants to know how big our haul was."

"And how was your haul today?" Trent asked.

The man looked at his companion not knowing how he should answer the hulking trespasser.

"Wrong answer, dipshit!" Trent depressed the power switch, again wondering how many times he'd have to do it. After a good long shock, he turned off the power. "How was your haul today?"

The second man answered again, despite his trembling. "Dammit, man! It was good, OK? You know what kind of trouble we're gonna be in with Dante for telling you this shit?"

"Don't you worry about Dante. I don't think he's gonna be around much longer. I've heard I'm not the only one looking for money. I just want to be the first one to get mine."

"You can take whatever we've got here, just don't tase us again, man!"

"How much do you have?" Trent asked.

"A couple grand."

"A couple grand?" Willy said, laughing. "I thought you said you had a good haul today."

"We did," the man said, "but Dante sends one of his girls to come pick up every night. She usually comes by around midnight."

Knowing he had to keep up the charade, Trent went in another direction. "OK, where's the money you have here?"

The man on the left pointed to a Nike shoebox on the floor. "In there."

"A safe deposit box. Very intelligent. Alright, you two sit tight as I make sure you're not bullshitting me."

Keeping the two men directly in front of him, Trent shifted around and glanced down into the box. It definitely looked like there was a couple of thousand dollars in assorted bills piled neatly inside.

"Here's what's gonna happen next, boys," Trent said. "You're gonna turn, face each other and give one another a big hug."

The second man cocked his head to the side. "What?"

Trent didn't even bother warning the men as he depressed the taser one last time. When the jolts ceased, both men had obviously met their limit and were ready to comply.

"Like I said," Trent continued, "I want you to face each other, give your buddy a big hug, and hold it."

The two men looked at each other not really wanting to know what was coming next. They did as instructed and glared back at Trent.

"Now, you with the arms on top I want you to straddle your homeboy."

The man hesitated only briefly then awkwardly climbed onto his friend's lap with his legs and arms wrapped tightly. Trent shifted the tasers so that he had both in his left hand, then reached into a large cargo side pocket and pulled out a handful of long black zip ties.

"If either one of you fuckers move, I'm gonna shock you until you're stupid for life. Got it?" Both men nodded and didn't budge as Trent expertly tied both set of hands and feet with the cables. "I hate to do this to you guys, but I can't have you running after me. Don't worry, as soon as your ladies wake up, they can cut you out."

He linked two zip ties together and looped it all the way around both men's necks. He secured a neck restraint by looping another zip tie between the two and cinching it down tightly. They weren't going anywhere without strangling themselves – not without help from their unconscious companions.

He finished by pulling out the taser wires and stuffing them, two cell phones, and two pistols into the cardboard box full of cash.

"Well, boys, thanks for your cooperation. And remember: Just say no to drugs."

Trent exited the way he came in and slowly made his way back to his concealed pickup truck down an alley a couple of blocks away.

He pulled out his cell phone and dialed Cal, who picked up on the first ring.

"Yeah."

"I think I got one of those breaks we were looking for," Trent told him.

"OK. I'll put on the coffee and wake up the boys. I'll see you when you get back."

"Roger, out."

Trent replaced his phone, started the big diesel engine and made his way back down to the compound.

Not bad for a former misfit, he thought.

CAMP SPARTAN, ARRINGTON, TN

After relaying the story – pausing once in a while for laughter – to the assembled group consisting of Cal, Brian, Andy, Travis and Neil, Trent went on to explain what he thought they should do with the stolen cell phones.

"It seems to me that West is pretty tight on cash. I doubt he'd want to miss any one of his pickups. My vote would be to set a little ambush for his cash girl and convince her to take us back to Dante tomorrow night. The problem is, now he'll know we're onto him if he calls one of these cell phones."

Cal turned to Neil. "Do you have any way to tap into these cell phones?"

"I thought you'd never ask. I can make these phones do things you could never imagine. When I'm done with them, they'll be singing like canaries."

"You wanna tell us how you're gonna do that or do I have to zip tie your ass like Top's buddies?"

Neil looked apologetic. "Didn't mean to be a smartass, Cal. So, here's what I'm gonna do. I'll take whatever info I can off the cell phones. I can pretty much guarantee they're disposables so their secrets will be limited. If we're lucky, I might be able to find the phone number West is calling from and then use the cell carrier's network to pinpoint which towers he's been feeding off of when he calls. That *might* give us a better idea of where he's operating out of. Again, no promises."

Cal nodded. "That's more than we had an hour ago. Do the best you can and get us close. I think the rest of us should get working on gear."

ABOUT FIFTEEN MINUTES LATER, Neil looked up from his laptop. "I've got something!"

The rest of the group crowded around to look over his shoulder. The entire screen looked like complete gibberish to all except for the excited computer hacker.

Neil pointed at the screen. "So, check this out right here. I told the program to look for the two numbers I tagged that were recently used by West. At least we know he's still in the area."

Cal stared at the screen not fully comprehending what he should be looking at. "Dude, do you want to tell us what the hell you're talking about? What is all that crap on the screen?"

"These right here are the periodic signals from the towers on the north end of Nashville," Neil explained. "All the recent pings are in the same area."

"So, we can see exactly where this guy is hiding," Brian said.

Neil shook his head. "Nope. This just shows us the general area he's hanging out in."

"How big of an area are we talking about?" Trent asked.

Neil looked sheepish. "About two square miles."

Cal clenched his fist in frustration. "That's like finding a needle in a haystack. Can't you do any better than that?"

"I told you this wasn't foolproof, Cal," Neil said. "It doesn't help that West isn't a total idiot. He's clearly utilizing multiple disposable phones and using them only when needed. The best shot we have is if he calls one of the phones Willy brought back; *or* we catch him moving out of the area he's been hanging out in."

"Shit." Cal dragged a hand down his face. "Look, we don't have much time before he realizes those cell phones are compromised. Anyone have any bright ideas?"

Andy shrugged. "What if we just give the guy a call? What's the worst that could happen? Maybe Master Sergeant Trent could play his 'give me my money' routine?"

"To what end?" Cal asked. "He'd just trash the phone he's got. No, we've gotta have a better plan to use these damn things to our advantage."

Cal picked up one of the stolen cell phones and started turning it over and over as he contemplated their next step.

"What if we get him to run?" Brian said suddenly.

Cal turned to the former Corpsman and waved for him to continue.

"What I mean is, set up some kind of loose perimeter in the area we think he's hanging out in. Then maybe Top can scare him enough to run into our net. It's not the perfect solution, but at least it's something."

It was obvious, after a few quiet seconds, that no one really loved the idea, but all were at a loss to come up with something better.

"So, let's say we get this guy out in the open," Andy said. "Then what? A *French Connection*-style chase through the streets of Nashville? I see way too many things wrong with the idea, but unless we can pinpoint his exact location and conduct a quick raid, I can't think of anything better."

Cal nodded and stroked his chin. "So, if we can't just catch him in the open, can we somehow lure him to another location and take him there?"

Trent checked his watch. "Cal, it's six in the morning and I really don't think—"

The silent buzzing of one of the confiscated phones cut off Trent's comment. Everyone looked down in anticipation as Neil carefully picked it up and looked at the caller ID.

"It's him."

Without hesitation, MSgt Trent grabbed the small phone and answered on speakerphone. "Yeah?"

"Yo, who's this?" Dante asked.

"A customer."

"Listen, asshole, put Jevon on the phone."

"Jevon ain't here. He went to take a leak."

"Then put Polo on."

"He's upstairs gettin' it on with one of the girls."

They could hear swearing in the background as Dante tried to figure out what the hell was going on. "Go get those idiots and tell them to call me back!"

The line went dead.

"Well, that buys us two minutes," Trent said. "Any ideas?"

Neil looked up from his computer. "I think I've got something. My tracking program was able to pinpoint West's location down to one square block. Is there any way we can get there fast?"

Andy shook his head. "Now that it's light out, I don't see how we can pull this off without the whole world knowing. I say we call him back and tell him we know where he is and see what happens. Cal, can we get some of your company assets up there like yesterday?"

Cal turned to his cousin. "Trav, can I get four teams of two in civvies and standard vehicles up to Nashville?"

"I'll have them out front in ten minutes."

"Let's split up into two teams. Me, Top and Neil will ride in Top's truck. Doc, can you drive your car up with Andy? I would rather keep you two a little farther back just in case."

Brian shrugged. "No problem."

"Alright, everybody grab your gear and any weapons you can conceal on your person," Cal said. "Top, do you still have some extra shotguns in the back of your truck?"

"Yeah."

"Why don't you go down with Doc and give him and Andy each one."

"You got it."

Trent, Brian and Andy left the room.

Cal turned to his tech guru. "Neil, can you bring your tracking gear on the ride with us?"

"Of course."

"Good. Now go put on some more operational shoes and let's get going."

Neil looked down at his Italian loafers. "I thought I had them on already."

―――

As promised, ten minutes later the teams assembled outside the Lodge. Cal gave everyone their instructions and patrol areas. Neil handed out small water-tight boxes to each team. Cal looked at him quizzically. Neil just winked back.

No one hesitated as they jumped in their respective vehicles and headed north.

NASHVILLE, TN

Cal looked into the back of the truck's cab to see if Neil was up and running. "You getting anything yet?"

"Nope. I probably won't get a damned thing until Top makes the next call. I'm worried this guy's gonna lose the phone and then we're shit out of luck."

"All right then, let's make the call, Top. Remember, keep him on the line as long as you can. Say anything you need to."

Although he was driving, MSgt Trent pulled out the stolen cell and re-dialed Dante's number on speaker. The other man picked up after the first ring.

"Where the fuck have you been?"

"I've been in my truck," Trent said coolly.

"What do you mean, you've been in your truck? I told that fool to have you give… Wait a minute, who is this?"

"This is the fool."

"What are you talkin' about?"

"The fool you owe money to, bitch."

Dante was silent for a few seconds. "Where are my two boys?"

"Don't you worry about them. They're nice and cozy."

Dante's voice rose in anger. "Fool, if I find out you killed them..."

"Calm down, Dante. I didn't kill 'em. I'm just after my money."

"Fool, I don't even know who you are, asshole."

"Fool or asshole? Make up your mind. And I told you, I'm the one you owe money to," Trent said again.

Neil poked his arm through the two front seats with a thumbs-up signaling that he'd caught the cell phone trail. He'd silently told them that he'd need about a minute after latching on to the signal before he could get a better location. The convoy was still about ten minutes from their target.

Now West sounded amused. "If I owed you money, you'd either be dead or on a payment plan by now. I don't know you. And if I don't know you, that means I don't owe you."

Trent glanced at Cal who gave him the keep going signal. "I said you owe me. I didn't say that you know me. It was actually one of your boys that I took care of over in the shitty little house in East Nashville. Motherfucker stiffed me out of ten grand last month when I came to deliver supply. I asked him to pay me and he told me to talk to you. Something about it being *your* business."

There was a pause on the other end as Dante weighed the new information. He wasn't an idiot. He wanted to keep all the customers he could get. Gangster or not, he was still a businessman.

"Look, fool, I don't know what that idiot told you but I never stiff my customers or my competition. This town is too small for that shit."

"That's what surprised me. I've been doing business with your guys for a while and this was the first time I ever felt cheated. So, what do we need to do to get me my money back?"

Trent looked at Cal who shrugged his shoulders as if to say, *I can't believe this guy is buying this.*

"How about I have a little talk with my boy and I'm sure we can get this thing worked out."

"How about I come over to your place and we talk about it?"

"Sorry, man, that I can't do. Give me a couple minutes and I'll call you back."

Trent looked at Cal again, who nodded.

"OK. Call me back."

The line went quiet as the call ended.

Cal smacked Trent on the shoulder. "Nice job, Top. I guess he took the bait."

"Yeah, but I wouldn't count him out yet. He's like a cornered rat. A *smart* cornered rat. I could almost see the wheels in his head turning. Did you see how fast he calmed himself down? This is one cool customer."

Cal looked thoughtful. "Yeah."

"So, have you figured out what we're gonna do with this guy when we get him?"

"I figured we'd just have to see how it plays out. I'm sure, with the experience you guys have had in the past, we can hatch up some plan to dump him on the police without anyone knowing it was us."

"Now you're thinking," Trent said. "We can't let him know it's us either. That would be bad for you *and* for the company."

Neil raised a small duffel bag on the seat next to him. "Good thing we've got a bag full of black masks back here."

There was silence for a minute as Cal digested the conversation and planned the upcoming action. Worst case, they would miss West. Best case, they would find him. Then what? Cal couldn't run from what he felt in his heart: He wanted to see West die by his own hands. The realist in Cal pondered the idea and knew it wasn't the logical outcome. He could not put his people in jeopardy or endanger their livelihood. Furthermore, he did not want to be known as the wayward son that brought down his dead father's company.

Think, Cal, think.

He'd just come to a decision when Neil tapped him on the shoulder. "Put this in your ear, the team's checking in."

Cal glanced back as Neil handed him what looked like a miniature hearing aid. "What do I do with this thing?"

"I forgot you haven't used one of these yet," Neil said. "It's one of my latest gadgets. The boys in the field love it. It's going to let you communicate with the rest of the team. You're the only one that everyone will be able to hear all the time until you tap the side there." He pointed to the slightly raised edge on the side of the earpiece. "Tap it once to talk."

"How powerful is this thing?"

"Thanks to my mad skills, it's got a range of just over a mile. The battery is another one of my designs and will give you about twenty hours of straight use without recharging."

"Nice."

Cal slipped the tiny piece of communication gear in his left ear. He tapped the side of the earpiece.

"This is Snake Eye Six, teams check in, over."

Each of the six teams, including Brian and Andy, checked in with their respective assigned team numbers.

"OK, listen up. We're about five minutes out. When you get into position, I want your baby birds on the fly, over."

Each team confirmed. The quick plan Cal had laid out for the team prior to departure was that each pair would have one of the spy drones for easier reconnaissance. Upon final check in each team would launch their Baby Bird – Cal had named the drones much to the chagrin of Neil, who thought they should be called something more sophisticated – and discretely recon the objective. It would be tricky in the light of day, but the miniature size of the Baby Birds decreased the likelihood of detection by curious civilians.

"Something's not right about this," Dante said to himself.

Two of the hired guns glanced up in confusion. Dante waved them back to their card game.

He mentally processed each of his customers and drug partners. He knew the two men running the operation that had apparently been raided by the mysterious caller. He'd made a quick call to one of his whores to go take a peek inside. The soonest she could be there was in ten minutes.

Shit, Dante thought. He didn't like other people having the upper hand. West didn't like owing people either. It seemed like ever since that damn thing with Shorty he was neck deep in favors. Yes, he was a criminal, but he liked to think of himself as a relatively honest criminal. His crew always delivered, and never dared tread on someone else's territory unless provoked —or if it was marked for acquisition by Dante himself. By keeping that tight rein on operations, N.O.N. had seen solid growth in income and recruitment since 2005. West did not want that to go to shit. So, what should he do about this caller he supposedly owed money to?

NASHVILLE, TN

Neil let out a victory whoop. "I've got him!"

"Where is he?"

Neil swiveled his laptop so Cal could see and tapped on the property address. Cal relayed the information to the rest of the teams: The net just got a lot tighter.

"We're five minutes out. Let's get him back on the phone just to make sure."

MSgt Trent hit redial.

Dante answered on the first ring. "Yeah?"

"Did you find out where my money is?"

"Not yet."

"That's not good, brother."

"I know, I know. Look, I'm working on it. It doesn't help that I can't get a hold of the two boys you handled."

"Not my problem, Dante. Maybe I should come by and visit."

"Look, man, I think you know that there's no way I'm gonna tell you where I am, so how about we just calm down and wait."

"I'm not so good at waiting, Dante." Trent pushed harder. "What if I told you your boys told me where you're hanging out?"

He looked at Cal and smiled. He could hear the bastard sweating.

THE COMMENT DISTURBED DANTE. Deep down he knew there was no way his crew had snitched. Hell, he hadn't even told them where he was hiding. He wasn't stupid.

At the same time, the paranoid part of Dante West made him peek out the front window of the house. He didn't see anything suspicious. Besides, he had a house full of firepower ready to defend himself. The problem was that he just couldn't shake the confidence of this deep-voiced caller.

"I told you, man, there's no way you know where I am," Dante said. "Give me another couple of minutes. I've got a girl going over to the house. In two minutes, I'll know which of my boys I need to squeeze to get your money."

"What if I told you I'm on my way to your place right now, Dante?"

"I'd say you're bullshitting me." West peered out the window again. The other men in the room had gone mute and were watching Dante.

"I don't bullshit, bitch. I'm gonna get my money one way or another."

West put his phone on mute and yelled at his crew. "Get up off your asses and pack your shit. I think we've got trouble coming."

The men started running around gathering their gear in a fairly organized manner. These men were not novices to danger. They already had their weapons at the ready as each headed for the back door and their escape vehicles.

Dante took his cell phone off mute. "I've had enough of this conversation, man. Even if you are on your way, I'm gonna be gone. I'll call you from another phone later, if I feel like it."

He finished the call and began thinking faster than ever.

THE CONVERSATION ENDED and the line went dead.

Cal tapped on his earpiece and started instructing his assault teams. "All teams, get the Baby Birds ready. Target is on the move, I repeat, target is on the move."

It was overkill to let his men know to prepare their firearms. These were veterans who didn't hit the latrine without a weapon. They'd be ready when asked to execute. Each knew without being told that action within a civilian neighborhood required extreme caution. Firepower wouldn't be used except as a last resort. Per standard operating procedure, each member was given multiple tasers in the event close contact warranted non-lethal intervention.

As they rounded the second to last turn approaching the address provided by Neil, Cal pulled down his ball cap to conceal his face as much as possible. He didn't think wearing a black mask in a neighborhood would be the most inconspicuous disguise. Besides, he wasn't planning on letting Dante get a look at him.

The others didn't bother with the masks either. No one really thought West would call the cops and describe them to a sketch artist.

Cal heard his earpiece beep and listened to team Three.

"Six, this is Three. I think we just saw our target roll by. He's in a nineties model maroon Honda Accord. Target is driving and there are four other targets inside. Big boys too. How copy, over?"

"Roger, let's launch all Baby Birds now."

Team 2, made up of Andy and Brian, chimed in. "Six, this is Two, we've got three other vehicles leaving the target address."

"Dammit. All teams, any ideas on how to exploit this situation, over?"

There was a pause as each team pondered the question they'd already been calculating. They all knew the danger of exposing themselves. A prolonged chase and shootout was not in anyone's interest. It was Andy who spoke up first.

"Six, I think we need to go with Plan B."

Plan B was to call the local authorities and give them a good location on the wanted gang leader. Cal wrestled with the thought. He wanted nothing else but to get the man who'd killed his beloved. But how could they take the man out without engaging a bunch of armed gang members in the middle of the city?

In the desert of the Middle East, he wouldn't have thought twice. The decision would've been easy. This war was a different story. His team wasn't riding to battle in armored vehicles and combat gear. They were pursuing a wanted criminal in the heart of America wearing normal clothes and carrying a few measly weapons. Cal knew what he had to do.

"Roger that," Cal said. "I'll make the call."

Cal picked up the disposable cell phone that Neil had provided at step-off and dialed the number for Nashville's Metro Police Department. He relayed the pertinent information to the operator then hung up twenty seconds later.

His head hung down for a couple seconds and then he looked at his friends.

Trent spoke up first. "Don't worry, Cal, the cops won't get this guy. We'll find him later."

Cal nodded and looked back at his cell phone. If only he could use it to call in some artillery support or even some 30mm mortar rounds. As he daydreamed, he heard reports from the teams. West was slipping through their fingers.

"Six, Two, the cars have split up onto different roads, over."

"Six, Four, still have eyes-on target with Baby Bird, over."

"Six, Three, still have eyes on target. Target is speeding up, over." There was a pause. "Six, Three, cops just spotted target's car. Wait... lights are on, target is speeding up, over."

"Six, Two, the two cars we're following just sped up too, over."

"Six, Four, target is outpacing Baby Bird, over."

"Six, Three, trying to casually keep up with the chase, but they're really moving now, over."

Cal looked up and tapped his earpiece. "All teams break pursuit and meet-up at rendezvous point Charlie, out."

His face covered in silent frustration, Cal took the earpiece out, bent toward the console, and turned on the police scanner.

"Where the fuck did this guy come from?" Dante accelerated through the red light. His four passengers looked back toward the trailing police cruiser.

One minute they'd been driving down Dickerson Pike matching

the speed limit, then some cop had lit them up and pulled up behind them.

Not easily scared, West was now completely spooked. First, the call from the mysterious money collector and now the cops were onto him? This was the fourth car he'd had since being on the run. All the tags were legit. The car was clean. What the hell was going on? Was it possible the guy on the phone was a cop?

As he let that thought tumble through his mind, he continued to accelerate and speed through intersections. He swerved to miss cars and put more distance between him and the now-fading cop car. He'd had each of his escape rides specially equipped with new racing engines straight out of *The Fast and the Furious*. The cops didn't stand a chance unless they got a helicopter up above. West wasn't going to give them that opportunity.

Being the savvy criminal that he was, he'd already planned out multiple contingencies for escape. Right now, he was on his way to one of his many safe houses where he'd pick up another ride and move from there.

With the police cruiser fast fading in his rearview mirror, Dante was already finalizing his plans for the operation later that day.

CAL WAS silent as he listened to the police described the inevitable outcome. The police helicopter was on the other side of town when the call was placed. By the time it came on station, West had evaded the lagging police cruiser.

Trent put a reassuring hand on Cal's shoulder. "There wasn't much more that we could've done, Cal."

"I know. It just pisses me off that he was so close and we couldn't do a damned thing."

"Now you know what the cops deal with every day."

"Yeah."

"Where to now?"

"Let's head back down south," Cal said. "Neil, can you radio the rest of the guys and tell them to head home?"

"No problem."

THE TEAMS MET BRIEFLY outside the campus headquarters building. There wasn't much to say other than a couple thank-yous from Cal so the crowd quickly dispersed.

"I wish we could've done more," Andy said.

Cal nodded. "I know, but it was the right call. Thanks for making it."

"No problem. Hey, you know what that reminded me of?"

Cal looked confused for a second and then the light bulb went on. "That patrol we were on with the sheepherders!"

Brian looked from Cal to Andy, then back to Cal again. "You jarheads wanna tell me what the hell you're talking about?"

Andy turned to Brian and explained. "Our platoon was running one of those crappy patrols on another hot-ass Afghan day. Well, all of a sudden, Cal looks to our right and sees two insurgents peeking over a little hill about a hundred yards away. We immediately take cover and call battalion to get some fire support. We get weapons platoon on the hook and tell them what we've got. The platoon commander was a buddy of mine and told me that if I wanted to have some big guns there was a pair of Cobra gunships a few clicks away. As you probably know, it's always fun to watch the Cobras fire some rounds, so my buddy patches me through. Right about the time the gunships get on station, my radio operator taps me on the shoulder and points back to the little hill. I look over there and I'll be damned if there isn't a fucking flock of two hundred sheep strolling up to the hill flanked by a couple of herders. The two insurgents decide to take advantage of the distraction. They actually run into the middle of the herd and hunker down with the sheep."

Brian laughed. "No way."

Andy beamed. "So, the Cobra pilot gets on the hook and tells me he can see the two insurgents but that he can't shoot because of the livestock and herders. I told the guy that we suspected the two bad guys were lying in wait so they could trip an IED. The pilot didn't care.

He said the rules of engagement were tight. He couldn't shoot up a bunch of local sheep because some paper pusher in the rear had decided it was bad for local relations. So what do we do? We had to just sit there and wait for the two guys to come out. We're sitting there watching as the two Cobras are literally hovering overhead, the two guys don't even shoot at them."

"I'll bet they were pissing their pants, though" Brian said.

Andy nodded. "We would've run over there except we were still waiting for EOD to get there so they could sweep the road for explosives. Well, even when the Cobras floated lower to try and scatter the sheep, the damned things stayed calm and the insurgents stayed with the sheep as they were guided toward the little town. I called everyone I could, but we couldn't get anyone else in on the ground in time and because of the IED threat. So, we had to watch these two guys mosey on into the sunset with their herd of sheep. That's what I felt like today."

Cal chuckled. "Now that I think about it, it's a pretty good comparison. Let's get back to the Lodge. I think I'm in need of a couple of fingers of The Famous Grouse."

As the friends hopped in their vehicles and made their way to the bar, Cal said a silent prayer to his beloved Jess.

Don't worry, baby, he thought. *The fucker's mine.*

PART THREE

N.O.N. SAFE HOUSE, NASHVILLE, TN

"Dante, the boys are all set and we have that van you wanted." West stared at the hulking messenger, one of the hired guns from New Orleans. He'd especially be glad to have this guy gone soon. West wasn't afraid of much, but being surrounded by a bunch of bouncers with guns, even vouched bouncers, made him antsy.

"All right, thanks," Dante said. "Tell your boys that we'll be taking off as soon as it gets dark. I want everyone on the level. No drinking or drugs. Clear heads for this last thing."

"We ain't idiots, Dante. We'll be ready to go."

West nodded and closed the door to his new bedroom. As he looked around yet another dingy room, he dreamed of the day he could live in luxury once again. *Just a few more hours. Just a few more hours.*

TRENT RAISED HIS FULL GLASS. "I'm limiting myself to one of these. My ass is draggin'."

Cal raised his own in salute. "Thanks for all your help today, Top. We wouldn't have even had a chance to catch West if you hadn't tracked him down."

Trent drained his glass and looked back at Cal. "We'll get the guy, Cal. Let's all get a little shut-eye and we'll hit the streets again tonight."

"Thanks, Top."

Trent nodded and, with surprising grace considering his size, hopped up from the couch and left the bar.

Brian motioned to the bartender. Cal had told him the guy was a former Marine sergeant major who'd come onboard after losing a leg in the first Gulf War and soon became one of Cal Sr.'s first hires. The bartender nodded back and walked around the bar with a half-full bottle of The Famous Grouse. He gave everyone in the group a healthy splash finishing with Cal.

"Thanks, Sergeant Major. How's the new book coming?"

"Slowly. Took me a while to get my rusty brain running again. Neil set me up with a laptop behind the bar so I can write while I work. Thanks again for that, Neil."

Neil waved nonchalantly. "Anything for my warriors, Sergeant Major."

Andy and Brian looked on intrigued. Andy spoke up first. "What's the book about, Sergeant Major?"

"It's the story about my time in the first Gulf War and how I lost my leg."

"If I can ask, how *did* you lose it?" Andy asked.

"I was off doing some long-range recon for Cal's dad and ran into a bunch of bad guys. Me and my spotter were able to take out the guys, but not before one lucky sonofabitch lobbed a grenade our way. I'm lucky that I only lost my leg. Hurt something fierce when my spotter dragged me a couple clicks back to our evac point."

"So, what made you write the story now?"

The bartender pointed to Cal. "That young man right there. He came back from the sand pit and, after a few libations he convinced me that *someone* would want to hear my story."

"As usual, the Sergeant Major is being modest," Cal said, leveling the other man with a look. "The book isn't just about that one incident. What he failed to mention, of course, was that he got a Silver Star out of that one because the bad guys in question were on their way to ambush one of dad's companies. He and his spotter took out almost the entire enemy party of twenty some guys with a sniper rifle and an M-203. The rest of the book is gonna be about his battle to regain active duty status after losing his leg. His fight to do that will really resonate with wounded guys coming back from war today."

"Yeah, well, I guess that's where it finally got me. If the book can help even one disabled Marine, how could I say no?"

Brian slapped Cal on the back. "It's good to know that I'm not the only one that doesn't seem to have the ability to say no to our fearless leader here."

"He takes after his father that way," the bartender said. "Never could say no to Colonel Stokes either. They must have some voodoo magic in their blood or something."

Cal shook his head and responded to the obvious compliment. "No, you've got it all wrong. I've just found that it's a lot easier to convince you guys to do things when you've had a couple of these."

He raised his glass to demonstrate the proper sipping technique for The Famous Grouse.

"Well, be that as it may, I'm still glad you made me do it, Cal. I'll get you the rough draft in a couple of weeks. You can tell me whether an old salty Marine with only a high school education can actually write."

He turned back to the bar and resumed his duties as the group settled in to finish their drinks. Cal couldn't let that last comment pass.

"The good Sergeant Major is, of course, being modest again. What he fails to mention, is not only did he regain his active duty status as a Gunny, but he went on to be one of the first Marine first sergeants to serve with a line company with a prosthetic leg. Then he went on to become a Sergeant Major while also finding time to earn two masters degrees *and* PT his battalion into the dirt. Don't let him fool you with that fake limp or high school education bit. He puts on his Cheetah prosthesis and he'll give Marathon Andy a run for his money."

As the gathered crew discussed recent events, Cal's mind began to wander. He replayed the day's action over and over. What could they have done differently? What if they'd kept following West and not called the cops? He finally filed it all away for future analysis, knowing that the team had done all that was possible without blowing their cover. It didn't matter, Cal was convinced that he'd somehow find West again very soon.

ON THE OTHER side of town, West's crew was finalizing plans for that night's operation. No one knew the location except for Dante himself. He'd given clipped instructions to his hired muscle. Although he didn't think there would be much resistance, his recent failures necessitated extreme caution. Each man merely nodded as they listened to his orders.

AFTER ADJOURNING FROM THE BAR, Brian and Andy headed back to their respective rooms. Neil and Cal headed to Travis's office to discuss options for continuing the search.

"So, what are you thinking about work-wise after we get this guy, Cal?" Neil asked.

Cal shrugged his shoulders, still not clear about where his path might lead. "I'm not sure. I want to see this thing out first, then who knows? Maybe I'll go on a long vacation."

Neil glanced empathetically at his friend as they walked. "Have you talked to Higgins yet?"

Dr. Alvin Higgins, PhD, was SSI's resident psychiatrist. He'd been a long-time member of the CIA's brain squad for years. He came to SSI after working with the company on a particularly hairy case a few years back. He was SSI's resident expert in all things intellectual, meaning he could either unwrap the mental wiring of criminals and terrorist leaders, conduct interrogations (he'd developed new and non-lethal techniques for the CIA for years), or help SSI employees and family members with any counseling they needed.

A pudgy man, a smidge over five and half feet tall, the affable Dr. Higgins had quickly endeared himself to the employees at SSI. Where some psychiatrists were aloof and borderline condescending, Higgins was the exact opposite. Jolly in a way that reminding you of Santa Claus, Higgins had actually been the reigning Saint Nick every year at company Christmas parties. Not really what you'd expect from a man who'd dedicated most of his adult life to the extraction of information from men's minds by all means necessary.

Cal shook his head. "No, I haven't seen him yet. Come to think of it, he'll probably be with Trav right now. Trav said he'd gather the inner circle to think this West thing out."

As they entered the headquarters building, the usual bustle of activity seemed like home to Cal. He'd never officially worked at SSI, but he'd practically grown up in these halls. At the same time, he always got the feeling that he was in the middle of a battalion headquarters in the field. Electronic maps and target dossiers were displayed on an impressive array of flat screen panels all along each wall. SSI remained on the tip of the technology curve; thanks, in no small part, to Neil and his team of techie geeks.

They headed to Travis' secure office. In reality, this entire building and any other SSI structure with any sort of information capability, was shielded from outside snooping by advanced electronic jamming and masking technology, once again courtesy of Neil's R&D team. The masking system was now being leased by numerous government facilities and a mobile version was also in development for field headquarters.

Cal entered Travis' spacious office not really knowing who to expect. He glanced to the eight-man conference table in the corner and found the party waiting. Two others accompanied his cousin. The group included the first female employed by SSI: company attorney Marjorie Haines. "The Hammer." Not only ferocious in court and deposition rooms, she was also an expert martial artist in Brazilian jiu-jitsu and kung fu. She'd been known to take down multiple new recruits on the fighting mat after a particularly trying day.

She'd entered SSI shortly after winning a case against the company. Travis and the rest of the executive team had been so impressed with her tenacity that they'd gone after her to fill the role of lead attorney. It didn't hurt that she could match many of the men in physical discipline, was a former prosecutor in the Navy JAG Corps, and a diehard patriot. She was, of course, well paid for her efforts at SSI and was considered one of the inner circle members. Today she was standing casually, her typical gray pant suit perfectly tailored to her athletic build. Her dark hair was pulled back in a sleek pony tail.

And next to Haines was SSI's head of internal security, Todd Dunn. Dunn was one of Travis' first hires at SSI and a beast. If there could be a human version of an English bulldog, it would be Dunn. A muscular barrel of a man and former Army Ranger, Dunn rarely cracked a smile, but could be absolutely depended on, as anyone who knew his story could attest...

DUNN

He had been a star in the Rangers, quickly rising through the enlisted ranks. Shortly after re-enlisting, his father had been diagnosed with cancer. Todd Dunn, now separated from his parents by a four-hour plane ride, did what he could to help his father. Because the family had little money and poor health insurance, the hospital bills continued to pile up. Dunn got a second job as a bouncer at one of the strip clubs outside Fort Bragg to make some extra money to send home. He was quickly promoted to head of security for his cold calculation and eerie calm during altercations. It didn't hurt that he could do the books better than the strip club owner. The new position allowed Dunn to make more money by getting a portion of the bartender and stripper tips.

One night on the job, a group of rowdy townies decided to make trouble with some drunken soldiers. The soldiers, obviously half in the cups but harmless, were easy targets for the small group of oversized rednecks. Taunted into brawling, the group of three soldiers were no match for the five rednecks. The one black soldier was apparently the target of a torrent of racial slurs hurled by the hulking antagonists.

As Dunn approached the group of brawlers with another bouncer, he noticed the butt of a pistol in one of the attackers' jacket pocket. *Shit. I'm gonna have the ass of whoever let that guy in.*

What started as a shouting match quickly escalated into a melee of flying fists. Just as he reached the guy with the gun, the man pulled the weapon on Dunn. Acting on instinct and training, Dunn closed the final foot, cupped his hands over his head, and pushed the weapon up over his head while simultaneously bending his knees slightly.

The diverted weapon fired and the loud boom echoed in the enclosed space. Patrons and employees screamed as they ran for the doorways. Dunn wrestled the pistol away from the man and clocked him in the temple with the butt. The man fell to the floor unconscious.

Dunn turned to see two of the three bloodied soldiers lying on the ground. The third was being dragged to the door by three of the massive rednecks. The two remaining antagonists turned on Dunn; one with a large buck knife and the other with a pistol matching the one in Dunn's hand.

Still calm but with pistol aimed at the gun-wielding redneck, Dunn made an attempt to diffuse the situation.

"Alright boys, you've had your fun. How about you drop your weapons before anyone really gets hurt?"

Instead of answering Dunn, the largest of the five attackers and, apparently, the leader of the burly band, yelled to his three companions dragging the soldier out. "Bring that nigger over here."

They did as they were told and brought the black soldier, blood pouring from his broken nose, to their leader. As the small group corralled, the remaining club security crew waited anxiously on the sidelines looking to Dunn for direction. *Shit*, thought Dunn. *How am I going to get these hillbillies out of here?*

The tough-talking leader grabbed his captive's shoulder with his hand and positioned the victim between himself and Dunn. Then he put the dazed man in a headlock and pressed the pistol to his left temple.

"What are you gonna do now, tough guy?!"

The rest of the man's cronies laughed evilly as they watched.

Dunn remained calm. "I'll give you one more chance. Put the guy down along with all your weapons and we'll make sure the cops treat you fairly."

The leader laughed. "Boy, you have no idea who you're dealing with. Now, I'm gonna give you thirty seconds to get all the money into a bag and give it to me. If not, your black friend here dies along with a couple more of y'all."

He waved his gun menacingly at the group of security guards. They could tell by his fierce look of determination that the man wasn't lying.

With a clear head, Dunn analyzed the situation. The redneck's last comment told him that the situation had just gone from bad to worse. What at first glance had seemed like a normal barroom brawl, had now escalated into an armed robbery. He knew it would take the local police a few more minutes to get there. Meanwhile, the huge hillbilly was counting down.

Dunn saw bloodlust in the man's eyes and doubted that many would go unscathed even if they gave in to his demands. To make matters worse, two more of the redneck crew had revealed small pistols that had apparently been taped to their lower backs. They all grinned wickedly as if daring someone to make a move.

"Twenty-two... twenty-one... twenty..."

Dunn looked at the club owner, who seemed to barely have the strength to stand. The rest of the employees were quickly gathering cash and wallets to present to the armed robbers. Dunn saw the leader's eyes flicker and a slight grin played across his mouth. The man was actually daring him to act.

"... twelve... eleven... ten... nine..."

Dunn took one last glance around the room and analyzed everything: the location of the armed men, the position of his security crew, the strippers cowering behind the stage curtain, the hostess squatting behind the club owner and the club owner hiding behind the bar.

"... three... two..."

Dunn kept his eye on the man's trigger finger and, just as the man started to say *one*, pulled back the trigger, fully intending to shoot the dazed soldier in the head. Dunn reacted on instinct and double-tapped the huge man in the face. Instead of waiting to see the result, he turned slightly left and double-tapped the other two armed men center-mass. Within a split second, the place was pandemonium again. The black soldier was covered in the now dead leader's blood and gazed up blankly at Dunn. The other two men whom he'd just shot were now writhing on the ground surrounded by security and being stripped of their weapons. The only redneck without a gun quickly dropped his knife in horror and threw up his hands.

The aftermath of the incident confounded and confused Dunn. Instead of being hailed a hero, Dunn was treated like a criminal. With two men dead and another two in the hospital, the local authorities had no choice but to fully investigate the situation.

Despite eyewitness accounts of all the club employees, the authorities could not prove that Dunn was justified in killing the man. He still remembered asking the police about it in the following days.

"Would it have been better if I'd let the guy shoot a man in the head *before* I shot him?"

The system was suddenly against him and the interrogator said as much. The police officer told Dunn that if that had been the case, they wouldn't be having this conversation.

"Look, kid, we don't make up the rules but the law is pretty clear. If this thing goes to court they can paint you into a cold-blooded killer. I already heard that the leader of those redneck boys came from some rich family. They're pretty connected around here and are already raising holy hell to get you the chair.

"But these guys were gonna kill," Dunn argued. "I could see it in their eyes!"

"I hear what you're saying, kid, but I don't make the laws," the detective repeated.

That same police station was where Todd Dunn first met the CEO of SSI. Travis was in Ft. Bragg visiting some contacts and got a whiff of the incident through friends in the Ranger battalion. After making a few inquiries, Travis decided to intervene. He made the visit under the guise of an attorney to gauge Dunn's personality. He walked out of the station knowing he'd just found a diamond in the rough.

Days later, Dunn found himself in a private jet being swept up to some campus in Charlottesville, VA. Apparently this company, SSI, had pulled a few strings and he'd been honorably discharged *and* all charges had been dropped. As he stepped off the plane in Charlottesville, he was met by Travis, now in his casual SSI clothing: outdoor gear and hiking boots.

Travis had apologized for the ruse in the police station and went on to explain what SSI was and find out whether Dunn might be looking for a new job. After coming to the realization that his career in the Army was over, Dunn was quietly overjoyed at the opportunity.

One final piece finalized the deal and Dunn's undying loyalty to SSI and Travis Haden. Not only did SSI welcome Dunn into their family, Travis also made sure that Dunn's father's hospital bills were paid off completely and that he received follow-up care from the top cancer specialists in the world. Eight years later, the old man was still in remission, and Todd Dunn was enjoying his eighth year as head of security for SSI.

CAMP SPARTAN, ARRINGTON, TN

"Where do we stand?" Cal asked.

"No blowback from the authorities," Travis said. "No one even knew you were there."

"How about that reporter? Did you get him off my ass?"

Travis sounded exhausted, but he pushed on. "We're still working on that. In fact, it was the Hammer that came up with a rabbit trail for him. It's a good one."

Haines glared at Travis for using her nickname. She was a modest woman despite her fiery spirit and having a nickname like the Hammer didn't help her sense of propriety. Luckily, she and Travis were good friends (and rumored at times to be lovers) and the comments usually rolled off her back.

"Let's just say I threw the guy a bone through an anonymous source and he might be pursuing another more lucrative news story," Haines said.

"I'm not following you, Marge," Cal said.

"It's another operation we're running. Let's just say it won't hurt our cause to have a reporter snooping around. It might actually help us flush a couple of bad guys out."

"So, you're not gonna tell me?"

Haines grinned. "Not yet. You haven't been officially sworn in or given us your blood brother handshake."

Cal shook his head. He always felt one step behind dealing with the Hammer.

Travis held up his hands. "All right, all right. Let's leave Little Cal alone. Todd, any inkling about where this West guy ran off to?"

"Nope. Once the cops lost him, he did a pretty good job digging another hole to hide in. I'm thinking he's probably got safe houses all over town."

"So, you're saying we've got nothing."

"Sorry, boss."

Travis sighed. "OK. So, what's our next move? Any ideas, Cal?"

Cal thought it over for a moment. He didn't really have anything concrete. Maybe thinking out loud would help.

"This last lead was all because of Top Trent. I guess we could send him out again and get him digging. Do we have any other guys that fit into that part of town?"

"We do," Travis said, "but from what you're telling me about this guy, I don't think he'll make the same mistake twice. What do you think, Todd?"

"I agree. I'll bet he made some quick calls to his network and told them to be on the lookout and armor up. I think if we send Willy and some more men up there they might be easy targets."

"What about your link to his cell phone, Neil?" Haines asked.

"Looks like he dumped it. He knew that's how we got a lock on him. That's a dead end now."

Just then the door opened and Dr. Higgins waddled into the room.

Dr. Higgins spoke so formally he almost sounded British. "Sorry I'm late, everyone. I wanted to make sure the file was ready to scan. Ah, hello there, Calvin."

"Hey, Doc! What file are you talking about?"

Higgins pointed a pudgy finger at Travis. "Ever since your attack, our fearless leader over there has had me building a dossier on Mr. Dante West. Mister Patel, will you pull up the file on this computer?"

"No problem."

Neil walked over to the 52-inch touch screen panel on the office wall and started tapping and scrolling. "Is it in the usual place?"

"It is. My friends, what Neil is about to pull up is not only all the police records we could find, but also my analysis of the man's mental abilities and motivations, along with some video surveillance Neil uncovered."

"Video surveillance?" Cal asked.

Higgins nodded. "Our resident wonder boy Neil was able to hack into some kind of database down in New Orleans. We found a thoroughly entertaining video of Mr. West robbing a local bank."

Travis huffed impatiently. "What are we supposed to get from that?"

"I don't know what you'll *get* from it," Higgins said, "but I was able to determine a lot about our adversary. I won't spoil it for you."

Travis rolled his eyes and looked back to the screen. Neil pulled up the main file. The first image showed a worn file folder with an old photo of West. He looked to be in his teens.

Higgins cleared his throat before diving into the report.

"This, ladies and gentleman, was Mr. West at age fourteen. It was his first formal arrest. From what we could gather, he was implicated in numerous other crimes since the age of ten but had never been caught or arrested. This tells me that Dante West is no fool. Even at a young age, the man was smart and cunning. Apparently, the only reason he was arrested in this instance was because one of his accomplices identified West as being the ring leader. As you'll see on the next page, the boy that snitched was later found brutally beaten in the juvenile detention facility. The informer ended up being paralyzed from the neck down as a result. It was assumed, naturally, that West was the culprit. Once again, the assault charge wouldn't stick to West. We can only assume that the incident taught the assaulted boy a lesson."

"Great story, Doc," Travis said, "but what does this have to do with finding the guy?"

Higgins held up a finger. "Patience, my dear boy. As I was saying, West seems to have a knack for staying under the radar. I looked back through his grade school records and found that in his early years he excelled in academic studies. One report even suggested he had an extremely high IQ, although his school did not have the means to test for it at the time."

Haines sat up a little straighter. "So, what changed?"

"Dante's father was killed when the boy was nine. It looks like his mother turned to drugs and prostitution shortly after. The state soon took Dante out of the home and placed him in a foster facility. It was apparently in that facility that he had his first taste of gang life. The reports from the foster home staff read like a novel. Good kid gone bad. They all talk about how smart he was, a natural leader. He used his authority with the kids to set up his own little gang. They started by stealing food from the kitchen at night and soon escalated to armed robbery. At the age of eleven, he ran away from the facility and never came back."

Higgins took out a handkerchief and wiped his forehead before continuing.

"From the age of twelve on, he was often brought in for questioning but, believe it or not, they could never charge him with anything. All the police reports detail the fact that he was always respectful, unlike so many of the other young toughs they'd interview. I got a laugh from one entry made by a detective who'd had the opportunity to interrogate West on more than one occasion. This detective actually recommended that the department stop bringing West in for questioning because the young man was, and I quote, 'a squared-away young man with communication skills far beyond the usual perps.' This officer actually submitted the recommendation to the D.A. The whole time they had no idea who they were dealing with."

Cal felt the anger rising in him. "Sounds like you're starting to admire the guy, Doc."

Higgins nodded without an ounce of regret. "Professionally, I do admire him. He is probably a borderline genius with the skill and cunning to elude the authorities. Anyhoo, where was I? West moved up through the ranks in New Orleans and, by his mid-twenties was a top Lieutenant. When Hurricane Katrina hit in 2005, all the local gangs scrambled to claim territory. West's gang came out on top with no small help from West himself. It was never substantiated, but I found two gang task force reports that alluded to West's part in the land grab. Then, all of a sudden, West was gone. Vanished. Through inside sources, the task force pieced together that, as a result of his success in the post-Katrina operation, West was given a promotion. He was tapped to expand the gang's influence to Nashville with the backing of his old gang. Think of it as franchising for gangs. For the last couple years, he's been growing a lucrative trade here in Nashville."

"What do you mean by lucrative trade?" Haines asked.

"It appears that West set up a more structured business than other typical gangs. He essentially uses the gang to protect his assets: drugs, prostitutes, protection, *et cetera*. In another life, Dante West might well have been a very successful businessman."

Cal's temper continued to rise. "Well that's not how he ended up, Doc, so I'd appreciate it if you wouldn't talk about him with such reverence."

Travis kept his voice calm. "He didn't mean anything by it, Cal. You know how Doc is. He looks at all these targets like an author treats a new novel."

Cal took a couple slow breaths. "I'm sorry, Dr. Higgins. I didn't mean any disrespect."

"It's OK, Calvin. I was only saying it's a shame West's talents were... *misaligned*. Sure, his upbringing could have been better, but I'll be the first to admit that we mustn't allow that to cloud our judgment of such a man. At some point in his life, Mr. West was presented with a choice as to how he wanted to deal with his unfortunate circumstances. He chose incorrectly. Don't worry, Calvin. We'll do our best to make sure we find Mr. West and bring him to justice." After the visible tension left the room, Higgins continued. "So now the question is 'What will Dante West do next?'"

"Any ideas, Doc?" Cal asked.

"West is a very capable leader and strategist. Looking back on his record, he's never made the same mistake twice. I think he's trying to figure out how to stay out of the hands of the local authorities while at the same time trying to hold his organization together. It's my professional opinion that Dante West is trapped and needs to do something audacious to break out or just sit back and wait. The problem with waiting is that he'll risk losing his associates and possibly lose a lot of his street business. No. I think he'll try to make a move."

"What kind of a move will he make?" Travis asked.

"Something that will solve his problems, get the police off his track, and get his business back. Maybe an assault on a rival gang? I just can't say for certain. What I can say is that Mr. West is not one to sit back and wait. He is a man of action. He is a man who's built his own destiny. He will not wait to see what happens. I think we need to monitor the police scanners and look into any turf wars or gang violence we might hear about."

Cal sat back in his chair, disappointed. "So, more waiting around."

"Yes, more waiting," Higgins said, looking down at him apologetically. "I suggest you all read his dossier and digest what you can. I am good at what I do, but you may find something I didn't. It's all I can think to do for now."

Cal nodded and moved to shake Dr. Higgins' hand. "Thanks for your help, Doc. I appreciate your insight."

"Not at all, Calvin. I'll continue my analysis and let you all know if I find anything new."

With that, Higgins waved farewell and left the room. Cal and the others had no doubt that SSI's resident mind specialist would spend many sleepless nights analyzing and reanalyzing West's file. Once on the trail, Dr. Higgins was a true bloodhound. He wouldn't stop until his quarry was found.

Cal turned back to the others. "Any other thoughts?"

"I'll do some digging, too," Todd offered. "Maybe my contacts within the police department and FBI can help. Couldn't hurt."

Haines stood up. "I'll run some checks through my court contacts. See if we can't run down some of his associates and squeeze some intel out of them."

"I'll reach out to some of my contacts, too," Travis said. "Let's all remember to be discreet about this. The last thing we need is that reporter catching wind of this."

The small group dispersed and Travis followed Cal out.

"Hey, Cal. Got a minute?"

Cal nodded and led the way to his father's office two doors down.

Even though it'd been years since his parents' deaths, the office was still in the same state that Cal Sr. had left it in 2001. The office was cleaned daily by a crusty old Marine who'd served with Cal Sr. in the early 1970's. Although now technically retired, the old Marine came in every weekday to reverently dust and vacuum "The Colonel's Office."

TILLY

Cal remembered first meeting the man years ago. Leonard Tilly had left the Marine Corps after serving in Vietnam. He'd been a machine gunner in then-Capt. Stokes's company. Back in those days, the military wasn't given the same place of honor as in the post-9/11 days. The proud Marine returned home to find protesters spitting at him and calling him names. Worst of all, upon returning to his family he found that his twin sister (the two had been inseparable from birth) now dressed in hippy garb and spewing the same propaganda he'd heard debarking the airplane ride home. Even after repeated attempts to make peace with his sister, he finally gave up.

Unable to settle in or even find a job, he learned to cope through drugs and alcohol. Instead of dealing with the pain and emotional grief, he internalized his pain and went into a quick downward spiral. Within a year, the poor man was living on the streets begging for money so he could buy a hit or swig. Leonard Tilly spent the rest of the 1970's and 1980's bouncing from shelter to shelter and bottle to bottle.

In the mid-90's Tilly had somehow wandered to the Nashville area. By that time, the Stokes family was back in Nashville and Cal Sr. was reestablishing his roots and expanding his business. One weekend as father and son were volunteering at a local shelter handing out food, Cal Sr. spied Tilly in the line. Now hunched, his body ravaged and aged by years of abuse, the prematurely old man shuffled forward in his oversized winter coat. On his left arm he'd sewn on a tattered Marine Corps emblem. Cal Sr. liked to chat with the people they volunteered to help and used the patch as his introduction.

"Nice patch you got there. Were you in the Corps?"

The crusty marine looked back at him suspiciously. "Yeah. So what?"

"I was in the Marine Corps too."

Tilly paused and tried to concentrate his gaze on his fellow Marine. Without thinking he blurted, "I was in Vietnam."

"Me too. Those were different times, weren't they?"

Finally, the man's smile cracked. Cal Sr. could see his filthy teeth, but also noticed the sudden gleam of remembrance in the man's eyes.

"They sure were. Different times."

Over subsequent visits, Cal Sr. made it a point to keep track of Tilly and check up on him. Cal remembered asking his father why.

"Because he will always be a Marine," his father said. "That makes us family. If he wants help, I'll give it to him."

The two Marines had quickly made the miraculous discovery that the homeless Tilly had once served under Cal Sr.'s command. Not surprisingly, Cal's father put great effort into helping "his Marine." Over time, Tilly agreed to enter a rehabilitation program paid for by the charitable arm of Stokes Security International.

After getting cleaned up and reunited with his family, he was offered a position in the newly built SSI complex just south of Nashville. After years of substance abuse, Tilly's mental capacity was now diminished. He was, however, extremely grateful for the chance to help maintain the grounds for SSI. Over the next few years, he became one of the company's most loyal employees. Refusing, even after numerous offers from Cal's father, to call Cal Sr. anything but Colonel, Tilly was once again home among his fellow warriors. He ate in the chow hall and shopped in the small PX. This was indeed his home.

Upon Cal Sr.'s death, Leonard Tilly wept openly as he demanded from Travis that he be allowed to maintain the Colonel's office as a sort of shrine. Travis had relented.

After officially retiring, Tilly was given a comfortable living space in one of the campus' small homes.

CAMP SPARTAN, ARRINGTON, TN

Needless to say, the office was spotless as Cal and Travis walked in. Cal often came to the office to sit and stare at the countless photographs all around the office. There were pictures of the family and of his time in the Corps. Anyone visiting the office could see that Cal Sr. had somehow found a way to merge his two families into one through the birth of SSI. It was his legacy and would serve as a home for warriors for years to come.

Cal still remembered what the place had looked like during construction. His father always enjoyed nature and had his office designed so that it appeared to be part of the outdoors. The office itself actually jutted outside the main structure of the building and close to the surrounding woods. It afforded the office a 180-degree view of the surrounding area. You could sit in the office early in the morning and watch the deer and turkey grazing below.

Cal walked around the large desk and sat in the cushy swivel chair. Travis took the seat in front of the desk. He always deferred to his younger cousin when visiting the office together.

"So, what do you think, cuz?"

"I'm thinking that I'm about tired of waiting," Cal said. "We got all geared up for that trip north only to have it fizzle out on us. It's just a little frustrating."

Cal answered while mindlessly opening drawers and peering in just as he had done as a teenager. He'd always been curious about what his father kept close at hand.

"I understand how you feel, but you've got to realize that this is the real world. Middle America. We can't just go around guns blazing shooting up the bad guys."

"I'm not an idiot, Trav. I'm just disappointed."

"I know, man. But listen, if nothing else, this is good experience for you for later on. If you decide to be an active part of SSI, you need to learn about the rules. You might as well learn them now."

"Alright, I'm game. Hit me with the high points."

Travis drew a deep breath. "OK. Like I told you before, these types of operations started a few years ago. We saw the need and we attacked it. Also, we were approached by certain entities that needed work done on the sly. We've always been really careful with whom we work. We are not vigilantes for hire. We are also not a tool for corrupt politicians or criminals. The work we do here in the states beneath the law is strictly regulated and kept under the radar for obvious reasons."

"So, who approves these missions?"

"Right now, me. Back in the day, it was your dad. There are only five of us within SSI that are actually involved in decision making for these ops. Todd Dunn and the Hammer are two of the five. Dr. Higgins is obviously in the loop. Last, but not least, is Neil. Between the five of us, we make the call whether to use company assets or not."

"What about the teams you send out to do the dirty work?"

"They are never, and I repeat, *never* in contact with any individual or group that initiates the mission. That's my job. I think I mentioned before that some of the people that tip us off are highly placed government officials. It is absolutely necessary that they maintain plausible deniability."

"Trav, I hate to say this, but you're starting to sound like you're running some kind of secret society. Do I have to learn the secret handshake too?"

Travis didn't laugh. "I'll give you the benefit of the doubt because of who you are, but this shit is serious. Now do you want to hear this or not?"

Cal threw up his hands in surrender. "Sorry. Go ahead, Grand Master."

A small grin spread on Travis's face. He was a man that rarely displayed anger, but Cal's comment had obviously hit a nerve. It was hard not to give his cousin a little ribbing every once in a while. Tough habit to break.

"Like I was saying, our sources are really funny about their involvement. We've obviously vetted everyone but we've always gotta be careful. That's why each mission is always reviewed by the five of us before we decide to make a move. Every angle has to be explored and the good and bad always have to be weighed. As a result, we don't greenlight every mission. Sometimes we decide not to act and our sources understand that. We can't be everything for everyone."

"So how do you decide which mission you do green-light?" Cal asked.

"There's no real formula. It really comes down to a couple of things. One: do we think we can get away with it without being exposed? Two: does the result of a successful mission, and its positive effect on this country, outweigh the possibility of failure AND exposure Three: does the mission live up to the standards of Corps Justice? If any one of those things can't be answered definitively, we don't move forward. Sometimes we'll go back to our sources and tell them thanks but no thanks and give them a recommendation on who should handle the problem."

"Can you give me an example of a mission you refused?"

Travis thought for a moment. "Three years ago, one of our sources came to us with an interesting dilemma. Apparently, one of the big Mexican cartels was hiring American engineers to dig these elaborate tunnels under the border. The problem was that law enforcement didn't have the manpower to track down the leads and exploit the intel, so they came to us. We looked at the intel and asked what they wanted done. Basically, they wanted us to shut down the operation. We ended up not taking on the mission, although we did provide them with some of Neil's toys because we didn't see the direct result it was having on American security. Now don't get me wrong, I'm not all about the cartels bringing their drugs into our country, but we just didn't feel like it was a worthwhile operation for the amount of effort we'd be putting in."

"So what if the cartels were running terrorists through those tunnels and not just drugs?"

"That would've been another story. We hate terrorists around here; especially the ones that try to sneak into the country. But you need to understand that we get A LOT of requests and we're only one company. As much as it sucks sometimes, we can't say yes to everyone."

"I think I've got a better picture now." Cal looked his cousin in the eye. "So, tell me how you think I'd fit into the equation."

"Honestly, I just don't have the time to run it anymore. It's not that we run a lot of ops, it's just dealing with our sources and going through the thought process. As CEO, it's probably best that I don't run it anyway. Too much visibility. I'll still be involved but I think you've got the brains and experience to run it."

"Trav, I'm a Marine Staff Sergeant. You're talking about running a covert arm of this company. I'm not sure I'm really qualified to do that."

"You'll have help. Dunn, Haines, Patel and Higgins to start. And don't forget that I'm not going anywhere either. Don't worry, we're not just gonna throw you to the wolves on day one. We'll ease you into it."

Cal was skeptical. "That sounds like what my company gunny said before I took over as platoon sergeant."

"This ain't the Marine Corps, cuz. SSI is a well-oiled machine. Besides, not to pump up your ego too much, but you've got a lot of your dad's talents. The guys around here already respect you and think you're part of the team. Anyone gives you grief, I'll deal with them. Plus, is there anyone else in this world that we could trust more to run our covert ops? I think not."

Cal mulled it over. Is this really what he wanted to do? He'd always respected his father's company and the men in it, but running what was essentially a division within a multi-billion-dollar corporation at his age was almost too much to fathom.

The sun had already set as he thought about what else to ask his cousin. Cal obviously didn't need the money. He'd considered going back to school, maybe heading back to UVA to finally finish his degree. He couldn't go back in the Marine Corps. It was still entrenched in two wars and he'd already gotten funny looks from those who knew about the Navy Cross. He loved the Corps but that chapter was finished. He couldn't go back.

Besides, this might give him the opportunity to actually do some good without being bogged down by rules of engagement or meddling by higher headquarters. He could think of a lot worse options out there.

"So, you're saying that at some point I'd have final say in any operation we take on?" Cal asked.

"Yep."

"Do we have a name for this quote, unquote division?"

"Not really. I call our inner circle the Fantastic Five but no one thinks that's very funny. I guess if you want to name it, you can. I wouldn't recommend going out and getting business cards though."

Cal nodded. The idea was starting to grow on him.

N.O.N. SAFE HOUSE, NASHVILLE, TN

Dante looked around at his underlings. All were armed and ready. They'd taken the remainder of the afternoon to inventory their gear and finalize plans.

"Any questions?"

The gathered men shook their heads. They knew the plan. It wasn't a complicated one.

"Alright, let's get going."

West led the way to the back of the house and out the door. Their vehicles were waiting and fully gassed. They'd all been serviced earlier in the week per West's instructions. He was not about to let a low oil light or a faulty transmission screw up this night's action.

The assault crew piled into their respective vehicles and cautiously pulled out of the driveway. After the episode with the police earlier, everyone was on edge.

The caravan made its way out of town and onto the interstate. It would be a short twenty-minute ride to their destination. West was almost giddy with anticipation. He calmed his nerves as he always did: by imagining a mental picture of a dead Cal Stokes.

CAL AND TRAVIS talked until the sun had fully set. There were still a lot of details to be ironed out once the former Marine had made his final decision, but Travis was confident that Cal would come around.

"So, like I said, Cal, sleep on it and we'll talk about it again over the next couple of days. Right now, your focus needs to be tracking down West."

"OK. Give me a day and I'll give you a decision one way or another. How about we—"

Cal felt his cell phone vibrate in his pocket. He pulled it out and checked the caller ID.

"I'd better take this, it's Frank. You wanna wait, or see you tomorrow?"

"I'll catch you in the morning," Travis said. "Give Frank my best."

Travis got up out of his chair and turned to leave. Cal picked up the call.

"Hey, Frank."

There was a pause on the other end.

"Frank can't come to the phone right now, if you'd like to leave a message please wait until the sound of the gun shot."

Cal's blood froze. He knew the voice well. He had heard it over and over in his brain since waking up in the hospital. Dr. Higgins had it right: Dante West had made his play.

Travis turned to wave goodbye and apparently noticed the pale expression on his cousin's face. He quickly walked back into the room and shut the door.

"What happened?" he whispered.

Cal grabbed a piece of paper and pen from the desk and scribbled: *It's West. He's got J's parents.*

Travis nodded and grabbed his own cell phone. He speed-dialed the emergency number for the SSI alert system. Within minutes, the entire internal management team would be assembled in the war room and the quick reaction force would be mobilized.

Cal turned his attention back to the call. "What do you want?"

"I guess I don't need to formally introduce myself. By the tone of your voice, it sounds like you already figured that one out."

"What have you done with Jess's parents?"

"Oh, nothing yet. Just a couple of bruises. Old man wanted to fight back so we had to smack him around a little."

"I swear, if you touch them—"

"Now let's not start making promises you can't keep, hero boy. How about we get down to business before I have to cut this call off."

"What do you want?" Cal repeated.

"I want *you*, Mr. Stokes. So, here's the deal. I want you to come meet me and some of my friends. If you act nice, we'll exchange you for the husband and wife. If you call the cops or do something stupid, they die."

"How do I know you'll keep your word?"

"You don't, but what other choice do you have? From what I've read online, you're the hero type. I seriously doubt you'll let these old-timers die."

What other choice did Cal have? At the moment, he couldn't think of another option than to agree. "OK. Where do I go?"

West relayed the address and Cal wrote it down.

"What time do you want me there?" Cal asked. His hand was shaking.

"Let's say one AM. That way we'll have the place all to ourselves. Come alone."

"I'll be there."

"See you then, hero."

The phone went dead and Cal stood and stared out the window. The moon was almost full and he could clearly make out the surrounding trees. The forest seemed eerily calm, as if anticipating the impending confrontation.

Travis gave Cal a few seconds to gather himself before he spoke. "What did he say?"

"He says he'll let them go if I give myself up."

Without a direct reply, all Travis could do was nod. He knew it was better not to give an opinion until the team had gathered. "I've already alerted the headquarters staff. They should be gathering in the war room right now. Let's go see if we can figure this out."

Cal managed to grab his notes and followed his cousin out the door. Doubts swirled in his mind as he tried to focus on some kind of solution.

His mind reeled at the twist. *How did I not see this coming?*

WILLIAMSON COUNTY, TN

Dante replaced Frank's cell phone on the kitchen table and turned to his prisoners. They were sitting on the floor flanked by two of West's men.

"Looks like your boy is gonna pay us a little visit. You both behave and you might get to go home."

Frank glared at the gang leader through hate-filled eyes. "You leave Cal out of this, you murderer!"

"Now, now, grandpa. That's no way to treat your host. Don't make me put you to sleep again. Better yet, how would you like me to give your lady a little time with a couple of my boys here?"

"You touch her and I'll kill you!"

Dante responded with a kick to the man's stomach. Frank doubled over and retched on the floor.

"Now, see what you've made me do? Like I told you when we took you out of your house, you keep your mouths shut and you just might make it out of this. If not, I can't make any promises."

He threw up his hands to accentuate his point, as if the choice were completely out of his control.

Frank looked up again and put his arm around his quietly sobbing wife.

Dante rubbed his hands together. "Now we've only got a few short hours to wait. My boys will take you back to the master bedroom and tie you up so you can get some sleep. I'll come get you when the time comes."

West waved a casual dismissal and the two guards pulled the prisoners to their feet and took them to the back of the house.

Dante turned back to the window and repeated the phone conversation over in his head. He'd always had the ability to find the calm within the storm. His analytical brain outshone any of his competitors. Many had underestimated his talents. His was a gifted mind that catapulted him up through the ranks. That, coupled with his ruthless tactics, would see him rise once again.

My redemption nears.

CAMP SPARTAN, ARRINGTON, TN

The SSI inner circle gathered in the secure conference room down the hall from where Cal and Travis had just been. Each member walked in quietly and waited for the information. This was not their first emergency session.

Travis took a seat at the head of the table and the rest arrayed themselves close by. Cal stayed standing as he continued to pace the length of the room.

"Cal," Travis said gently. "Why don't you give everyone a quick rundown of the conversation you had with West?"

Cal did in a tone that suggested his mind was already searching for possibilities.

"OK," Travis said, looking around the room. "We've got about four hours until Cal needs to be there. The good news is that as smart as West is, he has no clue that Cal's got SSI assets behind him. Anyone have any questions or comments?"

Todd spoke first. "I think we need a few teams to infiltrate into the area right now. We can take them in low with the two helos we have on site and drop them in about a mile away. Hell, there's so much farmland out there the launch will be easy. After landing the teams, the helos can take up station and give us some video using their infrared cameras. We should be able to get a damn good idea of who's with him and the layout of the place."

Travis nodded. "OK, get it done."

Dunn grabbed his phone, slipped to the corner, and made the call in clipped, whispered commands.

"What else?" Travis asked.

Neil was next. "I'll make sure all the teams have multiple drones at their disposal. They'll each be rigged with non-lethal darts. Might help take out some of West's friends."

Travis nodded and pointed to Dunn. "Go talk to Todd and make sure those guys don't leave without getting as many of your toys as possible. I mean it, Neil. Anything they need."

"Got it."

Neil got out of his seat and headed over to chat with Dunn.

"Who's next?"

"I know I'm asking the obvious," Higgins said, "but have any of you cowboys thought about how young Calvin is going to get out alive?"

"I'm not worried about that, Doc."

"I understand. You will, however, be going in unarmed into the lion's den, as they say."

"Doctor Higgins is right, Cal," Travis said. "It won't do anyone any good if West gets his hands on you."

Cal's voice was steel. "I don't care about me right now. I need to get them out of there. If that means I go in alone, then I'll go in alone."

"I know you're upset, cuz, but you need to take a step back on this one. If you don't, you'll be playing right into his hand."

Neil stepped back into his spot and snapped his fingers. "Dammit!"

"What?" Travis asked.

"I can't believe I didn't think of this before. I've got a couple of things that might be able to help Cal out."

"You want to elaborate, Mr. Wizard?"

Neil was full of energy. "Let me run down to the Bat Cave and grab a few more toys. It'll be easier to show you than to explain. I'll meet you guys outside."

He ran out of the room with an excited, almost childlike, grin on his face.

Travis shook his head. "I don't know sometimes with him. OK, so who else has a brilliant idea? Marge, you got anything?"

Haines thought for a second before she answered. "Clearly, you guys have the operational stuff taken care of. I'm just trying to think of the aftermath. Anyone give a thought to what we do with any bad guys you might capture or, worst case, kill?"

Cal answered immediately. "We take out anyone we need to. I'll deal with the consequences later."

Haines shook her head. "I know you're upset, but that's not how we run around here, Cal. We *have* to think about the next step. For instance, if we do take prisoners, what do you do with them? Especially if they've seen your face. We have to make absolutely sure that SSI is not linked to the rescue."

Cal blew out a breath. "Sorry, you're right. So how do you guys usually do it?"

Travis rubbed his chin. "If it's something overt like this we usually wear masks or face paint at least. It really depends on the situation. It'll be hard for you to do that. So, the question again is, what do we do with West and his henchmen?"

"I know I'm the most amped up about this, but what if, worst case, we just kill them all? I'm not a murderer or anything but these guys asked for it, right?"

"True," Travis said. "But then you've still have to think about the fallout. Disposing the bodies is no big deal. Jess's parents are another problem. We can't have them blabbing about this team of guys dressed in black coming to save the day."

"I thought Frank and Dad were good friends. Doesn't he know some of what we do?"

"Sure, but not at this level. I guess we just have to be careful about how much we expose them to."

"I agree," Haines said. "The less they know, the better. If it ever comes to sitting on the witness stand, I want them to have plausible deniability. They need to be able to say they didn't see anything and don't know anything."

Todd looked up from his phone and called across the room. "Hey, Trav. We've got the two helos warming up and we've got six two-man teams getting ready. I've got 'em suiting up in black with suppressed weapons and non-lethals. Along with night vision and Neil's toys, they should be good. Anything else?"

"Nope. That sounds perfect. Tell them we'll meet them at the helos in ten minutes."

Dunn nodded and continued to relay his orders through his cell.

"All right," Travis continued. "Let's all go grab whatever gear we'll need and meet back up outside."

Everyone left the room knowing it was going to be a long night.

CAMP SPARTAN, ARRINGTON, TN

The assault teams and supporting staff met ten minutes later at the PT field that doubled as an expedient landing zone. Andy and Brian were both suited up in identical black utilities. MSgt Willy Trent stood nearby talking with Dr. Higgins and Marjorie Haines. Todd Dunn was giving the assembled troops their final orders while Travis listened and chimed in periodically.

Neil wandered around the pairs of assault men handing out his goodies. Each pair nodded as they were handed their gift bags. They all knew Neil well and always liked getting to try out his array of new gadgets. These were all highly skilled operators with extensive real-world experience. Warriors, one and all.

Cal walked around the group not really knowing where to fit in. He was a key part of the operation, but he still felt disconnected. Everyone else knew their part and none had hesitated to come to his aid. It was in that moment, as he observed the silent preparation of each man, that he finally felt at home. A feeling of peace wrapped itself like a blanket around his body and mind. The clarity of battle suddenly enveloped him. He knew what he had to do.

He stepped up to the men that would put themselves in harm's way and asked for everyone's attention.

"I wanted to say a couple words before we step off. First, although I think I know the answer, any man that feels uncomfortable with the upcoming mission and the possible repercussions can leave right now."

He looked around at the gathered men and none stirred. Until someone chuckled. It was Travis. Then the laughs spread to the assault teams.

Cal knit his eyebrows together. "Didn't anyone ever tell you not to volunteer for anything?"

The snickers changed to outright guffaws as a smile spread across Cal's face. One of the men in the back row shouted. "We don't have a choice, Staff Sergeant. You sign our paychecks!"

Cal laughed. It was good to be with his family again. Another man in the front row joined in the ribbing, pointing at Travis.

"Shit, I didn't volunteer. The recruiter screwed me."

Cal held his hand up for silence. "As long as we understand each other, I just wanted to say thanks. I feel like I'm back with my Marines."

Another voice rang out. "Semper Fi, Staff Sergeant!"

A fourth man joined the chorus. "Ooh-rah, Staff Sergeant!"

Followed by a din of barks and backslapping, the men lined up to shake Cal's hand. He somehow held in his emotions of gratitude and he looked each man in the eye as they all quickly shook his hand and boarded their respective helicopters.

As the last man boarded, the pilots of each helo looked to Cal, saluted and lifted off.

Travis walked up behind Cal and put a hand on his cousin's shoulder. "Well I guess I know what your answer is."

"Yeah. I'm in."

IT WOULD BE a short twenty-minute car ride out to the location where West held his captives. It gave them a chance to finalize their strategy.

They had devised a plan that would both keep things simple and maximize their chances of success. Cal would drive MSgt Trent's truck to the rendezvous point while the others – Travis, Dunn, Brian, Neil,

Andy and MSgt Trent – would board one of the returning helos and fly to a nearby loitering area. It would allow them to monitor the situation and provide almost immediate support if needed.

Neil explained his new gadget to Cal and the others as he helped him put it on. "Just remember, since this is a prototype you'll only get one shot with it. It doesn't have the ability to recharge yet."

"Got it," Cal said. "One helluva way to field-test it."

"Yeah. You'll owe me a full debriefing when you get back."

Patel paused, and both men knew why. The tech guru had suddenly realized there was a high probability that Cal would not return.

"No problem," said Cal. "I can't wait to use it." He'd seen the change in Neil's demeanor and wanted to diffuse the sudden tension. Patel relaxed and slapped on his quirky smile once again. "You're a genius, brother.

Trent stepped up to them. "I'd really like to see the look on West's face when you use it."

Cal nodded. "To rehash really quickly: once I get eyes on Frank and Janet, I give you guys the signal and you send the teams in. I'll take care of West."

"Yeah. Just remember to keep your head down when our boys come crashing in," Trent warned. "I told Dunn not to use flash bangs so you should be good there. With any luck, those Baby Birds will take out a few bad guys. Hey, Neil, you got the helo cams up yet?"

Neil had resumed his position in front of the numerous computer screens. "Almost there. They just called in to say the insertions were successful."

"Can you patch that through your speakers?" Cal asked.

"Just a sec." Neil played out a few keystrokes. "Got it."

The small group looked over Neil's shoulder to see the live stream from the two helicopters. They'd positioned themselves at a distance and altitude that wouldn't allow their locations to be heard from the farm held by West and his crew.

"Spartan six, this is Spartan Mobile Two."

Travis answered. "Go ahead, Mobile Two."

"Roger, how does my video feed look, over?"

"Clear and pretty, Mobile Two."

"Roger, zooming in for a closer look."

The group stood transfixed as the pilot zoomed in on the main house. It appeared to be a one-story ranch. The infrared camera easily picked up the heat signatures in and around the house.

"Six, I've got what looks like twelve bodies on location. You getting this, Six?"

"Roger, Mobile Two," Travis said. "Can you really get in there with the zoom and pan around the house, over?"

The pilot did as instructed and panned from room to room. There were six people in the house itself. Four were in what looked to be a back bedroom or master suite.

"Zoom in some more on that back room, Mobile Two."

"Roger."

The screen enlarged and the team could see the white outlines of two people sitting on the ground and another two pacing around the room.

"That's gotta be them."

Travis nodded. "Mobile Two, can you give us a better look at the perimeter?"

"Roger." The video slowly zoomed out and panned around the property. "Six, I've got what looks like four teams of two patrolling the perimeter, over."

Silence reigned as the team continued to follow the moving video. Each man was analyzing the battlefield in a different light. They could already make out the patrol patterns.

"Are we patching this to the assault teams?" Travis asked.

Neil nodded. "I gave them some tablets that have the video streaming live. Each two-man team has one."

"Good. I want to make sure we're all seeing the same things."

They continued to watch the live feed knowing that the landscape they now observed would soon be underfoot.

THE FOURTH PATROL had just checked in. Nothing but a bunch of deer and turkey. His boys weren't used to farm landscape but none had complained. They knew better than to gripe now. West walked to the master bedroom and addressed the captive couple.

"You have about another hour until your hero gets here. Don't go thinking you're gonna try anything. Both of my boys here have orders to shoot you if you run. Don't worry though. I told 'em only to shoot you in the legs. It'll hurt like hell, but it's better than being dead."

The bound pair said nothing for fear of more beatings. They'd already silently agreed to wait until Cal showed up. They believed in Cal's abilities and, more importantly, Frank secretly hoped SSI would be involved.

"You ready, Cal?" Trent asked.

"Yeah. Thanks again for loaning me your truck."

Trent grinned. "No problem. I know if anything happens to it, you'll buy me something better."

"You bet."

Travis came over to join them. He had the look of brotherly worry already etched on his face. "Are you ready?"

"Jeez. How many dads do I have around here? I'm fine, Trav."

Travis shrugged, but he didn't look sorry. "Had to ask."

"I know."

"Anything else you need?"

"How about you have a nice glass of The Famous Grouse waiting for me when we get done?"

"You got it. But really, Cal, are you sure you're ready for this? You did just get shot like two weeks ago."

"I'm still a little sore and weak, but I'm not planning on doing any of the heavy lifting. I'll let the assault teams take on the bad guys."

"Good. Like we talked about, keep your head down and our boys will take care of the rest."

Travis patted him on the back. Cal nodded and jumped in the truck. He had to adjust the front seat to accommodate his smaller frame. Starting the engine, he looked back as his friends gathered next to the truck.

"Alright, boys, I'll see you on the other side."

He closed the door and didn't look back. Pressing on the gas, he wondered if this would be the last time he'd see them.

Dante played the scenario out in his head. He knew that the Stokes kid would probably try something. Hell, he'd try some little trick too if he was in the same boat.

It didn't matter though. The plan he had concocted couldn't even be foiled by an FBI raid. Revenge was fast approaching.

WILLIAMSON COUNTY, TN

Cal pulled into the dirt driveway that led to the appointed rendezvous point. He knew the assault teams were simultaneously tracking their targets and getting ready. Taking a deep breath, he drove the oversized truck up the lane.

Around a bend, he caught the winking beam of a flashlight. He figured it was probably two of the guards sitting by the interior fence. Sure enough, as he pulled up he saw two thugs armed with rifles flagging him down.

He slowed and approached the gate.

The guard's voice was hard. "Get out of the truck."

"OK." Cal complied and slowly opened the truck door. He came out with his hands raised.

"You have anything on you?" the guard asked.

"Just my cell phone."

The guard shouldered his weapon and expertly frisked Cal. He took out the cell phone and gave the other guard a thumbs-up. Then he turned back to Cal.

"Get in the truck. We'll be in the back with our guns pointed at your head so don't try anything stupid."

"I wouldn't think of it."

The three men climbed into the truck and one guard directed Cal to drive up to the house. Cal did as instructed and they made it to the modest structure without further interference.

The other guy in the cab ordered Cal out of the truck. For the second time that night, Cal carefully stepped out of the cab. He looked up to the porch and saw another thug standing in front of the door. He motioned for Cal to come closer. Once again, Cal was subjected to a thorough frisking. These guys weren't messing around.

The first guard handed Cal's cell phone to the house guard and walked back to the truck.

A third guard pointed at the house. "Go in through the door right there. Dante's waitin' for you."

Cal nodded and headed to the door trailed by the third guard. He opened it and stepped inside. The guard motioned to the right. Cal walked towards what he knew was the kitchen. As he moved, he imagined the assault teams quietly moving into their final positions, drawing beads on West's patrols.

He walked into the kitchen and tensed as he saw the familiar face of Dante West.

"Welcome to my humble abode."

"Where are Jess's parents?"

"Right down to business, huh." He yelled to whomever was in the other room. "OK, bring them out."

Cal heard footsteps and waited anxiously for his one-time future in-laws to appear. They shuffled slowly into the room. Jess's mother looked disheveled and scared. Frank's appearance made Cal's blood boil.

"Are you guys OK?" he asked, his voice trembling with rage.

"We're fine, son," Frank said.

"I thought you said they wouldn't be touched."

Dante shrugged casually. "It's not my fault the old guy wanted to put up a fight."

"You're going to regret touching them."

"I don't think you're in a position to do much threatening, white boy. So, anyone tracking you with that cell phone?"

"I told you I was coming alone. Now let them go."

Dante spoke to the guard with Cal's cell. "Take the battery out of the phone and give them to me."

The man did as ordered and gave them to Dante. West looked at it briefly then put it in his right pant pocket.

West pointed to his two prisoners and spoke to his men.

"Take these two out back and get rid of them. I'll take care of the hero."

Cal screamed. "You *motherfucker!*"

Cal lunged at Dante. The man side-stepped and watched Cal drop to the floor.

"It's time for you to take a nap, white boy."

West pulled out his pistol and slammed Cal in the back of the head. The last thing Cal remembered before blacking out was a foggy image of a screaming couple being dragged out of the house.

"Oh, shit." Neil said.

Travis leaned over his shoulder. "What?"

"Cal and West just disappeared."

"What do you mean they disappeared?!"

"One second they were there, clear as day, on the infrared video screen, then there was a scuffle and the two disappeared."

"Could they be in a basement?"

"It's possible, but we'd still have even a weak signal if they were in a typical basement."

"Wait," Andy said. "What if it's not a typical basement?"

Travis looked up at him. "What do you mean?"

"Neil, what does it look like on the screen when someone walks into a secured bunker?"

"They disappear."

Brian chimed in. "But this is a normal house."

"That's what it looks like from the outside," Andy said. "Neil, can you pull up the ownership records for the property again?"

"I've got it right here."

"OK. It says here that the property was quitclaimed over to some entity called Williamson Enterprises, LLC," Andy said.

"Yeah. I already looked that one up. It looks like a typical shell entity used to hold real estate."

"What if this LLC is controlled by West?"

Neil quirked an eyebrow. "You really think he's that sophisticated?"

"You heard what Dr. Higgins said. This guy's been underestimated his whole life. I think he owns this property and has built something under the property."

Travis held up a hand. "Is that even possible?"

"I wouldn't put anything past this guy, Trav. You better tell—"

Neil interrupted Andy. "Hey, guys, it looks like some of the guards are dragging Jess's parents outside."

Travis spoke into his microphone. "All teams, this is Six. Mission is a go. I repeat, mission is a go."

Silently in the dark night, each of the teams launched their quiet drones. Every man knew how critical it would be to hit their targets with their one and only non-lethal shot.

In staggered intervals, each team took out their targets with swift precision using the drone's dart capability, save one.

The pair dragging the prisoners outside got halfway to the backyard before one of the men was immobilized. The second gang member bent down to pick up one of his stumbling prisoners just as the dart meant for his neck sailed harmlessly high and into the side of the house.

Standing back up, he looked to his left and noticed his partner unconscious on the ground.

"What the fu—"

Two muffled rounds in the face silenced the man forever. The assault team moved in quickly to secure Jess's parents.

Each pair called in to Travis to report their success.

Travis spoke to his companions. "All of West's men are secure. One dead. They've got the parents and are moving to the evac LZ."

"What about Cal?" Brian asked.

Travis shook his head. "There's no sign of him. The house is empty."

N.O.N. UNDERGROUND FACILITY, WILLIAMSON COUNTY, TN

Cal awoke to find himself strapped to a two-wheeled dolly by a set of orange vehicle tie-downs. He was being carted down what looked like a narrow tunnel with intermittent lighting. It was cold, musty, and damp as he tried to get his bearings. Suddenly the dolly stopped and West stepped around to face Cal.

"You awake?"

"Where are we?"

"Where nobody will find us."

"Underground?"

"Not as dumb as you look, white boy."

"Where are you taking me?"

"I guess I can tell you now. Once my boys take care of your girl's parents, they're gonna join us down here. Then the fun starts. Before that happens, you'll get a little tour of my facility here."

Without further explanation, Dante moved back behind Cal and started pulling the dolly again.

Cal's eyes were wide as they kept moving farther into the hillside. They soon passed rooms full of marijuana plants and high-powered halogen lighting. It looked like they had one impressive growing operation down there. It was no wonder West could keep operating even on the run. Cal decided he'd try some questions.

"You want to tell me how you built all this?"

Dante's voice was filled with pride. "The economy's in the shitter. For the right price, we had some really good contractors down here building for a while. We even had a couple of consultants from the Army Corps of Engineers. I got the idea from something I read about a redneck here in Tennessee who built something similar for his weed-growing but got caught when someone noticed how much electricity he was using. We solved that problem. We're entirely off the grid. No one knows this place exists."

"What about the guys that built it? You can't keep their mouths shut."

"We were choosey about who we picked and where they came from. Shipped them in from a couple of states and kept them on property until they were done."

"Are you telling me they're still working?"

Dante chuckled. "Sort of. They're fertilizing the local vegetation now."

So that was it. He promised to pay a king's ransom and then he killed them. Higgins was right. This guy was smart and ruthless. Cal decided to keep trying to build rapport.

"How did you guys get around the power problem?"

"That was the easiest part. My boy in the White House decided to start giving out tax credits for new energy sources like solar and geo-thermal. We've got a huge geo-thermal footprint all around the underground tunnels. On top of that, we've got dedicated generators powered by everything from gas to solar. Not bad for a kid from the hood."

"Is this your only facility?"

"Now why do you think I'd tell you that?"

"I figure you're probably going to kill me, so what's the harm?"

"Fair enough. We've got a total of five of these babies scattered around Williamson County. Three are operational. We get to make our goods right under one of the richest counties in the nation. We're starting out with marijuana then we'll probably get into the meth business. That's what you white boys like, right?"

Cal was impressed by the size of the underground facility. The sheer magnitude of dirt moved illustrated the power of West's burgeoning empire.

The problem: How the hell was he going to get out?

THE ASSAULT TEAMS gathered on the front porch listening to Travis give orders. The incapacitated gang members had been quickly interrogated. Not one knew anything about the secret tunnel they'd just uncovered. Worse still, the one man who probably could've helped had been killed. He'd apparently been Dante's number two.

To complicate matters even more, the door they'd found behind the rotating shelving in the walk-in pantry was built like a bank vault. From what they could tell after a cursory examination, the steel door was some five inches thick. One of the assault teams was already trying to cut through the door. West had covered his tracks well.

Travis spoke up. "So, here's the plan: the assault teams will stay here and keep trying to cut through this damn door. Willy, you stay with them and lead the way in. The rest of us will jump in the two helos and take a look around. There's an exit somewhere, we've just gotta find it."

"What about Cal?" asked Andy.

"The best we can do is find him fast. There's no telling what West has planned for him."

CAL REMAINED silent as they neared their final destination. West wheeled his guest into what looked like a butcher shop mixed with a crude third world hospital clinic. Cal could feel the cold air and smell the residual stench of some kind of meat. The dolly came to a stop.

"Where are we?" Cal asked.

"This is my own private interrogation chamber. Over there, you can see some of my tools. Picked up the trade from this ancient voodoo man in New Orleans. Taught me some good tricks to get men talking. Really useful when you think one of your boys is a snitch."

Cal stayed quiet as he gazed around the room. He noticed an old rusted bedspring in the corner anchored to the floor and ceiling. Next to it was a pair of car batteries with cables. Next to the cables was a bench with an assortment of knives and tools. Everything looked well-cared-for and well-used.

"You want to tell me why you're going to torture me?" Cal asked.

"It's called revenge, brother."

"It's not enough that you killed my fiancé?"

"You killed my crew *and* you crippled my business. I owe you change."

Cal wasn't getting anywhere with his questions. He needed to try something else. When in doubt, try the frontal assault.

"For a guy as smart as you, I'd think a pussy move like attacking a harmless couple was a dumb move."

Dante froze. "What the fuck are you talking about?"

"Shit, Dante, I heard you were a pretty smart guy back in the day. I guess all that dope you've been slinging gets harder and harder to say no to."

"You don't know a thing about me, motherfucker."

"I know about your dad and how he died. I know about how your mom gave you up when you were a kid."

Dante stopped what he was doing. His eyes went wide then flashed with anger. He also registered a touch of unease in response to Cal's comment. How could this white boy know that? It was never in the papers. He'd made sure his past had been buried a long time ago. It was amazing what he could snag with a couple quick break-ins.

"You made that up."

"Oh really? Then ask me how I know that you've got a really high IQ and that up until the age of ten you were doing well in school."

"Who have you been talking to?"

Cal laughed. "You dumb shit. Obviously there are things about me that you don't know."

"You better watch your mouth. Looks like you forgot who's in charge."

"Really? I'd say in the next couple of minutes my boys are gonna be coming through that door over there."

"Who, the cops?"

"No, asshole. Tell you what, why don't we leave it as a surprise?"

West stared hard at his prisoner. "You a gang leader now?"

"Wanna try me?"

"You know why I don't believe you?" Dante said.

"Why?"

"Because I designed this place myself. Oh, I forgot. You were passed out when we passed through not one but three doors built like bank vaults. It'll take days to cut through that shit."

Cal tried to gauge whether the gangster was bluffing or not. Either way, one of them would be right soon. Cal could only hope that his friends would find him quickly.

MAIN HOUSE, N.O.N. COMPOUND, WILLIAMSON COUNTY, TN

"Six, this is Big Dog." It was MSgt Trent.

"Go ahead, Big Dog," Travis said.

"We've got a little issue here. We got enough of a hole cut to see through the other side with our fiber optics. Looks like there's another door on the other side some ten feet down the passageway."

"You're kidding me."

"You know I wouldn't do that, Six."

"Alright, keep working and we'll do the same. Let me know if you have any other ideas. Six, out."

Travis looked to his companions and gave them the news. West was surprising them at every turn. What looked like a straightforward mission now felt like a complete clusterfuck.

"Anyone else have any bright ideas?"

Andy rubbed at the back of his neck. "I think we need to start by getting half of your teams roaming the countryside. Who knows, they may get lucky and find the tunnel exit."

"What about the toy I gave Cal. You think he'll use it?" Neil asked.

"I'd think he would've used it by now," Travis said.

Andy looked worried. "OK. Then let's keep sweeping the countryside and see what we find."

The companions fell silent and continued to look out the windows with their night vision goggles. Each kept toggling back and forth between normal night vision and heat register.

Nothing yet.

WEST HAD GONE BACK to preparing things in the room. Cal was curious about why his captor hadn't called his goons yet. Maybe they worked off cell phones and the signal couldn't penetrate the underground lair.

Cal had one more ace up his sleeve: the weapon Neil had given him. The problem was its deployment would be tricky. He somehow had to get West to use the cell phone he'd confiscated. That would take some coaxing.

Think, Cal, think.

An idea popped into his head like a lightning strike. His plan wouldn't be easy and he'd have to feel some pain first. No matter. It was his only option. Cal gritted his teeth and steeled himself for the upcoming torture. He knew from talking with former POWs that everyone broke eventually. The body and mind could only take so much.

He would have to use that to his advantage.

"Are you gonna get started or do I have to torture myself, pussy?"

Dante looked back in surprise. "You still think you're gettin' outta this, don't you, white boy? Think again. Oh, and you may wanna watch your mouth and enjoy the last few minutes you've got."

"Whatever. Any second now my guys will be busting in that door over there."

"Not likely. The back exit to this place is impossible to find. Plus, this won't take long. I'll be outta here and leaving your body to rot after I'm done with you."

"So, are you going to tell me why you want to torture me? Not for nothin', but revenge kinda sounds like a bullshit answer."

Dante grinned. "At first it was all about revenge. You see, I can't let the asshole that put me on the radar and killed my boys get away with it. The second reason came to me a minute ago while you were running your mouth. I'm curious about these so-called secrets you say you have. It might be a good investment of my time to do a little digging."

Bingo!

Dante moved back to the dolly and pressed his pistol to Cal's temple. "Now I'm going to unstrap you and take you over to the bedspring. You try anything, I'll shoot you. You got me?"

"Yeah, I got you."

He released Cal slowly, not once allowing the gun to slip. He ushered his prisoner over to the bedspring that was now connected to the two car batteries. West methodically strapped Cal to the metal frame with zip ties on his ankles and wrists. Cal was spread-eagle, glaring at West and prepared for pain.

"I'll start with a low setting," Dante said. "I just want you to get a little taste."

West switched the machine on and Cal heard the buzz of electricity. Next, Dante grabbed the power knob and turned it to the first setting.

Cal's body seized and his eyes shut involuntarily.

This wasn't going to be fun.

TRAVIS WAS AGITATED. "All the teams just checked in. Nothing from the guys scouring the farm. Neil, are you finding anything in those property records?"

"Nothing. Obviously no plans were ever submitted to the local commissions for the building. Looks like he really did it on the sly."

"What about the police records? Any complaints for noise or blasting?"

"Already checked that and no. Besides, this property is just shy of a thousand acres. They could get away with a lot without ever being seen or heard."

"What about the topography?" Brian asked.

Travis turned to him. "What do you mean?"

"I know there's a lot of land in the hundred-year flood plain around here. I would assume that if West wanted a long-term facility he would've factored that in. Maybe we can find out which way the tunnel leads by taking away certain portions of the topography."

"Good idea. Neil, pull up all the topo maps with elevation and flood plain data. It's the only lead we've got right now."

WEST HAD JUST SHOCKED Cal for the third time. He had yet to ask a single question. It was obvious he was just enjoying seeing the pain register on the former Marine's face.

Cal, although in extreme pain during each shock, was starting to finalize his plan. It was a strange talent he'd uncovered while on the battlefield in Afghanistan. He'd found that in times of extreme pain and duress, his mind became hyper-focused instead of losing its edge and dissolving into fog. It was what had allowed him to keep going even after being wounded multiple times.

Within this clarity, he remembered hearing stories from former POWs from the Vietnam War and World War II. They'd survived by divulging mere snippets of the truth. They'd survived by effectively weaving lies within the truth. Cal was about to try the same tactic.

Cal was panting. "Are you gonna ask me any questions or just get your rocks off watching me shake?"

"Man, you must really have a death wish. You ready to die already?"

"No. I'm just ready to be done with your bullshit."

"Still hoping your buddies are coming to save your ass, huh?"

"That's right. And when they do I'm gonna strap you to this fucking thing and let you go a couple rounds."

"Hate to tell you this, boy, but that ain't gonna happen. How about we just get down to the questions. This time we're gonna play a new game. If I think you're not telling the truth, I turn on the machine again. If I *really* think you're bullshitting me, I'm only gonna beat on you a little bit."

Dante picked up a steel baseball bat from the corner and demonstrated practice swings. His grin returned.

"What, no knives yet?"

"Oh, those will come soon enough. So, let's get to the questions."

MSgt Trent pulled at the heavy steel door with all his strength. They'd finally cut around the locking mechanism. Sweat beaded on his brow as the door finally separated from the last bit of steel holding it to the lock.

The door swooshed open and the assault team quickly jumped into the space, guns at the ready, panning for targets.

The leader called out. "All clear!"

Trent eyed their next obstacle. "Does it look like the same kind of door as the first one?"

"It does, Top. You want us to start cutting again?"

"Do it."

The team leader nodded to his demolitions expert and the man moved quickly to the next door his cutting tools already in hand.

Trent spoke into his mic. "Six, this is Big Dog."

Travis answered immediately. "Go ahead, Big Dog."

"First door breached. Moving to breach door number two, over."

"Roger. Let me know as soon as you have an idea of what's on the other side."

"Roger, out."

Trent was praying there wouldn't be a third door.

West had begun the interrogation with some basic questions: date of birth, home address, sexual preference, etc. It was obvious that West was building some kind of rudimentary baseline to see if he was lying; sort of a gangster version of a lie detector test.

"Time for some real questions," Dante said. "How did you find out about me?"

"My company."

"What do you mean your company?"

"I own a company."

"What kind of a company?"

"A consulting company."

"This is your one and only warning. Stop trying to drag this out. You answer me or I'll make you answer it. You got me?"

"I thought I was doing damn well, asshole."

Without warning, West picked up the baseball bat and took a quick swing square into Cal's gut. Cal tried to dodge and somehow absorb the blow. His head sagged as the wind was knocked out of him.

"You've got thirty seconds to catch your breath and then you start answering."

Cal could feel his recent gunshot wounds throbbing and threatening to bleed again. He had to stay focused and buy more time. The only problem was how much more could he take.

Hurry up, Trav.

ANDY CROSSED his arms over his chest. "The best I can see is that the tunnel has to run this way under this ridge line. Any other way, they risk going into or at least skirting the flood plain."

"I'm still not totally sold on the idea," Travis said.

"I think West would've thought about this. The guy went through Hurricane Katrina and probably the flood of 2010 here in Nashville. He doesn't strike me as a guy that would take any chances."

"OK. So where does the tunnel dump out?"

"I say we start right over here by the Harpeth River. We might—"

"I just had another idea!" Neil interrupted.

"What?" Travis asked.

"Let's assume that West is using this place as some kind of drug manufacturing center. Even if he's able to mask the heat of his power source, he'll still need to have some kind of exhaust."

"Explain that."

"It's like a car engine. All that heat has to go somewhere. The intake and exhaust help keep the engine cooled. If West is using heat lamps, for example, that hot air has to go somewhere. It would be crazy expensive to have a self-contained system like they have in a nuclear sub. I'm betting they had to build vents to get the hot air out."

"Then shouldn't we see them with our heat vision?" Travis asked.

Neil shook his head. "Not necessarily. The scopes we use are calibrated to see obvious variances, like the difference between a person's body temperature and the ambient air temperature."

Andy cut through their conversation. "But then how do we see people at night when we use the same scopes in the desert?"

"There's still a difference between your body temp and the air temperature," Neil said. "It's just that the air's warmer."

"So how do we find these vents?" asked Andy.

"Let me see if I can patch into the helo's infrared system and recalibrate it for much smaller variances."

"All right, but do it fast," Travis said. "The longer we take, the less I like Cal's chances."

WEST WAS GETTING MORE and more excited as the interrogation went on. He'd already found out about SSI and Cal's stake as owner. Who would've thought he'd catch the heir to a billion-dollar company? The options started to whirl in Dante's head.

Maybe he could ransom Cal.

Maybe he could exchange his prisoner for money and weapons.

The possibilities were endless.

"You're in luck, rich boy. I'm thinking that you might just make it out alive today."

Cal looked up through puffy eyes and spit more blood onto the floor. His insides were on fire and his tongue felt like a puffed-up marshmallow. Every time he got shocked, he swore he'd bitten off another piece of his tongue.

Dante smiled down at him. "What's wrong? No more smartass comments?"

Cal's voice was thick when he answered. "What do you want me to say?"

"How about you give me the number to someone I need to call at your company? Maybe I can talk to someone sane there."

"I don't know the number. It's on my cell phone."

Dante glanced down at his pant pocket as if he'd forgotten the missing cell phone. He pulled the cell phone and battery out. "How do I know they won't track me as soon as I put this battery in?"

"Aren't you the one that told me cell phones don't work down here?"

"True."

"So how the hell would they track it?"

"OK. So, what's the phone number?"

"Call my cousin Travis. It's under T. Or wait, you can read, can't you?"

West shook his head and looked back down at the phone. He replaced the battery and turned the phone on. Cal watched expressionless, waiting for the perfect moment to reveal his surprise. He wondered if he'd even be able to reach the trigger Neil attached to his right molar with his tongue.

Neil had instructed him to tap the molar three times and the miniature flash bang he'd installed within Cal's cell phone would detonate. The problem now was getting his swollen tongue to react at the right moment.

Cal moved his numb tongue around in his mouth and spat another gob of blood and phlegm onto the floor. He looked back to Dante.

"This thing is asking for a password. What is it?"

Cal gave Dante the access code and instructed him on how to retrieve the correct phone number.

"You may want to try making the call from the phone. It's got enhanced signal strength and could work," Cal offered.

"I thought you said it wouldn't work down here."

"It's worth a shot. Might get you through faster, unless you have a better idea."

Dante glared at him for a moment and then shrugged. "What the hell."

Dante speed dialed Travis's number and held the phone up to his ear. Just as it reached his ear, Cal carefully tapped his molar three times.

The cell phone exploded.

West collapsed to the floor, his hearing in his left ear thoroughly wiped out. He lay unconscious as Cal tried to find a way out of his restraints. Neil had been very clear on the last point. West would only be incapacitated for a maximum of three minutes. Cal had to hurry.

ABOVE N.O.N. COMPOUND, WILLIAMSON COUNTY, TN

The team on the helicopter waited anxiously as Neil patched into the onboard system and clicked away.

"I've almost got it. There."

Everyone looked expectantly at the video monitor to see the change. Neil had been right. What had looked before like only a few spectrums now looked like a rainbow where every color bled into the next.

Travis' voice rose. "You want tell me how the hell this helps us?"

"Patience, Travis."

"I'm about out of patience, Neil. My cousin, your *friend*, is down there right now having that fucking gangster do who-knows-what to him. He might already be dead."

Andy placed a hand on Travis' shoulder. "We don't know that, Trav. Neil's doing his best. So, show us how this works, Neil."

Neil pointed to the monitor. "Now this is all just theory, but I'm thinking that if we zoom in close enough we might be able to see the vents."

Travis began to calm down. "What are we looking for?"

"It should almost look like a little fire," Neil said. "You know how you look at a flame say coming out of a pipe? I'm thinking if I got the calibration right, we'll be able to see that."

The group spent the next minute staring at the screen as Neil zoomed and panned over the terrain. Brian almost jumped out of his seat pointing.

"What's that right there?"

Neil leaned closer. "Let me zoom in. That looks like a vent! Now let me follow it up this way..."

"There's another one!" Andy shouted.

"Good job, Neil," Travis said. "Now keep following those vents and let's see if we can find that damned rabbit hole."

IN UNDER A MINUTE, Cal had somehow managed to scrape the zip tie on his left wrist almost all the way through on the rusted bed spring. He gave one last tug and the tie popped off of his bloodied wrist.

He glanced back down at the still unconscious West. His internal clock told him he probably had less than a minute to get out. He was in no condition to find out if his body could handle a hand-to-hand fight right now.

THE HELICOPTER CREW tracked the vents to a location just over a mile from the main house. There they found some kind of tiny structure that appeared to be a sewer drain. Travis decided to start the search on the ground there.

After hearing from MSgt Trent that there was a third steel door behind the second, Travis ordered Trent to leave two men to guard the house and bring the rest via helicopter to the possible tunnel exit.

Travis spoke to the pilot, pointing to an open spot below. "Put her down right over there in that field. We'll hump the rest of the way."

"Where do you want me?" Neil asked.

"Stay on the helo and give us updates from the air. Doc, I want you ready with whatever medical gear you have."

"Roger," Brian answered.

"Andy, how do you feel about going in first?" Travis asked.

"I'm game."

"OK. The rest of us will provide support."

The pilot spoke up. "Ten seconds to LZ."

"Roger," Travis said, surveying his team. "Let's go get our boy."

CAL HAD ALMOST REMOVED his last restraint when Dante started stirring. He looked up in confusion and shook his head trying to clear the cobwebs. Attempting to focus, he got up to his hands and knees just as Cal snapped the last zip tie off of his left ankle.

With speed that surprised Cal, Dante got to his feet and reached in his pocket. Staggering on unsteady legs, Cal snatched the baseball bat from the ground, swung it backhanded, and connected with West's firing hand just as he extracted a pistol from his coat.

The weapon fired and clattered to the floor as Dante clutched his hand.

He looked up at Cal. "You're gonna pay for that, boy."

Dante stepped backed and grabbed a wicked looking filet knife from the bench. Cal was trying his best to stay on his feet but his head was reeling. His body had taken a real beating. He had to focus. His life depended on his ability to stay on his feet.

N.O.N. UNDERGROUND FACILITY BACK EXIT, WILLIAMSON COUNTY, TN

Andy led the reinforced team up to the iron sewer grate that was mounted into the side of the hill. The crisscrossed iron bars were big enough to fit an arm through, but no way near big enough to fit a person. The stench was foul. He could see water draining out through his night vision goggles. It smelled like it came from a local cow farm. Sweeping the area, he looked for some kind of entrance. Where the hell was the exit? Looking back to his left he stopped.

"Did you hear that?"

Trent nodded. "Sounded like a muffled gunshot."

"Yeah. Came from inside the grate. You think you can move it?"

"Let me take a look."

Trent shouldered his weapon as the rest of the team provided cover. The huge man felt around the edge of the grate for some kind of release or handhold. Nothing. Next, he reached inside the opening and started methodically feeling along the inner edge. Halfway around he stopped.

"I think I've got a handle here but it's locked."

"Where are the hinges?" Andy asked.

"On the left side."

"You think we can blast through it with a little demo?"

"Won't that give us away?"

"I think it's a little late for that. Besides, I didn't like the sound of that gunshot a second ago."

Trent nodded his agreement. "OK. I'll go get the breach kit from our guys."

Andy nodded and looked back to the grate. *I hope it's not too late.*

THE TWO WOUNDED men circled each other trying to find an opening. They each eyed the pistol on the ground. The weapon would easily turn the tide.

West took a quick swipe at Cal. Cal dodged easily and shifted left as West moved closer to his lost gun.

"I can't wait to carve you up, white boy."

"You're the one with half an ear. Looks like I'm winning."

Dante put his hand up and touched the remains of his tattered ear. Although wounded, he was far from being out of the fight. The loss of hearing in his left ear wasn't going to stop him. West looked at his opponent with pure hatred. Only one man would be leaving alive.

West was convinced he would be that man.

THE TEAM STEPPED BACK and took cover as the signal was given that the breaching explosive was set. Andy counted down with his fingers and the demolition man pressed the button on the remote device.

At the same moment, the loud blast echoed through the trees.

Andy looked around the tree and saw that the grate was now resting on its hinges. They were in.

CAL AND DANTE looked toward the open hallway at the sound of the muffled explosion. Fear crossed Dante's face as he quickly calculated his options. He still had an extra escape route in case the back sewer was found.

Cal grinned. "I told you my boys were coming."

"They're not here yet," Dante said, but he sounded shaken.

As he spit out his last word, he lunged for the discarded pistol. A second later, Cal was also diving for the weapon. He was too late. As he descended to the floor, Cal could see Dante wrapping his hand around the pistol and turning his way. The world slowed as Cal stared down the barrel of his executioner.

THE TEAM RUSHED into the tunnel scanning and clearing as they went. They kept as quiet as they could, but the running water made it almost impossible. Andy pushed hard as he moved down the tunnel. Fifty feet down he found a door. Luckily, this one wasn't made of steel.

CAL LURCHED to the right as Dante pulled the trigger. Miraculously, the bullet somehow only grazed Cal's head as he descended the final distance to the ground. The side of his scalp burned from the bullet's passing. He ignored the pain and tried to knock the weapon aside.

Dante brought the pistol back around towards Cal. This time he wouldn't miss.

MSGT Trent barreled through the wooden door like a freight train. Andy came in right behind with his weapon leveled. He could see light ahead and heard the sound of another gunshot.

Instead of shying away from the gun, Cal embraced it... literally. He grabbed Dante's pistol hand and tried to angle the barrel up as he pulled the weapon closer to his chest.

A crash sounded from the hallway and Cal could see Dante struggling to keep his focus inside the room. For Dante West, the next few moments would seal his fate regardless of whether he lived or died. His only hope now was to exact his revenge before that happened.

Andy ran down the tunnel trailed by the rest of the assault team. His heart pounded as he readied himself for the scene he was about to encounter. Would Cal be dead? Rounding the corner his heart leapt as he saw his friend struggling on the ground with West. *Still alive.*

Dante's eyes widened as he glanced at the hallway to see men in black streaming into the room. The two men grappled on the floor, a fight to the death. The pistol remained lodged smack in the middle of the two. A hairs breadth either way and one man would be dead.

Cal and Dante lay locked in a deadly embrace, eyes blazing and desperate. West's finger still gripped the pistol trigger. Cal struggled to point the gun back at West. Cal saw his opponent pull the trigger twice and felt the loud double report of the gun.

The assault team watched helplessly, not wanting to take a shot for fear of hitting Cal. His friends each felt the two gunshots deep in their guts. They all screamed at once as Cal slumped to the floor.

EPILOGUE

CAMP SPARTAN, ARRINGTON, TN

The funeral was a private affair. All of Cal's and Jess's friends attended.

They'd decided to dedicate a new cemetery on Camp Spartan itself. With some heavy legal work by Marge Haines, they were able to get the approval of the state and local authorities. The deceased was family after all.

The grave site was situated on a lonely hill overlooking the rifle range. It afforded a magnificent view of the surrounding countryside. According to Travis, it was where Cal had taken Jess for their first picnic on the campus grounds.

Cal Stokes stood flanked by his closest friends, looking down at the casket holding his beloved Jessica. Although still gripped with grief, his head and heart had turned the page. She would never be forgotten, but Cal could live free of guilt. The death of Dante West had closed that chapter for Cal. He could now move on as Jess wanted.

The service was short but beautiful. Jess's pastor presided over the affair with grace and dignity. It never ceased to amaze Cal, as he stood surrounded by some of the fiercest warriors he'd ever met, that such men often held the most compassion and emotion. It was what allowed them to do what they did to the best of their abilities and protect fellow Americans that often criticized their methods and spat in their face. These were men of duty and honor.

Among the tear-stricken brave, he was finally home.

———

CAL SAID his final farewells to Jess's parents and split off to rejoin his friends. Travis cut him off before he got there.

"How you doing, Cal?"

"Still a little bruised up, but I'm OK."

"It's only been a week. You'll have plenty of time to heal now."

Cal's voice sounded absent. "Yeah."

"Hey, I know this might not be the best timing, but I've got some people I'd like you to meet."

"Here?"

"Actually, down at the Lodge."

Cal raised an eyebrow. "How about a hint?"

"It's a little hard to explain. Why don't you tell the guys we'll meet them at the bar in about an hour. The Sergeant Major's bringing out the good stuff."

———

TRAVIS LED the way down the second-floor corridor of the Lodge. Cal could see two burly men in suits standing outside one of the large suite doors. *What the hell?* He decided to keep his mouth shut and follow Travis's lead. *I guess I'll find out soon enough.*

Travis nodded to the two guards as one mumbled into his lapel mic. Following his cousin into the suite, he noticed the backs of nine men as they entered. Each man was dressed in casual attire but even their clothing couldn't dampen their air of dignity and power. They came in varying shapes and sizes but all seemed familiar to Cal and apparently with each other.

The tallest guest turned as did the other eight at hearing the sound of the door closing. Cal almost tripped as he recognized each and every man, not from personal acquaintance, but because in the suite stood nine of the most powerful American political leaders of the last two decades, including three former U.S. Presidents.

"Gentlemen, allow me to introduce my cousin, Cal Stokes. Cal, say hello to the Council of Patriots."

COUNCIL OF PATRIOTS

"COUNCIL OF PATRIOTS"

Book 2 of the *Corps Justice* Series
Copyright © 2012, 2018 C. G. Cooper Entertainment. All Rights Reserved
Author: C. G. Cooper

WASHINGTON, D.C

10:35AM, SEPTEMBER 11TH

Congressman Zimmer knew he was in deep shit. The last six months replayed in his mind as he swirled the remnants of his fifth drink in his glass. Ever since that episode in Las Vegas, his life had drastically changed. He remembered the incident like it was yesterday. Hell, he'd relived it every night in his dreams. He hadn't had one decent night's rest.

SIX MONTHS EARLIER, Brandon Zimmer, a promising first-term United States representative from Massachusetts, was on the rise. Barely thirty years old, Zimmer was no novice in the political world. He'd first accompanied his parents on the campaign trail as a newborn. His father, U.S. Senator Richard Zimmer of Massachusetts, employed young Brandon over the years in positions ranging from runner to assistant campaign manager.

After graduating from an elite private school, Brandon matriculated to the Ivy League. His father, a Harvard alum, pushed for his son to follow his lead. Brandon decided to rebel and go to Yale instead. He did attend Harvard for his MBA, however.

During his years in school Brandon excelled in academics and always elected to be part of the student council. Yes, politics was in his blood.

A year prior, Congressman Brandon Zimmer won the vacated congressional seat in his home district in Massachusetts. Despite being a staunch Democrat in a very blue state, he narrowly won. The early campaign looked promising and his staff expected a landslide victory. Zimmer had the good looks the media loved. He was also the son of a long-standing and extremely popular Senator.

Despite his status and the endorsement of his six-term father in the Senate, Brandon's playboy ways were soon splashed throughout social media. Pictures of Zimmer dancing with naked coeds at a Mardi Gras bash in New Orleans the year before almost sealed his fate. Soon other reports, photos and videos surfaced. It was only through the damage control of his staff and his father's wealthy backers that he was able to win the election.

After the fiasco, his father put his foot down.

"Son, this is your last shot. I will not come to your rescue again. You've got to learn to control your urges. Do you really want to give up everything we've worked for?"

Although he'd promised to leave his partying days behind, halfway into his first year as Congressman, Zimmer accepted the invitation of a small Japanese lobbyist who represented the gaming industry. Brandon first met Ishi Nakamura at Harvard Business School. They'd worked hard and played even harder. After graduation Zimmer entered politics and Nakamura entered the family gaming business in Las Vegas. They'd kept in touch over the years and always promised to visit.

Not long after Zimmer was sworn in he received a call from his friend. Ishi wanted to offer his congratulations and let Brandon know that he was now heading up his father's small lobbying firm, Ichiban Gaming. Brandon was honestly excited for his friend and mentioned that they should link up sometime soon.

Six months later, he received another call from Ishi.

"Hey, brother. Just wanted to let you know that we're having a couple of your peers out here in a week to show them around. Didn't know if you might like to join them. You could make some new friends and I can give you a tour of Sin City," Ishi invited.

Brandon moaned before answering. "I don't know. I'm on a pretty short leash around here."

"Come on. What happened to the Brandon that used to sneak weed into Professor Flannigan's lectures?"

The freshman Congressman chuckled, "I'm a member of the House now, Ishi. Being in the wrong place at the wrong time already bit me once."

"I know, I know. I'm just giving you a hard time. Look, consider it payback for all those times you hooked me up with your rejects. I promise to wine you and dine you and nothing else."

Brandon took a second to respond. What could it hurt? "Well, as long as we stick to food, shows and a little gambling…I guess I can go."

CONGRESSMAN ZIMMER WISHED he'd said no. The trip started out like any other fact-finding junket. Lectures and meetings followed by expensive dinners and more meetings. It all fell apart for Zimmer on the third night.

After a long day hobnobbing with local gaming contacts, Brandon needed a break. He slipped away and headed back to the swanky new hotel-casino, Zeitaku, owned by one of Ishi's clients. Ducking into one of the many bars he'd toured earlier in the week, he soon found a dark corner and made himself at home.

Halfway into his third martini, a gorgeous blonde walked into the almost deserted bar. *Wow. Look at the body on that one.*

She sat down at the bar and ordered a drink from the Japanese bartender. After a couple sips from her cocktail her eyes wandered around the nearly empty bar. Almost squinting, she caught Brandon's eye. She smiled sheepishly and went back to her drink.

Five minutes later the young woman walked towards the restroom but veered over to the Congressman's alcove.

"I'm sorry. I don't mean to bother you, but are you by any chance Congressman Zimmer?" she asked shyly.

It wasn't every day that Zimmer was recognized in public, but his ego always loved it.

He plastered on his best man-of-the-people-smile. "Yes I am."

The blonde smiled ecstatically. "I thought so! Do you mind if I sit down?"

Brandon gestured to the other seat. "Please."

Her name was Beth. She was also from the East Coast, and had gone to the University of North Carolina at Chapel Hill. They hit it off immediately after ribbing each other about the strength of their alma maters' basketball teams. Zimmer conceded that UNC was a perennial powerhouse on the court. His concession made Beth beam with pride.

They stayed in the bar until it closed, drinking countless martinis in the process. One thing led to another and the pair eventually made it back to Zimmer's penthouse suite.

The next thing Zimmer remembered was waking up with his face cradled in Beth's perfect breasts. He felt severely hung-over, but that was nothing new. *Must have been a really good night*, he thought.

Something felt strange as he started to move. He didn't remember getting into any kinky jello stuff, but his hands and midsection felt sticky.

His eyes were still blurry and he could just make out Beth's peaceful face. Man was she sleeping hard. He pushed himself off her naked body, looked down, and screamed.

Everything came into stark focus. Beth's beautiful body was completely dismembered. Her arms and legs had been cut off. A huge amount of blood was soaking the king-size mattress. Still screaming he looked down at himself and saw that he was covered in blood as well. Even worse, he raised his hands to his face and realized that his right hand held a long serrated knife, caked with congealing, sticky blood.

He screamed once more and fainted.

When he came to, hotel security staff was wandering around the bedroom. All were Japanese. They'd apparently wrapped him in a robe but neglected to clean off any of Beth's blood. He started to panic as he took in the scene. Beth's body was barely visible because it was surrounded by camera-wielding security crew. He even noticed one man casually taking videos of the room.

The cameraman noticed Zimmer awake and motioned to one of the other men. The man nodded and headed towards the fallen congressman.

The security guard walked over to Brandon and addressed him in heavily accented English. "Congressman Zimmer, I am head of hotel security. Would it be possible to take your statement now?"

Brandon didn't know how to answer. Was he going to jail? What the hell was happening?

"I'd like to call my attorney first," he forced out with as much conviction as he could muster.

The head of security nodded. "I understand, Congressman. However, this is a highly sensitive issue. I would recommend cooperating with us. Failure to do so could make the situation much worse."

"What do you mean by that?"

"Let me just say that you would not want these videos to get leaked to the police or the public."

Brandon's head started to clear as did his bravado. "Are you trying to frame me?"

The security man looked almost contrite and bowed before answering. "Of course not, Congressman. You do see our dilemma…"

He was interrupted by Ishi Nakamura bursting through the door.

"What is the meaning of this?!"

The guard bowed in deference. "Nakamura-san, I did not know that you were acquainted with the Congressman."

Ishi looked enraged. "Of course I am, you idiot. Does Mr. Saito know about this?"

"He does. Saito-san wanted me to take care of this personally."

Ishi calmed and replied, "Tell him that I am here and wish to speak with him."

The head of security bowed and stepped outside to make the call.

Ishi turned to his friend. "What the hell happened, Brandon?"

Brandon's composure slipped as he answered, "I...I...I don't know. Last thing I remember I was having a great time with this girl, and then I wake up straddling a corpse. What the fuck, man?!"

Ishi put a sympathetic hand on his friend's shoulder. "Calm down. I'll take care of this."

"How the hell are you gonna take care of this?! They've got my prints all over and they keep taking pictures!"

Ishi paused and looked squarely at Brandon. "Do you trust me?"

Still panicking, Zimmer couldn't think of anything else to say. "I...I guess."

Shaking his head Ishi scolded, "That's not good enough. Do you trust me?"

Brandon looked at his old friend momentarily, then nodded. "Yes I trust you."

The corner of Ishi's mouth turned up in sly grin. "OK. This won't be easy, but I may be able to call in a few favors. The owner of this hotel, Mr. Saito, is a client of my firm and a friend of my father. Let me see what I can do."

Now in tears, Brandon pleaded, "Do whatever you have to and get me out of this, Ishi."

THAT WAS SIX MONTHS EARLIER. At the time all he wanted was to be out of that bloody room. Congressman Zimmer never had time to think about the consequences. Little did he know how much that favor would cost.

TURKS AND CAICOS, PROVIDENCIALES ISLAND

9:00AM, SEPTEMBER 13TH

Cal stretched lazily on the king-size bed and looked across the huge suite. Neil was still monitoring the surveillance cameras. They'd been in Turks for just over a week, and had taken full advantage of the local amenities. That fact was clearly illustrated by the massive headache threatening to overtake Cal's attention.

Cal snapped his fingers at Neil. "Anything new?"

Not looking up from the monitor, the genius known as Neil Patel answered, "Nope. Our boy is still sleeping off his hangover."

"I feel like I should be doing the same thing."

Neil chuckled and looked back at his friend through his stylish Prada glasses. "You were pretty funny when Brian dragged you back in here last night. What the hell did you get into?"

Cal rubbed his hands over his eyes. "I was the idiot that thought he could match Master Sergeant Trent drink for drink."

MSgt Willy Trent was an enormous man. Standing just under seven feet with the physique of an NFL linebacker, Trent was a hard man to miss. He and Cal were both former Marines and competed in anything and everything possible. There was only one problem. Despite the fact that Cal was a very fit five foot ten former grunt and a deadly warrior, not many people could match Trent's athletic abilities.

Cal changed the subject, not wanting to make his headache even worse. "When does my shift start?"

"It's nine o'clock now. You're not on until eleven." Neil went back to his vigil and coffee.

Cal tried to shake the cobwebs. "Sweet. That gives me some time to marinate under a nice hot shower."

"You need it. You smell like a brewery," Neil answered sniffing the air.

Cal gave his friend a middle-finger salute and trudged off to the bathroom. As he soaked in the shower, his mind drifted. He thought about his entrance into his deceased father's company, Stokes Security International (SSI). Had it really been a year since he'd started working at SSI?

It seemed like only yesterday that he had accepted the position as head of SSI's covert division. His cousin, Travis Haden, was CEO of SSI and a former SEAL. He'd not only enticed Cal into taking the position, but had also allowed the former Marine to utilize SSI assets to avenge his fiancé's murder.

Cal had exacted his revenge in the gang leader's underground lair, not far from SSI's headquarters, Camp Spartan, just south of Nashville, Tennessee. It was a close fight (Cal had the scars to prove it), but he'd finally killed the criminal who'd taken his beloved Jessica's life.

He still felt the bitter sting of grief. It had lessened over time, but Cal still couldn't bring himself to start dating again. His friends knew it would happen in time, but no one pushed the issue.

Cal remembered Jessica's funeral. It was a beautiful ceremony on a bright sunny day. They'd buried her on the grounds of Camp Spartan, and Cal often took a jog up to her grave. He liked to think that Jess was now watching over him as he continued his journey with SSI.

After the funeral, Travis had introduced him to the men that would completely change his life's path: the Council of Patriots.

THE COUNCIL WAS COMPRISED of nine men. All were former U.S. political leaders, including three former Presidents, four senators and two congressmen. All were Republicans except for former President Hank Waller, a Democrat.

He remembered that first meeting vividly. They'd each introduced themselves then told him the story of their formation.

The Council had formed in the early 2000's after the disaster of 9/11. It all started with a couple of former political opponents playing 18 holes at the Army-Navy Country Club just outside of D.C. Both men were former presidents. Hank Waller was a two-term Democrat from California, and John Kelton was a single-term Republican from Tennessee. They'd been bitter rivals for years, but the presidency has a way of broadening perspectives. Waller and Kelton had collaborated on various relief efforts after their presidencies, and grew to respect one another. They'd become close friends despite their political leanings.

It was on that chilly May morning in Arlington that the two former presidents first conferred about the threats affecting the United States. What many Americans fail to realize is that retired politicians still maintain open lines of communication within the federal government, including sources within certain intelligence agencies. There are even times when sitting presidents call upon their predecessors for advice. Therefore, it was not surprising that the two friends were very well informed about the current dangers their nation faced.

Cal had interrupted the story to ask why any Democrat would even be caught dead with a former rival. He prefaced the question by pleading total ignorance about the political process and the players involved.

President Waller, the tallest of the group at around six foot five, chuckled and explained.

"You're not far off the mark, Cal. I won't lie to you. I was as liberal as they come when I first stepped into office. Funny thing about becoming President is that it humbled me. All of a sudden I was thrust into a whole new world. Yes, I had access to a lot before I was sworn in, but nothing prepared me for the reality."

Cal didn't understand. "What do you mean?"

"Let's just say it was like I'd been walking around with blinders on my whole life and then all of a sudden, they were gone."

Cal was beginning to understand. "So what changed for you?"

Waller laughed and spread his arms wide. "Everything. Now I was getting daily reports from our intelligence assets. I really began to think the intel guys were just trying to spook me, no pun intended. It seemed like every brief I got was about some communist faction or terrorist cell trying to wipe us off the planet. I suddenly realized how naïve I'd been."

"I'm confused, Mr. President. You took office back in the nineties. You just said the Council didn't form until after 9/11."

President Waller nodded, "First off, in this room we all go by our first names. We're all putting our necks on the line, including you. So start out by calling me Hank."

Cal was clearly uncomfortable by the request, but conceded, "OK, Hank."

"That's better. Now to answer your question. As a lot of my liberal predecessors have done, I moved away from the far Left toward the Center during my tenure. I couldn't make drastic changes overnight. People would think I was crazy AND I'd lose my electoral base. Hell, I'm not vain when I say I wanted to get reelected."

"So what else changed during your presidency?"

"I started listening."

"To who?"

Waller motioned to the entire group. "Everyone. It's a sad fact in the political arena that once you get a taste of power, you feel like you know everything. Now I wasn't totally close-minded, but I sure had an ego. I can tell you that now without being embarrassed. So I started listening to the experts, namely the operators in intelligence and the military. I really had no idea how smart some of you guys are."

President Kelton motioned to his colleague. "Let me chime in for a second, Hank."

Waller grabbed his drink and toasted his friend. "Have at it, Johnny."

Kelton toasted back, "I just wanted to tell Cal that our red-headed Democratic stepchild was not the only one to experience a wakeup call. I think if you ask each man in this room, he'll tell you about some event that opened his eyes to the threats confronting America."

Waller nodded and replied, "That's right. And I guess that's the point. The nine men you see here today experienced an awakening. First and foremost, we are all American patriots. We believe our nation is the greatest in the world. We are a beacon of hope for so many. We are also a perfect target."

"So you guys came out of retirement?"

Kelton answered, "I don't think politicians ever retire. We just move on to other things. You know, fundraising, support, opening libraries, consulting..."

"I'm assuming you don't publicize this group."

Waller shifted in his seat. "That's right. Could you imagine what would happen if the media found out that a bunch of retired politicians are working to save America? They'd either think we were a higher form of radical militia or just put us in jail. No, we won't ever be going public."

Kelton looked back to Cal, "Cal, we all take this risk willingly. We know that we can't just stand back and do nothing. I'm thinking that you would understand that more than most."

Cal nodded and thought about his recent out-of-bounds operation to take down the gang leader, Dante West, who killed Cal's fiancé the year before. Did these men know what he'd done?

Cal nodded seriously. "Okay. So tell me how I fit in."

"Well, Travis tells us that you're about to take over the reins with us," said Waller.

"I'm still not entirely sure what that entails," Cal shrugged.

"Obviously, we don't get together much, what with our Secret Service entourage and all. We usually have to come up with some excuse. This go-around, we're accepting Travis's invite for some hunting in the area. It's not the easiest thing to cart us around. But from time to time, we come upon certain intelligence that has to be exploited outside the normal channels. SSI has become one of the tools we use to go operational."

"So how did you guys find us?" Cal asked.

Waller took a sip of his drink. "I met your dad back in the nineties when I was in office. Didn't know him well at the time. SSI handled some of my personal security just after 9/11 too. The Secret Service was stretched so thin that they had to augment with outside personnel. Travis came down with the crew he'd assigned to me. We hit it off after he found out I liked duck hunting and football. When Johnny and I came up with the idea for this group Travis was the first person I contacted."

"But why SSI? Why not go through your old government contacts?" Cal prodded.

Waller answered with a shrug, "We tried. Believe me we tried. Problem was that in the aftermath of 9/11, all of our agencies were overwhelmed. We had to find another ally."

"So you guys met with Travis and then what?"

"He agreed to take a look at what we found. It took a couple times to work out the kinks, but we've got a better system now," answered Waller.

Travis, who'd kept quiet, finally entered the conversation. "Normally we communicate over a secure network Neil developed. The Council will send over the intel they want analyzed. We do some digging and give them our answer."

The look of incredulity gave away Cal's next question. "I may be stating the obvious, but this feels way off the reservation."

Waller lost all the humor in his eyes and responded seriously. "It is. Just like your Corps Justice."

Cal's eyes went cold for a split second. He'd have to remember that these were men of power. They were used to knowing everything. They knew about his completely illegal operation to take down Dante West. *Calm down, Cal. You should've been prepared for that.*

Waller nodded and continued, "Yes, we know about your dad's credo. That's actually what convinced us to go with SSI."

President Waller reached into his pocket and pulled out what looked like a business card. Cal knew what it was. He had an identical, if somewhat worn, version of the same card. It was the *Corps Justice* card his father had given him before his death. Cal took the ex-President's card and read it for maybe the thousandth time.

CORPS JUSTICE
1. We will protect and defend the Constitution of the United States.
2. We will protect the weak and punish the wicked.
3. When the laws of this nation hinder the completion of these duties, our moral compass will guide us to see the mission through.

Cal wondered quietly whether this was what his father had in mind. Taking out a ruthless criminal was one thing; doing the dirty work for a bunch of politicians was another story.

"I know what you're thinking, Cal. Never trust a politician, right?" Waller asked innocently.

The bluntness surprised Cal. "I...I don't mean to be disrespectful, but...yes."

Waller laughed. "We're gonna get along just fine. Sounds like a chip off the old block, Trav."

"He is," smirked Travis.

"Did your dad ever tell you the story about meeting me?" President Waller asked.

Cal shook his head. "I don't think so."

"Let me give you the abridged version. I think I mentioned earlier that we'd met during my presidency. Some of my top military aides had recommended calling in your dad for more intel on the Middle East. Saddam was being a real pain in the ass and SSI had assets all over Iraq. So your dad shows up and answers all of our questions. Then one of my more enthusiastic junior aides starts grilling your dad on the legality of how the information was obtained. I didn't really approve, but I let the conversation run its course. I wanted to see how your dad would handle it."

Travis chuckled, "You'll love this, Cal."

"He's right. Long story short, your dad proceeds to calmly dissect this young aide's political career, along with a few non-discreet details about his dirty private life. Your dad made it pretty plain that he hated politicians and completely embarrassed his accuser. I think the only reason he showed up that day was because he thought it was his patriotic duty."

"That sounds like dad," answered Cal with a chuckle of his own.

Waller continued, "I walked away from that incident with two thoughts: one, that your dad was a Marine through and through; and two, that I never wanted to be on his bad side."

Travis interrupted, "I've known these gentlemen for a while now, Cal. I wanted you to meet them today so you could see with your own eyes. They are not typical politicos. They're American patriots just like us."

Waller suddenly stood and pointed at the American flag in the corner. "Damn right, and we're gonna do anything we can to keep this country safe."

―――――

THERE WAS a part of Cal that still couldn't come to grips with his new life. If he could tell anyone what he did for a living, they'd never believe it.

Cal finished up his shower and dried off. It was time to get back to work.

WASHINGTON, D.C

10:40AM, SEPTEMBER 13TH

Congressman Brandon Zimmer was in no mood to talk. After a lot of soul-searching, he'd decided to tell his father about the incident in Las Vegas. He waited for the senior Senator to make the walk from his senate chambers. He'd instructed his small staff to take an extended lunch break. Father and son would have the office alone. Brandon tapped his foot nervously as he waited.

Senator Zimmer strolled into Brandon's office precisely ten minutes after their phone conversation. The elder statesman was the very picture of a political figure. Completely gray haired, his frame was still fit from vigorous daily exercise. He'd competed in triathlons in his younger days, but now whetted his competitive appetite on the tennis courts, typically throttling his peers. Senator Zimmer was a card-carrying Democrat, but was well respected on both sides of the aisle. He'd mellowed with age but his temper was still legendary.

Senator Zimmer cut to the chase. "So what is it this time, Brandon?"

Brandon tried to look his father in the face as he answered, "I've got a problem."

The Senator rolled his eyes. "What else is new?"

The young Congressman pounded his fist on the side table. "Dad, this time it's really serious."

Brandon knew better than to lie to his father, so he quickly ran through the details of Beth's murder in Las Vegas. Senator Zimmer stayed quiet during the most of the recitation. He only interrupted his son twice to clarify points.

As Brandon wrapped up his tale, Sen. Zimmer walked to the Congressman's large desk and sat down. He placed his hands on the desk and glared at his only son.

"Well Brandon, I'd love to know how you're going to get your tail out of this one."

LAS VEGAS, NEVADA

11:30AM, SEPTEMBER 13TH

The small group of men sat quietly in the windowless gloom of the hotel conference room. Smoke from carefully tended cigarettes curled towards the ceiling and hovered. They all knew each other. Theirs was a relationship kindled over years of collaboration. No man was younger than fifty-five.

They'd gathered as friends but considered each other family. In fact, some had betrothed their children to the offspring of fellow members.

Every head around the table digested the latest reports from their appointed leader. The time for decisive action was coming. The Empire of Japan would rise again.

TURKS AND CAICOS, PROVIDENCIALES ISLAND

12:02PM, SEPTEMBER 13TH

Cal adjusted the remote camera. After only an hour on surveillance, he was bored. The only way he could keep focused was to continuously pan and zoom the view. Not that he could complain though. He'd volunteered for the gig against Travis's objections.

As head of the newly dubbed Strategies and Contingencies Division (SCD) of SSI, Cal should have been at one of SSI's two headquarters, one south of Nashville and one outside of Charlottesville, Virginia. Travis, Cal's cousin and CEO of SSI, wanted Cal to coordinate his division's future plans.

Despite the conveniently unhelpful name given to SSI's newest branch, it was in fact the covert wing of the Stokes Security International. Unknown to the public and government agencies, at times SSI worked outside the law. Through its contacts, like the Council of Patriots, SSI gathered actionable intelligence that would otherwise go unused by law enforcement and even the most covert of government agencies. The reasons were twofold: first, the intelligence itself could never be used in a court of law because of the methods by which it was obtained and second, the secret division was only tasked with threats to the American homeland.

SSI's special operations brethren could take care of the international threats. Politicians were loath to deploy troops on American soil. That left agencies like the FBI, Homeland Security and local law enforcement to the task. Those agencies are still bound by law to employ due process and not infringe on individual liberties. The Patriot Act helped, but not in all cases.

It was Cal's father who had decided to help the cause. Instead of standing by, watching helplessly as America was devoured from both the outside and within, Cal Sr. decided to act. Employing his mantra of *Corps Justice*, he took his covert battle to the enemy.

Targets over the previous years included drug lords, terrorists, mass murderers, and more. The common thread? Each target knew enough about American law to skirt law enforcement. Technology had allowed the enemies of the United States to further entrench themselves into North America.

Cal Sr. realized the immense danger this would create for his corporation. He'd therefore carefully picked those involved for their sense of integrity, patriotism, and ability to choose right from wrong. It didn't hurt that one and all were former warriors from their respective branches of the Armed Forces.

Years later, it was Cal, Jr. who'd been tapped to exact this covert justice. It was a thankless job, but each man involved was used to serving his country and barely getting a pat on the back. To a man, the most important aspect was protecting America from growing internal threats. There was no sleep lost for their slain enemies. There was only the dream of a brighter future and a more secure America.

He was currently in Turks and Caicos with a small SSI surveillance team. Nothing fancy, just a week of staring at a camera and following a high profile target around the small Caribbean island. Since taking over the new division Cal had made it a point to get a feel for all operational aspects at SSI. He'd spent time with the insertion teams, the security teams, an unfortunate weekend with the VIP protection teams (Cal couldn't stand kissing up to snobby elite), the Research and Development Division headed up by his good friend Neil Patel, and finally the surveillance teams. Cal had also been through a majority of the training programs provided by his company, such as the close quarters combat training and the hand-to-hand training led by MSgt Willy Trent. He still had a green bruise from their last training session on the mats.

It had taken him away from the strategic planning Travis had wanted, but in the long run it gave Cal a better understanding of SSI's capabilities. As a Marine, he had to be familiar with all the parts of an operational unit. It also allowed him to be on the ground with the troops. It was one of the things he still missed about being in the Marine Corps.

He'd always known that SSI made a lot of money, but he never knew exactly where it came from. In its infancy, the bulk of the company's work came from security, training, and surveillance contracts. SSI still had a large contract force in Iraq and Afghanistan.

They'd slowly moved away from operational work and branched into cyber warfare and R&D. Not only did SSI provide equipment and weapons systems for the United States government, it also developed software and products for civilian corporations. With Neil in the lead, SSI had grown into a virtual factory of American commerce.

Cal was proud of the fact that his company now quietly led many of the most innovative brands in the world. Neil had even created a technology incubator that annually selected twenty technology start-ups from around the world, provided them with $100,000 for one year, mentored them through the rigors of launching, and allowed them to work in close proximity with either the Nashville or Charlottesville headquarters of SSI. The company would, of course, retain twenty percent of each venture.

Over the past three years, out of the sixty start-ups they'd sponsored, thirty-two were already profitable. Six had already been sold to the likes of Google, Apple, and GE to the tune of 150 million dollars.

CAL'S MIND wandered as he stared at the high-def screen. This stint had been more of a vacation than an undercover operation. The big fat target they were getting paid to monitor did little more than eat, sit by the pool, and sleep. Even his entourage rarely left the confines of the beautiful resort.

His cell phone buzzed silently in his pocket as Cal struggled to stay awake. He pulled it out of his shorts, looked at the caller ID and answered.

It was his cousin. "Hey, Trav."

"I heard a nasty rumor that Willy drank you under the table, cuz."

Cal laughed. "Ain't no rumor, Trav. I woke a sleeping giant and lost."

"I could've told you that would happen!" Travis laughed back.

"I know. You live and learn."

Suddenly serious, Travis asked, "Hey, something just came up. How quickly can you get back here?"

"Are you in Tennessee or Virginia?"

"Virginia."

"I guess I could catch a flight tomorrow. We only have two more days left on this gig anyway."

"I need you back sooner."

Cal was curious about the sudden urgency. "You wanna give me a hint of what's going on?"

"We've had a request from the Council and they're bringing an outsider to come see us."

An outsider? Cal couldn't think of who it might be. "Huh. Let me make a couple calls and see if I can't get out tonight."

"Call me when you know," Travis said and finished the call.

Cal replaced his phone and looked back up at the screen. The obese target was still lying in bed rubbing his rotund belly. Maybe it was time to go.

CAMP CAVALIER, CHARLOTTESVILLE, VA

7:45AM, SEPTEMBER 14TH

Cal walked into the Headquarters building of SSI's Charlottesville outpost, Camp Cavalier. He tiredly nodded to the guard at the front desk. Sporting a three-day beard and the remnants of a red-eye flight gone wrong (they'd hit foul weather upon take-off and landing), Cal was quite a sight.

The guard chuckled as he glanced up at Cal. "Good trip back?"

Cal smiled with a sigh. "You better watch what you say or I may walk close enough that you can smell me."

The guard put up his hands and shook his head. "No thanks. Can I help you with your gear?"

"I'm good. I'll just make a quick run down to the showers and get cleaned up."

The guard looked a little embarrassed to add, "Travis asked that you come to his office as soon as you got here."

"I'll tell him you told me, but I'll be damned if I'll walk in there smelling the way I do."

The guard shook his head again and waved, "Good luck, Cal."

Cal made his way to the staff locker room and took a much-needed shower. Ten minutes later he emerged wearing a slightly mussed pair of cargo shorts and collared shirt. It was the best he'd managed from his assorted island wear. There hadn't been time to stop and get anything nicer.

Oh well. They'd have to deal with it. Cal wasn't much for fancy appearances these days anyway.

He walked by Travis's secretary who looked at Cal with an arched eyebrow. Cal ignored the look with a nod and knocked on Travis's door.

"Come in," Travis barked from inside.

Cal walked into the large office and glanced at the sitting area. Travis was seated, facing two men dressed in impeccable suits. They looked vaguely familiar and had similar bone structure. *Father and son?* Cal thought.

"Cal, I'd like to introduce you to Senator Zimmer and Congressman Zimmer." Travis stood as he motioned toward his guests.

Cal shook both men's hands and took a seat next to Travis. The younger Zimmer seemed to be sizing him up almost disgustedly. Cal didn't like the vibe he was getting from Junior.

"Gentlemen, I'd like to apologize for my appearance. I hopped on the first flight I could bribe myself onto."

"Not to worry, Cal. We just appreciate you getting here so quickly," Senator Zimmer responded kindly.

Travis continued, "Cal, this meeting was arranged by some mutual friends. The Senator has a slightly sticky situation he'd like our help with."

Cal knew that "mutual friends" meant the Council of Patriots. No doubt the elder Senator knew one or more members. It was strange to be meeting with current members of the U.S. government. Cal couldn't wait to hear what this was all about.

"How can I help, Senator?" Cal asked.

"As Travis said, a mutual friend suggested I call you about a little problem my son has," the Senator answered cryptically.

"Little problem?"

"I believe my son is being framed, Mr. Stokes," Zimmer answered, suddenly serious.

Cal looked over at the younger politician then back to Senator Zimmer. "In what way?"

Senator Zimmer proceeded to tell the entire sordid tale. Cal simply sat in stunned silence. Congressman Zimmer looked like a beaten dog, eyes cast to the floor.

Cal finally answered, "I'm sorry, Senator, but I don't quite understand why you need our help. Wouldn't the Secret Service or FBI be a better fit?"

Senator Zimmer shook his head almost sadly. "Unfortunately, no. As much as I would love to see my son learn the lesson on his own, an episode of this caliber would not only destroy my son, but would also send untold ripples through Washington."

"I don't mean to repeat myself, Senator, but I'm still confused about what you want us to do."

"Find out who's doing this to my son."

Cal looked to Travis for guidance. He was in completely uncharted territory on this one. A murdered woman. A seemingly guilty Congressman. A famous Senator. What the hell was HE supposed to do? Never one to take the easy approach, Cal pressed on.

"It seems to me that if Congressman Zimmer would resign and turn himself in, all this would be a moot point."

Brandon Zimmer jumped out his chair and pointed at Cal. "Oh, you'd like that wouldn't you! I don't have to sit here and listen..."

"Shut up and sit down, Brandon! I'm sorry, Mr. Stokes. Apparently my son still doesn't appreciate the gravity of the situation."

Cal nodded skeptically. If they wanted the truth, he'd give it to them. It looked like Junior was about to have a nervous breakdown.

Cal continued, "Senator, let's say we do end up helping you, what do you want us to do once we've determined who the guilty party is?"

"I'm not asking you to do anything you're not comfortable with. What if we just start with finding out who they are. Once we have that, we can make a decision on which way to turn."

Cal thought for a minute. It didn't sound like anything too overt. Maybe it'd end up being a little surveillance. The one thing Cal wasn't looking forward to was dealing with Congressman Zimmer.

"I'll do it on one condition, Senator."

Sen. Zimmer's eyebrow rose. "And what would that be, Mr. Stokes?"

"Your son has to do EXACTLY what I say."

Over the strong objections of his son, Sen. Richard Zimmer answered with a wry smile, "Done."

CAMP CAVALIER, CHARLOTTESVILLE, VA

8:39AM, SEPTEMBER 14TH

"You could've given me a heads-up, Trav." Cal frowned at his cousin. The last thing he wanted to do was babysit a spoiled politician.

Travis smiled. "If I'd told you who it was and what they wanted, you would've figured out some way not to make it back. This way we both win."

"How do I win?"

"You get your first action with the Council. It's great that I've vouched for you, but until you prove yourself, they won't know what to do with us."

"But I thought we were in tight with these guys."

Travis walked over to his desk as he explained. "We've had contact with the Council off and on for last few years. The problem is that we never had anyone dedicated to utilizing their intel. I was their contact, but I also had to run SSI. It pulled me thin. Now that we've got you, we can put some muscle behind it."

"So what's my guidance going forward?"

"I'm not gonna hold your hand or look over your shoulder, Cal. In this case, I want to push you. Take a look at the file we've started compiling. I think you'll find some interesting tidbits about the Vegas underground. Plus, I completely agree with the Senator. Despite Congressman Zimmer's past, the whole bloody murder scenario isn't his M.O. He's being set up for something."

Cal realized he'd allowed his emotions to cloud his objectivity. Maybe Travis was right. Maybe there was something to the story.

"Okay. I'll handle it."

"Alright. Why don't you head down to Intel and see if you can't dig up anything else. In the meantime, come up with a team and a plan. Let me know if you need something special."

Cal walked out of Travis's office and headed to his personal cubicle. They'd offered him his father's office but he'd declined. The old man's office was more of a shrine now. Besides, Cal enjoyed the thought of working his way up the ladder and being with his troops.

The first thing he needed to do was pick his A-team. Then it was off to Sin City.

LAS VEGAS, NEVADA

2:48AM, SEPTEMBER 16TH

The workmen loaded the large packages into the nearly full semis. They were all getting paid hefty overtime for working through the night. It was almost three in the morning but the boxes weren't particularly heavy. There were just a lot of them. The only pain for the crew was dealing with the quiet little Japanese guy and his big Russian friend.

The smaller Asian man was obviously in charge. He gave clipped orders and maintained an intense vigil over the loading process. The large Russian looked bored as he gazed lazily around the small truck terminal. He hadn't made a sound except for the occasionally spit of phlegm over the metal railing.

"Hey boss, how much longer we got?"

Max Unger looked back at his worker. "Until we get all these trailers loaded, shithead. Now shut up and go back to work."

The worker grumbled and headed back to the smallest stack of packages. Max stole a look at the man who'd offered a tidy sum if the shipment could be processed in one night. Unger had almost refused, but the enticement of so much cash won him over. Even as he was anticipating his payday, Max Unger couldn't shake the feeling of unease as he loaded yet another stamped cardboard box. *What the hell is in these boxes?*

CAMP SPARTAN, ARRINGTON, TENNESSEE

7:37AM, SEPTEMBER 16TH

It took Cal two days to piece together an initial plan of attack and gather his team. He'd recalled Neil Patel and MSgt Trent from Turks. The other members of the advance team included his good friend and former Navy Corpsman Brian Ramirez. Brian was currently heading-up the battle-med research team inside Patel's R&D department. SSI focused heavily on new development not only to make money, but also to better support American troops serving around the globe.

Cal figured that the first thing to do was take a look around Vegas and see what cropped up. Dumb luck just might expose Zimmer's enemies without much effort.

The small team chatted quietly as Cal gathered his notes. He finally looked up. "You guys have a good trip back?"

"First Class is always nice when I'm not the one paying for it," Willy joked in his booming voice.

"Top told me all about your little competition at the tiki bar, Cal," Brian interrupted grinning. "I knew you were a dumb grunt, but waking the sleeping giant..."

Cal raised his hands in defeat. "I know, I know. I'll never live that one down. Let me run you through what we've got."

Cal recounted the Congressman's story. He also outlined Zimmer's past and what he'd been able to dig up about Ishi Nakamura, which wasn't much. Eyebrows were raised, but they waited for Cal to finish before asking questions.

"So the first thing we need to do is link Top up with Congressman Zimmer. You'll be tapped as his new bodyguard. We've already floated the story of some weirdo sending Zimmer some threatening letters. Now, Top, this guy might end up being a royal pain in the ass, but I need you to stick close to him," Cal instructed. "Neil, I'll need you to be around for technical support. Bring anything you think you might need. Brian and I will be posing as tourists. We'll take in the sights and do a little gambling. I want to see if we can weed out anyone following Zimmer. Any questions?"

Brian spoke up first. "Why only four of us? Don't you think we might need some more manpower?"

Cal shook his head. "This is just our initial reconnaissance. I don't want whoever's framing Zimmer to know we're there. The smaller the team, the less likely it'll be that we get spotted."

"You want me to do some more background on this Ishi guy?" Neil asked.

"Yeah. I couldn't find much. Seemed pretty normal on paper. His parents came over from Japan when he was a kid. Grew up in San Francisco. Did well in school. Met Zimmer at Harvard. A few jobs and internships here and there. Typical post-college stuff. I really want to know more about this company he works for."

"I'll get on it," Neil answered as he turned his attention to the mini-laptop perched on his knees.

Cal knew that if anybody could penetrate an organization with technology, it was Neil Patel. The certified genius wasn't just a whiz with gadgets, he was also a world-class hacker.

"Top, we'll fly you out to D.C. tomorrow. You can link up with the Congressman and then fly out to Vegas with him. Anything else?"

No one had anything to add. Everyone was already mentally coming up with their own game plan for the operation. Cal knew better than to get in their way. They were all proven operators. Even Neil was a warrior in his own way. All they needed was a quick snapshot. The rest would evolve once they got to Las Vegas.

LAS VEGAS, NEVADA

7:52AM, SEPTEMBER 16TH

"What is the status of the shipment?"

"The packages are ready and each truck is awaiting my order to depart."

"Do you expect the packages to be delivered by the time we requested?"

"Yes. We have allowed extra time in case of weather or some other unforeseen circumstance."

"Good. Then you may proceed with the delivery."

The older man's assistant bowed respectfully and exited the palatial suite. The master took another drag from his cigarette and gazed out at the desert landscape. Soon America would feel the pain and humiliation he'd long planned.

FALLS CHURCH, VA

1:46PM, SEPTEMBER 16TH

M Sgt Willy Trent stepped out of the taxi and paid the driver. It'd been an easy ride over from Reagan National. It still amazed him how close the nation's capital looked as you landed. You could see everything.

Unfortunately, this wouldn't be a tourist stop. His orders were clear: keep eyes-on Congressman Brandon Zimmer, 24/7.

He strolled up to the modest home and quickly scanned the finely manicured lawn. Access to the property looked easy. No obvious security. Strange. He'd have to change that.

Trent knocked and waited patiently for the door to open. He was surprised when Congressman Zimmer opened the door. *No interior security either?*

The good-looking congressman smiled and reached out his hand. "You must be Master Sergeant Trent."

"Yes, sir. Although most people call me Willy or Top."

"Top's the nickname you Marines call Master Sergeants, right?" Zimmer asked still smiling congenially.

"Only the ones they like, sir," Trent smiled back.

"Well, come on in. I'll give you a quick tour of the place and then you can fill me in on your team's plan." Zimmer ushered Willy in through the door and led the way to the back of the house, highlighting the layout as they went. The hallway opened up to a large great room that overlooked Lake Barcroft. Trent could see a couple families enjoying the early fall weather on their pontoon boats. He wondered quietly whether there was any security on the sprawling back lawn either.

"Can I get you anything, Top?"

"No thank you, sir. Maybe we should go over your itinerary."

Zimmer's smile slipped for a split-second, but was replaced quickly. Trent noticed. *Obviously this guy isn't used to being on someone else's schedule.*

"Why not? Tell me what you guys have come up with." Zimmer walked over to the closest armchair and took a seat.

Maybe this guy ain't as bad as Cal thinks. We'll see.

"First, sir, my orders are pretty clear. I'm supposed to be with you 24/7. No exceptions."

To Zimmer's credit, not even the faintest hint of anger crossed his face. "I understand, Top. I assume you already know the whole story?"

Trent nodded.

"Then you know I'm not really in a position to fight this. You guys are doing me a favor and I really do appreciate it. Democrat or not, I'm no idiot."

"No disrespect intended, sir. I've just always found that it's better to clear the air and manage expectations in the beginning."

Willy looked to Zimmer for questions but none came. "So to start I wanted to ask you some questions about your property here."

Trent grilled Zimmer for close to an hour. He quickly found that the security in the rented residence was decent but still lacking, despite the Las Vegas episode. The only things in place were a monitoring system supplied by a local vendor and a panic number provided to all incoming members of the House of Representatives.

It was clearly evident that the freshman representative was somewhat naïve about personal protection and surveillance. It wasn't unusual for unknown Congressmen to drive their own cars, but Willy got the distinct feeling that prior to the Vegas incident, Zimmer almost felt untouchable. Zimmer explained that he'd clearly been instructed by Ishi not to increase any security after the girl's murder. Brandon wasn't stupid. He knew the lack of security meant easy access for his blackmailers.

"Have you noticed anyone following you, anything strange?"

"Are you kidding? I see shadows everywhere now. I'd started to think I was really losing my grip on reality," Zimmer answered in a tone colored with panic.

"That's why I'm here, Congressman. I'll need to do some upgrades to your system here, but we'll do that through SSI, so whoever's watching you won't know. The next part of the plan is to take a little trip to Vegas. Cal wants to see if we can't get these rats out of their nest."

Brandon didn't want to go anywhere near Las Vegas. "No way! The minute I step into that place they'll be all over me. They've already had me back for a couple of mandatory meetings. Every time I feel like I'm the fish in the fishbowl. I'm surrounded and subtlety reminded of where I stand. I can't handle it!"

Willy shouldn't have been surprised by the outburst, but he was. He'd have to tread carefully on this one.

"Sir, as long as I'm with you, nothing will happen. Besides, we'll keep the visit as public as we can."

Zimmer wouldn't be mollified. "They'll see right through it. Why would I want to go out there anyway?"

"Cal's cooked up a story that we're floating out to the media. We've got contacts with prominent casino owners who are big political donors. One of them has a local job placement charity for disabled vets. He'd love for you to come out and help publicize it."

"What!? Those guys are all Republicans! I'll look like an idiot! I need to call my father on this before…"

"Sir, Senator Zimmer already knows."

"There's no way he'd approve this. I'll be a pariah!"

"Maybe you should look at it in a different way, sir. This group is all about job creation, helping military veterans and the local economy. You'd be doing a good thing."

"Cal's just trying to piss me off, isn't he?" Zimmer said dejectedly.

"I won't say that, sir, but maybe it'll be good for you. Besides, if you don't mind me saying, your political career isn't exactly shooting the moon right now."

Zimmer stared at his huge new bodyguard. The last thing he expected was a mountain with brains to show up on his doorstep. He'd assumed that Cal would send some dumb muscle-head to babysit him. At least he'd have someone to talk to now.

"You're right. When do we leave?"

EN-ROUTE TO LAS VEGAS, NEVADA

1:29PM, SEPTEMBER 16TH

Cal took the cranberry juice from the stewardess. "Thanks."

The pretty blonde looked down at him. "Not a problem, sir. Please let me know if you need anything else." Her gaze lingered for a second and then she moved on to serve other passengers.

"I think she likes you, brother," Brian Ramirez teased from beside Cal.

"Not my type, Doc."

"You haven't had a type for a long time, Cal. What happened to that girl you met at the conference we went to?"

"Who?"

"You know. The one with the nice ass. Sabrina?"

"Oh, Salina. She was alright. The long distance thing wasn't for me."

Cal took a sip of his juice. Would he ever be ready? He wasn't conceited; he knew he was good looking. Above average height, still boyish but with the build of a man. He just couldn't get Jess out of his head. She'd been the one. The one that stopped his heart for the first time. Now she was at eternal rest overlooking Camp Spartan.

Brian looked at his friend and read his thoughts. "Not ready are you?"

Cal shook his head. "Not even close. Every time I talk to a girl I feel like I'm cheating."

"That's natural, man. Forget I even mentioned it. So like I was saying before, where do you want to hit first?" The look of excitement on Brian's face almost made Cal spit out his cranberry juice. He looked like a kid going to Disney World for the first time.

"How is it that you've never been to Vegas before?"

"Never had the chance. Left home at eighteen for the Navy, saw the world, then ended up back in Nashville."

Cal didn't want to spoil it for his friend. Las Vegas had some great stuff to see and eat, but he could never shake the contrast of wealth and poverty every time he visited. Vegas was littered with lost souls seeking an instant fortune or last drink. It wasn't all bad. The city was doing some great things for the arts and large corporations. Zappos had recently relocated to the area.

"You know, we do have to do some work while we're there," Cal replied almost seriously.

Brian shook his head. "You said this was a recon mission. That'll leave plenty of time to get fat and happy. I've been reading all about the buffet at the Bellagio. Did you know that they have all you can eat lobster?! I'm gonna eat 'til I fall over."

Cal chuckled. "Alright, Doc. Haven't they let you out of the Bat Cave? You sound like you've been sequestered for the past month."

"We've just been really busy. I'm trying to get these new Robo-Tourniquets to MARSOC."

"Robo-Tourniquets?" Cal asked.

"Yeah! It's fucking brilliant. One of the problems we've had on the battlefield was proper ways of maintaining pressure on injured arms or legs. The tourniquets in med kits have gotten better, but you've still got guys pulling off bootlaces and shredding their utilities to tie-off wounds. A lot of times, by the time the evac gets to a field hospital, the limb can't be saved. We always knew that there was a pressure threshold to decrease blood loss while maintaining good blood flow. The problem is you can't always manually monitor that when you're getting shot at. That's why we built the Robo-Tourniquet."

"I think you lost me, Doc." Cal knew all about the project from Neil, but wanted to hear it from Brian. It was the first R&D invention the former corpsman had spearheaded himself.

"So you've seen those blood pressure cuffs you can buy at the store, right?"

Cal nodded.

"Basically, we started out with one of those. Neil helped me rig one so we could actually program in the optimum pressure for a given wound and body type, then the cuff does it automatically. We've tested it with my paramedic buddies at Vanderbilt and they love it. It takes away the guessing game and lets a total amateur save someone's life and limb."

Cal was truly happy for his friend. They'd met just over a year before. Cal the patient, Brian the nurse. Ramirez was there when Cal needed a friend most after the loss of his fiancé. Brian's faith in Cal turned into a strong friendship. He thought it was always funny how former military guys tended to bond if the initial introductions went well. Somehow they were able to skip a few levels of trust, bypass the B.S. and become buds.

After the episode with the gangster, Dante West, Brian was offered a full-time position at SSI. It wasn't a hard decision for him. Although he loved his job at Vandy, he still missed the camaraderie of the Navy and Marine Corps. SSI provided not only a challenge, but the brotherhood so many military vets long for after separating from the service.

Brian fit in easily with the team at SSI. Athletic like the rest, his easy-going attitude endeared him to even the most hardcore of SSI operators. It didn't hurt that Brian was also a Silver Star recipient for saving the lives of his fellow warriors in Iraq.

"Anything else you want to do in Vegas?" Cal asked.

"I heard about a few new clubs that could be fun. Maybe I can practice some of those counter-surveillance techniques Dunn's been teaching me."

Todd Dunn was head of internal security at Stokes Security

International. Dunn was also a former Ranger that rarely broke from his serious demeanor.

"Have you ever seen that dude disappear in a crowd? It's unbelievable!"

Cal knew most people underestimated the burly Dunn. What strangers never knew was the cunning and brilliance inside the soldier's mind. He looked like a typical meat-head but could easily run with the best tacticians in the game. Dunn wasn't a bad chess player either. He'd trounced Cal on more than one occasion.

"Yeah. I remember when I went through his Urban Escape and Evade course earlier this year. He took a couple of us to the Green Hills Mall. The place wasn't even close to being packed and we lost him in under a minute. Later he shows up with a detailed description of what I'd done for the whole time. Guy knows his stuff," affirmed Cal.

The stewardess appeared and asked if she could get the companions anything before landing.

"I think we're good..." Cal paused to remember the girl's name.

"Veronica," she replied with a dazzling smile.

"Veronica," Cal repeated, "thanks for everything."

She disappeared down the aisle and Brian took the opportunity to lean over Cal and get a last peek of Veronica's exit.

"You sure you're not ready yet?" Brian asked his friend.

WASHINGTON, D.C

2:10PM, SEPTEMBER 16TH

"Is everything in position?" the career politician asked into the secure phone.

"Yes. All teams are standing by for your authorization."

"Good. As we discussed, once I give you the go-ahead the operation must commence within twenty-four hours."

"Understood."

"I won't have any problems with your compatriots will I?"

"No. As long as you hold up your end of the bargain, you will soon be the next President of the United States."

The politician sat back and smiled. He'd waited a long time for this opportunity. He couldn't wait to show that moron in the Oval Office what a real leader looked like. "We've known each other a long time. Have I ever gone back on my word?"

The man on the other end paused. "We only wish to ensure all parties will move forward together. Once again, our nations will be allied on the same path."

The politician honestly didn't give a damn for his partner's motives. This was all about securing the American presidency.

"You provide what we agreed on and your little empire will rise again," he sneered into the phone.

"It will be done."

The politician replaced the receiver. The Democratic National Convention was right around the corner. This one would be absolutely historic. The nation and his party would soon be desperate for a new leader. *I'll be damned if I'll wait another four years.* Maybe it was time to write his acceptance speech.

LAS VEGAS, NEVADA

3:16PM, SEPTEMBER 16TH

Cal and Brian checked into their room at the Cosmopolitan Hotel and Casino. It was located in an ideal location at the end of The Strip. Close enough to Neil at the Bellagio, it was also within easy walking distance to Congressman Zimmer at Zeitaku just off The Strip.

Cal glanced at his watch. "Top and Zimmer should be flying in soon. Let's head over to the Bellagio and check out what Neil's got."

Although it was only early afternoon, Las Vegas Boulevard was already packed with tourists. The pair made their way through the throngs and finally arrived at the Bellagio.

"Wow! This place is crazy!" Brian exclaimed.

"You talking about all the people or the hotel?"

"Both! Is it always like this?"

Cal kept reminding himself not to dampen the mood. Brian needed to enjoy the experience.

"The hotel looks even more beautiful at night. We'll come check it out later. As for the people, I guess the cooler weather's really brought out the masses this year."

"Does it have anything to do with the convention?" Brian asked.

"Which one? They have a ton out here."

"Do you ever watch the news, jarhead? The Democratic National Convention."

"I get all my news on Drudge, Doc. Besides, why the hell would I care about the left side of the aisle?"

"We are helping out a Democratic Congressman. You know what The Hammer says. Do…"

"Yeah, yeah. Do your homework." Cal interrupted impatiently. The Hammer was SSI's lead attorney Marjorie Haines. She'd picked up the nickname not only for her ferocity in the courtroom, but also the way she regularly took down SSI operators on the training mats. It was rumored that she had an impressive array of vintage wines aging in her cellar, thanks in part to the lucrative bets she'd won from SSI warriors. As the only female employee at SSI (a distinction she was silently proud of and didn't care to share), there was always a challenge especially from cocky newcomers.

The Hammer was also meticulous about preparation. She knew more about impending ops than most of the men going into the field. It was a habit she hammered into her peers constantly. Haines was a valued advisor to Travis (it was also rumored that the two had an on-again off-again romance on the side) and the rest of the SSI leadership team. Beautiful and deadly, she was a force to be reckoned with.

"So when is the convention?" Cal asked.

"This week."

The two walked in through the Bellagio's main entrance and headed for the elevators. Cal glanced around casually, further honing his counter surveillance skills. He knew that Las Vegas casinos were some of the most guarded fortresses on Earth. It would be interesting trying to pick out the enemies among the sea of native security staff.

They soon reached Patel's door and knocked on it.

Pointing to the small peephole Brian asked, "You think that's one of his rigged cameras?"

The tech genius was known for weaving surveillance gear into anything he could. It also made him one of the most successful pranksters on both SSI campuses.

"I'll bet it is," Cal answered. "What the hell's taking him so long?"

He knocked again. Nothing. Strange.

Cal pulled out his mobile and dialed Neil's number. Patel picked up on the third ring.

"Yeah?"

"Were you asleep?"

"Cal?"

"Yeah, jackass. We're right outside your door!"

"Oh, sorry. I'll be there in a sec."

Cal looked down at his phone and shook his head.

"He did get here yesterday, Cal. I'll bet he was out gambling all night," Brian said smirking.

The door opened and a bleary-eyed Neil peered out.

"Sorry guys. Pulled an all-nighter."

Brian beat Cal to the punch, "How much did you win?"

"What?" asked a clearly confused Patel as he stepped back into the room, Cal and Brian following.

"How much did you win at the craps tables last night?" Brian repeated.

"Oh! I wasn't gambling, Doc. I was getting all this set up." Patel motioned to the impressive array of equipment lining the room.

"Holy crap, Neil!" Cal piped, "Are you having an Xbox convention in here?"

"I wish. Figured we'd need as much horsepower as we could get. It was a real pain getting it shipped and setup yesterday. At least now I've got everything I'll need to work remotely." Neil scratched his disheveled hair and fixed his expensive eyeglasses. His handsome Indian face was lined with two-day-old stubble. "You guys hungry?"

"We just grabbed a quick bite at our hotel," Cal explained. "You wanna order up some room service or give us a quick rundown of where we're at?"

Neil gave food a serious thought as he felt his stomach grumble. He knew better than to make his friend wait though. They'd know each other since their days at the University of Virginia, and Neil knew Cal could be an impatient and stubborn ass when he wanted to.

"Let me give you a brief summary and then I'll get some food."

Cal nodded and followed Neil over to the main bank of computer screens.

Patel sat down, logged in, and started clicking away on the mouse. Pictures popped up on multiple screens.

"Okay. Based on the information I got from Congressman Zimmer, I've started my analysis on this gaming consultancy: Ichiban Gaming. The only intel I've gathered on them is from their website and public records. I've got a couple of my crawler programs making some inquiries now." Neil pointed at the far left screen. "This guy right here is the Congressman's friend, Ishi Nakamura. Looked up his records and so far everything checks out. It does seem a little odd for him to be such a big fish at Ichiban at his age. Then again, it's his father's company so you never know."

Cal interrupted. "This guy is dirty, Neil. No way could he call off the hounds at a murder scene without having some pull. Do whatever you need to do to find out more."

"Already on it. I'm pulling his banking history right now. With that, I can track where he's been. Should know more soon."

"Okay. I'm going to Zimmer's hotel to take a look around. Do you have my order?" Cal asked.

"Yeah, it's all in that box." Neil pointed to a black case, about two feet by four feet in size, laying on the nearest chaise lounge.

Cal kneeled down and opened the case. Inside were three pistols and plenty of ammunition from the SSI armory. Nothing less than a .45. Cal ignored them. Walking into a Las Vegas hotel armed wasn't the best thing. Instead, he snagged one of four knives and pulled it out of the sheath. The blade, six inches in length, was pointed and razor sharp on both edges. He'd heard about these particular blades in one of his favorite novels and decided to order them a few months earlier. It was a small weapon but effective in a pinch. More importantly you could strap it to your wrist and carry it concealed. Retrieval was easy and deadly. After the attack in Nashville the previous year, Cal never left home unprepared. Although he would've loved his trusty Springfield XD pistol, the blade would do.

He looked up at Ramirez, pointing at the remaining weapons. "You want one?"

"I'm good. I'll stick with my pennies," Brian said, patting his jean pockets.

Brian was talking about the two sets of rolled pennies, one in each pocket. They weren't as good as a firearm, but very effective in a fist-fight. Besides, Ramirez wasn't a stranger to hand-to-hand combat. He'd spent plenty of time in the Principal's office as a kid. Going to an all-white (save one) school in Nashville hadn't always been the easiest. There were always a couple of rednecks that wanted to pick on his Hispanic heritage. They soon found out that the little beaner was a scrapper, thanks to hours of practice in the boxing ring.

Cal took off his sport coat, strapped the knife onto his left arm, and put his coat back on. "You ready, Doc?"

"Let's go."

"FATHER, the Congressman will be landing soon," Ishi bowed to his father.

Kazuo Nakamura, a slightly overweight man, looked at his son with pride. To think that all their plans were finally coming to fruition. Years of planning. Congressman Zimmer was the icing on the cake. Yes, delivered by their contact in Washington, but designed and executed by Ishi.

"Good. Ensure our eyes are always on him," he said as he stroked his graying goatee.

"Yes, Father. There has been one new development." Ishi offered cautiously.

"And what would that be, my Son?"

"It seems that the Congressman has a bodyguard with him."

"How did you find out about this?"

"Our contact sent me an encrypted email an hour ago. Apparently, the Congressman contacted a company called SSI to provide security."

"What?! The fool! You assured me that this would not happen."

"I warned him, Father. There is more."

All vestiges of Kazuo Nakamura's calm façade disappeared. "What else has he done?!"

"Our contact also alerted me to the fact that there might be additional SSI personnel coming to Las Vegas to conduct surveillance. He was only able to provide a brief profile of one man, a Calvin Stokes, Jr. Mr. Stokes is the heir to the company's founder; his deceased father."

Kazuo stroked his beard, thinking. "Did he provide a physical description?"

"He provided a picture from his military record. Calvin Stokes is a former Marine."

"Provide the photograph to the security staff at each of our hotels. If this Calvin Stokes sets foot in one of them I want him followed and apprehended...quietly."

"Should I use one of our teams?"

"No. Use our Russian friends. They know how to be discreet."

"Yes, Father. I will take care of it."

"Is there anything else?"

"No, Father."

"Our time is coming, my Son. Do well and our family will soon attain new heights within the empire."

LAS VEGAS, NEVADA

7:40PM, SEPTEMBER 16TH

Dusk was falling as the young man prepared. He splashed cold water on his face and looked into the bathroom mirror. His strong chiseled jaw was now covered with a shaggy beard. His blonde hair, once cut to military precision, hung to his shoulders. *I look more like a mountain man these days*, he thought. He finished in the bathroom and walked into the bedroom to collect his clothes and his weapons. Maybe tonight God would answer his call.

Brian and Cal hadn't found anything of interest at the Congressman's hotel. There were some exclusive gambling rooms filled with foreign high-dollar players and two swanky Japanese restaurants, but nothing that stood out. At least now they had a better idea of the lay of the land.

Cal did not want to be in the hotel when Trent and the Congressman arrived. They'd already arranged a separate meeting outside of enemy territory for the next day.

The darkening sky found the duo walking the strip, meandering with the crowds. There wasn't any work to do tonight so they'd decided to see the sights.

"You want to hit that new club over by Caesar's? I think it's free before ten."

"Which one is that?" Cal asked as he swerved to avoid one of the thousands of leaflet purveyors trying to get the attention of wandering tourists.

"Motown Moscow. It's some kind of fusion of Jazz and Communism. Rumor has it that an ex-KGB agent runs the place."

"Motown Moscow? I don't know, Doc. I'm not a huge fan of jazz."

"Come on, Cal. Where's your sense of adventure? Maybe they'll have one of those crazy, frozen vodka bars with Miles Davis playing on top!"

"Okay, okay. But if I get hit on by some seven foot tall Russian troll…"

"Don't worry, man. It'll be fun. I promise to get you home before midnight."

Brian led the way after quickly glancing at his smart phone's mapping app.

"You're sure it was him?" Ishi asked into his mobile phone. He listened for the response. "Good. Have the Russians follow and get rid of them."

A pre-emptive strike would impress his father. If things were coming as close to fruition as his father thought, now was the time to take action.

"Are you sure we're going the right way? I think we're too far off The Strip, Doc."

"Hold on. Let me check again."

As Brian checked his phone, Cal got the nagging feeling that they were being watched. He casually glanced around, taking in the crowd. Nothing jumped out. Maybe he was tired. Just as he turned back to his friend, he caught someone's eye. The man's gaze lingered a breath too long. Something about the bearded man set off alarm bells in Cal's brain.

"We need to move, now."

Brian looked up from his phone. "Huh?"

"Don't look around. Just act casual. We've got a tail. Bearded giant about forty yards back."

Brian took Cal's cue and followed. They weaved in and out of the packed sidewalk. *Let's see how persistent this guy is*, Cal thought as he quickly turned down a small side street.

As soon as they entered the street, Cal knew he'd made a mistake. What he'd thought was a street was just one of the many service entrances to a casino. No exits unless the back door happened to be open.

"Shit," Cal whispered.

"This is a dead end, Cal."

"I know. Just keep going."

"Why do you think this guy's following us?"

Cal had no idea. Money? Random thuggery?

He stole a quick look back. The bearded giant had materialized with two enormous companions. *Maybe it's time to find out what these guys want.*

Cal nudged Brian and said loudly, "Dude, this isn't the right way!"

Brian took the cue. "Crap! Sorry. I think we turned one street too early."

They swung around and saw that the three giants had quickly closed the gap. Twenty yards separated the two parties.

"Hey, fellas! You guys know how to find Motown Moscow?" Cal asked cheerfully. Maybe the whole thing was a fluke.

Instead of answering, the three men kept walking forward. Their wide frames moved in unison. They fanned out to surround Cal and Brian. As they stepped closer, a van screeched to a halt at the opening of the service alley. The side door banged open and two more men jumped out.

"I guess these guys don't want to talk," Cal mused.

"Yeah. Any ideas?"

"Hey diddle diddle?" It was a private joke. Marines were fond of saying 'Hey diddle diddle, straight up the middle', to explain a full-frontal assault.

Brian nodded and put his hands in his pockets. He gripped his weapons casually. "You sure we can't talk about this guys?"

The bearded giant spoke for the first time in a heavy Russian accent. "No talk. Now we crush you."

"Whatever you say, Ivan Drago. I think..." the words stuck in Cal's throat as he noticed a figure climb over their attackers' van and jump down on the two men waiting for their companions. As he fell, the shaggy stranger pointed two tasers at the backs of his targets. Their muted screams and Cal's gaze drew the attention of the three hulking men. They turned their heads. Cal and Brian took advantage of the distraction and attacked.

Cal unsheathed his knife and dropped into a squat, simultaneously slicing a clean line through the man's left knee. The man screamed in surprise and bent to grab his injured leg. As he did, Cal sprang up pulling the man's head down as he drove his knee up into the Russian's nose. The man collapsed unconscious.

Meanwhile, Brian went to work on the giant on the far right. As a combat veteran, Brian knew there was rarely such thing as a fair fight. Use any advantage you can. Instead of trying to reach a swing at the man's head, Ramirez directed his uppercut at his groin. The man quickly joined his companion on the ground.

The bearded giant was the only one who had a chance to retaliate. As Cal turned back to the last attacker, the wild looking stranger sprang on the larger man and landed a brutal blow to the man's temple with what looked like a short billy club. Game over.

"We need to get out of here," said the longhaired newcomer. Cal noticed that the man was barely breathing heavy. His posture looked almost animalistic in its grace.

Not wanting to wait around for the authorities, Cal agreed. "You lead the way..."

"Daniel."

"You lead the way, Daniel."

The three men rushed to the end of the alley, replacing their weapons as they ran. Once they got to the van, they squeezed around back and disappeared into the moving crowds.

After silently following Daniel for fifteen minutes, the trio approached an old apartment complex. Daniel walked up the only flight of stairs and opened the third door.

He ushered his guests inside and turned on the lights.

The apartment was small but spotless. It was sparingly appointed. No pictures, just a small kitchenette, bathroom, an old bed and some books on a shelf. It looked much newer than the exterior.

Daniel took off his trench coat and placed it on the bed neatly. As he did Cal noticed the large tattoo on the man's left arm. It was the trademark skull and arrowhead of Marine sniper units with the motto: 'Swift, silent, deadly.'

"You're a Marine?" Cal asked.

"I was," Daniel answered quietly as he moved to the kitchen sink and washed his hands.

"Me too."

Daniel didn't respond except with a silent nod.

Cal thought of what to say as he studied the other Marine. The young man looked fit and muscular. He probably stood just over six feet with dirty blonde hair and beard. Cal guessed that the guy couldn't be more than thirty years old. *Where'd this guy come from?*

Daniel turned back from the kitchen and spoke. "How'd you get involved with the Russians? Gambling debts?"

Cal was totally confused. "You know those guys?"

"I know WHO they are. They're hired thugs. They split their time between security duty and breaking knee caps," Daniel explained.

"Let's back up a minute, man. First off, I'm Cal and this is my buddy Brian. He was a corpsman so we all call him Doc."

The three men shook hands. "I'm Daniel Briggs."

"I guess we forgot to say thanks, Daniel," Brian added. "How'd you happen to be nearby anyways?"

Daniel took a second to respond. How had he known? How did he ever know where danger was? Some might call it a gift. To Daniel it often felt like a curse. He didn't know how to explain but he tried.

"You guys spend any time over in Iraq or Afghanistan?" he asked.

Both men nodded.

"You ever have a hard time sleeping?"

"I don't, but I have plenty of friends that do," Cal offered.

"Same here," Brian added.

Daniel paused again, praying that he was doing the right thing in telling these strangers about some of his darkest secrets.

"Well, I'm one of the ones that couldn't sleep. Tried alcohol for while. Didn't take. Neither did the prescriptions. Then I found God. Now I help other people."

Brian and Cal looked at each other. Who was this guy? He'd obviously had some post-traumatic issues. They both knew that a lot of returning veterans had PTSD symptoms. Some of the most successful found healing through counseling and religion.

"So what are you doing on the streets of Las Vegas?" Cal asked.

"Long story short, I felt led here. I'm from Florida. Hopped on a bus one day. Vegas was where my bus ticket ran out. I've spent the last few months doing odd jobs during the day and walking the streets at night. I make sure tourists aren't getting taken advantage of. The thieves and con artists are pretty easy to spot if you know what you're looking for. I've just been waiting."

"Waiting for what?" Cal and Brian asked at the same time.

"Something else. I know God will tell me when it's time to move on."

Cal respected the man's conviction. "So what about those guys tonight? How'd you know they were coming after us?"

"Vegas is actually a pretty small town. Once you've been here for a spell, you start to know the characters. I've seen these guys on collecting duty before. They work for that Japanese-themed hotel behind the Bellagio. Usually it's just two of them. When I saw them tonight, they looked like they were on a mission. I decided to follow. You know the rest," Daniel finished.

Cal and Brian stood silent for a second. So they'd been detected at Zimmer's hotel. But what was the motive? Questions started rolling around in Cal's head. How'd they pick out Cal and Brian? Why come after them now? Who told them? Cal had a sneaking suspicion that Congressman Brandon Zimmer had opened his big fucking mouth. He'd have to have a little talk with the arrogant prick.

Cal filed away his thoughts for later. Back to Daniel Briggs. What do you say to a guy that looks like a crazy mountain man and spends most nights playing hero on the streets of Sin City?

Both friends were obviously curious about the man's past.

"So you were a scout sniper in the Corps?"

"Yeah. I'd never picked up a rifle before boot camp. My drill instructors said I was a natural," Daniel explained without a hint of arrogance. "Once I finished up the School of Infantry in Lejeune, I got picked up to go to sniper school."

"How many tours did you do?" asked Brian.

"Iraq once and three times to Afghanistan. Spent some time with MARSOC too."

So this guy had been around the block a few times. Cal would have to find out some more details from his contact at Headquarters Marine Corps.

"If you don't mind me asking, what was your PTSD trigger?" Brian asked.

It didn't look like Daniel minded the question. If he'd already admitted to having sleeping issues, Brian figured he'd probably open up about the rest. It didn't hurt that Cal and Brian had similar backgrounds: brothers-in-arms.

"It wasn't the killing. I never had a problem with that." He paused to gather his thoughts. "The guys we took down were bad dudes. Most were insurgents from across the border. Some of the best shooting I ever did was over-watch for battalion. I knew I was saving Marines' lives. It was my last tour when things went to shit. Some of our teams were getting attached to special ops groups. They wanted to double the number of snipers they were taking into the zone. So we're on this op in the middle of shitland Afghanistan. Real nasty urban area. Full of Taliban and Al Qaeda fighters. We'd just inserted with a team of four SEALs. As soon as we fast roped to the ground and the helo banks left, insurgents took it out with a couple of RPGs. The SEALs told us to find some high ground to get a better vantage point, and they took off for the insurgent position. We tried to get indirect fire or close air support, but higher wouldn't allow it because of the large civilian population. Me and my spotter got into one of the compounds and found the best view we could. We watched as those SEALs leapfrogged all the way to the enemy pos. It was pitch black, but we could see that two of the guys were already wounded. Those brave sons-a-bitches kept assaulting and cussing out higher over the radio. I'd just setup my Barrett .50 cal as I watched all four SEALs get mowed down by a truck-mounted machine gun. I started unloading on the fuckers. It was like shooting fish in a barrel. They kept streaming out, trying to get the bodies of our SEALs."

"Pretty soon they realized where our shots were coming from. They turned their fire on us. I have no idea how long I was shooting. My spotter, Grant, got hit in the shoulder almost right away. He kept calling out shots though. Finally some fucker gets smart and they start lobbing mortar rounds at us. We started pulling back into one of the only two story buildings in the area. Grant was wounded but still doing okay. Then he got hit with an AK round in the leg. Went right through his femur. Blood everywhere. I lugged my .50 cal on one shoulder and dragged Grant under the other arm. We get in the bottom floor of this building and all hell broke loose. It sounded like two or three mortar tubes thumping rounds onto us. We somehow got to the lowest part of the building before it collapsed."

"I don't know how I didn't get crushed. Grant did though. His other leg was completely smashed under the rubble. Grant tried not to scream as his leg pumped more and more blood onto the dirt floor. I applied a quick tourniquet and tried to make him comfortable. I remember telling him that someone would be there soon. Man, was I wrong."

"For the next two days we listened quietly as the insurgents searched the rubble pile. I don't know how they didn't get to us. I could even hear the fuckers cheering. Found out later that they'd mutilated the SEALs' bodies and hung 'em up outside where we were trapped."

"Our radio got lost in the explosion, so we were shit out of luck there. I kept telling Grant that we just had to stay quiet and some of our boys would be there soon. He was delirious with pain for a day. I tried to keep him awake but he finally passed out. A day later, I couldn't find a pulse."

"He died in my arms. We'd been friends since boot camp. I was the best man at his wedding. I barely had a scratch on me. A day later, I heard a lot of firing and then troops talking English. I screamed and screamed until they pinpointed where I was. They brought in the engineers and got us out. I found out later that the enemy had been waiting for us. Apparently some American politician had opened his mouth and word got to the right people on the other side. We didn't have a chance."

"I spent a lot of time afterwards wondering why. I'd drink my way into a dark tunnel and wonder: why not me instead of Grant? Why did he have to leave his wife and kid? Why do politicians leak secrets? The answer I found was simple: It's not up to me. The Man upstairs has some kind of plan. Maybe he was saving me for something. All I can do now is try my best and live up to the second chance."

Cal and Brian stood quietly, digesting the story.

"So how do you sleep now?" asked Cal.

"Like a baby most nights. I still have bad dreams every once in a while. Mostly they're memories of Grant slowly dying in my arms, repeating his wife's name over and over. He looks more like an angel in my dreams now."

"I appreciate you telling us. We've been in the shit a few times, too. How about you come have a drink with us so we can thank you properly?" asked Cal.

"I don't drink alcohol anymore, but sure. How about tomorrow night?"

They exchanged contact information and Cal promised to call Daniel the next day to confirm. Cal and Brian said their goodbyes and walked outside.

"You think we should change our hotel room now?" Brian asked sarcastically.

LAS VEGAS, NEVADA

9:30PM, SEPTEMBER 16TH

The large bearded Russian stood almost at attention. Ishi Nakamura paced back and forth in front of the giant.

"How is it that you let these two men get away?" Ishi asked once again.

"I told you, Mr. Nakamura. We were not expecting the third man. We also did not know the capabilities of the targets. That information could have been useful. I now have two men in hospital," grumbled the hired thug.

"I don't care about your men, you idiot. We pay you a lot of money to take care of such simple tasks. I still can't believe five military-trained men couldn't take down two targets," Ishi continued as he paced.

"Technically, it was three m..."

"Shut up! Just shut up!" Ishi screamed. "Now I want you to be ready the next time I call. If you need to find more men, do it. Meanwhile, I'll clean up this mess."

Ishi dreaded the next conversation with his father. Nakamura-san would not be amused.

CAL AND BRIAN called Neil as soon as they left Daniel's apartment. He'd get them another suite at the Venetian by the time they packed their gear. It was a little farther away, but owned by a friend of the company.

"The reservation will be under your Alpha aliases," Neil instructed. Each operator at SSI was assigned three aliases (Alpha, Bravo and Charlie) for contingencies. "I suggest you boys get some rest for tomorrow."

"Thanks, Dad," Cal retorted. "We'll see you tomorrow, Neil."

He replaced the phone in his pocket and followed Brian through the door at the Cosmopolitan.

"You still happy you tagged along, Doc?"

"Who me? I'm used to your crazy adventures by now, man. What's next? Naked stripper assassins parachuting through our glass windows at the Venetian?" quipped Brian.

"I sure as hell hope not. You'd be too distracted by the naked girls to defend yourself."

"Very funny, jackass."

They got in and out of their room quickly. There really hadn't been time to unpack so grabbing their bags was easy. Cal put the Do Not Disturb sign on the outside of the door. They'd let the reservation run its course for the next two days, just in case.

Cal led the way down the back staircase and headed for the service exit.

DANIEL BRIGGS KNELT NEXT to his bed. The adrenaline finally seeped from his system; he was exhausted but happy. He took a moment to say a quick prayer. When he finished, he stripped down to his boxer briefs and fell right to sleep.

LAS VEGAS, NEVADA

7:08AM, SEPTEMBER 17TH

Congressman Zimmer and MSgt Trent arrived late the night before. It was a bright morning that promised to be clear and beautiful. Not a cloud in the sky.

Zimmer padded into the living area just after 7:00am wearing some gym shorts and a t-shirt. Trent had to admit that the man didn't look like a pansy. He seemed to be in good shape. Maybe in another life he could've been in the military.

Trent was shirtless but already dressed in gym shorts and running shoes. He'd sprawled his massive frame over the long couch overlooking the outdoor pool. Creeping up on the big four oh, Willy Trent was still as fit as any professional athlete. At one time, he'd been drafted into the NFL. He soon found another calling with the Marines.

"You sleep okay, Top?"

"Just fine, sir."

"You ready to hit the gym in a few minutes?"

"Yes, sir. I'll throw on a t-shirt and we can go."

Both men finished getting ready then headed to the workout facility.

AN HOUR LATER, they headed back to their suite.

"I don't know about you, Top, but I needed that," stated a completely sweat-soaked Zimmer.

"Yes, sir. Always nice to start the day off with a good workout."

"What time are we meeting Cal this morning?"

Trent looked at his watch. "He called while we were in the gym and pushed it back an hour. Apparently they had a little situation last night. He's trying to get a read on it before we meet."

"What kind of situation?" asked Zimmer.

Trent shrugged. "He wouldn't tell me over the phone. I guess we'll find out soon enough."

Getting back to their suite, each man split off to their respective rooms to shower and change.

Brandon was putting his pants on when his personal cell phone rang. He looked down at the caller ID.

"Hey, Dad."

"How are things going, Son?"

"We got in last night. We'll be meeting Cal soon."

"Good. Any progress on their investigation?" the Senator asked.

"I'm not sure yet. I'll know more after we meet, I think."

"Now you remember, Son. Let those boys do their job. From what I hear, they're very good at what they do."

"I know, Dad. I'll behave."

"Call me when you know more," Senator Zimmer instructed.

The line went dead. Brandon tucked the phone into his pocket and finishing dressing. Zimmer hoped it would be an uneventful day.

MSgt Trent led the way down to the lobby. He scanned the area and ushered the Congressman toward the main exit. Just as they were about to step into the revolving doors, someone called out.

"Brandon!"

Trent and Zimmer turned around. Ishi Nakamura approached with a pair of security guards. Zimmer plastered a happy look on his face and waved to his old friend.

"Hey, Ishi."

Nakamura walked up and hugged him. "How come you didn't call me when you got in? I would've sent up some champagne or something."

"It was late when we got in last night. I didn't want to bother you."

"You're never a bother, my friend. Remember, you are MY responsibility."

Trent detected a slight flare of a threat in Nakamura's tone.

"God, I'm sorry, Ishi. I forgot to introduce you to my new bodyguard. Willy Trent, this is my old friend, Ishi Nakamura."

The two men shook hands. "Good to meet you, Mr. Trent. Can I call you Willy?" Ishi asked pleasantly.

"Mr. Trent would be just fine, sir."

Ishi's face fell for a split second. He recovered and said, "Once a Marine, always a Marine, eh, Mr. Trent?"

"That's right, sir. You can take the man out of the Marines, but you can't take the Marine out of the man."

Ishi laughed. "Ha! I like that. Either way, welcome to Las Vegas and let us know if the hotel's security team can help in any way."

Ishi turned to Congressman Zimmer. "Brandon, I've got some people I'd like you to meet later today. They're big donors and are helping with the planning for the Democratic National Convention. How about we grab dinner tonight?"

Zimmer looked to Trent who nodded. "Sounds good. What time should we meet you down here?"

"Let's make it seven thirty."

"Alright, we'll see you then."

The two men shook hands again and went their separate ways. As

Nakamura passed the concierge desk, his phone buzzed. He picked it up.

Ishi answered in Japanese. "Did you see your target?"

"Yes."

"Good. Make sure he's taken before my dinner with the Congressman. I want no mistakes."

"Yes, Nakamura-san."

Ishi ended the call and continued to his office. *It's time to teach Brandon a little lesson.*

TRENT HAILED a cab and held the door open for Zimmer. Five minutes later, they were getting out in front of Caesar's Palace. During the ride, Trent spotted two vehicles following them from the hotel.

"Sir, I'm gonna need you to do exactly as I say," Trent murmured to Zimmer.

"Huh? What's going on?" he whispered back.

"Just keep walking toward the main entrance over there. Don't look around. We've got a tail."

"Is it someone from the hotel?" Zimmer asked calmly.

"Yes. Now we're gonna do a little extra walking. Follow me."

Trent slipped in front of Zimmer and started weaving his way through the morning crowd. Brandon followed closely.

Willy pulled out his phone and dialed Cal.

"Yeah?" Cal answered.

"We've got extra friends trying to wreck the party. Let's move to the backup location."

"I'll see you there."

Trent pulled his phone away from his ear and walked faster. Zimmer was having a hard time not running just to match the Marine's long stride. They walked quickly around the curved drive. Trent walked up to a cab and hopped in, Zimmer right behind.

Willy instructed the driver to go to Circus Circus at the north end of the The Strip.

"What the hell is going on?" Zimmer whispered.

"I think your friend Ishi sent some of his goons after us. Not sure if it's just to keep an eye on us or what. I didn't want to take any chances."

"Should we even go back to the hotel later?"

"What choice do we have? Let's focus on getting to this meeting first. Maybe Cal will have something for us." Trent continued to watch behind them. He couldn't pinpoint anyone following, but that didn't matter. He'd learned long ago to trust his sixth sense. Right now it was blaring like a foghorn.

Ten minutes later, the cab pulled out of the congested corridor and pulled up in front of the aged Circus Circus. Trent paid the driver then followed Zimmer over to the front entrance.

"We're supposed to meet Cal and Brian in front of the Krispy Kreme stand in the Slots of Fun side of the casino. Stay close now, Congressman."

No sooner had they stepped off towards the entrance that they both felt a pinch on their necks. At first, Trent thought it was a horse fly bite. That was until Zimmer collapsed to the pavement. A large limousine pulled up beside them. The last thing Trent saw before he fell unconscious was the rushed steps of four men running his way.

"Where the hell are they?" Cal thought out loud.

"Have you tried calling him again?" Brian asked.

"Yeah. Three times. There's no way Top left his phone in the hotel room."

"Want me to go outside and take a look?"

"No. Let's both go. Maybe they just got caught in traffic."

As they walked, Cal texted Neil to track the GPS locator in Trent's phone. All SSI phones were rigged for tracking.

They stepped out into the sunlight and looked around. No sign of Trent and the Congressman. Cal's phone buzzed.

"What did you find, Neil?"

"The locator says Trent is standing right in front of the main entrance to Circus Circus."

"Hold on. Let me walk that way."

Cal pushed past a group of drunken gamblers and headed to the front of the casino.

"Do you see him?" Neil asked.

"Not yet. You sure you've got it right?"

"I'm showing a full signal. No way this thing is wrong."

Cal started jogging. His anxiety increased as he reached the sidewalk leading into the building. Both men looked all around.

"Cal, look!" Brian was pointing at the ground.

Lying on the ground next to a pair of broken sunglasses was MSgt Trent's cell phone.

"Holy shit. Neil, message Trav and have him send in the contingency team."

Cal ended the call and sprinted to catch a cab.

CAMP SPARTAN, ARRINGTON, TN

12:16PM, SEPTEMBER 17TH

Travis Haden addressed his three closest advisors: Todd Dunn, Marge Haines, and Dr. Higgins, SSI's resident psychologist. He'd just run through the details from Cal.

"So, Cal just called for the contingency team. I think we better prep for the worst. Any questions?"

Marge Haines started, "What do we have on books as far as Trent's security with Zimmer?"

"I can answer that," Todd Dunn said. "We tasked him out as a VIP security contract. By the way, I just got confirmation that the contingency team is in the air."

"Good," Travis nodded. "What else?"

"Who else knew about the security arrangement?" Haines asked.

Dunn shrugged. "We'll have to assume that Zimmer's immediate support staff knows. Senator Zimmer is also in the loop."

Dr. Higgins raised his hand. "Have you thought about a possible leak, Travis?"

"I've thought about it, but don't have a clue who it could be."

"I think it's fair to assume that the operation has been compromised and we're dealing with a larger threat than we initially believed," Higgins intoned professionally.

"I think you're right, Doc. First, Cal tells me about getting attacked by these giant Russians. Now, Top and Zimmer are gone. I think we need to alert the Council and start putting some more pieces into play."

"Is it time to involve the authorities?" Haines asked.

"Let's give Cal a little time. I find it hard to believe that this Japanese group would dispose of Zimmer so soon. I think something else is brewing," Travis said.

"I concur," agreed Dr. Higgins. "It looks like our new enemy is taking extreme measures to keep us out of the picture. Do we have any thoughts on their motive other than to blackmail Congressman Zimmer?"

"Neil's working on it right now. I think Cal said he was close to getting into the Ichiban system," answered Travis.

"Seems like a long time for Neil to crack the code," Dunn noted.

"Yeah. I think these Ichiban guys have some serious horsepower under the hood. I'm not liking it," answered Travis. "Let's meet up again in an hour. Maybe we'll have some good news from Vegas by then."

CONGRESSMAN ZIMMER WOKE up to a splitting headache. He tried to open his eyes but realized they were covered by a blindfold. His arms were numb and bound to the chair he was tied to. *Where the hell am I?*

He tried to shift into a more comfortable position and heard a chair squeak.

"Hello?" Zimmer croaked. He noticed his throat was bone dry.

"I thought we talked about expectations, Brandon?"

"Ishi?"

"Yes. I don't think you understand the position you've put me in. We saved you from public embarrassment and possibly life in jail. You repay us by ignoring our rules and taking advantage of our friendship," Ishi explained smoothly.

"What the hell are you talking about, man?"

"Let's start with your bodyguard. If you were worried about personal security, why didn't you contact someone within your government?" Ishi asked.

"No one listens to a first-term Congressman. They'd think I was just being paranoid."

"Okay. So why didn't you ask us for additional security?"

Zimmer almost laughed. He might be a little naïve, but he wasn't stupid.

"Look man, I know I owe you guys a lot, but this is ridiculous. I'm sorry if I broke the rules. If I'd known how much of a problem it would be, I wouldn't have hired Trent."

"Well, you won't have to worry about Master Sergeant Trent anymore."

Brandon's stomach went to his throat.

"What did you do with him, Ishi?"

"Oh, you'll see him soon enough. He's being employed in a more… entertaining way. Are you almost ready for dinner?"

"Tell me where Trent is, Ishi."

"ENOUGH! I'm not the little punk you knew at Harvard, *Congressman*. You can't push me around anymore. From now on you do exactly as I say. Is that understood?"

Brandon knew he couldn't win this fight. He decided to keep his mouth shut and bide his time. At the moment, his own safety didn't seem so important. His main thought as Ishi untied his arms was: *Where is Willy Trent?*

MSgt Trent opened his eyes. Where was Zimmer? He quickly surveyed his surroundings. His prison cell was a small windowless room. The space was about ten by ten, the floor concrete. They'd laid him on an old cot with a thin, musty mattress. Trent struggled to his feet. His head pounded. What the hell had they knocked him out with? He remembered the last seconds before passing out. He remembered Zimmer going down. *Where the hell is he?*

Once his mind cleared, he realized they'd taken his clothes. The only thing covering his extensive frame was a stylish loincloth. His captors had also attached a thick collar around his neck. *What the hell?* He flexed his neck and felt around the edges of the leather collar. It felt completely locked in place. Trent thought he detected a small antenna on it as well.

Take a deep breath and think, Willy.

Over the years he'd been in some strange situations. This one was definitely taking the cake. He must look like an overgrown Zulu warrior right now. What was next? A spear and shield? *Someone's gonna pay for this shit.*

As he pondered payback, a robotic voice sparked to life from a hidden speaker.

"In ten minutes, you will be escorted to the weapons room."

"Say what?" Willy yelled back at the faceless voice.

"Prepare yourself."

There were no further instructions. Trent stood baffled. What the hell was going on?

―――

CONGRESSMAN ZIMMER'S clothes were waiting for him. Following Ishi's instructions, he changed and used the bathroom to clean up. They'd given him five minutes.

Five minutes later a Japanese man, dressed in a butler's uniform, entered the room.

"Congressman Zimmer, Nakamura-san has requested your presence." The man bowed waiting for a response.

"Okay. I'm, uh, I'm ready to go."

Zimmer followed the man through a short maze of doorways. He occasionally glimpsed a window. The night outside was pitch black. The building felt part industrial part high-end hotel. Where were they? He never saw an exterior door. No easy way out.

Reaching the end of the hallway, the butler opened a heavy oak door. He held it for the Congressman who stepped in alone.

"Ah, here he is!" Zimmer recognized Ishi's voice in the dimly lit room. He looked around and found himself in an elegantly appointed dining room. A group of older Asian gentlemen were gathered near a large plate-glass window.

Brandon put on his best politician smile and stepped into the gloom. "Hey, Ishi."

The men in the corner stopped talking and stared at the freshman Congressman from Massachusetts. *Who are these guys?* They were giving him the creeps with the way they looked at him.

"Congressman Zimmer, please let me introduce you to my father and some of his associates," Ishi said loud enough for the room to hear.

Brandon followed Ishi to the group. He went to glance at the large window, but the light beyond flicked off as if on command.

"Father, this is my good friend Congressman Zimmer."

Kazuo Nakamura stepped forward and shook Zimmer's hand. "It is a pleasure to finally meet you, Congressman. My son has told me so much about you." He smiled almost conspiratorially.

"Please, Mr. Nakamura, call me Brandon."

"Very well." He turned to his associates. "I won't bother to tell you all their names, but let me introduce you. These men are my closest friends. They are all captains of industry and leaders of Japan. We trace our family roots back to the days of the samurai, through the rise of our Empire during the Second World War, and now Japan's rebuilding. Together we've known both loss and success. In short, they are as close as family."

"It's very nice to meet you all," Brandon said respectfully.

"Do you enjoy hand-to-hand combat, Brandon?" asked Ishi's father.

"I've watched a little Mixed Martial Arts on television. It's okay," Brandon answered.

Kazuo Nakamura chuckled. "Ah yes. Your country calls it MMA. Well, what we have tonight is MUCH more exciting than your MMA. Can Ishi get you something to drink, Brandon?"

"Uh, sure."

Congressman Zimmer's mind swirled. He had a sinking feeling about the night's festivities.

A buzz sounded and the door to MSgt Trent's cell opened. No one entered.

"Follow the hallway to the left and enter the weapons room," the voice overhead ordered.

"Sure would be nice if you said please," Trent shot back. When he didn't get a response he entered the illuminated hallway. He walked slowly toward the weapons room. At set intervals he could now see other cell doors and video cameras installed above. Trent waved to the cameras and kept walking.

Reaching the only other open door, he peeked in. Inside was an impressive array of weapons displayed in stainless steel racks. Not the typical weapons Trent was used to seeing in armories. There were no firearms. All types of swords, spears, and tridents waited on one side of the space. The other side housed shields of varying sizes, along with nets. There were two of everything. Trent whistled quietly and looked up at the closest camera.

"Impressive shit you have here, fellas."

"You have five minutes to arm. Take your weapons of choice and make your way to the door at the other side of the room," the voice ordered.

Trent surveyed the racks. Being a lead instructor at SSI, he had experience with a multitude of arms. That included weapons of opportunity; everything from lead pipes to broken beer bottles. He finally found what he wanted. Ignoring the larger items, he picked up two identical blades. *Fuck it. If I'm going out, I'm going down swinging with a couple KA-BARs, baby.* The former Marine Master Sergeant took an overhand grip on both.

He cracked his neck to both sides, shook the tension out of his arms and legs, walked to the opposite end of the room and waited.

Congressman Zimmer tried to be cordial as he mingled with the group of successful Japanese elders. He couldn't put his finger on it, but it felt like they were subtly trying get his take on the American economy. There were little comments like: "Would you say the dollar is more favorable than the Euro?" "What will new housing starts be next quarter?" "Will Congress re-examine its stance on internet gaming?"

Taken separately and outside the current situation, they might be innocent questions. He'd heard them all before. And yet, he sensed a well-concealed urgency in their tone. What the hell were they after?

These were men of substance. All seemed to have a fierce determination lying beneath their passive facial expressions.

A quiet gong rang from some unseen corner.

"Gentlemen, please direct your attention to the arena. Our festivities are about to begin," the white-haired butler announced.

Congressman Zimmer followed the excitedly murmuring crowd to the large window. As he found a spot, the area beyond the glass slowly illuminated. The arena was about one floor below their vantage point. It looked like a smaller version of the gladiatorial rings he'd seen in Italy. The floor was even covered in sand. *What the hell is this?* Zimmer thought.

Kazuo Nakamura made his way over to Brandon, with Ishi in tow. He addressed Zimmer in a measured tone.

"What you are about to see is usually reserved for our private enjoyment. You see we were all warriors in our past lives. Now we must feel the sting of a blade or the blunt side of a shield vicariously through others. This facility was built especially for such events. We felt that in your current...situation...it might be useful to have you enjoy this as well."

Nakamura turned to the butler and nodded. The servant pressed a small button on the wall and a door in the arena opened. Zimmer watched as a huge man entered the small arena. From his vantage point, Brandon could swear the man stood almost eight feet tall. He was covered head-to-toe in tattoos. In his right arm, he carried an enormous spiked club over his shoulder. Turning to the viewing window, the behemoth bowed.

His host explained, "The warrior you see below is a very special part of my family. Years ago, we established a sort of an orphanage on the island of Samoa. We took very good care of the orphans. The children were rarely placed with new families and most became employees within our companies as they aged. Some, like this man, are recognized for their fighting prowess. We start them in combat training from the age of seven. This one, he calls himself Poktoo, has an amazing proficiency for killing. He has never been bested. What do you think of my Poktoo, Brandon?"

"He's very, uh, large," Brandon answered hesitantly. He wanted nothing to do with the huge fighter.

Nakamura laughed aloud. "Indeed he is, Brandon. Now would you like to see our other fighter?"

"Sure, I guess."

Nakamura nodded again to the butler who pressed another button. The door opposite Poktoo slid open and another warrior exited. This dark-skinned man looked large as well, but not even close to the enormity of the first fighter. Zimmer looked closer and inhaled quickly. *Holy crap! That's Trent!*

"As you now see, Brandon, that is your friend William Trent. Not only did we want you to be entertained..." Nakamura paused for effect, "...we also wanted this to be a lesson of what can happen if our instructions are not followed in the future."

Congressman Zimmer could only watch in horror as Trent paced into the center of the sandy arena and prepared for battle.

THE DOOR to the arena slid open and Trent peered in. *So now I'm a damned gladiator. The boys at home will never believe this one.*

He stepped into the ring and tested the sand. It wasn't very deep but it would impede quick movement. Trent looked across the arena at his opponent. *That's one big dude. Maybe I should've brought more than my KA-BARs.*

The huge tattooed guy was looking up at the big window waiting for something. *I guess that's our audience. I wonder when they're gonna tell us to...* Trent couldn't even finish his thought as a loud GONG sounded and the monster charged.

"Hey, Cal, I've got something!" Neil yelled into the next room.

Cal sprang up from his laptop and ran into the living room.

"What's up?"

"After I got into the Ichiban system, I started trying to pinpoint anything that might help us. I still can't get into their super secure stuff, but I was able to hack into their logistics software."

"How does that help us?"

"Well, their logistics package deals with everything from ordering toilet paper to tasking employees."

"Come on, Neil. Get to the point."

"Sorry. Okay, so one of the things they track is their transportation system. Apparently they have a fleet of automobiles ranging from delivery trucks to stretch limos. They'd built this thing so that when an order goes into the system, the schedule is automatically synced with the smart phone of the first available driver."

"How again does this help us?"

"In order to complete the request, the input must include a start and finish destination. I'm looking at today's requests and there've been one hundred and thirty-two. Sixteen of those requests start at different locations but end up at the same destination."

Cal's impatience was visibly growing.

"We don't have time for this, Neil. How does that help me find our guys?"

"I'm almost there. The destination of these sixteen requests is at this location, about twenty miles outside of Las Vegas." Neil pointed to a map on one of his computer screens. "I'm not finding any hotels or amenities in the general vicinity. The only thing public records show is some industrial property owned by a subsidiary of Ichiban Gaming, LLC."

"You sure about this?"

"I mean, I can't confirm that our boys are there, but it seems like a good place to start."

Cal thought for a minute. If they went into some industrial complex, guns blazing, the local police would be all over them.

"How long would it take us to drive there?" Cal asked.

"It's almost 8:00pm so I'd say...thirty minutes, forty max."

"Okay. Message the contingency team and tell them to get in their vehicles and meet me in the parking garage in five minutes. I'll grab Brian and take him with me."

"You want me to come?" Neil asked hopefully.

"No. I'll need you here to help coordinate and break everything down if this thing goes to shit. Remember what we discussed, priority goes to keeping SSI out of the papers," instructed Cal.

He didn't wait for Neil's response. Running to the bedroom, he grabbed his .45 with three extra magazines and stowed them in his sport coat. Grabbing his keys off the side table, he bolted for the door.

HE'D ALREADY BRIEFED his four team leaders. In addition to Cal and Brian, there were sixteen men waiting to step off. They piled back into their four vehicles, a mixed bag of standard rentals armed with silenced weapons and a variety of breaching equipment.

"How sure is Neil that this is the place?" Brian asked Cal.

"I'd say around ninety percent. It's really all we have so we've gotta go."

Cal started the car and pulled out of the parking spot. Every vehicle had the target address programmed into a GPS. They would each take slightly different routes. No need to be a bigger target than necessary.

They pulled onto Las Vegas Boulevard. The streets were jammed with revelers. It was imperative that they get off the main drag quickly. Cal's small strike force could be stuck for an hour on the packed thoroughfare if they weren't careful.

THE POLITICIAN HANDED his boarding pass to the airline attendant. It would be a nice flight out to Las Vegas. First class was always comfortable. The flight would probably be the last he'd ever take on a commercial airliner. Next stop: Air Force One.

THE HUGE SAMOAN bellowed and swung a wide sweeping blow at Trent's head. Willy barely had time to duck and roll to the side. *This guy is fast.* Trent thought.

His opponent completed the swing with a graceful 360 degree spin. *Must be some island fighting style.*

Poktoo growled and looked at Trent. I'll bet he's used to killing dudes with the first swing.

The trick with big boys was to either take out their legs or take them out from afar. He didn't have a gun so he'd have to take it close. Unless...

Trent rushed Poktoo with some tentative downward stabs at the man's midsection. He needed to get the man off-balance. Willy roared as he tried to sweep his enemy's left leg. Their shins connected and... nothing. The Marine looked up in shock as the tattooed devil grinned down. Before Trent could react, the deadly club came up, butt end first, and slammed him in the chin.

Willy flew back, the darkness threatening to overtaken him. He heard muted cheers from the observation deck as he struggled to his feet.

He stumbled back and shook away the stars. *Okay, shithead. No more games.*

Poktoo had taken the time during Trent's stumble to throw his arms up in a victorious roar. As he looked back down at Trent, the former Marine cocked the KA-BAR in his right hand and stepped into a powerful throw. Willy knew from experience that the KA-BAR wasn't the most balanced throwing knife. As luck would have it, he'd recently won a few bucks off former Delta guys at SSI. They'd bragged about their hot shit knife throwing skills. They used some little blades that were about as big as a man's hand. Being a Marine and sick of their bragging, Trent insisted on using a KA-BAR. After hours of practice, he'd perfected his throws with the larger blade. He could hit the bull's-eye on a log target fifteen yards away. Poktoo was maybe five yards from him.

The giant Samoan barely had time to register surprise as the razor sharp blade entered his open mouth and entered his brain stem. His eyes opened wide as he crumpled to the floor.

"One shot, one kill, motherfucker. Oorah," Trent mumbled.

He turned around and yelled at the observation window. "You got another one, assholes?!"

The robotic voice returned. "Congratulations, champion. Drop your weapon and proceed to the open door."

Trent looked toward the door that was even now sliding open. He decided enough was enough. Switching the remaining KA-BAR from his left to right hand, Willy threw the weapon at the window. He heard a muffled yell as the blade bounced harmlessly off the reinforced glass.

Instead of further instruction from the speaker, Trent heard a beep on his large collar. For the second time that day, he collapsed unconscious as an electric charge mercilessly racked his body.

As the KA-BAR entered his champion's mouth, Kazuo Nakamura screamed in rage. "NO!!"

Zimmer's concern for Trent was replaced with barely concealed exultation. Considering the circumstances, it seemed like such a small victory, but a victory nonetheless.

"Order that man to his cell now!" Nakamura screamed.

The invisible voice did as instructed. That was when Trent decided to throw his knife at the spectators. Brandon almost laughed out loud as, collectively, the men all ducked.

There were angry shouts as they directed their ire at Kazuo Nakamura. Zimmer couldn't understand anything they said, but he got the sense that they were like a crowd who'd paid good money for a prize fight and then watched a ten second knockout.

Nakamura and his son tried to calm the heated guests. Soon they were ushered out of the observation room and into waiting vehicles by apologetic staff. Zimmer followed behind and watched. As the powerful men were loaded into their respective vehicles, a small troop of beautiful women exited the industrial building and filed in with them. Doors closed and the limos departed. *What the...?*

"Brandon."

Zimmer turned around and found Ishi waiting next to a Cadillac Escalade. "It's time to head back to the hotel. I'll drive."

Congressman Zimmer nodded and moved to get in. He stepped up to Ishi. "What are you going to do with Trent?"

"He'll stay alive as long as he's winning."

Zimmer nodded and looked down at his shoes. Without thinking, he cocked his right arm and slugged Ishi in the temple. His former friend collapsed to the ground. Zimmer shook the tingling out of his hand and waited to see if Ishi would get up. He didn't.

I've gotta get Trent. With a quick glance around, Congressman Brandon Zimmer ran for the building's open door. He didn't have a plan, but he couldn't leave the Marine behind.

OUTSKIRTS OF LAS VEGAS, NEVADA

8:25PM, SEPTEMBER 17TH

"We're about two minutes out," Cal announced as he looked at his watch. He felt a sense of dread that they might be too late. He never should have let Zimmer and Trent out of his sight. Maybe if he'd put some kind of tracking device on them, then just maybe… No. He couldn't start thinking that way. Trent was a big boy and more than capable of handling the assignment. They'd all underestimated the threat.

Cal pulled up to the rendezvous point. It was in a small depression just off the narrow two-lane highway. One of the other teams was already there and had spread into a hasty security perimeter. The hiding spot was about two hundred yards from the target building. The plan was to get eyes on it, see if they could detect the presence of their two missing members, and then act accordingly.

The operation had to be fast. No one wanted the local authorities in the picture. SSI couldn't afford the publicity.

"Any updates?" Cal asked the team leader on station. He was a small Hispanic with a long beard that he liked to braid into dual strands. Everyone called him Gaucho, sort of a Spanish version of a cowboy. The man was a former Delta operator and carefully reckless, hence the nickname.

"We got here about five minutes ago. Saw ten to fifteen stretch limos buggin' out from the other side of the building. Couldn't make out Top in the crowd."

"Any signs of life in the building?"

Gaucho shook his head. "Haven't been able to tell. You want us to go take a look, boss?"

Cal peered into darkness. "The other teams will be here in a second. I don't want to waste time waiting on recon. How about you head over there with your boys and scope things out? We'll be right behind you."

"Got it, boss." Gaucho rushed back to his team and gave hushed instructions. The group of four took off at a jog. They knew what to do.

Two minutes later, the remaining teams pulled up. Cal gave the men a quick rundown of the scheme of maneuver. A minute later, the small assault force spread across the barren terrain, anxious to find out the fate of MSgt Trent.

ZIMMER DIDN'T SEE anyone in the hallway. He didn't know where to go, but he correctly assumed that the holding cells were on the lower level. Running, he tried opening each door he reached. Every one was locked.

After a couple minutes of random wandering, Brandon stopped and got his bearings. *I don't have much time*, he thought. Just then, the butler from the observation room exited one of the hallway doors.

"Congressman, how may I help you?"

Well, at least they haven't alerted the security staff yet.

"I, uh, think I left my cell phone up in the observation room." The excuse sounded lame but the man seemed to believe it.

"I would be happy to get it and bring it to you in your vehicle, sir," the butler replied respectfully.

"That's okay. Just point me the right way and I'll grab it." Zimmer tried to act as nonchalant as possible. The last thing he needed was to have the butler in tow.

"I am afraid that is not possible, Congressman. Visitors cannot travel alone inside the building. Now if I can escort you outside…"

Zimmer's patience ran out. Instead of letting the man finish, he closed the gap and delivered a vicious uppercut into the unsuspecting man's stomach. The butler doubled over. Zimmer caught him on the way to the floor and propped him up against the wall.

"Now you listen to me," Zimmer whispered into the man's ear. "You take me to my friend right fucking now."

The man still struggled to breathe but nodded his head. Zimmer felt remotely guilty for assaulting the aged servant, but he didn't have many options at the time.

"Which way?" asked Zimmer.

His captive pointed to the door he'd just exited.

"Is it locked?"

The man nodded.

"Give me the key," ordered Zimmer.

Half bent, the butler obliged by giving the Congressman a key ring and indicating which one to use. Zimmer grabbed the key with his right hand and the back of the man's collar with his left. Half dragging his guide, Brandon unlocked the door and moved inside.

ISHI CAME TO. Lying just outside the open door of the Escalade, he struggled to get his bearings. He suddenly remembered Zimmer's fist connecting with his head. *Shit! Where is Zimmer?*

The younger Nakamura rose and looked around frantically. His vision was still blurry and he stumbled back against his vehicle. Just as he regained his balance, he looked up and saw what looked like a line of men approaching the building from about fifty yards away. Was he seeing things? The men jogged closer and Ishi panicked.

Jumping into the driver's seat, he started the large SUV, put it in drive, and gunned the gas. He squealed out of the parking lot as he fumbled for his cell phone.

"Shit. Who was that?" Cal asked in a whisper. No answer came. He knew time was up. The first team to the building had already reported seeing employees through the upper level windows of the large industrial complex. They'd approached from the opposite side and found a door. Gaucho had already taken care of the lock with his pick set.

Cal didn't like going in blind, but what choice did they have?

The teams stacked up just outside of the unlocked door. Cal nodded to Gaucho, who winked back.

The small man opened the door quickly and the teams filed in, weapons drawn.

Miraculously, Zimmer and the butler didn't run into any other staff on the way to the holding cells. What Brandon didn't know was that after the commotion of the fight, Trent was swiftly thrown unconscious into his cell and the remaining security staff had run upstairs to assist the unsettled guests. They'd then been tasked with riding along as an added precaution. The building was, therefore, currently undermanned.

Zimmer stepped up to Trent's cell. To the right of the door was a small red button that the butler said would open the portal. Brandon pressed it and looked inside. Trent had been uncaremoniously tossed just inside the door. He seemed to be stirring.

"Top!" Zimmer whispered as loudly as he dared.

Trent turned his head slowly and looked at Zimmer through foggy eyes. "That you, Congressman?" he croaked.

"Yeah. Can you make it through the door? I don't want this damned thing to lock us both in."

The tough Marine nodded and got to all fours. He bear crawled through the doorway. Once out, Zimmer grabbed the butler, shoved him into the room, and closed the door. He double-checked just to make sure the lock was secured.

"Do you think you can walk?"

"Yeah." Trent stood on slightly shaky knees and shook his head. "I've gotta get this collar off. I could live without another one of those shocks."

Despite the gravity of the situation, Zimmer chuckled. "Come on. Let's get out of here."

Zimmer led the way, still not running into any Japanese personnel.

"Where did everyone go?" Trent asked.

"I don't know. I think...did you hear that?" Zimmer whispered.

Trent nodded and nudged his way into the lead. They could see a bend just ahead. It sounded like muted footsteps coming their way.

"Let's go find out who that is."

Zimmer looked at the huge black man, still wearing only a loincloth. "You think that's a good idea, Top?"

"Trust me, Congressman. Whoever that is, they're in for a world of hurt." Trent cracked his knuckles and sprinted off toward the bend.

THE ASSAULT TEAM hadn't run into any resistance. While that seemed odd, no man complained. They'd searched most of the lower level. Eventually they came to a section that looked older yet well-maintained. Gaucho looked back at Cal for direction. Cal gave a thumbs-up.

They moved swiftly down the corridor, checking doors as they went. All were locked and there didn't seem to be any need to open them yet. They approached a bend as Gaucho signaled the group to stop. Listening carefully, they clearly heard something. Was that bare feet running their way? Weapons readied, the elite team of SSI operators waited calmly for the approaching runner. The sound got closer when all of a sudden, MSgt Willy Trent, resplendent in his stylish loincloth, rounded the corner and skidded to a halt in front of Gaucho.

"Well I'll be damned. What's goin' on, Gaucho?" Trent asked.

Muted laughs rose from the normally disciplined men. The relief they all felt was almost palpable. They had their man back. Just as Cal walked up to see Trent, Congressman Zimmer trotted around the bend. Cal looked past his friend and pointed his finger at the politician, "You son of a bitch, I thought I..."

"Whoa, whoa, whoa. Hold up, Cal," Trent said calmly as he held his friend back. "If it weren't for the Congressman, I'd still be locked up in this Japanese dungeon. Lay off, alright?"

Not easily dissuaded, Cal took a step back. He still couldn't shake the feeling that somehow the Congressman was responsible for the setbacks they'd suffered.

Turning away from Zimmer, Cal addressed his men. "Get us the hell out of here, Gaucho."

The team leader nodded and guided them out without anyone saying another word.

ATLANTA, GEORGIA

11:49PM EST, SEPTEMBER 17TH

Tom Jablonski pulled his rig into the distribution hub. Driving from Las Vegas wasn't hard. He'd made similar trips for years. It didn't hurt that he was getting paid a serious bonus for arriving on schedule. He wished every cross-country trek was as lucrative.

Waving to the security guard, he pulled up to the guard shack. An extra spotlight blazed on and cut through the midnight blackness.

"Paperwork please," asked the tired looking, middle-aged sentry.

The driver handed over the manifest.

The guard reviewed the documentation and checked his computer to see which terminal to direct the driver to. "Head over to Thirty Seven. Honk once or twice for the loading guys," the man instructed. The bored security guard handed back the paperwork and waved the semi through.

Jablonski was familiar with the routine. He'd been to the hub earlier in the month. Pulling into Terminal 37, he honked twice. He knew from experience that the loading crew would take a minute. Working the graveyard shift meant napping when you could.

After a couple of minutes, three men made a slow exit from the terminal building. Two headed for forklifts and one headed to the truck.

Jablonski hopped out of the cab and handed off his paperwork. After a second to review, the foreman with sleep in his left eye looked up.

"Says you got some electronics set for priority shippin'." Jablonski couldn't tell from the southern drawl whether it was a question or a statement. Better to be nice and get out of here quickly.

"Yeah. I think they're cell phones."

Surprisingly, that perked the foreman's interest. "Hey, they aren't those new smart phones everyone's waiting in lines for, are they?"

"I don't know, man. They just tell me where to take 'em," Jablonski replied.

"You mind if I take a look? My kid's been buggin' me about getting her one of those damned things. I ain't gonna shell out four hundred bucks for one though!" the man flashed the driver a dirty grin.

Jablonski had seen this same routine countless times. *Oops a pallet fell off the truck and a couple pieces fell out.* But Tom was an honest driver. He'd never stolen from his shipments and once scolded his own son when he'd suggested doing so.

"Hey, man, you think we can just get these things unloaded so I can go? It's been a long haul."

The foreman looked at the truck and finally nodded. "If you can get the back unlocked, I'll have my boys get 'er done in a half hour."

Tom Jablonski thanked the man and headed to the back of the trailer. Another hour and he'd be in bed, counting his cash bonus.

LAS VEGAS, NEVADA

11:03PM, SEPTEMBER 17TH

The SSI operators made it back to the Bellagio without incident. Along the way Trent and Zimmer relayed the entire story of their capture and the arena battle. Cal wouldn't admit it, but he was surprised by the Congressman's decision to go back for Trent. It would've been really easy for him to get in the car with Ishi and head back to Vegas. Instead, he'd returned to the lion's den and saved Cal some precious time.

Cal, Brian, Neil, Trent and Zimmer were all comfortably seated in Patel's suite. MSgt Trent looked refreshed after a hot shower and highball of Famous Grouse. He continued his story. "I'll tell you what, Cal, these are some sick fuckers. Who the hell does that kinda shit anymore?"

Cal sipped his drink and pondered the same thing. What had they stumbled on? Underground fights to the death, women for hire, a blackmailed politician; the whole thing sounded too farfetched to be true. He still had more questions for Zimmer.

"Congressman, did you recognize any of the men you met?"

Zimmer shook his head. "They never gave me any names. I'm thinking these guys may be more behind the scenes."

"Any other impressions?"

The Congressman took a sip of his drink and let the question sink in for a second. "I'm not gonna lie to you. Most of the time, I was scared shitless. I got the feeling that I was some kind of pet to them. They looked at me like...I don't know how to describe it. They were looking down at me. It felt like..."

"You were less than nothing," Trent completed.

"Yes. Talk about xenophobic. These guys stick with their own kind," Zimmer finished, still wondering where everything was headed.

Cal stood up and walked to the window. "From here on out, the Congressman stays with us."

"But what about Nakamura's instructions?" Zimmer asked on the verge of panic. He could only imagine what would hit the media without his cooperation. The bloody videos would quickly destroy his life.

"Do you really want to go back with those guys?" Cal asked almost angrily. "My job was to find out who these guys are and to keep you safe. I can't do that unless you stay here. For now, we need to take the chance. Maybe we call their bluff. I have a feeling that you're an important part of their plan. I don't think they'll jump the gun."

"How do you know that?" Zimmer blurted. "How do you know they won't take those videos and plaster them all over the Internet?"

"I don't, Congressman. It's called a calculated risk. Besides, it'll all be a moot point soon."

"Why is that?"

"Because we're gonna take these motherfuckers down."

―――

AFTER SOME FURTHER PLANNING, the team dispersed to their new rooms. They were all exhausted and they'd have an early morning wakeup call to start executing Cal's plan.

In all the commotion, Cal had completely forgotten to call Daniel Briggs. Despite the late hour, he figured the sniper might still be awake. He swirled the last remnants of his drink as the phone rang on the other end.

"Cal?"

"Hey, man. Sorry I didn't call earlier."

"Everything okay?"

"I wouldn't really say that, but they're better than they were a few hours ago."

"Anything I can help with?" Daniel offered.

"I don't know, man. Tell you what, why don't you come by my hotel room at eight tomorrow morning. By then we'll be done with our meetings and I might have some questions about Vegas that I'll need some insight on."

"No problem. I'll be there fifteen to eight."

Cal chuckled. "Once a Marine..."

"Always a Marine," finished Briggs. "Every gunny I ever had told me that being on-time was being late."

"Me too, Brother."

Cal relayed the hotel and room number and they said their good-byes. *What the hell am I gonna to do with the scruffy sniper?*

Next, he placed a call to President Waller. The man was still awake and requested they conference in the other members of the Council of Patriots. After five minutes, everyone was on the line and Cal gave a rundown of everything that had happened.

"How soon until Neil gets all the way into Ichiban's network, Cal?" Waller asked.

"I'm not sure, sir. He's having some trouble because of the level of sophistication."

"Any thoughts on what they're after?" asked President Kelton.

"None yet, sir," answered Stokes. "I'm not getting a good feeling about the convention though. Is there any way we can get it postponed until we know more?"

Waller answered first, "Can't do it, Cal. As much as I hate to put so many people at risk, we don't know if that's their endgame yet. Just make sure you keep us in the loop and we'll alert the authorities if needed."

There were a couple more questions from the Council, but nothing was really resolved. They were all anxiously waiting to see where the investigation would lead. They'd learned to be patient men during their time in office. It was a trait that Cal didn't have. The Marine in him wanted to take out the enemy...now.

LAS VEGAS, NEVADA

6:47AM, SEPTEMBER 18TH

After a couple hours of sleep, the SSI team met over a mound of room service food. Cal had reluctantly allowed Zimmer in on the meeting. In for a penny, in for a pound.

"Neil, please tell me you have SOMETHING we can work with," Cal mumbled through a bite of chocolate croissant.

Neil looked like he'd been without sleep for a week. His usually impeccable dress was marred with countless wrinkles and more than one food stain. It wasn't like the computer geek to go this long without cracking into a system.

Patel yawned and waved away a coffee refill offered by Brian. "Okay. So like we talked about before, Ichiban Gaming's main source of legitimate income is from consulting. Early this morning, I finally got past their last firewall. You wouldn't believe how far these guys reach. They've got contacts all over the world."

"Anything we can use?" asked Trent.

"I'm not sure. What I can tell you is that in recent months they've consolidated a lot of their assets. At first glance it looks almost random, but these guys are pretty methodical. They've divested the majority of their American stock and now own a huge portfolio of real estate and commodities like gold and silver."

Zimmer chimed in. "That's nothing new, is it? Haven't the Japanese had a huge interest in our economy since the eighties?"

"Yes, but this is one entity. I'm also seeing a lot of dead ends. They're reporting internal expenditures that are getting spread across hundreds of banks around the globe. A hundred grand here, a few million there... Since they're a private company, they don't have to make this stuff public."

"Can you see where the money's going?" Cal asked.

"Of course, but it would take me weeks to track the end accounts. Most likely they're wired to an initial banking center then routed again multiple times. It's a real maze. I wouldn't be surprised if they had some internal system for tracking their stuff. There's no way I can access that unless I'm inside their server room."

"How hard would it be to get inside that room?" Cal's mind was already running with possibilities.

"Almost impossible," Neil said matter-of-factly. "Besides, I'm sure they probably have some kind of kill switch to destroy all the evidence in case of an investigation."

"Either way, I think we need to try. Any other ideas?" Cal looked around the group. No one could think of anything better. It was a classic dilemma. They had one of the smartest computer geniuses on the planet, plus nearly unlimited technology at their disposal, but what they really needed was boots on the ground. The CIA was learning the same lesson the hard way. Human Intelligence (HUMINT) was invaluable.

"Let's let this sink in for a couple hours. Meet back here at noon. Don't worry, lunch is on me," Cal deadpanned. It was already after 7:30am and he wanted to make a quick call before meeting with Daniel. He excused himself and headed to his new room across the hall.

He dialed a number and entered the bedroom as he waited for someone to pickup.

"Andrews."

"Andy, it's Cal." Capt. Bartholemew Andrews was Cal's former platoon commander from the fleet. They'd seen a lot of combat together and each had a Navy Cross and wounds to prove it. When they were SSgt Stokes and 1stLt Andrews they had grown close after saving each other from the clutches of death, on more than one occasion. No one ever called Capt. Andrews by his given name. He'd always gone by Andy to his friends.

"Hey, Cal! What's going on?"

The last time they'd been together was during Jessica's funeral. Being assigned to the Marine Silent Drill Team kept Andy pretty busy.

"They still have you serving canapés for the Commandant?" The Marine Silent Drill Team was stationed at Eighth and I, the traditional home of the Marine Commandant. Extra duties for assigned officers often included attending cocktail parties with visiting VIPs.

"All that crap stopped as soon as I went to Silent Drill. Where are you calling from?" Andy was one of the very few people outside of SSI that actually knew what the company did behind the scenes. He'd even been a part of the extract team that had infiltrated Dante West's tunnel system and rescued Cal a year ago.

"Me and a couple of the boys are in Vegas doing some work."

"No shit!? We're heading out there tomorrow for the big convention."

"Which one?"

"The Democratic National Convention."

"Really? I thought you guys just traveled to do shows at football games."

"Usually we do. Apparently, the President pulled a few strings and might've threatened to end a couple careers. He wants to look really presidential for his re-election." Andy's disgust was obvious.

"Maybe we can get together. You think you'll have time?"

"You kidding? We always make time to get out when we're on the road. It's one of the few perks we have."

"That's great. Hey, I was wondering if you could do me a favor?"

"You want me to get a signed picture of Chesty for you?" Andy laughed. Chesty was the name given to the Marine Corps mascot, an English bulldog. The name was a tribute to a Marine Corps legend,

Gen. Lewis "Chesty" Puller. Every young Marine learned about Chesty in their first days of boot camp.

"Very funny. No, I was wondering if you could look somebody up for me."

One of the advantages of being near Headquarters Marine Corps was the ability to access information about almost any Marine.

"You actually caught me about to log-off of my work computer. Who do you want me to look up?"

Cal gave him Daniel's name and told him that Briggs was a scout sniper. Using his name and Military Occupational Specialty (MOS), the corresponding record popped up after a couple of clicks.

"Got it. What do you want to know?"

"Just wondering what his current status is. Guy told me he got out with PTSD. Wanted to get a better feel for him."

Cal waited as the Marine Captain scrolled through the record.

"Did multiple tours overseas. Wow. He's got over a hundred confirmed kills. Where'd you meet this guy?"

"I'll tell you when you get out here. What else does it say?"

"Honorable discharge as a sergeant, and...wait a minute," Andy clicked on a note under the Awards section. "Holy shit."

"What?" Cal asked, thinking the worst.

"He's nominated for the Medal of Honor."

"Really?! For what?"

Andy skimmed through the citation and read the highlights to Cal. It sounded like the story Briggs had told him. He'd failed to mention that in the firefight he'd probably killed close to fifty insurgents. What was even more impressive was that it was the SEAL Team Commander that put Briggs in for the nation's highest military award.

An additional note added that the sniper's fire was verified by a UAV that had loitered long enough on station to get video of the entire gun battle.

"Thanks for checking on that, Andy."

"No problem. You need anything else?"

"Nope. Just give me a call when you get in."

"Will do."

Cal placed his phone on the wet bar. *What the hell am I going to do with this guy?*

DANIEL BRIGGS KNOCKED on Cal's door precisely at quarter 'til eight. Cal opened it and invited Briggs inside.

"Can I get you anything?"

"No, thanks."

"Any more interesting nights on the street?"

"Not yet."

"I wish I could say the same."

Briggs cocked his head in concern. "Anything I can help with?"

"I'm not sure." Cal didn't know how much he should tell Briggs. On one hand, he knew he probably wouldn't say anything. Most Marines knew how to keep their mouths shut. On the other hand, SSI's mission in Las Vegas was completely off the reservation. If anyone so much as caught a whiff of what they were doing, it could spell real trouble for Cal and the company.

"Do you mind if I ask you a couple questions first?"

"Sure." Briggs nodded.

"Okay. First, anything I tell you today you can consider Top Secret. Cool?"

"Cool."

"Second, what's the deal with the CMH?" CMH is short for Congressional Medal of Honor.

Daniel's eyes went cold. "How did you find out about that?"

"I have ways of finding out anything I need to. You okay with that?"

"Why were you checking up on me?" Briggs accused.

"Wouldn't you do the same thing? You meet this guy that looks like he just stepped out of the jungle and he saves your life. Oh, AND he's a Marine?"

Daniel's temper cooled and he actually laughed. "You're right. I guess I forget how I come across sometimes."

"If it makes you feel any better, I don't like to go into many relationships blind. With the resources I have at my disposal, I usually checkup on everybody I can. So you want to tell me about the CMH?"

After a brief hesitation, Briggs explained. "Apparently the SEAL Commander put me in for it. I don't want it."

"Why not?"

"The damned thing makes it sound like I'm a fucking hero. I'm not. A hero would've saved those guys." Cal could see tears coming to his eyes.

"It's just recording what you did, Daniel. From what it sounds like, you deserve it. And that's coming from a guy who knows a thing or two about awards Marines don't want."

Daniel looked. "What do you mean?"

"Let's just say I won an award for killing some bad guys and saving some buddies. I'd give it away if it meant getting my Marines back. It took me a long time to acknowledge the fact that I did something heroic. I don't think I'm a hero either. I did just what they trained me to do: kill the enemy and take care of my Marines. The faster you come to that realization, the faster you'll heal, man."

Briggs nodded thoughtfully. Was this the missing piece? Was God finally answering his prayers?

Cal went on. "I want to introduce you to some of my guys. We're all part of a company called Stokes Security International; SSI for short. My dad started it a few years back after he got out of the Corps. Who knows, maybe you'll like it enough to stick around. We can never have enough lead-slingers around."

Cal smiled and was pleased when Daniel did the same. He was on unfamiliar ground. Of course he had the authority to hire new employees, but he hadn't yet. Cal just got the feeling that there was something to Briggs that could really complement his team.

He gave Briggs a quick rundown of what SSI did but decided to leave out the covert aspect. Better safe than sorry for now. They talked for a few more minutes. Cal was impressed with Daniel's knowledge of Las Vegas. Like a true sniper, he'd evaluated the area with a cunning eye.

Cal gave his new friend a quick brief on what they were up against.

He left out the details concerning Zimmer's blackmailing, and kept it to the threat coming from Ichiban.

"How about you join us for lunch at noon? I can introduce you to the rest of the guys and maybe you can poke holes in our plan."

Daniel accepted the invitation and excused himself to run a few errands.

Cal watched him go, all the time wondering if he'd just found a diamond in the rough.

Ishi had spent the morning trying to run damage control. His father had flown into a murderous rage at the news of the escape. It was only the impending coup that had finally calmed the incensed Nakamura.

"From now on, you will not leave Matsura's sight!" Kazuo Nakamura pointed at the third man in the room. The small man smiled and bowed to his master.

"Matsura has already coordinated our deliveries. It is now a simple matter for him to monitor the situation. I have talked to our contact about recent events. He assures me that he can provide information that will eliminate the threat of this Calvin Stokes."

"What kind of information, father?"

Nakamura glared at his son. "It will be provided to Matsura when I receive it."

"What about the Congressman?" Ishi dared to ask.

Father smiled at son. "I have taken care of Congressman Zimmer. He is no longer your concern."

He walked away. It was a dismissal.

Ishi's embarrassment was complete. His failures laid bare, the young Japanese felt afraid. Would his father keep him from the coming glory? Just as he had the thought, he shook it off. His father wouldn't throw him to the side. Ishi was his only child. Since the day of his birth, they'd groomed him for this moment. Ishi would listen to his father for the time being. Soon enough, he would exact his vengeance on his family's enemies. His father would come to see that all his training was not in vain.

The SSI team met at noon. There were no immediate updates from Neil. Cal was desperate for more intel on the Ichiban organization, so he allowed Neil to keep clicking away while the rest of the group talked.

He'd started the meeting by quickly introducing Briggs to his team. It was clear that Zimmer wasn't happy about having an outsider involved, but he wisely kept his mouth shut. After hearing the story about Briggs coming to Cal and Brian's aid, the Congressman couldn't disagree that the sniper might be a valuable asset.

"So now that we have a lock on where Ichiban houses its main servers, we need to get in there and see what we can find. As of now, we don't have anything concrete on these guys. At least nothing we can take to the Feds," explained Cal. "We know they've augmented their own security staff with some Russian thugs. Me, Brian, and Top are compromised. We won't be able to set foot in any of their hotels. That means it'll be up to Gaucho's guys."

Gaucho raised his hand. "How much money are you gonna give us to hit the tables, boss?"

The assembled men all laughed. Leave it to Gaucho to keep it light.

"I'm not giving you a fucking penny, Gaucho," Cal joked. "I heard about your shitty luck in Tunica."

Everyone laughed again. The Hispanic commando did like to spend his time off at the Mississippi casinos. Contrary to what Cal said, he often came home with pockets bulging.

Briggs raised his hand and the room went silent. Up to that point, he'd said little more than hello to the elite team. They all sensed a warrior in him, even without knowing about his exploits.

Cal pointed at him. "Whatcha got, Daniel?"

"I was wondering if maybe I could be one of the guys going into that hotel."

Everyone looked to Cal. It's not what he'd expected. "I really just brought you here for a little Vegas insight. I'm not sure I feel comfortable putting you in harm's way."

"I'll stay out of the way. It's just that I know these places a lot better than these guys. No offense, fellas." He looked around the room to nods of agreement.

"Okay," Cal assented, "Gaucho, use Daniel however you need. I'd prefer he sticks to recon."

Gaucho nodded and patted Daniel on the back.

"Okay, any other questions?" Cal asked his men.

"You want me to stay with the Congressman?" Trent asked.

"Yeah. Make sure that we..."

"Oh shit." Everyone turned toward Neil. He was clicking his mouse frantically, pulling up multiple screens.

"What is it, Neil?" asked a concerned Cal.

"They just posted the murder scene video on YouTube."

Congressman Brandon Zimmer paled and looked close to vomiting.

"I guess they just called our bluff," Cal offered conversationally.

AFTER DANIEL and the contingency team left, the remaining men crowded around Neil's computer screen. The video was exactly one minute long. There was no sound, only a flickering subtitle: *"Woman butchered by popular politician. More details coming soon."* Zimmer cringed as Beth's naked body flashed into focus. Luckily they'd decided to blur her face, for now. The camera panned around the dismembered body and bloody bed. No one said a word.

I can't imagine waking up to that, Cal thought. Although he'd resisted it before, he now allowed a shred of sympathy for the Congressman's predicament. Cal was pretty sure the man standing next to him had not been the culprit of the gory scene replaying over and over again on the computer screen.

"DID you really think that was necessary?" the politician asked Kazuo Nakamura.

"The Congressman forced our hand. He was given explicit instructions. He decided not to follow them. Now he will know that we are very serious about exposing him." Nakamura took another sip of his green tea. Posting the video had been a gamble, especially in the presence of his current guest, but he had to maintain his position of power.

"Very well. How is the rest of our little agreement progressing?" asked the politician, between sips of his own tea.

"The upcoming convention is proving to be a problem."

"Why is that?"

"The Secret Service is being extremely diligent. We are concerned that all the pieces will not be in place on time."

"You assured me that this would not be a problem. What do we need to do to remedy the situation?" the politician asked through gritted teeth. He'd put a lot of faith in the Japanese businessman. They were too far along to turn back. Besides, he'd waited long enough for his day in the national spotlight. Only yesterday, he'd listened as the blithering idiot in the White House had bowed to yet another foreign dictator. The President had become a foreign policy nightmare. It was time for strength within the Democratic Party once more. *FDR must be rolling in his grave,* the politician thought, not for the first time.

"I think we can handle the Secret Service. I am, however, concerned with this SSI organization. Do you have the information you promised?"

The politician smiled. He'd called in a lot of favors for the contents in the manila envelope. There'd also been some substantial bribes to loosen the tongues of some ultra-patriotic federal agents. Nevertheless, the information contained in the envelope would not only take care of the SSI problem, but would bolster the politician's new platform as President. Yes, it was time to clean the skeletons out of the closet. America would be a shining example of strength and transparency. No more pansy pandering to terrorists and third world countries. It was about time America had a real democratic leader at the helm.

"Everything you need is in this envelope. Do not release the information to the public until the hour we discussed. You may, however, use the information to dissuade SSI from further involvement near our little operation."

Nakamura finally smiled to his guest. He would have to remember how ruthless this man could be. Unconcerned, Nakamura knew he had enough evidence to condemn the man should the politician decide to cast the Japanese aside. Besides, the packages that were presently being delivered were his organization's ultimate insurance policy. The two men were connected for better or worse.

THE COUNCIL MEMBERS sat in stunned silence as the YouTube video replayed across their screens for the second time. Pres. Waller pressed STOP and addressed the group via video conference.

"So as you can see, the ante's just been upped. I'll be heading out to Las Vegas soon for the convention. I'm planning on having regular contact with Stokes. Once I know more I'll get you an update."

The members of The Council of Patriots disconnected from the call. To a man, no one would correctly predict the final outcome of the coming drama.

LAS VEGAS, NEVADA

9:12AM, SEPTEMBER 18TH

The Democratic Party converged on Las Vegas. The convention began in two days. Congressman Zimmer had already gotten ten phone calls from staffers and fellow Congressmen traveling to Vegas. They all wanted to ask if he'd watched the YouTube video and see if he had a guess as to who the murderer might be. He'd laughed off the questions and asked whether they were the guilty party.

He dreaded every call. His paranoid mind kept telling him that they knew it was him. Zimmer knew they didn't, but he wondered what they'd say when they found out he was involved. They'd crucify him. He didn't think badly of them for it. He knew he would've done the same thing a few months ago. They were as clueless as he'd been.

Zimmer remembered watching all those documentaries about Americans spying for Russia during the Cold War. He wondered how many of those spies were just normal people being blackmailed into betraying their country.

His phone buzzed again. It was his father.

"Hey, Dad."

"I assume you've seen the video?"

Brandon cringed. "Yeah."

"So what are our friends doing about it?"

"They're looking into it, Dad."

"We need to meet, Brandon. Where are you staying?"

Brandon told him. "I'll be there in thirty minutes."

Congressman Zimmer looked down at his phone. The last thing he needed right now was an ass-chewing by good ol' dad. Zimmer walked to the wet bar, poured himself two fingers of bourbon, and drained the glass.

He walked back to his laptop and watched the crime scene video for the twentieth time. It was already up to just over one million views.

THIRTY MINUTES LATER, Senator Zimmer walked into Brandon's hotel room. He was handsomely attired in the latest golf wear.

"I've only got twenty minutes, Brandon. I'm meeting some colleagues at the Wynn for eighteen, so give me the rundown quickly."

Brandon summarized the events of the past forty-eight hours. Once again, his father didn't interrupt. Brandon knew his father. He'd already be formulating a contingency plan in his head. One of the reasons Senator Zimmer was such a long-standing politician was his ability to think five steps ahead and outmaneuver his opponents. The last true electoral test he'd had was fifteen years earlier when a grandson of JFK decided to try his hand at politics. Voters longed for the dynasty of the past, but the Zimmer machine soon killed the young man's chances. Past dalliances were unearthed and witnesses were paraded onto every morning show on Massachusetts radio and television.

No one could trace the attack back to the Zimmer camp, but they all knew. Mess with the crafty Senator and he'd make your life hell.

Richard Zimmer had mellowed a bit with age. He was comfortable in his position. He'd brokered deals for billions of dollars of government aid and contracts to be funneled to his home state. The voters loved him.

"What does Mr. Stokes have in mind for fixing this problem?"

"Dad, I want to say something, but I think it'll piss you off."

"Out with it, Brandon," growled an increasingly impatient Sen. Zimmer.

"I'm considering turning myself in. I think Cal and his team have done what we asked. I don't feel comfortable putting them in any more danger."

Visibly surprised by his son's request, the Senator took a moment to respond.

"I appreciate you trying to take responsibility for the situation, Son. It seems as though you've grown a bit this week. That being said, I do not think this is the right moment to go to the authorities. I've already privately consulted our attorney and he seems to think that the evidence wouldn't hold up in court. However, in the court of public opinion you would be crucified. I think that's the risk we need to take. With the Presidential election so close, we need to be careful."

Brandon wasn't sure if he agreed with his father. And yet, he was a little relieved to hear that should the worst happen he might not go to jail.

"So what should we do?"

"Let's see what Cal's team comes up with. Maybe they'll get lucky and get their hands on the evidence. Until we give them a shot, let's sit tight and wait."

Once again, Brandon couldn't really argue with his father. The only thing worse than the video was the waiting.

DANIEL LEFT the hotel and headed to a nearby storage facility. Walking up to the glassed entrance, he typed his personal entry code. Briggs went almost to the end of the straight hallway. His unit was the second to last on the left.

He pulled out his key and unlocked the rolling door, sliding it up. Daniel quickly entered the eight by ten unit and closed the door behind him. He'd rigged a custom lock inside the unit so he could stay undisturbed. After locking the door he turned around and surveyed his unit. Everything was neatly stacked. Just after getting to Las Vegas, he purchased several large metal storage containers. They were each about two feet tall by two feet wide and stretched four feet in length. The damn things were heavy as hell, but sturdy and impregnable by all but the best thieves.

Briggs unlocked the box on the far left and opened the lid. He had a variety of weapons neatly arrayed in mini racks. Since moving to Las Vegas, he'd methodically stocked his private armory. Once or twice a week, he visited a different outdoor store. Occasionally, when he had enough cash, he'd head to a gun shop and pickup a new firearm. Briggs never bought in the same place twice.

The box he examined contained mostly smaller weapons. Other containers held his long rifles. He wouldn't need those, for the time being.

Daniel unslung the backpack from his shoulder and set it on the ground. He picked out a couple of things he thought he might need in the next few days. His sixth sense started to prickle again. He could feel the coming tension. It was the same feeling he used to get before going on a particularly dangerous op.

Although Cal made the current action sound routine, Daniel thought otherwise. There was a storm brewing and the Marine in him wanted to be in the middle of it. Standing in the hotel with Cal and his compatriots, Daniel started to feel at home.

The last time he'd felt this comfortable was when he'd finally won the respect of the acting platoon sergeant of his first scout sniper platoon; a crusty old Gunny who looked like he'd been in the Corps since the days of General Lejeune. The man was a career Marine and respected by every enlisted Marine (and the smartest officers) in the battalion. His most commonly used words were 'shit' and 'fuck'. Like any good Gunnery Sergeant, he was a hard man to please. If you ever expected a compliment from the Gunny, you'd be waiting until the second coming of Jesus.

They'd just completed a grueling training evolution at Twenty Nine Palms. It was the lead-up to Daniel's first combat deployment. He'd shot like a pro all week. In addition, his infiltration into the simulated enemy's camp, the subsequent mock killing of their entire battalion staff, and his successful extraction, earned the platoon outstanding marks from the training officials. The Commanding General had even taken a turn commending the brave sniper team.

The old Gunny had turned to Daniel after the final debrief and imparted some of the sweetest words Daniel would ever hear in the Marine Corps: "Well, Briggs, looks like you're not the shitbag that I thought you were. Now go pack your shit. You're a fucking sniper now."

Briggs remembered the crusty old bird fondly. They'd become as close to friends as the Gunny would allow. Tragically, the brave Marine died early into their second tour in Afghanistan. He died a hero, standing in the open, calling in close air support to destroy a heavily manned enemy position while his lifeblood flowed freely from his right arm that was no longer there.

As he did whenever remembering the man, Daniel said a silent prayer for the old warrior. He knew Gunny was up in heaven giving Jesus a run for his money.

He grabbed another couple pieces of survival gear from a separate box and locked everything back up.

Leaving the storage facility, Daniel Briggs walked with a steadier step. He was a man on a mission. He was a man going home.

MEMPHIS, TENNESSEE

9:15AM, SEPTEMBER 18TH

The FedEx employee almost laughed out loud as he read the order form. Some businesses just didn't know how to ship merchandise. Take this one, for example. They'd literally paid double to have their packages delivered by 11am. They could've saved half if the same delivery was scheduled for two hours later. *Stupid*, thought the delivery supervisor.

He processed the shipment and scheduled the smaller parcels for local carriers. They'd be gone in under an hour. FedEx knew how to get stuff in and out, fast.

EIGHTH & I, WASHINGTON, D.C

9:22AM, SEPTEMBER 18TH

"Everything ready to go, First Sergeant?" Capt. Andrews asked his senior enlisted Marine.

"Yes, sir. Second platoon is waiting by the gate."

"Good. How about we head that way?"

Both Marines, attired in civilian clothing, stepped off toward the company van. They were booked on a commercial flight with the rest of their platoon. Leaving from Reagan National would be easy. In about seven hours, they'd be unloading their gear in Sin City.

THE WHITE HOUSE

"Mr. President, I've got your itinerary for the convention."

The tall president reached for the printed sheet.

"I thought you were gonna start sending these to me on my iPad, Bobby," the President teased his junior aide.

Bobby Johansen flushed in embarrassment. It was true. He had promised to "stop killing trees" as the President liked to say. Unfortunately, being swamped with the planning for the trip to Las Vegas, Johansen forgot to deliver the itinerary electronically. It hadn't helped that he'd gotten an email from that Asian guy when he arrived at the office. Something about a delivery coming in later today. He wished he'd never gotten in that mess during the campaign stop in Columbus. Now he had his unlikely savior asking random questions about the President's toys. The President loved new technology. He was known to spend hours scouring social media sites.

None of the inquiries were incriminating. Hell, Johansen didn't want to lose his job! No, the Japanese guy owned a technology company; something to do with cell phones. He wanted to get the inside scoop on possible upcoming government contracts. It seemed to Johansen that the man wanted to be able to brag to the public once the President received his newest smart phone prior to the official release. The guy seemed nice enough. He had helped Bobby out of that little matter with the Columbus police.

Johansen didn't see the harm. Hell, maybe he could even get a free phone out of the deal.

"So can you send this to my iPad, Bobby?" the President woke Johansen from his thoughts.

"Oh, yes sir. Sorry, sir. I'll send it to you right now."

LAS VEGAS, NEVADA

9:52AM, SEPTEMBER 18TH

Daniel hurried to his apartment and rushed to the bathroom. He quickly trimmed his beard and then shaved it off completely. He tied his hair back in a ponytail. Next he took out his one pair of decent jeans and threw on a form-fitting, black t-shirt. He finished the look with a weathered gray sport coat his mother bought him when he'd gone home for his dad's funeral. *I look halfway normal again*, he thought, as he stared into the bathroom mirror. *Mom would like to see me like this.*

He linked up with Gaucho's team twenty minutes later. They were all dressed in varying levels of stylish party attire. No one said anything about his appearance, but he thought he saw Gaucho smile in approval.

Briggs gave the men a quick rundown of the target. They were impressed by the level of detail in his presentation. One of the operators, dressed in an expensive Armani suit, asked Briggs how he knew so much about the place.

"Let's just say I've had a whole lot of time to visit most of the Vegas establishments. Zeitaku's relatively new, so I don't know what your plan is to infiltrate the secure areas."

Gaucho answered the question, "Neil gave us one of his toys."

Daniel didn't have a clue what the man was talking about. He knew Neil was the good-looking Indian guy with glasses. Briggs assumed he was just a computer geek that worked for SSI.

"I don't get it. What toys?"

Gaucho laughed. "Sorry, Compadre. I forgot that you don't really know our man Neil. His dad was some rich Indian dude. He built a big telecom company or something in the nineties. Well, Neil grew up working in his dad's workshop. By the age of ten, the kid could fix or build more shit than his dad's best technicians. So when Colonel Stokes brought Neil to SSI, he put him in charge of the company's R&D shop. You give the guy a problem and he comes up with the solution."

Briggs still looked confused. "Okay. So what about the toy he gave you?"

Gaucho motioned to the dark-haired operator standing next to him. The man handed what looked like an oversized CD case to the team leader. Gaucho pulled out a large disk and held it up. It was about eight inches in diameter and about a third of a centimeter thick.

"This is what Neil came up with for one of our little problems. We kept going on ops where the only way we could see through a door was either to knock it down or use one of those fiber optic cameras."

"What does it do?" Briggs asked.

"You ever see one of those kids toys where you unfold the paper and it turns into a snowflake or something?"

"Yeah, I think so."

"Well, this thing transforms into a ball. Then we can drive the thing on a smart phone loaded with the right software."

"But isn't that pretty obvious if somebody sees it on the other side?"

"I ain't told you the best part. We've been testing a lot of this new camouflage shit. You know, the electronic stuff that makes you look like a chameleon? So anyway, Neil used that technology on The Sphere."

"The Sphere?"

"That's what we call it. Neil came up with some crazy name like Techno-Gyro-Camo-Something. We're all dumb grunts. The Sphere works better for us." Daniel knew they were anything but dumb.

"So this thing can camouflage itself?"

"Yeah. It blends with its background. You can be looking right at it and barely see it. Kinda looks like a mirage. We can also flatten it out with the push of a button. Then it's almost totally invisible. It's not foolproof yet, but it's worked pretty well so far. Saves Bam Bam over there..." he pointed to a large man with bowling ball biceps, "...from having to bash in so many doors."

"So what else can it do?" Daniel was fascinated by the advanced gear. What he would've given to have some of those over in the desert.

"It's got a built-in camera so we can steer it and we can record to the cloud. Neil programmed a couple more features, but we'll save those for later."

"Cool. So where do you want me?"

"I've got you paired with Bam Bam." He turned to the rest of the team. "Let's get a quick comm check before we step off. I don't want my calls to go to voicemail."

The men chuckled and started checking their communication gear. They kept it simple and used cell phones. Most of their communication would be done via text. Only emergencies would be relayed via actual phone calls. They'd picked up the pay-as-you-go phones from a couple local pharmacies earlier.

Daniel checked his new phone and smiled. It felt good to be among warriors again.

"CAL, Gaucho just checked in. They're starting to head out," Neil updated the small command group.

Cal looked over at Brian, Willy, and Zimmer. "So to recap, Top, you stay here with Neil and the Congressman. Brian and I will head to the café across the street from the target."

"Why do I have to wear the chick disguise?" complained Brian.

"Neil thought you had the better hips," Cal answered with a grin. "It's better than having to wear this fat suit." Cal patted the belly of his twenty-pound fat suit. There was a prosthetic nose and pair of glasses to go along with the trucker hat he had perched on his head.

"Let's get ready and head that way."

Brian nodded and went into the bathroom to change into his drag outfit. He wasn't happy about it, but he knew that even his mother would never recognize him AND it was much easier to hide weapons under the many layers of his outfit. At least he wouldn't have to wear lipstick.

They walked out of the hotel room five minutes later. Brian walked uncomfortably in his patent leather combat boots. "I swear, if you ever make me do this again, Cal, I'll…"

"Relax, Doc. Next time, we'll get Top to wear the chick getup."

Brian laughed at the absurdity of the mental image. At seven feet tall, there was no way MSgt Trent could pass for a woman.

"If I'm dressing up as the woman, you're paying for dinner."

Cal laughed despite the severity of the situation. They were going into the heart of Indian country. Hopefully, all they'd be doing was observing. The last thing he wanted to do was chase the enemy around Las Vegas in a fat suit.

TAMPA, FLORIDA

11:02AM, SEPTEMBER 18TH

The young intern met the mailman at the door.

"Got a couple packages for your office. Here, I'll just put 'em in a box for you. Leave the empty container outside tomorrow."

The staffer took the box and looked down at all the labels. She'd planned on leaving early. She was jumping on a plane tomorrow with the rest of Congressman Unger's staff. The past week seemed a blur of planning and scheduling. Her boss was a second-term member of the House looking to get re-elected. Despite the President's waning popularity, Unger still wanted to get to Las Vegas early and be in as many photos with the incumbent as possible.

Her daddy, a rich Florida businessman, secured her a position through a couple of well-placed donations. When she'd first started working at the Congressman's office, she'd started a casual relationship with the twice-married Representative. His second wife was on the way out, and the staffer was on the way up.

Three months earlier, Unger off handedly mentioned that she should consider dating other people. He threw out some excuse about the re-election and trying to reconcile with his wife. She'd been offended but took it in stride. If she ever wanted a political career, she needed to have a level head. Besides, the Congressman wasn't fun anymore. He'd almost become a recluse in recent months. In fact, she thought, it all started with that trip out to Las Vegas in May. Strange.

She lugged in the mail and sorted through the junk. Picking up a small package, she inspected the label. *Opel. I'll bet this is that new phone he wanted me to order for him.* The pretty intern walked into the Congressman's vacant office and set the package on his large desk. On second thought, she grabbed a sticky note and wrote *"Let me know if you need help using this"* with a smiley face. It was better to keep all of her options open. Maybe Las Vegas would be a chance to climb back into his bed.

She left the office, already planning on which skimpy lingerie to pack.

LAS VEGAS, NEVADA

11:11AM, SEPTEMBER 18TH

Minutes after Cal left to monitor the raid, there was a knock at Neil's door. He was so engrossed with his work that he didn't hear the knock or see the manila envelope slide under the door.

GAUCHO'S TEAMS had already entered Zeitaku at staggered intervals. Some were in pairs of two, others as threesomes. It would be up to him to penetrate the casino's labyrinth with their little toy. They would only have one chance. It couldn't be wasted.

The team leader found the access door right where Neil had described. He glanced around casually and picked out a couple of his men. They were doing what they did best: blending in. Moving to the door, he rolled his suitcase behind. If anyone asked, he was looking for his room. His luggage was actually full of clothes. Tucked in the side pocket was their little surveillance tool.

Once next to the access point, he stopped and parked his bag. Luckily, there weren't any security guards nearby. There were, however, plenty of cameras. The drop would need to be smooth. Gaucho had just the thing. He'd tucked a map in front of the folded surveillance piece. Unzipping the side pocket of his suitcase, he extracted the map, keeping The Sphere covered right behind.

Staring at the travel guide, he used his peripheral vision to detect any wandering eyes. Nothing. Without taking his eyes off the map, he depressed the small power switch on the covert surveillance unit. He could just barely feel it vibrate as it powered on.

Gaucho waited five seconds more, mumbled a few curses for the sake of the cameras, turned quickly, and "accidentally" dropped the map. It fell perfectly flat, The Sphere safely on the ground. He bent over, still cursing to himself, and picked up the map. As he stood, he placed a perfect kick behind the barely visible disc and it slid under the door.

Taking his time with the map, he finally folded it up and slid it into his pocket. Next, he pulled out his phone and texted *GO* to Cal, Neil, and the rest of the team. He headed to the only place on the main level without cameras: the bathroom.

"HE'S IN," Cal whispered to Brian. They'd been at the little café long enough to have half their coffee.

"So how come we can't control that thing from our hotel?"

Cal took another sip of his coffee, then answered. "The signal won't go that far. We've gotta be pretty close to direct it."

"How long do you think it'll take?"

"As long as Gaucho can keep the thing moving, it'll probably be around twenty minutes. Thirty tops."

"So tell me again how that thing is gonna help us?" Brian asked between glances across the street.

"Neil thinks that if we can get close to their internal servers, he'll be able to tap into them. I think he's using The Sphere to send a signal at close range. Once he does that, Neil says we'll have unlimited access to their entire network."

"I guess we better pray that the batteries don't run out."

Cal snorted and went back to pretending to read something on his cell phone. Soon he should be able to see the feed from the surveillance unit. This thing had to work. He had a feeling the Japanese contingent was planning something big.

Gaucho settled into the handicap stall at the end of the bathroom. He propped his suitcase against the door and pulled out his phone. Switching on the display, he brought up the appropriate app. While he waited for it to load, he plugged in a pair of headphones.

The screen changed to a large green button. He pressed it. A few meters away, The Ball ballooned into a sphere. Gaucho could now see through the tiny camera. It was an unremarkable hallway that looked huge from the small camera's perspective.

He texted to Cal and Neil: *YOU GETTING THIS?*

They both replied: *YES.*

Following the small map Neil had drawn, Gaucho guided the silent vehicle to its destination.

Neil watched his creation move closer to Ichiban's server room. He wished he could be driving the thing, but Cal had insisted on keeping him at the hotel. He was too valuable to put in harm's way. Neil agreed on some level, but he always ached to be with the guys in the field. Sometimes he went along in a support capacity, but they never let him near the action.

He stood up and did some quick stretches. Once they were in the server room, he'd be busy trying to dissect the network. Might as well get in some exercise.

Ever since arriving at the hotel, he'd averaged two to three hours of sleep per night. In order to stay awake, Neil would occasionally do a couple sets of push-ups or burpees, just to get the blood flowing and jumpstart his brain.

As he lowered himself down to the ground for the first of fifty fast push-ups, he spied the manila envelope at the door. Curious, he stood up, walked to the door, and opened up the envelope.

It contained a simple message: *WE KNOW ABOUT THE COUNCIL*

Neil cursed and ran to his phone.

―――

CAL WATCHED as Gaucho carefully guided the remote vehicle through the winding maze. Two times he'd quickly swerved around walking employees who were oblivious to the spy camera's presence. He almost jumped when his phone buzzed with the incoming call. He looked at the caller ID. *What does Neil want?*

He put the phone to his ear. "What's up?"

"We've got a problem."

"Tell me something I don't know, Neil."

"I just got a message," Patel knew the capabilities of agencies like the NSA. Nothing you said on a cell phone was safe anymore.

"Can't this wait?"

"No. I need you back here right now."

Cal looked at Brian and shrugged. "Okay. I'll be there in ten."

Ramirez looked at his friend. "What's going on?"

"No idea. Apparently, we're in another shitstorm. Neil won't tell me until we get back to his suite."

"You want me to stay here?"

Cal thought about it. On one hand, having an extra pair of eyes might be useful. On the other, Gaucho's boys were more than capable.

"No, come back with me. I might need your help."

Brian waved for the waitress to bring the check while Cal texted Gaucho to let him know he'd be off station. What else could be added to this little adventure?

―――

TEN MINUTES LATER, the costumed duo entered Patel's suite. Neil motioned them over to the scattered papers on his makeshift desk. The first thing Cal noticed was the note from the envelope: *WE KNOW ABOUT THE COUNCIL.*

"What the fuck?"

"I told you it was bad. It gets worse though, Cal." Neil pointed at the contents of the mysterious envelope. "I think they're trying to tell us something."

"What are you talking about?"

Neil exhaled. He knew he had to keep his friend calm. "I think they're trying to say that we better leave or they'll expose the Council."

"But there's no way they could know about it, Neil!"

"Well, apparently someone pieced it together. It doesn't look like something you could take to court, but they sure could cause a stink."

"How the hell did this happen?" Cal wondered aloud.

THE CROOKED POLITICIAN started his investigation into the secret group nearly two years before. It all started as an accident. The aspiring President wasn't new to Washington. Over the years, he'd fought hard to head certain committees and cement important relationships. Very diligent in his planning, the long-serving federal servant knew the importance of building a resumé. He now chaired one of the highly coveted intelligence oversight committees.

On this particular occasion, a certain suspected terrorist cell was tracked to the United States by federal agencies. The problem was that The Patriot Act could only do so much. The President had already given explicit instructions that action would only be taken against suspected terrorist cells at home or abroad if the reviewed intelligence proved that the party was guilty beyond a reasonable doubt. Intelligence is rarely absolute. There isn't always a smoking gun. To make matters worse, cells operating in America had become very skilled at evading authorities and masking their activities.

One of the favored ways these groups stayed out of the reach of the law was to conduct clandestine meetings in mosques. Terrorists knew the American President drew the line at entering these holy places of worship. One of the pillars of his election was to repair the American relationship with the Muslim world. What sounded like a noble goal had turned into an open invitation. Ever since the Presidential inauguration, foreign fighters who'd managed to enter the U.S. flocked to mosques and made them their base of operations.

This particular cell, though new on the intelligence radar, was already very accomplished. Recruitment in the Detroit area increased alarmingly. As one of the hardest hit areas as a result of the recent economic downturn, young Arabs were easy targets.

The politician remembered grilling the FBI representatives that stood before his committee. He couldn't believe they were incapable of doing anything. Their reply was always the same: "Our hands are tied."

He'd thought the agency would somehow get creative. It scared him to think that America's enemies could so easily infiltrate his country. Something must be done.

A week later, he happened to run into former President Hank Waller. The two men were members at the same exclusive country club in Annandale. They'd been acquaintances in the halls of Washington for years. Over martinis, they caught up on each other's lives and commiserated on the trajectory of the American economy. Smoking cigars in the member lounge, the politician broached the subject of terrorists on American soil. Waller's brow furrowed. He could tell something was bothering his old colleague.

The politician proceeded to rail against the current President's asinine policy of treating terrorists like prisoners of war. He went on to describe a laundry list of potentially important operations that never launched just because the President wanted to be careful about offending the international community.

"Damnit, Hank. This man is making us look like a bunch of pussies!"

Waller calmed his friend and asked if there was anything he could do to help. Maybe a friendly meeting with the new President?

"That won't help. He's got his guard of cronies that make sure no one rocks the boat. During the election, he was all about reaching across the aisle; working together to affect change. Now he won't talk to a soul if his staff catches wind that they're trying to push an opposing agenda. The man is playing emperor in his ivory palace!" huffed the tired politician.

He'd continued by describing the case of the suspected terrorist cell in Detroit. "I mean, they are on OUR soil and we can't lift a finger until they jaywalk or murder someone. It's ludicrous."

Waller hadn't promised anything. He'd simply told him that if he ever needed to vent again, his door was always open. After all, he was retired. Both men laughed and promised to stay in touch.

The politician didn't think about the conversation until two weeks later. FBI reps were set to give his committee an update on the Detroit operation. What he received was far different.

"Sir, just this morning, we found out that the Detroit terror cell has been...well, it's been eradicated," informed the obviously confused FBI agent.

"What do you mean it's been eradicated, Mr. Pratt?" the politician questioned suspiciously.

"Well, sir, the two leaders of the cell and their top lieutenants were found this morning in front of their mosque."

"And...?"

"They were all dead, sir."

The politician sat back and digested the news. Certainly the FBI hadn't had anything to do with it?

"Were we involved, Mr. Pratt?"

"No, sir! In fact, we got the tip into our regional office at five this morning. I think we knew about it before the mosque did," Pratt paused, seemingly trying to formulate his next comment. "There's more, sir."

"More? I can't wait to hear this, Mr. Pratt." The politician rolled his eyes turning to his colleagues.

"This was a warning, sir."

"How so?"

"Each man lying on the ground held a large poster board with a message and a package. I have a picture for you here, sir."

"Why don't you save us some time and read it, Mr. Pratt," the politician recommended impatiently.

"It says 'America welcomes all races and religion. What we don't tolerate is terrorists trying to kill our country and our people'."

The committee sat back in shocked silence. Although quietly rooting for the vigilantes, the politician understood the possible fall-out.

"Thank you, Mr. Pratt. If you'll please leave copies of your documentation we will call on you again soon."

The politician had tried not to rush as he'd taken his assigned packet. It seemed that whoever had murdered the terrorists had first done their homework. Each man had a name tag stuck to his shirt. They were given names like PEDOPHILE, COWARD, and BLASPHEMER. In each package, they'd included the evidence to explain their nicknames. One man had a DVD showing close to six hours of the dead man having sex with ten-year-old prostitutes. The next man's package contained a thumb drive with hours of audio. Each recorded conversation was the dead man talking with one of his colleagues. They were laughing about the naïve recruits that strapped bombs to their bodies. The man actually said, "I would never be stupid enough to do that. They are so easy to convince in this country."

The transcripts went on and on. These men were obviously guilty. To cap it all off, the killers also provided audio, video, and schematics recovered from the deceased terrorists. The plans detailed an operation soon to be executed. They were targeting public elementary schools. The captured video showed the terrorists casing local educational institutions at the start of the school day. Based on the information provided, the FBI had already raided the terrorist safe house and uncovered crates of automatic weapons, RPGs, and hand grenades.

The politician was impressed by the daring killers. Whoever had conducted the investigation and the subsequent killings were professionals. Someone was secretly doing things right.

Over the next week, more and more intel was mined from the contents of the Detroit safe house. No one cried for the loss of these men. Surprisingly, once the truth of the dead terrorists' background and operation leaked to the press, the local Muslim community understood and calmed. They knew it was a warning to other would-be terrorists and not a threat to them.

The politician marveled at the effect of the killings. While listening to the testimony of countless FBI representatives, he started to wonder how the initial investigation leaked to the covert masterminds.

During one particularly boring hearing, the conversation with President Waller popped into his head. *Could it be? Is that the leak?* At first, the politician chided himself for his indiscretion. A plan formulated in his mind. Maybe if he let another piece of actionable intelligence slip to Waller, the problem would take care of itself.

The politician had found out long ago that in the corridors of Washington's elite, there was no such thing as knowing too many of other people's secrets.

That night, he carefully went over every supposedly dead-end operation he knew about. These would commonly be called 'cold-cases' in a police department. He liked to call them 'grey cases.' They lived in a grey area where either the evidence could only be collected through less than legal tactics or the suspected criminal was untouchable due to the person's station or status under current law.

Federal agencies hadn't 'officially' given up on them, but the mix of current regulation and the sitting President made convictions nearly impossible. After much reflection, the politician knew the perfect case to leak.

THE NEXT DAY, he placed a call to Hank Waller's office. Because of his status in Washington, he was immediately patched through. During the brief chat, the politician never mentioned the Detroit operation. Instead, he invited President Waller to play eighteen holes at the Army-Navy Club the next week.

Waller quickly checked his schedule and confirmed that he could make the tee time.

The following week, the two competitive men, surrounded by a roving Secret Service team, did their best to out-putt and out-drive each other. After the ninth hole, the politician steered the conversation to the increasing problems on the U.S.-Mexico border.

"It's pretty pathetic that the President has his attorney general crucifying these border guards. Did you hear that last week we actually had one of our outposts shelled?"

Waller looked up in surprise. "As in mortar shelled?"

"Yes," the politician knew he had Waller's attention. "The drug cartels are getting their hands on anything they want. What's next, heavy artillery?"

"Why aren't we doing anything about it?"

"These guys aren't idiots, Hank. They sit just on the other side of the border and wage war. We don't cross the border because Mexico is our ally. Problem is, the Mexican authorities are completely overwhelmed. They've got their hands full in major cities where hundreds of people are being murdered in broad daylight. What do they have to gain by helping us protect OUR border? Hell, a lot of their revenue comes from illegal immigrants coming over here and shipping money back to Mexico."

"So why doesn't the President put the screws to Mexico? I know we've done some joint ops before. We can help them if they need the help."

The politician laughed. "Are you kidding? When was the last time you saw the President put the screws to any foreign leader? I think the only country he's had a real pissing contest with is Israel. And they're our allies! No, he doesn't like making waves. He'd rather send drones into Pakistan than bitch slap a neighbor."

"That sounds pretty harsh," Waller scolded.

"It's the truth, Hank. Come on. You've been in the hot seat. You know how it goes. Give these guys an inch and they take a whole country."

The politician went on to tell the ex-President about the powerful cartel that was changing the face of the border war. Led by a secretive gangster, the expanding organization now played gatekeeper for other cartels looking to ship their illegal goods into America. The mortar attack was suspected to be the work of the same cartel.

Waller listened intently. The politician wouldn't know until nearly a month later that Waller had passed the information on to a secret band of warriors.

THIS TIME the results of the clandestine operation came from the DEA representative to the politician's committee. The man described, in detail, the load of intel that had recently been anonymously sent to their office. As a side note, the DEA man reported that the head of the border cartel had recently been found and gagged outside the regional Mexican police headquarters. Attached to the man were ten kilos of cocaine and enough video evidence to incarcerate him and his associates for hundreds of years.

So these covert warriors weren't just killers. They had the ability to deliver criminals alive to the authorities when appropriate.

The politician filed the thought away. He then set about having his contacts get him information on President Waller's conversations and travels. He hadn't known the exact identity of the organization conducting the covert operations, but he would soon.

The highlights of the almost two-year secret investigation filled the space the size of a large manila envelope. It was a pity he'd have to break up the party, but it was for the greater good: America's future.

CAL AND BRIAN sifted through the contents of the envelope. There were pictures of Council members together at various locations along with snippets of conversations. It sounded like someone had paraphrased after listening in. Maybe some of their Secret Service Agents?

All the documents felt more like a precursor. They were incomplete. Something was missing. What was it? What were they getting at? They seemed to be saying, "If you think this is a lot, just wait until you see what else we've got."

Maybe it was just a fishing expedition. Maybe whoever 'they' were didn't know anything. They were making one point painfully obvious: by delivering the envelope right to their suite, they knew where they were AND they knew about their connection to the Council of Patriots.

Cal picked up the secure phone next to Neil and dialed a number from memory. It was a number he swore he'd never use. He waited as the secure connection went through.

Hank Waller answered, "Yes?"

"Mr. President, we have a problem."

LAS VEGAS, NEVADA

12:28PM, SEPTEMBER 18TH

The group of Japanese men sat around the conference room table, chatting with colleagues as they waited for their host to begin.

Kazuo Nakamura looked around the room and remembered days long gone. These men truly were like family. Their histories were forever intertwined.

Kazuo's father, Akemi Nakamura, had been close to fifty when his son was born. His first wife, who'd left him childless, died six years earlier. His second wife was twenty-five years his junior. He'd married her simply to produce an heir.

The second wife produced a son, but died from complications during his birth. Young Kazuo was raised by an elderly housekeeper and occasionally allowed to enter his father's world.

At the age of nine, Kazuo awoke late one night. He heard loud shouting from the other side of the house. Being in a traditional Japanese home, most of the doors were literally paper-thin. He crept towards the commotion and peeked through a small hole in one of the door's panes.

He observed his father and four other men sitting around their chabudai dining room table. His father pointed at one of the men across the short table and yelled, "You know how that makes us look! You take advantage of the American contracts, but you will not be social with them!"

The man kept his head bowed in deference and tried to explain. "But, Nakamura-san, these Americans will do more business with us if I find the time to eat dinner with them or…"

"NO! I SAID NO! You must never associate yourself with them outside of business. We will use them for now, but soon Japan will be ours once again. The next time…"

The elder Nakamura stopped in mid-sentence. Even at close to sixty years of age, he was still physically commanding. Not a day passed that Kazuo's father didn't practice in the family dojo. Looking straight at Kazuo, he sprang up and moved to the door. Young Kazuo knew there was no sense in running. He'd felt his father's wrath before.

The elder Nakamura's hand shot through the thin papered pane, grabbed his son by the back of his head, and threw him into the room. He'd proceeded to methodically beat his son. There would be no cuts or bruises on his face or hands, but his torso would be black and blue for weeks. He was sure that his father had broken at least two ribs in the process.

The next day, his father walked into his room. Kazuo was at his desk doing his homework.

"Come with me," his father ordered.

With a wince, Kazuo rose and followed.

They entered the family dojo and the old man turned to his son. "Have you learned your lesson?"

"Yes, Father."

"Good. The next time you are caught spying…" he let the threat linger as he turned to the small shrine situated in one corner.

He grabbed two sake glasses, filled them, and handed one to his son.

"I have a story to tell you, son. Drink first, then we talk."

Kazuo did as instructed and gulped down the fiery liquid. It was his first taste of sake, but far from his last.

His father produced a pile of papers from a locked compartment under the small shrine. Kazuo looked at him anxiously.

"Have I ever told you the history of our family, My Son?"

"No, Father."

Akemi Nakamura nodded and spread the papers on the floor then knelt. Son followed. The first thing young Kazuo noticed were the pictures of his father. He was always standing in uniform. He knew his father has served in World War II, but he didn't know in what capacity.

"I was very young when I entered my first military academy," his father began. "At that time, we had a very strong force. Because my father was a prominent politician, I was given the choice of where to serve. After excelling in my studies and training, I was selected to serve with our Military Police. We were called the Kempeitai. I was recruited to be part of their elite interrogation unit. I trained extensively with the German Abwehr. Some of my friends flew to Italy to train with the Italian Military Intelligence called the Servizio Informazioni Militare, or SIM. It was a wonderful time in our history. The Empire reached farther than we ever had in our history. I spent much time in China and the Pacific islands. We captured and tortured our enemies. I was a very good interrogator. They called me Akemi. Do you know what that means, my son?"

"I think it means Beauty of Dawn, Father."

"That is correct. Now, what is on our national flag of Japan?"

"A rising sun, Father."

"Yes. I was named Akemi because of my cruelty and success. My fellow soldiers saw my actions as bringing about the new dawn. The rise of the Empire of Japan."

"But, Father, is Akemi not your real name?"

"It is now. That is another part of the story. As I was saying, we conquered wherever we went. Our warriors could not be stopped. The Pacific Islands, China, and Australia were all within our grasp."

Nakamura's eyes clouded. "That all changed with the invasion of Pearl Harbor."

"I thought that was a great victory for our people, Father."

"It was, my son. But it was only one battle. And that small victory awoke the American giant. Yes, we fared well at first. I still remember the newspapers filled with sinking American warships. It was a glorious time to be Japanese. But, after a time, the Americans recovered. Soon they were shipping unlimited resources to the Pacific. Our warriors fought valiantly...but, of course, you know the rest."

Father and son sat silent for a moment. Akemi seemed to be gathering his thoughts again.

"After the war the Americans came looking for war criminals. I knew that what I did was in service of the Emperor. It did not matter to the Americans. They tracked down many of my friends. Most were hung or shot."

Kazuo's eyes went wide with wonder. "What happened to you, Father?"

"I was eventually caught. Luckily, I had forged documents with my new name, Akemi Nakamura. My other stroke of luck was that anyone who witnessed what I'd done was now dead. That is, all except for a few of my men. Some were captured and some escaped. The gentlemen you saw last night were four of them. I was imprisoned until no evidence could be produced to prosecute me. I found a new home and started my new life. Over the years, I found some of my old comrades. Most have new names as well. We meet periodically to reminisce about the old days and talk of the future."

Kazuo stared at his father with awe. His father had been a great warrior of Japan, just like the mighty Samurai he learned about in school.

THE NEXT TIME his father's friends came for a visit, Kazuo was invited. He was always instructed to sit and stay quiet. A trend quickly emerged in Kazuo's mind. They were planning something. What was it?

Soon, with the approval of the elder Nakamura, the other men started bringing their own sons to the gatherings. Kazuo became their leader. Not only did they spend time together at the Nakamura household, they would run in the hills and play Samurai. Little did he know then that gatherings for monthly dinners would one day become what it was today.

He forged those relationships through his teenage years and his father slowly prepared him for the future. There was always the lesson of putting Japan first. They talked for hours about their ancestors as they trained in the dojo. Kazuo remembered those days fondly.

Then came the day when the military police came to his home. By some cruel twist of fate, the modern day version of the Japanese Kempeitai had found his father's true identity. Enough evidence was presented at the trial to lead to a swift prosecution. The war criminal, Akemi Nakamura, and his associates were killed by a Japanese military firing squad at the age of sixty-eight.

No one thought to question the children.

KAZUO NAKAMURA ASSUMED leadership of Japanese outcasts. Instead of mourning, he turned his sights on the ultimate goal: returning the Empire of Japan to its former glory. He had two enemies to confront: first, the current Japanese leadership and second, the United States. He saw the two as being the parties guilty of killing his father. He would not forget.

He led a delicate balancing act in the ensuing years. Nakamura pursued his education both in Japan and in the United States. Instead of being outwardly hostile to non-Japanese, Kazuo encouraged his small band to branch out. They learned about their enemies and entrenched themselves in both the Japanese and American political systems.

Nakamura's patriots slowly grew over the years. Now, there were close to twenty men in the inner circle. The influence of the group extended throughout the Japanese and North American economies. They studied their enemies and gained leverage whenever possible.

Kazuo relocated to America when his son was born and raised Ishi as an American. They'd first lived in San Francisco, then moved east and settled into Wellesley, a quiet suburb of Boston. At the age of nine, his son was indoctrinated into the group. He'd been an apt pupil.

By dumb luck, Nakamura had stumbled upon what would become one of their greatest assets. During Ishi's freshman year of private high school, he'd become friends with the son of a famous celebrity. At first, the strict father had forbidden the relationship. He didn't want his son THAT Americanized.

One of Kazuo's strengths as a businessman was to always search for the silver lining of unintended consequences. For years, he'd tried to figure out how to infiltrate America's capital. So far, he'd only achieved marginal success. His son's high school friendship gave him another idea. What if his son and the children of his compatriots became the friends of prominent politicians? He decided to try an experiment. First, he made discrete inquiries.

The next morning, he instructed Ishi to begin cultivating a relationship with the son of a long-standing U.S. Congressman. The two were in the same private high school but had never mingled in the same groups. Later that day, Ishi returned home to tell his father that the Congressman's son had rebuffed his attempts at friendship.

After a severe rebuke, Kazuo calmed down and gave his son more to work with.

"I want you to do anything you need to. Find out if the boy uses drugs. Maybe he likes girls and alcohol. Observe without being obvious."

Ishi agreed and the next day came home with the expected details.

"Father, I followed the boy and his friends at a discreet distance and found that they do like marijuana. In fact, I saw them smoking behind the football bleachers."

His father smiled. "Good work, my son. We have our way in."

Over the next week, father and son crafted a scheme to get Ishi into the boy's clique. Through his contacts, Kazuo Nakamura purchased medical-grade marijuana. He had Ishi practice smoking the drug in order to understand its effects and to learn how to maintain control. The next week, Ishi joined the boys behind the bleachers.

The Congressman's son, a fat spoiled teenager, confronted Ishi. "We don't want Japs hanging around us."

His friends laughed, but Ishi ignored the comments. Instead, he pulled out a carefully rolled joint, lit it, and took a long hit. The boys' eyes opened wide and menace changed to wonder.

"Where'd you get that, Jap boy?" asked the Congressman's son.

The young Nakamura looked straight into the boy's eyes and pointed at him. "First, my name is Ishi," he paused to take another hit. He could almost see the boys salivating. "Second, you want some?" He motioned to the boy with his joint.

"What is it?"

"It's something special."

"Is it laced with something?"

Ishi shook his head. "Nope. Just some shit stolen from a government lab."

The other boys all looked to the Congressman's son. They knew what his father did. They waited for him to lead.

The boy smiled and grabbed the joint hungrily. "I think you're gonna fit in just fine around here, Ishi."

It was a huge lesson for the Nakamuras. They now understood how their targets could be manipulated. Simply find their vice and exploit it. It was a formula they continued to use. Nakamura instructed his Japanese compatriots to do the same with their children and their businesses. Soon, their results surpassed Nakamura's wildest predictions. Blackmail was a powerful tool.

After doing some research, Kazuo found another interesting weakness he could exploit. The sons of prominent bureaucrats tended to follow in their fathers' footsteps. Over the years this phenomenon created families that would become political dynasties. It was time to attack the governmental elite.

During college, Kazuo Nakamura chose Ishi's target: The Zimmer Dynasty.

THE NAKAMURA'S ultimate victory neared. Their blackmail list stretched far and wide. Leading Japanese politicians and businessman, hungry for additional international market share and respect, had privately endorsed Nakamura's bold plan. In exchange for crippling the American machine, they would push through the reform needed to bring Japan back to superpower status. Yes, it would mean some minor disputes in Asia. But the ends justified the means. Besides, they would have the tacit approval of the next American President. The Empire of Japan would rise again.

BACK IN HIS POSH SUITE, the politician ran the details through his mind. He wished the coup didn't involve the Japanese, but that was now beyond his control. So far, they'd succeeded in their planning. If worse came to worst, he could always point the finger back at them.

Grabbing his gin and tonic, he sat down and prepared for the mayhem.

LAS VEGAS, NEVADA

1:34PM, SEPTEMBER 18TH

President Waller and Cal decided that meeting to review and discuss the packet was worth the risk. Cal agreed to meet the former President in under an hour.

Meanwhile, Neil had successfully hacked his way into the Ichiban internal servers. He was now downloading the mountain of information for his software to start analyzing. Patel also had a team ready to assist at his office back at SSI headquarters.

Because of the fact that the enemy somehow knew their location, Cal had a dilemma. What they needed to do was move Neil and all his equipment. The problem was that they needed it up and running.

Instead of relocating, Cal instructed Gaucho to pull his troops back to the suite and secure it completely. Barring a cruise missile, the suite would be untouchable.

On a whim, Cal decided to bring Briggs along. The guy knew the city and the best way to navigate it. There was a reason he was a "scout" sniper.

The two Marines set off for the meeting with Waller. Rather than follow the outdoor walkways, Briggs cut a path through the casinos. It was possible to travel through much of The Strip without even stepping outside.

Cal casually swept his gaze as he'd learned in Todd Dunn's challenging counter-surveillance course. He couldn't detect any tails. Daniel pressed on.

The pair finally reached the small room that Neil had just reserved at the Treasure Island Resort and Casino. They wouldn't need it for long, which was good. Waller had come with minimal security and in a casual disguise. Luckily, ex-Presidents weren't highly important targets or his Secret Service staff might have denied the last minute request.

Cal nodded to the large man in jeans standing outside the door.

"Sorry, sir. I was instructed to only let you in," the agent said.

Cal looked at Daniel. "Do you mind waiting out here?"

"Nope. See you in a minute."

Cal opened the door and approached the next agent, who quickly frisked him. He pointed to Cal's wrist that had his knife strapped to it. Just as the agent went to make a comment, Waller came out of the bathroom.

"He's fine, Jimmy. Why don't you wait outside?"

The agent looked like he was about to object, but instead nodded and stepped out.

"So, what are we dealing with here, Cal?"

Cal pulled his backpack off, extracted the manila envelope, and handed it to Waller.

Sitting down at the coffee table, President Waller took out the evidence and spread it out. His left eyebrow arched as he quickly perused the collection.

"Somebody's been doing their homework, haven't they?"

"Yes, sir."

"Do you guys have any idea who might be behind this?"

"I'm new at this whole thing, Mr. President. I don't know who you've had contact with in the past. My concern is that some of your security detail could be the issue."

Waller stared at Cal for a moment. "I really hate to think about that, Cal. How realistic could it be?"

Cal had thought about it on the way over. "The way I see it, Mr. President..."

"Come on, Cal, it's Hank in here, remember?"

"Yes, sir. Sorry, Hank. Anyway, it is possible that someone could have taken these pictures and gotten audio from a long way off. The problem is, how did someone know where to look? I'm assuming whenever the Council meets, the number of people that know the itinerary is minimal?"

Waller nodded.

"Well then, there has to be someone on the inside."

Waller stood up and walked to the window. "You know how bad this pisses me off? It reminds me of all the times Trav warned us about OpSec. He kept telling us that at some point someone would figure things out. How bad do you think this is?"

"I made a secure call to Trav before coming over. They're running some scenarios," answered Cal, unsure of what else the President wanted him to say.

"I want YOUR opinion, Cal. Does this kill us?"

"You really want my opinion?"

"Yes."

"Okay. I figure we have two options: One, pack up, head home, and let the Zimmers deal with their own mess."

"You know that's not what..."

"Hold on, sir. Let me finish."

"Sorry. Go ahead."

"Second, we can find the leak and plug it."

"And how do you propose we do that?"

"It'll be risky, but I think the rat is about to surface. The other thing I wanted to tell you was that we honestly believe there is going to be some kind of attack or demonstration during the Democratic Convention."

Waller's eyes went wide. "What? How is that even possible? I've been to these things for years. I'm sure the Secret Service has buttoned up the city pretty tight."

"A week ago, I would've agreed with you. But after what I've seen here, I'm not so sure. Hell, these guys found us and, more importantly, figured out about the most secretive group outside of the U.S. government. They've got resources and they aren't afraid to use them."

"So, what's the next step? Should we alert the Secret Service?"

Cal knew he was taking a risk, but he had confidence in his team. "I think we should see how it plays out. Let's say we give the Secret Service an anonymous tip that'll hopefully get them even more attentive. Meanwhile, me and my team find these fuckers and take them out."

Waller looked at the young man. If he felt any doubt, he didn't show it. "Travis was right."

"What do you mean?"

"We need more Marines in this world."

CAL AND WALLER ironed out a few more details. The ex-President would alert the rest of the Council and have them start thinking about potential leaks. Even though he wasn't close to the current President, Waller still had duties to perform for his Party. Over the next couple days, he would be called upon to attend to the Convention. It would keep him busy, but they agreed to stay in close contact.

Daniel and Cal left the meeting room and headed back. Thinking to himself, Cal barely noticed the passing landscape. He grabbed his phone and dialed Neil.

"Yeah."

"Tell me you've got something, Neil."

"You're not gonna believe this shit. They've got…"

"Hold on. Don't say anything on this line. We'll be back in a few minutes."

"Okay. I'll have a brief waiting for you."

Looking down to replace his phone in his pocket, Cal almost ran right into Briggs. Daniel had casually stopped at a slot machine and placed a quarter in the slot.

"What are you…?"

"Don't look up," Daniel interrupted.

Cal did as told and glanced down at the game. "What's going on?" he whispered.

"Looks like those goons found us again. Three o'clock. I saw at least two of 'em. I'll bet there's more," Daniel answered casually.

"How the hell did they find us?"

Briggs answered with a shrug. If he was concerned, he sure as hell didn't show it.

"What's our next move?" Cal asked.

"I've got a Marine buddy that works on the security team here at Treasure Island. Let me call his cell phone and see if he can get those fuckers off our tail."

Daniel continued to feed quarters into the slot machine as he pulled out his phone and dialed a number.

"Hey, Rick. I've got a favor to ask. You working right now?"

"Yeah, man. What's up?"

"You know those Russian goons that work over at Zeitaku?"

"Ivan Drago lookin' motherfuckers?"

"Yeah. They're in your casino right now and they want to put their hands on me and my friend. Anything you can do to help?"

Daniel could hear Rick already moving through the casino. "I'm on it, brother. Where are they?"

Briggs told him where they were and hung up.

"So who was that guy?" Cal asked.

"Rick was a grunt in my first battalion. Helluva squad leader. Saved his ass a couple times."

Cal's respect for the sniper kept growing. He might be a good friend to keep around.

Two minutes later, Cal heard a commotion. He turned to see a group of ten security guards surrounding the hulking Russians.

"I don't know why you bother me. I here to spend money!" the Russian leader bellowed.

"I'm sorry, sir, but we've received complaints that you've been harassing some of our customers," the head guard informed respectfully. "I'll need you to leave at once, sir."

"I no bother no one, jarhead!" the giant snarled. "Maybe I bother you, instead."

Rick, the former Marine, looked around at his nine guards near the three Russians. "You're more than welcome to try, sir, but I'm not so sure about your odds."

The huge man looked around and weighed his options. His instructions were clear: find Cal Stokes and kill him. It had been one of Ichiban's hookers that had spotted Stokes one casino back and alerted the team. The fact that the man was within earshot only angered the thug further.

"You hear from me again soon, jarhead. We go now."

Rick nodded and motioned for the other guards to escort the trio out. As they moved to the exit, he turned around and headed over to Daniel and Cal.

"Hey, brother. How goes it?" he asked, as he shook Daniel's hand.

"Good, man. Hey, I want you to meet a buddy of mine. Rick, this is Cal."

The two men sized each other up, as only Marines can do, and shook hands.

"Thanks for your help," Cal offered.

"Not a problem. I owe Snake Eyes a couple of favors."

"Snake Eyes?" Cal asked curiously.

"It was my call-sign on patrol," Briggs explained. "While I was in Afghanistan, my mom sent me the whole G.I. Joe DVD cartoon collection. Snake Eyes was always my favorite character and some of the other Marines found out about it and the nickname stuck."

Rick laughed. "Yeah. Dude would come back from an op and sit there and watch those fucking cartoons over and over."

Cal joined in the laughter. "I remember those. I guess the name fits for a sniper."

Briggs nodded. "Thanks again for the help, but we've gotta go."

"No problem, man. Stay in touch, okay? By the way, I like the new look!" He pointed at Daniel's ponytail and hairless chin. Briggs smiled and they all said their goodbyes.

"How close are we?" Cal asked his partner as they descended another set of escalators.

"Not far. About five minutes."

They walked out a back service exit and into an alleyway. Neither

Marine saw the small Japanese man, requisite tourist camera slung around his neck, casually looking their way.

"He found them, Father," Ishi informed.

"Good."

"What are his orders?"

"Tell him to kill them, quietly."

Ishi texted the command into his phone: *TAKE OUT THE GARBAGE, QUIETLY*

The Japanese assassin read the text and smiled inwardly. It had been too long since he'd used his skills. Kenji Matsura looked completely harmless. Dressed in a pair of old pleated pants, checkered shirt, and thick glasses, Matsura looked like one of a thousand Japanese tourists wandering the streets of Las Vegas.

His deadly abilities were hidden by his almost feminine. Born into a family of warriors, Kenji Matsura was what some might call a modern day ninja. An expert in four types of martial arts, he was also a veteran of the Japanese Defense Force. Most people didn't know much about the Japanese military. This was mainly due to the fact that after World War II part of the peace treaty declared that the Japanese people could no longer field an army. In recent years, the treaty's provisions had relaxed and Japan had even sent troops to help in the Middle East.

Matsura was part of the first unit sent. Unbeknownst to the public, a group of Japanese military officers had formed an ultra-secretive commando unit within the Defense Force: Unit 47. Through his amazing ability and family connections within the military (certain military officers were privy to portions of the plot orchestrated by Nakamura), Kenji Matsura was assigned to Unit 47.

It was in Iraq where Matsura finally utilized his skills. He was given free rein to track down and kill insurgents and suspected terrorists. His results overshadowed his ruthless tactics. Matsura often worked alone and slaughtered whole families. He'd finally been reined in and sent home.

No matter, Matsura thought. He'd been trained by the Army and battle tested in the desert, but it was Kazuo Nakamura who'd become his true master. Like a brilliant general, Nakamura had recognized Matsura's abilities and put them to frequent use. Many former rivals now called the cemetery their home, thanks to Nakamura's scheming and Matsura's death dealing.

He'd been warned about the prowess of Cal Stokes. It didn't bother Matsura one bit. Other great warriors had tried to kill him before. He'd slaughtered them all. It was time to put another notch on his sword.

———

DANIEL SENSED the approaching danger a split second before it happened. They'd just entered the rear entrance to the pool deck of the Bellagio, music blaring and bumping from the poolside DJ booth, when he grabbed Cal and threw him into the bushes.

The suppressed pistol round grazed Daniel's chest as he spun around for cover. He reached for his concealed pistol as he fell.

———

MATSURA COULDN'T BELIEVE he'd missed. He'd had Stokes in his sights, been completely quiet and concealed, yet the man with the blonde ponytail had sensed his presence. The assassin wouldn't make the same mistake again.

———

CAL GLANCED at Briggs from behind a short wall. Daniel pointed to where the shot came from and he nodded. Why had he not brought his pistol? As if reading his mind, Briggs showed Cal a second pistol. The Marines were about twenty feet apart, but at least they might have a chance of each sporting a weapon. Cal peaked out cautiously and heard a shot fired in response. He quickly whipped back and the bullet hit exactly where his head had just been.

This guy was good. What to do now? Cal texted the team: *ONE MAN SHOTS FIRED BY THE HOTEL POOL SEND HELP*

Hopefully, Gaucho would understand his text.

———

Daniel took a steadying breath and said a quick prayer. He'd been in similar situations before. It almost always came down to decisiveness, daring, and a little bit of luck. Briggs counted down the seconds as he watched the assassin move closer.

———

Matsura now had two suppressed pistols, one in each hand. He was an expert with both hands. Keeping his weapons pointed at their respective targets, he stalked forward. Two kills in a day was a walk in the park for the warrior.

———

Gaucho and Neil looked down at their phones at the same time. "Shit!" The room full of operators looked up. "I need four of you right now. Weapons concealed. We're going down to the pool."

The five men sprinted out of the suite, past their surprised sentries, and into the stairwell. Gaucho hoped they'd make it in time.

———

Briggs made his move, diving out from cover, low to the ground, facing his attacker. There was maybe fifteen feet between the two men. Matsura was faster, his two rounds on a perfect collision course with Daniel's chest as the Marine's double-tap went off a split second too late.

Matsura smiled as the bullets hit their target. He felt two stings on his shirt. Had he been shot? Looking down quickly, his eyes squinted in confusion. Instead of seeping blood, he saw two yellow paint splatters.

Just as he turned to find his second target, he realized his folly. The blonde man's dive had been a diversion. He'd sacrificed himself so that Stokes could flank the assassin. The Japanese killer had walked too close. He should have stayed back. During the quick exchange, Cal had taken advantage of Daniel's diversion and crept forward behind the tall privacy bushes.

He sprang up from his squatting position, knife leading the way. The blade went into the assassins left ear to the hilt. The Marine twisted the blade as the man struggled for a moment, and then folded to the ground.

After quickly making sure the man was dead and taking his two suppressed weapons, Cal ran to his fallen friend.

Gaucho's men rushed out onto the pool deck just as the muffled shots went off. The guests looked at them in confusion, most too absorbed in their drinks and the loud music to notice the commotion. The SSI team rushed to the source of the shots.

Cal bent down to his new friend. Daniel had signaled what he'd wanted to do, but Cal had shaken his head. This wasn't the sniper's fight. He'd seen the rounds hit. He could only hope that his injuries weren't fatal.

Cal rolled Daniel over and noticed that the wounded man was clutching his stomach. He looked up at Cal. "Did you get him?"

"Yeah. Don't move. We need to get you to the hospital."

"For what?" It was obvious the sniper was trying to catch his breath. They had to get him out of there soon.

"You got shot, man. Don't move. My guys should be here in a second."

As if on cue, the five team members spotted them and hopped over the fence. Gaucho reached the pair first. "He shot?"

Cal nodded. He then pointed to the Asian assassin. "We need to get that body out of here. Can your boys take care of it?"

Gaucho nodded and barked quick orders over the booming music.

Cal started peeling off Daniel's shirt so he could find the entry wounds. When he did one of the bullets rolled off of the sniper's Kevlar covered chest. Cal looked down in confusion.

Daniel gasped as he explained. "I was trying...to...tell you. It just hurts...like a...sonofabitch."

"You lucky fucker," laughed the short Hispanic, shaking his head.

"Wait," Cal stopped, "I didn't hear your pistol shots go off."

Daniel smiled. "These are...paintball...guns." He handed one to his friend.

"You crazy fucker," muttered Cal in admiration. This guy had real balls. "Come on. We've gotta get out of here."

Between the two of them, Cal and Gaucho helped Daniel up. He was still in pain but regaining his breath quickly. They all stowed their weapons under their shirts and headed back into the hotel as the disposal team went to work taking the body to a inconspicuous drop-off location.

What else could go wrong today?

LAS VEGAS, NEVADA

3:05PM, SEPTEMBER 18TH

"What the hell happened down there?" Neil blurted as the trio walked back into the suite.

"Someone just tried to take us out," Cal explained. "Please tell me you found out something that'll help us nail these assholes."

Daniel peeled off his Kevlar vest and grabbed some ice as Neil and Cal went over to the bank of computers.

"So, I think we've hit the motherload. These guys are into a whole lot of dirty business. You're not gonna believe how deep this goes."

"Start at the beginning while I grab a drink, Neil. You want one?"

Neil raised a Red Bull and shook his head.

"Okay. Brief overview: Ichiban Gaming is neck-deep into blackmail. It looks like they've got at least twenty Congressman and five Senators in their pockets. Pretty even between Democrats and Republicans. While that may not seem like a lot, they also have over one hundred political staffers under their thumbs. Not to mention lower level government employees. They've got these people on everything from alleged murder to heavy drug use. And that's just the government stuff!

I haven't even started pulling out the database of civilians that are on their extortion list."

"So what are they trying to do with all these people?"

"I haven't gotten to that quite yet. My system has to translate everything from Japanese into English. I've probably only uncovered about a quarter of it so far. It'll take some time to unravel."

"Neil, I know I don't need to tell you this, but the shit's about to hit the fan. I'd really like to know more as soon as we can," Cal requested, not unkindly.

"I know, Cal. I'm working as fast as I can. Even my technology has its limits." Neil exhaled in frustration.

"I understand. We just need something we can act on right now. How about you print me off a list of those top politicians so I can take a look. Maybe we can give somebody a heads-up. I mean, I'm not sure how we should handle this information yet. As much as I'd like to make a bunch of Washington-types look like idiots, I'm not so sure America needs that right now."

"Why don't you talk to the Council about it?"

"Our friends are a little busy right now. I think I'll wait until we know a little more about what the exact threat is. Where are Zimmer and Top at?"

Neil pointed up. "I got them a room right above us. Trent's got him cooped up in there for now."

Cal looked over at Briggs. "You good to walk?"

"Yeah. I'll be okay."

"Neil, we're headed up to have a little chat with the Congressman. Can I take those names with me?"

Patel handed him the two sheets of paper and the former Marines headed for the door. Cal had no idea what to do next. There was a large piece of intel they were still missing.

As they reached the stairwell, Cal's cell phone buzzed. It was Captain Andrews.

"Hey, man. Are you here?" Cal could hear slot machines on the other end.

"Yeah. We just landed. You have time to grab a drink?"

Cal glanced at Briggs. "I'm not sure, Andy. I think I'll know more in a few minutes."

"Everything okay?" Andy asked in concern.

"You know me. Never a dull moment."

Andy laughed. "Yeah, don't remind me. All right, give me a call when you know. I have a meeting with the planners at nine, but I'm free until then."

"You got it. I'll talk to you soon."

Cal put the phone back in his pocket and opened the stairwell door.

"Who was that?" Briggs asked.

"Just another Marine buddy. He's a Captain with the Silent Drill Team. Can you believe they're out here to do a show for the Convention?"

"You're kidding me! I thought they only did shows at football games and stuff."

"That's what I said! I guess someone pulled some strings to get them out here. Maybe it'll be..."

Cal stopped when Daniel grabbed his arm. "What if they're part of this?"

"What do you mean?"

"I mean it seems more than a little odd that the Silent Drill Team is performing at a political rally, doesn't it?"

Maybe Daniel's right. But how could they be involved?

"I guess, if nothing else, I can give Andy a heads-up that there could be a threat."

Briggs agreed. "I don't think any of us can be too careful right now."

Cal climbed the last few steps to the next landing and turned to his new friend. "You sure you want to be a part of this mess?"

Daniel grinned. "Are you kidding? I haven't had this much fun since Ramadi."

Cal smiled and clapped the sniper on the back. He'd be a good man to have around. Hell, in the span of less than a week, he'd already saved Cal's life twice. Too bad the man didn't drink or he'd be getting a lot of free booze.

THEY STEPPED INTO THE SUITE. Trent and Zimmer were playing cards at the dining room table.

"You want in, Cal?" Trent asked over his shoulder.

"We need to talk." The seriousness of his tone made both men turn.

Cal sat down at the table next to Zimmer. The Congressman glanced down at the sheets of paper. "What's that?"

"Neil hacked into their system. We don't know everything yet, but hopefully we will soon. I need your help, Congressman."

Brandon looked at Cal. It was the first time the Marine had asked him for anything.

"How can I help?"

Spreading the list on the table, Cal explained. "These are the names of other politicians and government employees that the guys behind Ichiban have been blackmailing. Some of them are long-standing. Some are new to the list. The problem is, we don't know what they're being used for."

"I'm still confused. How again do you want me to help?"

"I need you to remember whether this Nakamura guy ever asked you for anything. Did he try to get any information out of you? Did they try to get access to secure files or facilities? Anything out of the ordinary?"

Zimmer sat back and thought about the last six months. At first glance, nothing stood out. He'd thought at the time that Ishi was just working up to asking him something. It always felt like there was a request right around the corner. After all, why else blackmail a Congressman unless you want something in return?

"Not that I can remember. They kept it pretty professional."

Cal knew there had to be a goal. "Did they ever give you anything?"

Zimmer shook his head in frustration. "No. Honestly, I don't remember them trying to manipulate me other than that morning with Beth."

Cal pointed to the list. "Do you recognize any of these names?"

"Of course. Some of them are very powerful men."

"What about a connection. Do you serve with them on any committees? Do they run in the same social circles?"

Zimmer thought for a second. He really wanted to help, but he was the new guy in Washington. He wasn't useful to the old stalwarts yet. "No. I've met the Senators before because of Dad, but I really only know two or three of the Representatives on that list."

It felt like it was just beyond reach.

Daniel interrupted Cal's reverie. "You mind if I take a look at the list, Cal?"

"Have at it."

Cal slid the list across the table. Briggs looked down at the list with Trent. Cal was right. Nothing jumped out. Then an idea popped into the sniper's head: what if it wasn't WHO they were but WHERE they were? Each name had a two-letter abbreviation for the state they served. Daniel scanned the list again, simply focusing on the geographical locations.

The others noticed his increased concentration.

"What do you see, Daniel?" Cal asked.

"I'm not sure, but I think there's a connection with the states these guys represent."

He read the states out loud. "Ohio, Florida, Virginia, Nevada, Iowa, Colorado..."

"Wait a minute," Zimmer interrupted, "those are all swing states!"

Cal looked over at the Congressman in confusion. "Like for the election?"

"I'm not sure about Colorado, but I'm pretty sure the rest of those states are a toss-up right now. But, how could they have known that before the election?"

Cal didn't have a clue, but at least they'd latched on to something. "So you're saying that the Presidential candidates are fighting over these states?"

"Do you ever know what's going on in politics, Cal? Even I know this stuff," Trent teased.

"What can I say? I vote, but in general, politics make me want to throw up. No offense, Congressman."

A week earlier, Zimmer might have fought for his profession. Now, he understood the Marine's point of view. Looking at the blackmail list proved how dirty politics could be.

"Don't worry about it. Right about now it makes me want to puke, too."

The response surprised Cal. Maybe the Congressman really was coming around. He turned back to the list. "Okay, so are we in agreement that these guys might be trying to rig the election?" Nods around the table. "If that's the case, why go to all the trouble? If they want the President to get re-elected, why not just dump a bunch of money into the campaign?"

No one had an answer. What they didn't know was that there would soon be another candidate in the race for President.

AFTER CALLING SSI headquarters and updating Travis and his staff, the four men walked down to Neil's suite. They were all energized by the recent revelation. These Japanese guys had some balls.

As they walked, one question kept nagging at Cal: *Where was the leak?*

THE POLITICIAN SMILED into the mirror. Tomorrow would be a very big day. As long as Nakamura kept his end of the bargain, he'd have the election wrapped up in a matter of days.

LAS VEGAS, NEVADA

3:17PM, SEPTEMBER 18TH

Kazuo Nakamura called the number for the third time. It wasn't like his prized assassin not to check in. Still no answer.

Ishi looked on with interest. For years, Matsura had been a thorn in his side. The man never said much, but Ishi could see his influence growing. Sometimes he felt like his father treated the assassin more like a favored son. Secretly, he hoped the man disappeared.

"Have you tried him again?" Nakamura asked his son.

"Yes, Father. He's not answering calls or texts."

"Maybe he is busy disposing of the bodies."

"I think we need to assume the worst, Father."

Nakamura shot his son a murderous glare. "What do you mean?"

"With all due respect, Father, I think we've underestimated our adversaries again."

"I've sent that man out alone to kill five men at once before! He does not fail!"

Ishi bowed to his father, silently relishing the old man's lack of composure. "I know he has never failed, Father. Maybe he finally met his match."

Kazuo Nakamura paced back and forth, hoping his phone would ring. "We had them within our grasp! We've taken care of the Secret Service and the FBI. How is it that Stokes is evading us?"

Ishi knew he had to steer the conversation back to the task at hand. "Father, tomorrow will be the start of a glorious new path for our people. Perhaps we should focus on that, instead."

His father looked at him with an uncertain gaze. "Of course. Of course, you're right, my son. We must get back to finalizing our plans for tomorrow's festivities."

Ishi nodded and pulled out the chair for his father. Both men sat down and returned to the drawing of the Las Vegas Convention Center.

CAL CHECKED the caller ID on the dead assassin's phone. "Same number. Did you get a lock on the signal yet?"

Neil shook his head. "I don't know how they're doing it, but I can't pinpoint where the call is coming from."

"I thought you had that super duper tracking system."

Patel shot his friend an exasperated look. "I do. Problem is, the number isn't registered anywhere. It's like a ghost."

"Maybe I should call him and ask him where he is," Cal offered.

Instead of replying, Neil gave Cal the finger.

"Take it easy on him, Cal." Trent moved closer. "But maybe you're on to something. Hey, Neil, would it help if Cal got the caller on the line?"

"Of course, but once the guy hears it's not the dead dude, he's gonna hang up. I need him on the line for more than a second."

"Maybe Cal can piss the guy off and get him to start talking. How long do you need him on the line?"

Neil wasn't sure. He'd never run into a number that he couldn't track. "I don't know. Maybe thirty seconds?"

Trent turned to Cal. "You think you can get under the guy's skin?"

Stokes grinned. "That's my specialty. Just ask Neil."

Patel gave him the finger again, then refocused on the tracking program.

FIVE MINUTES LATER, everybody was ready. Gaucho had two of his four man teams loaded into their vehicles in the parking garage. Neil sat poised at his computer, ready to track the call. Cal picked up the dead man's phone. "Everyone ready?" There were murmurs of assent around the room.

Cal nodded and dialed the number.

NAKAMURA GLANCED AT HIS PHONE. The call was from Matsura. He breathed a sigh of relief and answered.

"Where are you?"

"In hell," Cal replied.

Nakamura's eyes went wide. "Who is this?"

"Somebody you don't want to fuck with."

"Where is my employee?"

"Oh, you mean the dead guy?"

Nakamura couldn't believe what he was hearing. Had they really killed Matsura?

"Where is he?"

"I told you. He's probably having a nice little conversation with the devil right now."

"You will pay for this! I will unleash all..."

"Now listen here, asshole. I think it's about time you and I had a little chat. I'm sick of having to kick the crap out of all your goons."

Ishi kept motioning for his father to end the call. The manufacturer had promised it was untraceable, but it was stupid to take the chance. The elder Nakamura ignored him. His pride demanded he confront the cocky American.

"So you are prepared to have me release all our evidence to the authorities?"

"That's where you keep misunderstanding. I could give a shit about a bunch of politicians. Let them fend for themselves. What do you really have? Some pictures of old guys hanging out and talking? That's all retired politicians do!"

Nakamura didn't know how to respond. His contact had assured him that the contents of the envelope would scare off the meddlers.

"I think you are the one misunderstanding me. There will soon be a shift in your puny world. An avalanche is about to cover your little company. I will destroy you."

Cal laughed. "You're welcome to try, buddy. Thing is, next time why don't you show up to the party instead of sending one of your cronies?"

Ishi finally grabbed the phone out of his father's hand and ended the call.

"What are you doing?!" Kazuo Nakamura screamed.

"I'm saving you from making a big mistake, Father. Is it not you who is always telling me to keep my emotions out of business? We are too close to victory to lose our tempers."

Nakamura took a deep breath. His son was right. He wasn't used to having things not go his way. He couldn't remember the last time he'd failed at anything. It was an unsettling feeling.

"I'm sorry, son. Thank you for putting things in perspective."

Ishi nodded and handed the phone back to his father. "Should we go back to our planning?"

Nakamura nodded and returned his attention to the Las Vegas Convention Center diagram.

———

"Did you get him?" asked Cal, expectantly.

"No."

"What do you mean? I swear I had him on the line for over a minute, Neil."

"I know, but they're using some really new technology. I didn't even get a blip in my program."

"Shit," Cal muttered to himself.

Zimmer walked over to the pair. "Did you really mean what you said about not caring about the politicians?"

Stokes looked into the man's eyes. "We weren't talking about the list, Congressman. It's something else." They'd chosen to keep any talk of the Council away from Zimmer.

"Something you can't tell me about?"

"Yeah."

"Look, I'm in the middle of this thing too. I think you need to..."

Cal's eyes flared. "I think you need to remember that we're here to save YOUR ass, Congressman. The last time I checked, I wasn't the one who got caught with his pants down. Last time I checked, me and my guys are the ones getting shot at. Now, if you want me to lock you in a room until this is over, I'm happy to do it."

"How dare you...?" Zimmer started to respond before Trent stepped between the two.

"Alright, fellas. How about we all take a breather and chill out. I think we could all use a little food and a good stiff drink."

Cal and Zimmer continued to stare at each other. Brandon was the first to walk out of the room, followed by Trent.

Stokes watched the two men go. He couldn't wait to be done with Zimmer.

LAS VEGAS, NEVADA

4:42PM, SEPTEMBER 18TH

Cal dialed Andy's cell number.

"Hey, I thought you would've called earlier."

"Yeah, sorry. Had a little unexpected...incident," Cal explained.

"No problem. You want me to come your way or can you come meet me?"

"Where are they putting you guys up?"

"We're staying at the MGM Grand."

"I'll come see you. Mind if I bring a couple friends?"

"Sure."

Cal woke Brian, snoozing in the recliner.

"Hey, we're going to see Andy." Brian just nodded. "You wanna come too, Daniel?"

"I'm in."

"Alright, let's go in five minutes."

Everyone prepared to leave. They wouldn't be walking the streets of Vegas unarmed anymore. This time Cal and Brian would be bringing their security badges and concealed carry permits. It was one of the perks of SSI's VIP protection division.

Cal knew he was running a risk by hitting the street again, but he had to warn Andy. Besides, he had his lucky charm with him: Daniel Briggs. He'd started analyzing how he could best utilize the sniper in the future. Maybe Briggs would become his vigilant companion like Travis Haden to his father and Todd Dunn to Travis. In his line of work, Cal could never have enough expert warriors around.

Five minutes later, the trio walked out the door. Each one hoped they wouldn't run into more Ichiban goons.

THEY ARRIVED at the MGM Grand without incident. Instead of trying to take back routes, they'd decided to walk through the most congested public areas. With the Democratic National Convention starting the next day, the sidewalks were overflowing with revelers.

Cal wondered how the convention attendees would feel if they knew about the imminent threat to the big party. It was par for the course and he knew it. Most Americans lived in blissful ignorance knowing nothing about the silent forces of good and evil at work all around them.

Andy opened the hotel room door and invited everyone in. Cal introduced Daniel to the Marine Captain. The two men shook hands and did the Marine size-up.

"Can I get you guys anything?" Andy asked.

"I'd kill for a coffee and a beer," Cal sighed.

"In that order?"

"How about just the beer?"

Andy nodded and took orders from the other two. Once they'd gotten their drinks and taken a seat, Cal told the whole Vegas story to his good friend.

Capt. Andrews didn't interrupt; he just shook his head in amazement time and time again. Cal finally finished. "So I really wanted to make sure you got a heads-up. As you can see, there's some squirrely shit going on around here."

"That's the understatement of the year," Andy commented.

"Have any ideas? Anything we haven't thought of?"

Andy took another swig of beer and contemplated the question. There were too many possibilities to consider.

"I'm just thinking out loud here, but what if it's all a wild goose chase? What if they're throwing you guys red herrings just to keep you away from what they're really trying to do?"

Cal shook his head. "I don't think so. This is shaping up to be something big. We really think the Convention is the trigger."

Andy wasn't convinced. During his time with the Silent Drill Team, he'd seen the capabilities of the Secret Service and the FBI. They'd probably spent months investigating every scumbag in a twenty-mile radius of Las Vegas. These guys knew how to do their homework. The last thing they wanted on their watch was a dead President. There wouldn't be a weapon anywhere near the leader of the Free World.

It was Daniel who broke the silence. "Captain, how about anything out of the ordinary? Is there anything they've asked you guys to do during your routine that you don't typically do?"

"Well, most of our routines are pretty similar. Sometimes our entrance is a little different. Like this time, they're keeping us a secret. You know how they have those big stages for the Super Bowl, where the singer comes up through the floor? Well, they wanted to do that, with a twist."

"What kind of a twist?" Daniel asked, suddenly feeling the hair on the back of his neck stand up.

"They've got this huge trailer that they're gonna pull out. Think of a semi trailer, only like four times as big. So they put us in there, a cannon booms over the speaker system, the sides of the trailer flip down, we're standing there ready to kick ass, and then we march out onto the floor. It's actually pretty cool. We've been practicing it for weeks. We'll have one last run-through tomorrow morning."

They were all impressed. Twenty-four Marines in dress blues made a beautiful sight. The Silent Drill Team as the surprise entertainment would be a big hit.

"Who've you been coordinating that with?" Cal questioned.

"Some woman on the President's event planning staff."

"Do you remember her name?"

"Sure. Janet Riley."

"Why do I know that name?" Cal thought aloud.

"Because she's on the blackmail list," Daniel answered.

Janet Riley, a pretty brunette from Los Angeles, pored over the itinerary for the upcoming convention. Taking the reins in the early spring, Riley brought her Hollywood talent and flash to the President's campaign. Over the past fifteen years, Janet had climbed tooth and nail up the competitive Los Angeles public relations ladder. She'd landed her dream job two years earlier as head of PR for one of the largest studios in L.A. The job included the added benefit of rubbing elbows with some of the biggest influencers in the entertainment industry. During the day she submitted news releases and coordinated publicity for the studio's biggest stars. By night, she networked with Hollywood elite at movie premiers and after parties. She was very good at her job.

It was at one event that she'd met the President's campaign manager. They'd hit it off and kept in touch until the day the campaign needed a new Events Coordinator for the election. She'd worked out a leave of absence from her studio and joined the campaign trail. It wasn't as glamorous as Hollywood, but Janet felt like she was doing her patriotic duty.

Her mind was swirling. She had so many moving parts for the Convention. Sometimes she wondered how she'd be able to keep it all together. To make matters worse, they were doing things a little different this year. Typically, the convention floor was full of constituents for the entire event. For this DNC, the first day would be more entertaining. The lower level would be empty, except for the entertainment and an occasional 'Rah Rah' speech from party leaders. They'd booked three of the President's favorite bands to start. The Marines would really kick things off toward the end of the night. The President wanted the tone to be patriotic, hence the many strings pulled for the Silent Drill Team to perform. In the end, everything would come together. It always did.

Riley looked at her watch. Her stomach grumbled as she thought about the lunch she'd missed and the dinner that would probably also be skipped. She had just a couple of hours before the Marine Corps reps came to the convention center to walk through the space. They'd requested the meeting to finalize the show's particulars. Janet had enough on her plate and wished she didn't have to go. These Marines were perfectionists though. They wanted to make sure every detail was ironed out prior to show time. Riley cursed them and their efficiency.

To make matters worse, the President had just requested to be at the dress rehearsal the following morning before any of the crowd showed. He wanted to see the Silent Drill Team run-through and spend a couple minutes mingling with the Marines. Capt. Andrews would not be happy with the change. At least they wouldn't have to contend with a large Secret Service presence in the morning without a crowd being there.

In another hour, Janet would head down to the convention floor. After that, she'd walk back to the hotel for one final meeting. The guy from Ichiban Gaming had called earlier in the day. He said he had another small request for the convention. Janet wanted to be done with the guy. He gave her the creeps, but she couldn't really deny the request. After all, he had pulled her out of that little situation back in L.A. four months ago. She never should have listened to her girlfriend and gone to that party. Janet knew there would be drugs all over the man's house and she had been secretly battling addiction for five years. In the end, she gave in and got wasted. It was only by a stroke of luck, and the help of that Japanese guy, that she avoided landing in jail.

He'd asked for nothing in return, until two months before the convention. She felt obligated to help because she was in his debt. The request wasn't out of the ordinary. So the guy wanted one of his companies to do some of the work at the convention. Who didn't? It was a big deal to be one of the vendors for a political rally. Besides, the bid was competitive so technically Riley wasn't doing anything wrong. It was her call which companies would be hired to setup for the week's events.

EVERYONE IN THE ROOM FROZE. Had they just found a piece of the puzzle?

"Are you telling me that I'm about to go to a meeting with someone on that list?" Andy asked incredulously.

"Looks like it. But the question is, what is she doing to help these guys?" wondered Cal.

"I'm seriously thinking about calling my boss and pulling the plug. Am I the only one that's getting a really bad feeling about this?" Andy asked.

No one answered. They all felt the same way. There was only one direction this was going: downhill.

"Andy, how about you go meet with Ms. Riley and see what you can find out? Who knows, maybe you'll stumble onto something. Who's going with you?"

"My First Sergeant and my squad leaders."

"Good. Starting now, I don't think you or your Marines should be traveling alone. Can you get that word to your men?"

"Sure. I'll call their rooms right now. Anything else?" Andy asked his friend.

Cal couldn't think of anything. "I don't think so. Just keep your eyes open and let us know if you notice anything fishy. Can you give me until tomorrow morning to make the call about cancelling the show?"

Andy wasn't so sure. His sixth sense told him to pack up his boys and head back home. "I guess. But you better be damn sure you're doing everything you can to find out what they're planning."

"We're all over it."

They said their goodbyes and left Andy to make his calls. Cal hoped that they would have a better idea of what they were dealing with by tomorrow's deadline.

"MAKE sure the Riley woman follows your directions. Remember, we cannot afford another failure."

The Japanese man bowed to his employer. Kazuo Nakamura sat

back in his chair as his underling departed. In less than twenty-four hours, everything would change. He looked forward to returning to Japan as a conquering hero.

WASHINGTON, D.C

8:42PM, SEPTEMBER 18TH

"Are you ready to go, Mr. President?" the head of the Commander in Chief's protection detail asked.

"Sure am." He stretched as he rose from his chair. "Sam, we've really gotta tell the Air Force One boys to stop booking these late flights."

The Secret Service agent chuckled. "Well, sir. You know it makes it a lot easier for the airports when we're not stopping traffic in the middle of rush hour."

"I know. It's just that the kids never get enough sleep when we fly after nine pm. You'd think that after four years they'd be used to it."

"Yes, sir."

The President glanced at his new smart phone and sighed at the time. "Well, I guess we better get going."

He followed his detail out to the waiting caravan.

LAS VEGAS, NEVADA

8:45PM, SEPTEMBER 18TH

Capt. Andrews and his small Marine contingent showed up at the Las Vegas Convention Center fifteen minutes early. He'd given word to keep their eyes and ears open without giving details. The Marine Captain didn't look like much to strangers, but his Marines knew the boyish face belied a fearless warrior and strong leader. His gaze remained serious as they toured the staging area.

"What the hell is that?" Andy pointed to the two identical trailers waiting side by side.

"We had to bring in a backup, Captain," answered Janet Riley as she strolled in, hands full of paperwork. "The last thing we wanted was to have the first one crap out and then be dead in the water."

The explanation made sense to Andy. Anytime Marines did a dog-and-pony show for VIPs, they liked to have backups, just in case.

"So which one are we loading into?"

"The one on the right. It's got a small green sticker on it. The backup is on the left with a small red sticker on the entrance ramp."

"Why don't you guys go inspect the trailers while I have a word with Ms. Riley."

His Marines split up and set about testing the mechanics of the two trailers.

"How can I help you, Captain?" Riley asked tiredly. She was ready to wrap the meeting up. It would've been easier for the Marines to just do their inspection without her, but Andrews had requested her presence.

"Are we still a go for the practice run tomorrow morning?" Andy could barely conceal his suspicion of the woman. He wasn't used to holding his tongue. If so much wasn't riding on him to keep his mouth shut, he'd call the woman out right now.

"Uh, yeah, with one change."

Crap. Here we go, thought Andy.

"The President wants to watch the practice run and then come meet your Marines."

It wasn't what Andy had expected. Being part of the world's most famous drill team, he was used to visits by the President and other foreign dignitaries. Considering the strings the White House had pulled to get the Marines there, it wasn't surprising that he wanted to have a quick photo op.

"Alright. I don't think that'll be a problem. Where will he be during the dry run?"

Riley pointed to the far end of the ground floor. "My workers are going to set up a couple of chairs for the President. That's where you guys should finish before you march off, right?"

"Correct. So just forget the about face and march off?"

"If that's okay," Riley requested politely.

The Marines wouldn't mind meeting the President. He was, after all, their President. He wasn't a bad guy and it was rumored that he'd really taken a liking to the Silent Drill Team.

"Sure. If we can make it quick though. I want to get my guys out of their uniforms and taking a break before tomorrow night. We'll be cooped up in that trailer long enough."

"No problem. I think they've only got ten minutes scheduled for that anyway. Anything else I can answer for you?" added Riley, hopefully.

"Not that I can think of. Thanks for meeting us down here. If it's okay, we'll just spend some time walking the arena. You don't need to be around for that."

Riley was grateful. "Sure. Take as much time as you need."

Andy thanked Riley for her assistance and she departed for her room next door at the Hilton. Maybe she'd have a few minutes to take off her high heels before her next meeting.

10:10PM

Andy walked back to his room after a couple of last words with his Marines. They'd all be ready to hop in the vans at first light. The boys knew better than to hit the town tonight. Regardless, he'd passed the word that everyone was to remain in their rooms until the morning. They could party tomorrow night after the show.

He pulled out his phone and dialed Cal.

"Hey, you find out anything?" Cal asked eagerly.

"Not really."

"No changes?"

"Just some minor things."

"Like what?"

"They've got a backup trailer for the show and the President is coming to our practice tomorrow."

"Is that out of the ordinary?" Cal wanted to shut down the show before the Marines were put in a bad situation.

"Not really. It's actually not a bad idea to have a backup trailer. That thing is frickin' huge. We'd be screwed if one of tires went out or the mechanical door stopped working. As for the President visiting, I don't see anything wrong with it. Sometimes the bigwigs want to meet us beforehand because after the real show it's total chaos," Andy answered honestly.

"What about the Riley chick? Was she acting strange?" There had to be something.

"Nope. Looked a little stressed out, but I would be too if I had her job. Sorry I couldn't help, Cal."

"It's not your fault, man. Thanks for keeping this quiet. We'll get to the bottom of it before tomorrow night's show. Wait, do you think you could get me and Briggs and a few other guys in for the practice run tomorrow? I'd like to see the layout and take a look around."

"Let me call one of the Secret Service guys that I just talked to over there. I don't think it'll be a problem as long as you don't come armed and keep your distance from the President."

Cal laughed out loud. "No offense, Andy, but I'll pass on meeting the President."

Andy chuckled. "Cool. I'll call you back as soon as I know."

The call ended and Andy dialed the Secret Service agent's number.

"Hey, Pete. I've got a favor to ask."

11:13PM

Congressman Zimmer was just getting ready to hop into bed when his cell phone rang. It was his father.

"Hey, Dad. What's up?"

"Are you ready for the Convention?"

"You still think I should be going with you?"

"Of course. I need you there with me. By the way, there's a slight change for tomorrow. I know I told you we wouldn't need to be at the convention center until five, but I just got a call from the President. He's going to the venue early to watch the Silent Drill Team practice. He invited us to come along to watch and stick around to chat afterward. I think he's going to try to get me to be Secretary of State again. I'll have to tell him no, but you can't refuse a Presidential summoning."

"Why don't you want to be at State, Dad? I thought it was something you'd pushed for before?"

"Maybe with Hank Waller in office, but the current President and I don't exactly see eye-to-eye on much these days. You remember that little argument we had about our CIA assets in Jordan?"

Brandon did remember. His father had grown into a hugely popular figure among intelligence and military personnel. Despite his political affiliation, he was a staunch defender of a powerful armed forces and a robust intelligence arm. The tiff with the President about Jordan had been about the President's decision to pull half of the CIA's human assets stationed there in exchange for a larger drone and signals intelligence presence. Sen. Zimmer had argued that while technology certainly augmented the intelligence gathering process, spies and informants were absolutely necessary. The President, still pushing for full withdrawal from Afghanistan, didn't relent. His closest advisors still professed the increased use of technology because it protected American lives.

Sen. Zimmer almost screamed in the President's face that if it weren't for intelligence community's boots on the ground, Saddam Hussein and Osama bin Laden never would have been found. In the end the President won and twenty-five CIA personnel were pulled out of Jordan. A week later, the coup in Syria caught the American government by surprise. One of the duties of the withdrawn CIA staff was to monitor the situation within the Syrian government. They'd even found seven exiled Syrian officials living in Amman, Jordan, and convinced them to be American informants. Each man still had extensive networks inside Syria. A day before the coup, all seven men disappeared. It was later determined, the lack of American protection around the men had allowed their capture and subsequent murder.

No, Sen. Zimmer would respect the office, but he could not serve directly under the man. Their ideological differences were too extreme.

"So why do you want me to come with you tomorrow?" Brandon asked.

"I think I'm gonna need a little moral support, Son. Besides, it wouldn't hurt for you to mingle with him a little bit. He is the President."

Brandon wasn't sure. He'd have to check with the SSI guys. Then again, what could it hurt?

"Will it be okay to bring Trent with me?"

"Is that your bodyguard?"

"Yeah. It's kinda one of the requirements you signed me up for."

The Senator thought about it for a second. "I don't see why not. I'll call the President's office and have them add him to the list. What's his full name again?"

Brandon relayed Trent's full name and former military rank. What would Trent say about meeting the President?

"I'll have my driver come pick you two up at six thirty."

They ended their conversation with a quick goodbye. Brandon walked into the adjoining living room and found Trent flipping through the TV channels. "Anything good?" Zimmer asked.

Trent answered without looking up. "Nope. It's all commentary on the Convention. This damn TV can't even get me the Falcons game replay."

"Hey, something's just come up."

Trent muted the television and looked at Zimmer. "What's up?"

"My dad got invited to meet with the President tomorrow morning. He wants you and me to come with him."

"What? Cal's not gonna like that."

"I know his attitude isn't your fault, Top, but Cal's being an ass. I don't really care what he thinks right now."

Trent had spent enough time with the Congressman to know that the man had truly experienced a wake-up call. More than anything, the comment was a reaction to his most recent conversation with Cal.

"Congressman, I know you two got into it, but Cal's trying to do the right thing. Put yourself in his shoes. He has to protect you PLUS all the rest of us. All I'm saying is that it's a lot of pressure and you might want to give the guy a break."

Zimmer exhaled. He knew Trent was right. Brandon had grown to respect the SSI men immensely. He trusted their judgment and promised himself that, if allowed to stay in office, he'd never lose that perspective. There were secret men and women, true patriots, that laid their lives on the line so that men like him could do their jobs and America could remain free. It was something he couldn't forget.

"I know," Zimmer replied. "But, this is really important. Have you ever met the President?"

"Nope. They don't let many big dudes like me around the White House, unless you just won the Super Bowl."

"Well, this is your chance. I'm sure Cal will be good with it as long as you're with me. Do you mind asking him? I don't think he's ready to talk to me yet," Zimmer almost pleaded.

The Marine thought about it. On one hand, he was sure Cal would be pissed. It really wasn't smart to let the Congressman out until everything blew over. On the other hand, they'd be surrounded by Secret Service agents AND he'd get to watch the Silent Drill Team. What could go wrong?

"I'll talk to Cal."

"Thanks, Top. You won't regret it," Zimmer smiled.

11:47PM

Cal put his phone down and closed his eyes in frustration. Another wrinkle.

"Okay, guys, one more change. That was Top on the phone. Seems as though the Congressman got himself invited to the party. He'll be at the convention center during the rehearsal tomorrow morning, too. I told Top to stick to his ass like glue."

Brian and Daniel looked up from their card game. "So who's going with you tomorrow?"

"Andy called back and said he could only get two passes from the Secret Service. No offense, Doc, but I think I'm gonna take Daniel with me."

Ramirez waived off the apology. "No biggy. That means at least one of us can sleep in tomorrow."

"You cool to come with me?" Cal asked Briggs.

"No problem. I guess we won't be taking any weapons." It was posed as a question.

"Yeah. We can leave them out in the car. I'll bet they'll have that place pretty buttoned up before the big show. I'm more worried about tomorrow night. Why don't you guys hit the sack? I'm just gonna go over that new list Neil gave us. I want to memorize as many faces as I can."

Daniel and Brian finished their game, cleaned up, and went to their rooms. Cal watched them go, wishing he could do the same. It was already midnight. He'd be up for at least two more hours, poring over the files Neil kept digging out of the Ichiban network.

1:25AM

Cal had just dozed off when a natty-looking Neil Patel tapped him on the shoulder.

"Hey, what's up?" Cal asked groggily.

"I just found something I think you need to see." The earnestness on Neil's face shook the fuzziness from Cal. He followed Neil to the computer station.

He watched as Neil pulled up a file. "So, earlier I found the original video file of the murder scene. Remember that in the one posted to YouTube, no one else was shown and the girl's face was blurred? Well, this one I'm about to play was put together not only with clips of the Congressman, but also with a full view of the woman's face. You ready to watch it?"

Cal knew they'd find some video like this, so he wasn't sure why Neil was being so damn serious. "Is there something you're not telling me?"

"I need you to watch the video first. Then I'll tell you what it all means."

Cal knew Neil wouldn't waste his time, so Cal nodded to his friend. Patel pressed the Play button.

Cal watched as the cameraman walked around the body. It was similar to the shots he'd already seen online, but this time it showed a full view of the woman's face. She was undoubtedly beautiful. She actually looked peaceful, despite not having any of her limbs attached. *She must've been drugged*, Cal thought.

Next, the camera panned over to Congressman Zimmer. He was lying unconscious, naked, and covered in the woman's blood. The sharp knife had obviously fallen out of his bloody hand and sat inches from his gory appendage.

Holy shit!, Cal thought. He couldn't imagine waking up to that. It reminded him of the iconic horse head scene from *The Godfather*. But this was different. This was a dismembered person. *Maybe I need to cut Zimmer some slack.*

The video finished and Neil looked up at his friend. "So what was your takeaway from that?"

After pausing for a moment to gather his jumbled thoughts, Cal replied. "First thing is maybe we can find out who that girl is. I also just realized Zimmer really went through some crazy stuff there. I'm surprised he's not in the nut house after that."

Neil agreed. Working with SSI, he'd seen some gory crime scenes. This was something different though. You could almost feel the detached brutality and evil of whoever had killed, then cut the poor girl up. It reeked of someone who had absolutely no regard for human life.

"You're right about finding out who the girl was. I ran her through the FBI's facial recognition system..." Neil had a way of hacking into any government agency he needed at the moment, "...and I got a match."

"Just tell me the punch line, Neil," ordered Cal impatiently.

Neil hesitated, "Her name was Patricia."

"I thought Zimmer said her name was Beth."

"Apparently, she wasn't telling him the whole truth."

"What's her last name?" Cal asked, totally intrigued.

"Waller."

"Waller? Is she related to President Waller?"

Neil nodded. "She's his daughter."

"Oh shit!"

LAS VEGAS, NEVADA

1:30AM, SEPTEMBER 19TH

Cal hesitated before grabbing his phone. Who to call first? He was in completely uncharted territory here. Should he call President Waller first? Should he call Travis and get his opinion? His sluggish mind struggled to come to grips with the latest information.

How in the world had she just happened to run into Congressman Zimmer? And, more importantly, why did she call herself Beth? Was she part of a larger Japanese plot?

It was too much for his tired mind to unravel alone. He needed help.

Reluctantly, he grabbed the secure phone and placed a call to SSI headquarters. He asked the man on duty to patch him through to Travis's encrypted line.

Ten seconds later, Travis was on the telephone, voice heavy with sleep. "What's going on, cuz?"

"We just got some news that I don't know what to do with. I need your help."

Travis was suddenly awake. It was rare that his cousin called to ask for anything. This must be big. "What's up?"

Cal told him about Waller's daughter.

"You've got to be shitting me! Have you told him yet?"

"No. That's why I'm calling you! What am I supposed to tell him?"

Travis had no clue. In the military, trained teams were sent to the homes of troops killed in action. Luckily, during his time with the SEALs he'd never had to pull that duty. How in the world do you tell an ex-President that his daughter was murdered and now being displayed all over the Internet?

"This is a big fucking mess, Cal."

"Tell me about it. So what do I do?"

"I think you need to call him and request a meeting right now."

Cal couldn't think of anything better. If it had been his daughter, he'd want to know right away as well.

"Okay, I'll make the call."

"Let me know if you need my help."

Cal killed the connection and dialed Waller's number. He picked up after one ring. Apparently, he was used to calls in the middle of the night because he sounded wide awake.

"Hey, Cal."

"Hello, sir. I've, uh, got some news that I need to share with you," Cal started hesitantly.

"Can you tell me over the phone?"

"No, sir. I think I better head over to your place, if that's okay."

"You think that's safe?"

"I'll bring a couple of my guys with me. If you can just make sure your detail knows we're coming."

"No problem. I'll see you in a few."

The call ended and Cal gazed out the window. He could clearly see the happy crowds enjoying the warm night air, hopping from casino to casino. Cal wished he were with them. Instead, he had to deliver the worst news possible to a President of the United States.

2:13AM

He'd woken up Daniel and the two met up with three guys Gaucho sent over. They hurried down to the parking garage and loaded into the rental car. Fifteen minutes later, they arrived outside Waller's hotel. Cal and Daniel hopped out and headed in.

Waller met them at his door and let the two Marines in. The three men were alone, the security detail stayed right outside the suite. Waller's wife was asleep in the adjoining bedroom.

"So what's going on, Cal?" President Waller was in an expensive blue robe. Even past one in the morning, the man looked put together.

"I think we better sit down, sir," Cal requested.

"I take it by your tone and the fact that you've forgotten to call me Hank that this is pretty serious."

Cal merely nodded and took a seat on the large sectional. Waller had weathered more crises than most men will ever have to endure, but the look on Cal's face sent prickles up his spine.

"Sir, we found out who the girl is in Congressman Zimmer's video."

By the look on his face, Waller was starting to put the pieces together. "Just tell me, Cal," Waller asked quietly.

"It's your daughter Patricia, sir."

Waller stared at Cal blankly. He hadn't seen his daughter in almost a year. She'd left for Los Angeles almost three years ago to pursue a career in acting. He and his wife had scattered contact with their only child. In fact, it'd been almost eight months since they'd last talked.

Shortly after arriving in L.A., Patricia had sent her security detail home and refused any more money from her parents. She was going to make it on her own. A part of Hank Waller was proud of his daughter for stepping out and being independent. It was often hard for the children of well-known politicians to have real lives. Waller was happy she'd chosen her own life.

He allowed her to live without the bodyguards, but still secretly kept tabs on her with a private security company. A few months after her independence, he'd received word from the owner of the company that his daughter had fallen in with a disreputable crowd of young actors. All played wholesome characters on TV and film, but in their private lives gorged on heavy drugs and explicit sex. Waller was crushed. He'd thought his daughter would have better sense.

Upon receiving the news, Waller and his wife hopped on a flight to California. They'd tracked down Patricia, who'd by then taken up with a local movie producer twice her age. It was obvious that she'd taken to the drug lifestyle, her skin hanging loosely from her pretty figure. Hank Waller almost cried when she'd first come to the door. He was losing his baby.

Her parents confronted the issue and threatened to have her committed. The intervention hadn't gone well. Patricia stormed out of the house and disappeared. For weeks, the security company couldn't track her down. Then three months later, Patricia had shown up on their doorstep completely out of the blue. She looked clean and healthy. He almost didn't recognize her at first. She'd grown into a beautiful woman. Hank and his wife cried as they hugged and welcomed her home.

Over lunch, she'd told them the entire story. In short, she'd fallen in with the wrong crowd and allowed them to manipulate her. She was embarrassed but owned up to her shortcomings.

"Most of all I'm sad that I worried you guys," she'd told her parents.

The weekend was perfect. They'd cancelled everything and spent time as a family. That had been eleven months ago. Then she'd apparently gotten a job with a Hollywood PR firm. Traveling extensively, contact had been rare, minus the occasional quick text hello. They'd wondered about the lack of correspondence, but just figured she'd been busy.

Hank Waller put his face in his hands. "How could this have happened?" he asked to no one in particular.

Cal didn't know what to say. Once again, he was in completely unfamiliar territory.

"Is there anything else I can do, sir?"

Waller looked up, the misery plain in his watery eyes. And yet, a spark of anger seethed. "You find whoever did this to my little girl, Cal, and I'll help you destroy them."

2:33AM

Cal and Daniel left the President with his quietly sobbing wife.

"You think they'll be okay?" Daniel asked. He hadn't said a word in Waller's posh suite.

Stokes knew Waller was a strong man. You can't be President without having an extra gear. Still, the man was human. He wondered how it would affect Waller's performance at the convention.

"I'll think they'll pull through."

"I'll pray for them."

Cal nodded. He appreciated having Daniel's calming influence around. In response, Cal also said a silent prayer for the Wallers.

3:07AM

They finally made it back to the Bellagio after fighting through the drunken crowds. Everyone was headed to the closest food joint before heading in for the night.

"Thanks for coming, Daniel. I'll wake you up in a few hours."

Briggs patted Cal on the back and headed off to get what sleep he could.

Cal took one last look out the large panoramic window. The lights of The Strip shone brightly in the dark desert. He hoped the morning would be uneventful.

The Marine set his alarm and fell back onto the over-sized couch. One of the benefits of his time in the Marine Corps was the ability to sleep anywhere, anytime. Cal was asleep in less than two minutes.

LAS VEGAS, NEVADA

5:02AM, SEPTEMBER 19TH

The First Sergeant had just called Capt. Andrew's room to wake him. Andy kicked his legs off the bed and walked to the bathroom. The details of the day's performance were already aligning themselves in his brain. It would be a very busy day.

5:42AM

Cal's alarm went off just as he slipped into one of his recurring dreams. He'd just found out that his parents had died and he was running to the Marine recruiting office. Problem was, in his dream, he just kept running and running. He never got close to his final destination.

He shook his head and looked up to see Daniel sitting across from him, apparently ready to go.

"How long have you been up?"

"Since five-thirty. I'm showered and ready to go."

This guy was good. He'd have to remember that. "Alright, give me a minute to rinse off. You mind making me a cup of coffee?"

"No problem."

Cal trudged off to the spacious bathroom and turned the shower to cold. He needed to shock his system. Today would be a long day and Cal needed a clear head. He held his breath and stepped into the frigid downpour.

5:49AM

"Are your men in position?" Kazuo Nakamura asked his compatriot.

"Yes, Nakamura-san. They are prepared to die a warrior's death," the man barked earnestly to his master.

"Hopefully, it will not come to that. We will need many men when we take back the empire. Have you made arrangements for myself and my son?"

The man relayed the plan. Nakamura was satisfied. They would have a front row seat to the coming carnage.

He examined the Nambu pistol in his hand one last time. It was a gift from his father. Somehow, he'd been able to keep it hidden from the authorities. He'd told young Kazuo that the pistol had served him well in the Great War. Many enemies had lost their lives to the simple weapon. Nakamura's eyes flared as he imagined using it against his enemies. Yes, today would be a day to remember.

5:56AM

Capt. Andrews looked at himself in the mirror. Even though it could be a royal pain sometimes, he still loved his dress blues. It made him feel like a Marine. As an afterthought, he walked into the bedroom and grabbed the shopping bag Cal's friend Daniel had brought. He'd given it to Andy just before leaving.

"Don't let Cal know, sir, but I thought you might need these."

Andy had looked into the bag, and found a Sig Sauer 9mm pistol, along with two replacement magazines full of ammunition. He silently thanked the sniper for his forethought.

Taking the weapon from the bag, he placed it uncomfortably in his back waistband. There wasn't much room inside the form-fitting uniform, but he didn't care. He wasn't going in naked. Andy deposited one magazine into each of his front pockets.

After looking at himself in the mirror one last time to make sure his weapons weren't obviously visible, he made his way out to the waiting vans.

LAS VEGAS, NEVADA

6:15AM, SEPTEMBER 19TH

The Marines filed into the convention center, carrying their rifles at port arms. Andy wished they'd been able to bring ammunition for the damn things. He still had a really bad feeling about their upcoming performance. It felt like they were walking into an ambush.

He chatted with the two Secret Service agents at the main entrance, waiting for Cal to arrive. Two minutes later, Stokes walked up dressed in black t-shirt, sport coat, and designer jeans. *So that's Cal's new uniform*, Andy thought. Cal had offered his good friend a position at SSI, but Capt. Andrews wasn't ready to leave the Corps. He came from a military family. His father and grandfather both retired from the military. Andy figured he would probably stay in for one more tour and then get out. After all, he did have bright prospects as a civilian. SSI was a good place for a warrior to end up.

"Hey, Andy!" Cal called cheerfully, Daniel walking smoothly beside.

Andy handed Cal and Daniel their visitor passes as the Secret Service agents did a quick frisking of both men. "Easy, boys. Your mama know you do that at work?" Cal asked.

The large agent chuckled as he finished frisking Cal with a hard smack on the ass. "Have fun, jarhead."

"Army?" Cal asked the muscular man, rubbing his rear.

"SEAL."

"You know what they say, sailor…?"

"What's that, knuckle-dragger?" the agent asked with a grin.

"What happens in the Navy, stays in the Navy," Cal commented innocently.

The agent's partner laughed and ushered the two Marines into the convention center after taking their cell phones for safekeeping.

Cal and Daniel looked around in amazement. The place was huge. It took them a full five minutes of brisk walking to get to the main event area. They didn't run into anyone else. The convention would kick off a little after 5pm with doors opening at 3pm. It looked like everything was ready and waiting for the impending visitors.

They finally reached the staging area where the Marines were waiting. Cal let them get ready as he and Daniel first examined the trailers and then walked to the entryway leading into the arena. The exhibition space was about the size of a football field. The Silent Drill Team would have plenty of room to maneuver, even with the huge trailer. Cal could make out the short row of chairs on the opposite end of the field where the President would be sitting. He hadn't arrived yet.

Capt. Andrews walked over. "They said you guys can grab a seat on this side of the arena." He pointed right over his head where seating was arranged stadium style.

"Sounds good. What time does the show start?" Cal asked.

"We load into the trailer at quarter 'til seven. They close us in and wheel us into the arena five minutes later. Why don't you guys head up to your seats and I'll see you after the show?"

Andy headed back to his Marines who were carefully being inspected by their squad leaders. They wouldn't be caught dead with even a speck of lint on their uniforms, even if it was practice.

Cal and Daniel took the set of stairs up to the landing where two folding chairs were clearly marked with "Jarhead #1" and "Jarhead #2" written on pieces of white paper.

"Those Secret Service guys sure are funny," Cal noted wryly.

From their seats, they could observe the entire field. It would give them a perfect view. He pointed to the highest point at the opposite end of the arena. They could see the two Zimmers and Trent filing into their row. Cal waved but couldn't catch Trent's eye.

The only thing not in view was the staging area. Little did they know that that was where they should have been looking.

6:27

Trent took the lead as he escorted the Senator and Congressman to their seats. Senator Zimmer had elected to keep his security detail outside. He'd reasoned that the Secret Service would already have the area sufficiently canvassed and secured.

Out of habit, MSgt Trent glanced all around the huge space. He saw Cal and Daniel at the far end of the hall. He waved and Cal motioned back.

Continuing his scan, he looked at the new VIP boxes. He didn't see anyone prepping. Strange. Just as he moved his gaze past the last window, he caught a flicker of movement in the skybox closest to the President. Probably just a cleaning crew, he thought as the figure disappeared again. The Senator was right; the Secret Service should have this place buttoned up tight.

Trent finished his inspection and looked back at the center of the arena. He looked forward to seeing Marines in dress blues again.

6:29AM

"Get back, you fool," whispered Nakamura harshly to his son. They were comfortably situated in recliners at the back of the skybox closest to the President.

"He didn't see me, Father," complained Ishi. He was getting tired of his father's paranoia. He'd be glad when this day was over.

"That black man looked back this way..."

"But he's staring at the ground floor again, Father. Let's just sit back and watch the show."

Kazuo Nakamura was too close to accomplishing his long-planned mission to relax. His contacts within the ownership of the convention center had paid off. Rather than having a lot of crew prepping the morning of the event, they'd pushed hard to get all the prep work done the day before the event. Nakamura's compatriot who controlled the event coordinator, Janet Riley, had 'requested' that she get the crew out by midnight in order for them to "get rest before the big event." It was a simple request and had seemed reasonable. Riley had complied willingly.

The lack of workers had allowed the Japanese imperialists to stage their people earlier that morning. The absence of building personnel would also mean fewer witnesses.

Better that the American people hear the news on this morning's telecast, thought Kazuo Nakamura. His people would be gone before the authorities had any inkling of the event. Yes, he had planned it perfectly.

6:40AM

"All right, ladies, everyone in the trailer," barked the First Sergeant. They methodically walked up the ramp and into the expanded trailer. There was interior lighting, but it was still like walking into a coffin.

Capt. Andrews and the 1stSgt were the last to enter. Andy threw the small Asian crewmember outside the door a thumbs-up and held down the control until the ramp was closed. They were now safely ensconced in the large trailer...or so they thought.

6:43AM

The crewman looked around to make sure no one else was around. He was alone. Quickly he typed into his cell phone: *LOAD*.

Ten seconds later, a platoon of seemingly identical Marines entered the staging area from a back entrance. They wore the same uniforms and carried the same M-1 Garand rifles. The only difference was the slightly increased weight of four of the weapons due to the live ammunition inside.

They marched quickly into the backup trailer just as the loud music started booming in the arena. As the ramp door closed, a man in a Marine Captain's uniform turned to the crewmember and snapped a quick salute. The crewmember returned the salute and pulled out a small remote control. He flipped the safety switch and pressed the red button. His duties accomplished, he slipped out a rear exit and drove to the private airfield outside of Las Vegas.

6:45AM

Capt. Andrews was giving the Marines last minute instructions when the booming of the convention theme song shook the trailer. "All right, Marines. That music means we have one minute. Right about now, the President is having a seat in the arena. I know some of you guys would love to give the President a hug, but please resist the temptation."

The Marines laughed with their commander as they fixed their bayonets. When the trailer sides flipped down, they'd be arrayed facing out, bayonets at the ready, as if about to ward off a horde of enemies.

"Let's all get into position," the First Sergeant barked over the loud music.

Andy shifted the pistol in his waistband one last time. The damn thing kept digging into his back. *Maybe I was being a little too paranoid*, he thought.

Just as he moved to the center position, the trailers lights flickered.

Andy looked up and squinted. Was that steam coming out of the ceiling?

6:48AM

"Whew, we just made it," remarked the President.

"Sorry about that, Mr. President. It's Howie's first time in Vegas," the lead Secret Service agent explained jokingly. Howard Grant was the President's driver for the day and a Secret Service veteran of almost twenty years. Contrary to his boss's comment, Grant knew the streets of Las Vegas intimately.

It was actually the President's daughters that had kept them from leaving on-time. They'd insisted on an extended breakfast with Dad. Never one to deny his beautiful girls, the President had relented until his detail leader had discretely tapped on his watch.

The President sat down as the music rose to its first crescendo.

LAS VEGAS, NEVADA

6:50AM, SEPTEMBER 19TH

The oversized trailer moved out of the staging area. It paused at the entryway to the arena and waited for the correct point in the music.

"Good. They got it to the door. I'd love to see the look on the President's face," Nakamura noted to his son.

Ishi didn't bother to respond. He kept his eyes glued to the arena. Father and son anxiously awaited the show.

Half of his Marines were already lying unconscious on the floor.

As Andy had noted the gaseous substance coming out of the trailer's ceiling, he somehow had the wherewithal to take a deep breath. Without opening his mouth, he'd silently tried to gesture to his

Marines. His First Sergeant was the first to comprehend and took in a deep breath before the fumes hit.

By the time the mist had moved down past the Marines' necks, some had already collapsed. Andy scrambled to get back to the ramp and engage the opening mechanism. When he got there, the Marine Captain could barely hear his Marines hitting the floor as the powerful gas assaulted their nervous systems.

In the back of his mind, he somehow recognized that keeping his breath in seemed to help. He'd always read that the more powerful chemical weapons entered the body through the skin and not through the airway. Andy had no way of knowing if that were true or not. It was like those videos the government used to show about how to react when a nuclear explosion occurs. Was it real or just made to make it seem that you "could" survive such an event? Was this gas agent the same way?

It had been close to a minute since he'd first inhaled. He pounded on the ramp release button. Nothing happened. He tried again and again then pounded on the ramp itself. Nothing. They were trapped. Almost all of his Marines were on the ground. Through the mist he could just make out his First Sergeant stumbling his way over the platoon of unconscious Marines.

―――

"Looks like they had to go with the backup trailer," Cal noted.

"Huh. Good thing they brought it," Daniel added.

A second later, a cannon in the music boomed loudly and the trailer flaps folded to the ground. The platoon was arrayed in a large oval, some kneeling in the front row, the second row standing; all were arrayed outward with bayonets fixed and presented toward the crowd.

"Wow! That's pretty sweet," yelled Daniel over the music.

Cal agreed. He'd never seen the Silent Drill Team doing anything like this before.

As they watched, the platoon of twenty-four reformed into a column and marched down onto the field.

THE FIRST SERGEANT had finally collapsed to the floor after banging on the ramp with Capt. Andrews. No one was coming to help them. Just as he started to lose his breath, he remembered the pistol in his waistband.

Andy quickly aimed toward the ramp. *Where to shoot?* The mist was clearing so at least he could see where he was aiming. Then he remembered the two hydraulic pumps at the bottom of the ramp that powered the door. Maybe he could shoot them out and push the ramp open. He only had ten rounds in each magazine so he had to be as accurate as possible. Luckily, the trailer sides were made of aluminum instead of steel. At least he'd have a chance. He fired five shots into the bottom of the left side of the door then moved to the right. His lungs ached as he realized he'd depleted almost a minute and a half of air. His limit was fast approaching.

CAL AND DANIEL watched as the Silent Drill team did its opening tricks in the middle of the field. All of a sudden, he noticed something. "Are those guys all white?" he yelled to Daniel.

Briggs squinted. "Yeah, where are all the black guys? And...wait... are they all Asian?"

Cal's eyes widened as he thought he heard something. He looked at Daniel who suddenly stood up. "Gunshot!" he yelled.

Without another word, the companions ran for the stairs.

THE PRESIDENT WAS ENJOYING the performance. He loved the Silent Drill Marines. But there was something he couldn't put his finger on. They seemed sharp, but not as precise as he'd seen them perform before. *And I thought they had some African-American Marines*, the President thought privately.

ANDY HAD one more magazine but was out of breath. He shoved the ramp with all his remaining strength. It started creeping open.

CAL TURNED the last corner and sprinted towards the trailer. He could see a hand sticking out of the side of the door. Daniel joined him as they ran to the trailer and started pulling the ramp down. Simultaneously, they noticed the vapor and quickly held their breaths. Soon the door was open enough that they could pull Capt. Andrews out. He hungrily gasped in clean air as they dragged him farther from the trailer.

Andy pointed back at the chamber. "There's an...emergency release...lever under the...left side of...the trailer that...unfolds the sides."

Cal and Daniel didn't hesitate as they ran back to the trailer to save the other Marines. Holding their breath once again, the two men pulled with all their might on the release lever. They felt a hard click and the trailer flaps started folding down slowly. By the time the flaps lowered, Andy had rejoined his friends.

"We need to get out there and help the President!" Cal yelled over the din. Andy had no idea what Stokes was talking about. He had no way to know about the Marines' imposters. Cal and Daniel bent down and extracted similar objects from their boot heels. Andy couldn't make out what they had in their hands. He followed closely behind Cal and Daniel as they sprinted to the arena.

MSGT TRENT WATCHED the show silently. Although he'd been impressed by the Silent Drill Team's appearance, the rest of the show seemed a little lacking. He'd have to give Capt. Andrews a hard time about that.

THE REPLICA SILENT Drill Team moved toward the President's position in four precise columns. They'd marched in step until they were twenty yards from the President. On silent cue, the platoon halted and four squad leaders from the rear marched out and to the front of the formation. Instead of doing the standard weapons inspection routine with two pairs, the planners had elected to go with four pairs. The squad leaders commenced the silent inspection, hurling weapons back and forth; making a show of inspecting the barrel and chamber of each gun.

Then, at the same moment, the four squad leaders grabbed the rifles. After doing a precise about-face they kneeled and aimed their weapons at the President. The Secret Service agents barely had time to react as the rounds came downrange.

AS THE FOUR squad leaders knelt on the ground, Trent sprang out of his chair. He vaulted whole rows as he extracted his pistol from his holster.

He was so intent on the unfolding carnage that he didn't even notice the two politicians following from behind.

BRANDON CAUGHT it a split second after Trent. Without thinking, he followed the Marine, albeit less gracefully. Zimmer was surprised to see his father following, too.

OUT OF THE corner of his eye, Nakamura saw Trent jump out of his seat. "Let's go, Son," he ordered.

"What? Out there?"

"Yes! Now get up!"

Kazuo Nakamura pulled the Nambu pistol out of his coat pocket and walked toward the arena. There were very few people who could ever claim the killing of an American President. Nakamura wanted to be one of them.

―――――

CAL, Daniel, and Andy sprinted toward the opposite end of the arena. They could just make out the President and his security team falling to the ground. *Shit, shit, shit*, Cal thought as he ran for all he was worth. He had no idea what they'd do once they got there, especially without weapons, but they'd die trying. The anthem music continued to pound overhead as the three Marines closed the gap. There were twenty-four fake Marines between them and their goal.

―――――

TRENT FIRED as he leaped the eight feet down to the arena floor. It wasn't a particularly well-aimed volley, but he centered his front sight post on the mass of men in dress blues. Remarkably, his rounds hit two of the squad leaders and the rest of the bullets flew into the platoon. With twelve shots, he'd incapacitated six men. There were still eighteen men for Trent and his friends to take care of. Trent hit the ground floor and ducked for cover. He quickly reloaded and focused his attention back on the platoon.

Where the hell were the rest of the Secret Service agents?

―――――

AS THEY NEARED THE PLATOON, several of the imposters fell to the ground, clutching wounds. *What the hell?* Cal thought. He ignored his own question and said a silent thanks that the platoon hadn't turned around yet. They were all still oriented toward the President.

He gripped two small composite blades he and Daniel had

extracted from their boots. It was a little gift from Neil before they'd left. Patel knew the Marines wouldn't want to go in naked. The small weapons wouldn't do much against ranged weapons, but hand-to-hand they would come in handy.

The three Marines closed the final few feet with only four blades, a pistol with eight rounds, and a pissed off attitude. *Three against twenty-four*, Cal thought, *What else is new?*

He screamed as he pulled the first man back by the head and slit his throat.

AFTER A SILENT PRAYER, Daniel followed Cal into the fray. Where Cal was ferocious, Daniel was more methodical as he quickly cut a swath through the crowd. By the time they'd gotten to the middle of the group, the Japanese imposters were refocusing on the pair of maniacal Marines in their midst.

POSSIBLY BECAUSE OF the after effects of the gas or the constricting uniform, Andy couldn't keep up with Cal and Daniel. An experienced triathlete and marathoner, Andy gritted his teeth and tried to move faster. By the time he'd reached the bloody scene, his two companions had already dispatched a good portion of the phonies. The men on the outside of the formation turned inward and leveled their M-1's at the marauding Marines.

Andy screamed in anger and started firing.

TRENT COCKED his head in confusion as the platoon fell apart and focused their attention inward. *Huh?*

Not one to look a gift horse in the mouth, Trent left his covered position and closed the remaining twenty yards, firing as he ran.

NAKAMURA'S EYES widened as he watched his elite guard get slaughtered. It couldn't be. They'd made sure to dispatch the security agents first. Who were these other men?

Ishi answered for him, "It's Stokes!" he yelled, pointing into the chaos.

Kazuo Nakamura growled in rage and ran to the stairs leading down to the arena.

JUST AS HE pulled his blade out of another man's brains, Cal felt an excruciating burn along the left side of his torso. He turned just in time to see a Japanese man in dress blues, M-1 Garand aimed straight at him. The man smiled and then the side of his head blew off, instantly killed by the hollow-point round from Andy's weapon.

"Keep moving!" Andy yelled over the booming music.

Cal nodded and looked around. There were only four men left. He finally realized how they'd done it when he saw MSgt Trent pull up. The Marines had no idea why they'd been so lucky.

What they couldn't know was that the squad leaders had been the only ones to be given special ceremonial rounds engraved with Japanese lettering for the WWII era weapons. It was a small vanity that the prideful Nakamura had insisted on, thinking that the one clip per squad leader would be sufficient considering the complete lack of security. He'd underestimated the Marines.

None of the four remaining Japanese had ammunition. If it bothered them, it didn't show. They were standing in a tight formation, bayonets pointed at their enemies.

"Put the rifles down!" yelled Cal at the four men.

Instead of complying, the enemy on the far left yelled something in his native tongue. His warriors charged.

Kazuo Nakamura peeked around the corner. He watched and smiled grimly as his four remaining loyalists charged. It would be an honorable death.

As quickly as possible, he made his way to the American President, pistol at the ready.

They were out of rounds. Just like their ancestors at Belleau Wood, the trenches of Okinawa, and the jungles of Vietnam, the four Marines moved to meet their enemy.

Congressman Zimmer climbed down to the ground floor. His father had opted to take the stairs. He ran toward the prostrate President, not realizing the Nakamuras were stalking in right behind him.

The eight men met in a clash of steel and flesh. Both sides were highly trained and deadly. The hulking Trent was the first to dispatch his opponent by dodging the man's bayonet stab and then the butt of his empty pistol onto the top of his opponent's head. The powerful blow crushed the man's skull and he collapsed to the ground. Trent turned for a new target.

Andy wasn't so lucky on the far right. Still woozy from the trailer episode, he just missed a parry and got a nasty cut deep into his forearm. The assailant kept stabbing, trying to gut the Marine Captain. All Andy could do at the moment was dodge the stabs until there was an opening or the challenger overcommitted.

IN THE MIDDLE of the group, Cal picked up a bloody Garand rifle from the ground and charged his foe. The two adversaries thrusted and parried. Taking a step back, Cal flipped the rifle over in his hands and gripped the weapon like a baseball bat. With tired arms screaming in protest, he swung the butt end of the rifle at his rival's head. The man scrambled to bring his own rifle up vertically to block the swing. He never had a chance. The swing was too powerful. The Marine was too mad. The stock of the M-1 blew through the parry and smashed into the man's head. Game over.

NEXT TO CAL, Daniel surprised his foe by throwing one of his knives straight at the man's face. It was a pretty harmless throw, and Briggs would've been lucky if the thing had done any damage. But that's not what he wanted. The Japanese raised his rifle to block the projectile. He heard the satisfying clang as the weapon bounced off harmlessly. However, this action gave Daniel the distraction he needed. Going to the ground, he did a quick roll and thrust his remaining blade into his target's abdomen. The man dropped his weapon and grabbed his stomach. Daniel extracted the dagger and drove it up through the man's throat. He gurgled as the sniper twisted the blade through the man's neck. The imposter fell to the ground, dead.

ANDY WAS STRUGGLING to keep up with his enemy's thrusts. He'd gotten two more deep cuts on his arms trying to deflect the longer bayoneted rifle. Out of the corner of his eye, he saw Trent step behind the remaining Japanese soldier.

The lone warrior noticed Andy's glance and turned to face his new threat. Too late. Like an anaconda, Trent's enormous arm wrapped around the man's throat and squeezed. The man dropped his rifle and scrambled to tear the giant's grip off his windpipe.

Before he could do so, MSgt Trent twisted the man's head violently and severed his spine. He discarded the imposter on the ground.

In unison, the four Marines turned toward the President. They saw Brandon Zimmer bending down to check on the American leader. They also noticed the two Japanese men approaching the Congressman from behind.

LAS VEGAS, NEVADA

7:01AM, SEPTEMBER 19TH

Brandon Zimmer bent down to check on the President. The leader of the free world moaned and rolled over, gripping his left arm. He was alive! Wounded, but alive.

"Hold on, Mr. President, I'll help you get your arm wrapped."

"What...where are my...?" the President tried to ask.

"Let's just get you out of here first, Mr. President," Zimmer yelled over the music that still reverberated loudly overhead.

The President grimaced as he tried to sit up. Brandon couldn't believe he'd survived the firing squad. He got the President to his feet.

"Walk away from the President!" yelled a voice behind him.

He turned to find Ishi and his father walking closer. The elder Nakamura was pointing a small pistol right at Brandon.

"Fuck you!" Zimmer yelled as he stepped to shield the President. Kazuo Nakamura changed the angle of his weapon and shot the Congressman in the leg. Brandon fell on top of one of the dead Secret Service agents and screamed, clutching his shattered patella.

CAL and his three friends stopped short when Zimmer was shot. They were four men against two, but Nakamura was the only one with ammunition. He saw Senator Zimmer at the entryway, opposite the Japanese. Cal motioned for the Senator to stay where he was. Richard Zimmer ignored the hand signal and walked purposefully toward the President.

AS IF ON CUE, the music overhead ended. The four Marines poised to make a run for the President. Kazuo Nakamura leveled his weapon at the President and addressed his adversaries. "If you want the President to live, you will stay back."

They didn't doubt him.

Senator Zimmer approached the President from behind and put his right arm around his boss' opposite shoulder. "How are you, Mr. President?"

"Zimmer? What...what's going on?" asked the President in confusion.

In response, Senator Richard Zimmer pulled a pistol out of his left coat pocket. "Well, Mr. President, I hate to tell you that this will be your last day in office."

"What are you talking about?"

"Well, let's just say I'm sick of your pansy-ass. I think it's time for a new world leader."

The President looked at the head of the Senate Intelligence Committee in shock.

"Don't look so surprised, Mr. President. It's truly unbecoming of an American President to be so afraid of death."

The President steeled his gaze. "You'll never get away with this."

Sen. Zimmer chuckled. "That's where you're wrong, as usual, Mr. President. You see, by the time the smoke settles, all of you will be dead and I'll be the last one left. The Party and Americans will flock to me in their grief. Losing an American President is a small price to pay for getting our national pride back."

Before the President could respond, Kazuo Nakamura cut in. "Enough of this, Senator. Let me kill him so that we can catch our flight home."

Richard Zimmer looked back at Nakamura with barely disguised contempt. Yes, he had been useful, but maybe it was time to end their relationship. He leveled his gun at the Japanese businessman. "I think maybe I can do this without you now, Nakamura-san." Without another word, he aimed at Nakamura's son and fired two rounds. The bullets slammed into Ishi's chest.

"Father..." he said quietly as he reached for his father, instead falling to the ground.

"You will pay for that..."

"Oh, what are you going to do? Shoot me with that shitty little Nambu? Did your father give you that before he died, Kazuo?" the Senator asked, smirking. He knew all about Nakamura's familial past.

"How dare you...?" seethed Nakamura.

"Oh shut up, you Nip. Did you really think that I was going to let you build your little empire? You've got to be fucking kidding me. If I'd known..." Zimmer stopped talking as he noticed Nakamura laughing almost uncontrollably.

Zimmer's face colored. "What are you laughing at?!"

Nakamura continued to howl crazily. Everyone watching thought the man was cracking up. Finally, he quieted and looked back at his mole in the American government.

"I'm laughing because I read you so well, Senator."

"What are you talking about, you idiot?"

"I knew you would double-cross me. Yes, you've become a very upstanding public figure in the last twenty years. But does anyone remember your early days? The days when the Irish mob bankrolled your election? How many favors did that cost you? And only to have that same mob investigated and put in jail years later. Tsk, tsk. No, Senator. You and I are more alike than you might think," Nakamura smiled.

"I am nothing like you. You know what, I'm done..."

"No, Senator, I have one more surprise for you."

Zimmer looked back in confusion. He thought he covered his bases. *What does this little Japanese prick have up his sleeve?*

"While you were so concerned with weaving your little plot to take over the Presidency, we were quietly making deliveries to your beloved Representatives."

"I have no idea what you are talking about," replied a flustered Zimmer.

"We know about the new Opel smart phones that everyone wants. You Americans will soon wait in line for days for this little piece of technology," Nakamura held up his own Opel smart phone. "You know that we've established a large network of blackmailed American government officials over the years. Well, our experts in Japan were able to acquire a single shipment of phones and retrofit them with a little gift."

Zimmer's eyes narrowed. "This was your insurance policy?"

"Yes, now you understand! You see, if my son and I don't arrive for our flight in thirty minutes, my people are ordered to detonate the devices," Nakamura said smugly.

"Detonate?" Zimmer asked.

"Why, yes. My staff is very crafty when it comes to technology. What you don't know is that we've been secretly developing a higher grade of explosive that is undetectable by scanners or your bomb dogs. Quite impressive, really. This explosive was inserted with remote detonating software onto the Opel smart phones. We've already confirmed delivery to over one hundred of your Senators and Congressmen. There are also over two hundred other important business leaders and government workers who received the phone over the last two days. They were very happy to get an early version of the phone. In fact, if I'm not mistaken, even the President has one of our phones in his pocket. Now, I'm not sure, but wouldn't it be difficult to be President and run a country without half of your elected officials? Not to mention all the businesses that would suddenly be without their leadership."

"You son-of-a..."

"Let's not call each other names, Senator. Why don't we just finish our business and move on to more glorious times for both of our countries?"

"So what are your terms?" Zimmer asked through gritted teeth. He'd hoped to be rid of the Nakamuras and not have to follow through on all the silly promises he'd agreed to.

"Simply this: I kill the President, all his friends over there..." he motioned to the four immobile Marines, "...and I walk out of here with my son."

"What about my son?" Zimmer asked, warming to the idea.

"Take him with you, as long as you think he can keep his mouth shut."

"I'll take care of my son. How do I know that you won't detonate those phones if I let you go?"

"You don't. But it would be much better for me to run the new Empire of Japan with the help of a healthy American ally. Besides, I'll be more than happy to give you a detailed list of all the recipients of our...upgraded phones once we land in Tokyo."

"What am I supposed to do with this mess?" Zimmer motioned to the piles of dead men.

"We'll use the same story we agreed upon. Those men were a rogue terrorist unit aligned with the growing Chinese communist threat. My government will be very apologetic and supply information corroborating your claims. We already have the documentation produced. It will all be taken care of."

The senior Senator from Massachusetts wasn't sure, but he didn't have much choice.

"Okay. If your son is still alive, take him and..."

His comment was cut short by six loud gunshots from the handgun Congressman Zimmer had taken from one of the dead Secret Service agents.

Kazuo Nakamura looked down at his pockmarked chest and dropped his pistol. Very slowly, he gazed up as blood seeped out of the corner of his mouth. His final mumbled comment, as he fell dead, was muffled by Ishi's crying.

"What have you done, Brandon?" Zimmer asked his son in shock.

"I was sick of listening to the little fucker."

Brandon struggled to stand on his one good leg. He managed to get up and face his father and the President. The Senator's pistol was pressed to the side of the President's head.

"What now, Dad?"

"Shoot him."

Brandon raised his gun and fired two shots.

LAS VEGAS, NEVADA

7:11AM, SEPTEMBER 19TH

The Senator's lifeless body crumpled to the floor as Cal rushed to help the President. He looked up at the Congressman in surprise. "How'd you learn to shoot like that?"

"Didn't I tell you that Dad made me join the Yale pistol team?" Zimmer deadpanned. He still couldn't believe he'd done it. He'd killed his own father.

Cal shook his head in wonder as his friends surrounded the President. "Mr. President, would you mind if I borrowed your phone?"

The President looked embarrassed that he'd forgotten the small bomb in his pocket. He carefully extracted the phone and handed it to Cal.

Stokes grabbed the Opel phone and dialed a number from memory.

"You think you should do that, Cal?" Brandon interrupted.

"You heard what the man said, Congressman. We have almost thirty minutes until this sucker explodes." He turned his attention back to the phone and dialed a number from memory. The other end picked up after the first ring. "Neil, we have a problem."

LAS VEGAS, NEVADA

5:00PM, SEPTEMBER 19TH

The five friends sat on the large couch and watched the kickoff of the Democratic National Convention. Within a minute, Neil was snoring soundly.

"Poor guy. He's been up since we got here," Brian observed.

Cal yawned and went to stretch before remembering the stitches in his side. "Son-of-a..."

Everybody that was awake chuckled. Cal looked around the room, still amazed that they'd all made it. It had been a close call, but in the end, the technological genius of the imperialist Japanese hadn't come close to matching the skill of Neil Patel. Rather than search through the haystack for the trigger, Patel simply wiped out Ichiban's entire system. He had, of course, already made a copy of all the files for future use. For now the threat was no more.

With the help of the President's phone call to the Japanese Prime Minister, all of Nakamura's associates were being rounded up as they arrived back in Japan. In Las Vegas, the Secret Service gathered up the Russian clan under Japanese contract. Rather than postpone the convention, the President was patched up, the convention center cleaned, and the show continued.

It was decided between Zimmer, the President, and Cal that allowing the convention to run as planned would be what America needed. Cal had to give the President credit. Rather than use the whole episode as a stepping-stone in the election (if the entire plot got to the public, they were all sure the incumbent would receive more than his fair share of sympathy votes), he chose to direct the Secret Service to keep the whole thing quiet. They'd mourn for the dead soon.

It was also agreed that certain stories would be concocted for the various deaths and injuries the team had endured. The President would pretend that he'd fallen and dislocated his elbow while dancing with his little girls. Congressman Zimmer, who received a personal invitation by the President to sit in his skybox, would tell his staff and the media that he'd shattered his knee mountain biking.

The Opel smart phones were also being quietly "recalled" through coordination with the FBI.

To further show his gratitude, the President agreed to let the Silent Drill Marines skip the convention. They'd all regained consciousness almost an hour later. By that time, the arena had been cleansed by the Secret Service and the Marines were moved to a new location in another part of the convention center. It was explained that an exhaust valve had leaked and rendered them all unconscious. The Marines were all smart enough to realize they'd never smelled anything like exhaust, but let it go when they were carefully warned by Capt. Andrews not to say anything about the incident. It hadn't hurt that the President had stopped by and apologized for the malfunctioning trailer.

As for Senator Zimmer and the Nakamuras, Ishi died just before Neil killed the Ichiban network. He never uttered another word as he watched Brandon help coordinate the cleanup. Ishi's body was later disposed at a local crematorium. Senator Zimmer and Kazuo Nakamura were transported by SSI personnel to a local pet crematorium. Their ashes were already scattered to the desert wind.

Just before he went into surgery to have his knee repaired, Congressman Zimmer chose the story to end his father's life. He was lucky to have a team of top orthopedic surgeons flown in by the President.

He whispered it to Cal just as the Versed started to kick in, his smile giving away his drugged state. "Tell the media that my Dad died humping a hooker."

Cal snorted as they wheeled the Congressman back to the operating room. Maybe that guy wasn't so bad after all.

He made a call to Travis and floated Zimmer's idea.

"How about we just tell them he had a heart attack?" Travis offered.

"Sounds good."

Cal hung up the phone and wondered what would've happened if they really had leaked the hooker story.

Ten minutes later, Cal's cell phone rang.

"Hello?"

"Hey, Cal, it's Brandon."

Before his surgery, Congressman Zimmer had made Cal promise that he'd call him by his first name.

"Hey, man. How ya feeling?"

"Anesthesia's almost worn off and they've got me on some good pain meds. Can't feel my leg, so that's good."

Zimmer paused as he fought for the right words to say.

"Cal, I just wanted to thank you again for all that you've done. I...I don't know what would've happened if you hadn't been there."

"No problem. That's our job, remember?"

"Yeah, I know, but I was a real..."

"Don't worry about it. Trust me. I'd have been surprised if you hadn't been an ass when I first met you. You would've made me feel bad about talking so much crap about your political affiliation."

Zimmer chuckled and paused again. "Cal, I...uh...was wondering if you could do me one more favor."

"What's that?"

"I was wondering if you could go with me to see President Waller."

LAS VEGAS, NEVADA

11:36PM, SEPTEMBER 19TH

P resident Waller entered his suite and stared at the two guests sitting in his living room.

"Will there be anything else, Mr. President?" his Secret Service agent asked.

"No, we're good Kurt. Thanks."

The imposing bodyguard nodded and walked out of the room.

"Thanks for waiting for me, gentleman," Waller said stiffly, "the President wanted to have a word with me."

He walked to the wet bar and chose a bottle of Jack Daniels. After pouring himself half a tumbler, straight up, he headed over to the leather sectional and took a seat.

"What did you want to see me about, Congressman?" Waller asked impatiently.

Brandon had thought about what he would say to the father of his murdered lover. What could he say?

"I…I just wanted to say I'm sorry…and that if you want me too…I'll turn myself in to the authorities," Zimmer stammered uncharacteristically.

Waller sighed and his face softened. "Now, why in the world would you want to do that?"

"I just thought that after what happened to Be...I mean, Patricia..."

"Let me stop you right there. First, you were both consenting adults. Second, the fact that she was being used as a pawn by that Japanese murderer..." his eyes hardened then mellowed again, "...it wasn't your fault, son."

"I know, but I keep thinking that if I'd recognized her or if..."

"Don't talk about what ifs, Brandon." Waller said in a fatherly tone. "Patricia was a big girl. She made her own decisions. There's no way you could've known who she was. She'd changed a lot since my days in the Oval Office. Besides, I'm guiltier than you are in this whole thing."

"Why is that, sir?" Zimmer asked in bewilderment.

"Well, I'm guilty for not keeping a better eye on my little girl. I got too busy and didn't follow up like I should have. If I had made the effort of spending more time out west, I'm sure I'd at least known SOMETHING was going on. But more important to this discussion, I'm guilty of leaking our organization's existence to your father."

Cal, with Waller's permission, had already told Zimmer about the Council.

"Now, sir, I don't know how..."

Waller held up his hand. "Let me finish. Once Cal told me it was your father who was scheming for the Presidency, all the pieces fell into place. I remember every conversation I had with Richard. I'm the one who gave him the opening. I'm the one who almost got us all thrown in jail. So you see, it's really up to YOU whether I should turn MYSELF in."

Cal and Brandon stared at the man in complete shock.

Cal broke the silence. "Mr. President, you know that I would never..."

"It's okay, Cal," Waller soothed, "I know you'd never turn me in. It's one of the things about you and your guys. Dependable to the last man. You would never expose a secret operation. I only wish we had more men like you. So, I guess the ball's really in the Congressman's court, isn't it, Brandon?"

Zimmer didn't know what to say. He'd come here hoping to apologize and dreading the possibility of going to jail. Now, a former President was asking HIM if HE should go to jail.

"Mr. President, if there's one lesson I've learned through this whole ordeal, it's that there's a reason for secrets. I didn't know how important it was until this week. It's also imperative to have men like you and Cal fighting the good fight, taking it to the enemy day-in and day-out. I never understood that before. Call it ignorance maybe. I don't know. But my eyes have been opened to a whole new reality. I only hope that I have the chance to go back to Washington and do what's right for this country."

EPILOGUE

CAMP SPARTAN, ARRINGTON, TN - 9:47AM, SEPTEMBER 24TH

Cal and Daniel rounded the last bend and slowed their pace down to a jog.

"How's your side feel?" asked Briggs.

The doctors had told Cal not to excercise for two weeks because of his stitches, but he just had to go for a run and get the crud out. His wound was burning, but his body felt great. He hadn't had a chance to work out in weeks.

"It's okay. Just feels good to get out on the trail, you know?"

The sniper nodded, barely even winded.

"Hey, I'm gonna go over to the barracks and get cleaned up. Wanna meet for lunch at eleven?" Daniel asked.

The day after the convention massacre, Briggs accepted a position at SSI. He hadn't even hesitated as Cal extended the invitation and a handsome compensation package. Internally, Daniel was overjoyed. His prayers had been answered and he'd found a new home.

His duties weren't completely ironed out yet, except for being Cal's constant companion, but the sniper was already making a name for himself on the live fire range. The operators around the campus all started calling him Snake Eyes.

He'd made one request as they'd said their goodbyes to the President in Las Vegas: that the President stop the processing of his Medal of Honor. Daniel still felt as if he didn't deserve it. The President finally acquiesced. Two days later, a small package arrived at Camp Spartan for SSI's newest employee. Daniel opened the box and found a Medal of Honor along with a note from the President. It read:

> *"Sgt. Briggs, I understand your reasons for not wanting this medal, but I must tell you that you are wrong. You are a hero to this nation and your sacrifices will always be remembered. I will keep my promise and not publicly give you this award. But, I did think that you should have this from a very appreciative Commander in Chief and a grateful nation. Semper Fidelis and God Bless."*

He'd only shown it to Cal who nodded and patted his friend on the back. As a Navy Cross recipient, Stokes knew how Briggs felt.

"Yeah, I'll see you there at eleven," Cal replied.

Daniel broke off towards the barracks and Cal continued on.

Winding up by The Lodge, a large log cabin style hotel for visiting VIPs, Cal noticed a black SUV parked out front. He wasn't expecting any company.

"I wonder who that is," Cal thought out loud.

He sprang up the steps and headed for his room on the second floor. It was great not having to drive to work. Before he got to the bank of elevators, he heard someone call his name.

"Cal!"

He turned around to see Congressman Zimmer, leg braced and walking with a cane, coming his way.

"Hey, Brandon, what are you doing here?"

"You know, I thought I'd stop by while I was in the neighborhood."

Cal laughed. "Seriously, what are you doing in Nashville?"

"I was wondering if we could have a little chat."

"Sure. You mind coming up to my room?"

They talked about how the Congressman's rehab was going and Cal bitched about his stitches while they rode the elevator and then walked to Cal's suite.

Cal held the door for Zimmer.

"Wow! Nice place you've got here," Zimmer admired as he looked around.

"Yeah. One of the perks of being an owner, I guess." Never one to beat around the bush, Cal dove right in. "So, how can I help?"

Zimmer winced as he took a seat on the closest chair. "Well, there've been some developments in my political career," he said cryptically.

"Don't tell me there's another psychopath trying to blackmail you!"

"Nothing that much fun. No, I've been approached by the Democratic Party to run for my dad's open Senate seat in Massachusetts."

"Well that's great, isn't it?"

"Sure, but it's not a given. I'll have to run in a special election. I'm so young that I don't know if I'll win."

"What's the worst that could happen, you still get to be a Congressman?" Cal joked.

Zimmer laughed. "Yeah, I know. But I'm just not sure if I'm qualified."

"I don't mean to repeat myself, but how again do you need my help?"

"I wanted to ask you, as a friend, whether you think I should run for Senate."

Cal was floored. *Why is he asking me? How am I qualified to give that kind of advice?*

"Look, Brandon, you know I stay way outside the political stuff. I wouldn't know the first thing about..."

"I guess I'm just asking if you think I have a shot."

Cal looked at his newest friend. They had been through a lot. He wondered how else the universe could've thrown the two men together.

"In my humble, dumb grunt opinion...I think you should do it. I mean, you're not half the asshole your dad was."

They both laughed at the macabre reference.

"Okay. Thanks, Cal."

"No problem. But, I'm sensing there's something else?"

"There is. I've been invited to a new club."

"What, like Army-Navy?"

"No. President Waller has asked me to be a part of the Council of Patriots."

Cal couldn't conceal his surprise. "I don't understand."

"Well, Waller figured that I already know about it and now I'm in a better position to help. He's even gonna quietly put his political backers behind my run for Senate."

"But, all the members are RETIRED politicians. Isn't that putting you in a precarious position?"

Zimmer was suddenly serious. "Two weeks ago, I had a really different view of how the world works. Now I know that groups like the Council exist for a reason. They're part of the solution not the problem."

"And you're okay with the way we go about exploiting the intel we get?"

"You're really asking ME that?" Zimmer asked with a sad grin. "Have you already forgotten what I did in Vegas?"

Cal would never forget Zimmer shooting his own father in the face. He was still surprised that it had been the Congressman who had killed the two masterminds of the conspiracy.

"Alright, alright. I get it. So, that brings us back to the original question: how can I help?"

"I've been tasked by the Council to bring you this." He handed over a single sheet of paper.

Cal skimmed the summary and looked up.

"Anything else I should know before we start looking into this?"

"President Waller figured you'd want to do some research first. How about we…"

The two turned as a loud ringing sounded in Cal's makeshift office. "Sorry, that's my secure line. Let me go grab that."

Stokes trotted over to his small desk and picked up.

"Stokes."

Zimmer watched as Cal's face went blank.

"Are you sure?" His face gave away his total shock. "Okay, I'll be right over."

Cal hung up the phone and didn't say a word.

"Is everything alright, Cal?"

"No." Stokes answered as he rhythmically clenched and unclenched his fist.

"What happened?" Zimmer asked with concern. He'd never seen the normally unflappable Marine in such a state.

Cal turned to the Congressman with dread-filled eyes.

"Neil's disappeared."

PRIME ASSET

"PRIME ASSET"

Book 3 of the Corps Justice Series
Copyright © 2013-2016, 2018 C. G. Cooper Entertainment. All Rights Reserved
Author: C. G. Cooper

GRAND TETON MOUNTAIN RANGE, WYOMING

5:49PM, SEPTEMBER 28TH

The shivering was gone. Adrenaline coursed through his body, fueling survival. The huge grizzly bear took another swipe as the young man retaliated with a short swing with his torch. Sparks flew as the errant swing grazed the side of the small alcove.

The bear didn't flinch. Instead, it pushed its head into the opening and unleashed a deafening roar. The grizzly's hot breath assaulted the trapped man as he tried to make himself as small as possible against the back of the hole. There was nowhere to go. He'd lost all his weapons except for the burning torch that was now almost out. What he wouldn't give for even a small knife. The only thing saving him from instant death was the fact that the bear couldn't fit through the alcove's entrance. But its claws could, and they'd already torn a jagged cut into the man's winter parka. It wouldn't be long until the bear figured out how to get more.

The man had no idea how the animal had followed him onto the narrow ledge. He'd underestimated the bear's tenacity and hunger. The park ranger had warned about the bears being hungrier than usual this year. Something about a shortage of berries. Shaking the thought from his head, the man reviewed his options. There were none. The best he could do was to wait and see if his attacker would leave. But that was unlikely given his current position.

The early fall blizzard continued to blow in as the bear tried to widen the opening. Suddenly, and without warning, the bear pulled its head out and turned around.

What's he doing? thought the man.

He chanced a peek out of the man-sized hole and watched the bear as it sniffed the air, almost looking like a dog as it searched.

The young man wouldn't have another chance. Squeezing out of the hole, the loud wind mercifully masking any sound, he stood not three feet from the distracted grizzly. He'd never make it if he took the path. The bear would win. Making up his mind, Cal Stokes sprinted the four feet to the ravine's ledge and jumped.

TETON VILLAGE, JACKSON HOLE, WYOMING

TWO DAYS EARLIER, 4:24PM, SEPTEMBER 26TH

Days earlier, Cal Stokes and Daniel Briggs landed in the small Jackson Hole airport. If asked, they were in the area for a two week hunting trip.

Cal was in his early thirties, good-looking and just under six feet tall. He was dressed in jeans, boots and a distressed t-shirt. His brown hair was covered in a trucker's ball cap. After getting his bearings, he left his companion and proceeded to the Enterprise counter.

Briggs, a couple inches taller and a former Marine sniper, stayed behind and waited for their luggage. He shook out his shoulder length blonde hair and tied it back in a ponytail. Out of habit, he glanced around casually while bending down to retie his hiking boots. No obvious surveillance other than the airport security cameras. Five minutes later, Briggs hauled their four bags and two weapons cases out the sliding doors.

The temperature was still in the upper sixties as Briggs took a deep breath. He loved the outdoors. He'd never been to Wyoming. Now was his chance. As the newest employee of Stokes Security International, Daniel was also his employer's unofficial bodyguard. On SSI's official ledger he was listed as 'Security Contractor 3982.' The company did a lot of personal protection and surveillance overseas and had a legion of former military contractors around the globe. To any prying eyes, Daniel was one of them. To the majority owner of SSI, Calvin Stokes, Jr., he was a trusted advisor and friend.

Cal pulled up in a black Ford Excursion. After loading all their gear into the back, the two Marines got in. Briggs keyed the hotel's address into their GPS as Cal made a phone call.

"Trav, we're on our way to Teton Village." Travis Haden was CEO of SSI, a former Navy SEAL and Cal's cousin.

"Good. Trent, Dunn and Gaucho's boys are spread out on the next couple flights. They should all be there by noon tomorrow."

"Thanks again for setting that up. Any updates on Neil?" Neil Patel, one of Cal's best friends and SSI's head of Research and Development, had disappeared two days earlier. He'd been in Jackson Hole for a small conference with some of the world's top technology firms. It was an annual invite-only-event and Patel's third year attending. Haden had received a call from a friend attending the conference. The guy told Travis that Neil hadn't shown up for his lecture; something about the importance of battlefield innovation on civilian product development. The man was frantic because the entire group of enrollees was waiting anxiously for Patel's popular talk.

It wasn't like Neil to miss anything. After calling Patel's cell and hotel room repeatedly, they couldn't track him down. Finally, Travis placed a call to the hotel security staff and convinced them to search Neil's room. The head of security conducted the search personally. Neil's room was empty. Despite an unmade bed and used hotel toiletries in the bathroom, all of Patel's personal belongings were gone.

Due to the sensitive information Neil stored in his genius-level brain, Travis initiated a complete lockdown of SSI's systems. In spite of Patel's insistence to the contrary, Todd Dunn, SSI's head of internal security, had warned against allowing one of SSI's key assets to travel alone. Always planning for the worst, Dunn came up with a backstop: Neil was required to have a micro transmitter (of Neil's own design) surgically implanted in his ankle. It would lie dormant until needed.

The transmitter allowed SSI to turn on the tracking feature and find Patel anywhere in the world.

The first thing Dunn did after getting the news from his boss was to turn on the tracking device. Nothing happened. That meant one of three things. One, the device malfunctioned. Two, Neil disabled the device. Three, someone had kidnapped Neil, extracted the transmitter, and destroyed it.

They had to plan for the worst. First, it wasn't natural for one of Neil's gadgets not to work. He'd tested it on multiple subjects, and it had always performed above expectations. Second, Neil had no reason to take the thing out. Third, Patel was a big target. If someone wanted to find a goldmine of technological knowledge, Neil was a human treasure trove. With his near photographic memory and world-class hacking skills (he regularly trolled the vaunted systems of organizations like the CIA, MI6 and FBI just for fun), he was an invaluable asset.

On the surface, things remained calm. Travis thanked the hotel security team and apologized for the inconvenience and had given them the excuse that he'd just found out that Neil left early due to a death in the family. He gave the same story to the colleague who'd called to ask about Patel.

Behind the scenes, SSI worked overtime. Not only was Patel a vital part of ongoing SSI operations and R&D, but, like a seasoned CIA station chief, Neil knew everything. His capture and the exposure of SSI's covert operations would mean disaster not just for the company, but for various players within the American government. There were implications all the way up to the President. It wasn't a scenario Travis wanted to have play out.

"Did you have Neil's guys go over the list of people attending the conference?" Cal asked.

"For the third time, yes, cuz. We're doing everything we can on this end. We haven't even had a whiff from any of our sources."

Cal huffed in frustration. He knew the headquarters team was doing everything they could, but Cal wasn't a patient man. Travis had even placed a secure call to the President to give him a heads-up. Because of Cal's recent rescue of the American President, the politician promised to help however he could.

"Sorry. I'm just worried."

"You and me both. I've been wracking my brain trying to figure this thing out. Have any wild ideas on your flight out?" asked Travis.

"I had too many ideas. Name one group of bad guys that wouldn't want their hands on Neil. It's like having the ultimate cyberweapon."

The two men were silent for a moment as they both tried to envision the possible fallout. It wouldn't be good. They had to get Neil back.

Cal switched gears. "How many people knew Neil was coming out for this conference?"

"Obviously everyone attending. That's just under fifty people. Then, of course, there's his staff here and our leadership team. Seventy-five people tops?"

Seventy-five people. It could be worse. "I assume you've already got our people doing background checks on all of them, right?"

"Yeah. Nothing yet. There are some competitors we need to take a closer look at, but I think the guy that organizes the conference has already done a pretty good job vetting attendees."

Cal figured that was the case. These were high-profile executives. Most of them probably had the equivalent of Top Secret clearances in the tech world. Still, at this point, everyone was a suspect.

"I've got a really bad feeling about this, Trav. Please let me know if you find out anything new. Me and the boys will hit the pavement here."

"No problem. Let's stay in touch."

Cal ended the call and put his phone in the cup holder. He'd hoped to have something to go on before starting the search. Best case, they'd find Neil soon. Worst case, someone had already shipped him off to another country.

NEIL SAT SHIVERING in his small cell. He was wrapped in an old olive drab wool blanket. It wasn't much, but it warded off some of the chill.

The only light in the room came from a tiny window the size of a brick. He'd already tried banging on it but the damn thing felt like it was a foot thick. One of the guards paid him a visit after checking the window and gifted him with a hard jab in the sternum. The spot still hurt.

He laughed at the pettiness of the recollection. Compared to the rest of his predicament, the blow was a minor inconvenience. Neil had a bad feeling about why they'd kidnapped him as he'd walked back from the sushi restaurant two nights ago. It made it even worse that they'd known exactly where his remote locator was. That was, until they'd taken care of it.

Neil reached down to the neatly bandaged stump that used be his ankle and winced. At least they'd had the courtesy to knock him out and supposedly had a real doctor cut his foot off. *Look on the bright side, right?*

He sat back and adjusted his Prada eyeglasses. Neil wouldn't be walking out anytime soon, but he started to prepare mentally for whatever horrors awaited him. A small part of his subconscious hoped Cal would come bursting through the door at that very second.

"YOU'RE SURE?" Nick Ponder asked into the phone.

"Yeah. They just landed. You want us to follow them?"

"No. I've got another team waiting in Teton Village. We already know they're staying at Hotel Terra. With the slow season it'll be easy to keep tabs on them. I want you to stick around and let me know when the rest of their guys land."

"Okay, boss."

Nick Ponder, a fifty-five year old former Green Beret, hung up the phone. He stood up from his simple metal desk and stretched his hulking six foot six frame. Over the past few years he'd grown out his beard into an unruly black tangle. He kept his head shaved bald. Being imposing and ruthless were two of Ponder's gifts. He'd learned it in the military and carried on the tradition when they'd kicked him out in 1996, and he'd started his own company.

He still worked out daily and could best most men half his age. Seven years ago he'd relocated his company headquarters to Wyoming.

Ponder enjoyed the wilderness but liked the secluded fortress much more. There wasn't much he couldn't do out here. It was perfect for staying under the radar.

After the little incident with that prick Calvin Stokes Sr. back in 1999, business was harder to come by. Before that, Ponder was a growing force within the mercenary world. At that time, he'd leveraged his contacts to recruit close to one hundred men and had them deployed to most of the world's shitholes. Well, at least the ones where some little dictator needed some real warriors to protect him.

Looking back, he knew his expansion into protection for the Mexican drug lords had been stupid. It'd seemed so easy though. The money was ten times what the majority of security contracts were. If it weren't for that fucking Marine Colonel, he'd probably be smoking Cohibas in Antigua right about now.

It was gravy up until he got the ultimatum from one of his competitors. He still replayed the conversation in his head whenever he didn't get a contract he thought he deserved.

"NICK, this is Calvin Stokes with Stokes Security. I was wondering if you had a minute."

Ponder's head was full of cocaine sampled from his client's latest shipment. He only knew Stokes by reputation. The guy was a former Marine and apparently a real hard-ass. "What can I do for the Marine Corps, Colonel?"

"I'm not sure how to relay this, so I'll just go ahead and say it. We've been hearing rumors that you're providing protection for the Jimenez cartel." Stokes let the accusation hang. If Ponder had been clear headed he might have handled the situation differently. He would've denied it.

"So fucking what? Even Mexicans need protection!" Ponder laughed out loud at the joke.

Col. Stokes exhaled. He'd hoped to have an intelligent conversation with Ponder. Yes, The Ponder Group was technically competition, but a certain respect was assumed between American security contractors. He'd never dealt with Ponder directly, but had heard stories of the man's exploits, both in and out of the service. The Army had drummed him out at the rank of Major after a little 'situation' in the Philippines. The unofficial report, provided by Stokes's contact at the Pentagon, gave vague details of how Ponder had singlehandedly slaughtered the families of five men suspected of being conspirators in a planned terror attack. Ponder had freely admitted to the atrocity and thrown it in his superiors' face. He even called them cowards for not doing the same.

Apparently the rumors were true, and the idiot had just admitted it.

"Look, Nick, I was just giving you a courtesy call before I turn this over to the authorities."

"What the fuck are you talking about?!" Ponder yelled into the phone.

"Without going into the details, I'll tell you that we've been doing some contract surveillance work for a Federal agency. I'm bound by our contract to give them everything I have," Stokes explained.

"Bull-fucking-shit! You're trying to torpedo my ass! I'll have your ass..."

"No, you won't." The cold menace in Stokes's voice cut through Ponder's cocaine high. "Like I said, I'm calling you out of professional courtesy. Either you wrap things up or prepare for the Feds to come down on you. It's out of my hands."

IT WAS the one and only conversation he'd ever had with SSI's founder. He'd heard the prick died on 9/11. Asshole.

None of it mattered anymore. He was about to make his retirement. One last op and he'd be fucking rich. They might have to fend off some of the competition but that didn't matter. Ponder was on his home turf. Plus, with the promise of a king's ransom coming his way, he could afford to up his firepower a bit.

Unfolding his huge frame from the desk chair, he walked over to the large bay window overlooking his horse corral. Maybe he'd take a ride after visiting with his prisoner. It was time to make sure his little investment paid off.

HOTEL TERRA, TETON VILLAGE, JACKSON HOLE, WYOMING

5:39PM, SEPTEMBER 26TH

Cal threw his bag on the twin bed. The room wasn't huge but more than comfortable. Outside they had a little balcony that afforded a beautiful view of the ski runs. Too bad they weren't on vacation.

"How about we go get some food."

Daniel agreed with a nod. "Where do you want to eat?"

"Let's stay close. How about that restaurant right across the quad?" Cal pointed through the window. "What does that say? The Mangy Moose Saloon? I could use a beer and a steak."

"Yeah, okay." Briggs grabbed the small backpack that Cal had recently discovered carried an assortment of reserve ammunition for his concealed weapons. Daniel took his new role as Cal's security seriously. Always the first through the door, Briggs kept a vigilant eye out for his new boss. Hell, in the first week they'd known each other he'd saved Cal's life no fewer than three times.

The two Marines walked down to the first floor and stepped outside. It was a short walk across the outdoor common area to get to the Mangy Moose Saloon. The place had an old log cabin feel and fit right into the Wyoming wilderness vibe of the trendy Teton Village development.

There weren't many patrons as they walked into the two-story establishment. Briggs paused at the door and scanned the tables. He did a once over of the Japanese couple sitting nearest the stage and the four guys dressed in riding gear sitting at the bar. No threats. Satisfied, he led the way in.

It was open seating, so Daniel chose a small table with a good view of the bar and dining area. A pretty, Nordic-looking waitress stepped up just as they were sitting down.

"What can I get for you, gentlemen?"

"Do you have any local IPA on tap?" Cal asked politely.

"Sure. Sir, what can I get for you?" she asked the blonde-headed sniper.

"I'll have a Diet Coke, please."

As the waitress walked back to get their drinks, two men walked into the restaurant and headed to the bar. Neither man looked toward Cal and Daniel, but the hair on Briggs's neck stood straight up.

They were both wearing well-worn outdoor clothing. The first man was skinny, of average height, with slicked back black hair and a wind-burned face. His beak nose was the feature that made him really stand out.

His companion was a full head taller and walked in with a swagger. He took off his grey beanie, shook out his light brown hair and sat down on the barstool.

"Give me a shot of Beam." He ordered loudly enough for Daniel to hear across the room. His smaller partner quietly took a seat and ordered a beer.

Briggs didn't know the men, but he knew the type. It was the way they carried themselves. These guys were former military, and they radiated danger to the highly attuned Marine. *Wouldn't be surprised if they're armed too*, he thought.

"Don't look behind you," Briggs mentioned casually to Cal, "but I think we've got a little trouble. Two new friends just sat down at the bar."

With his back to the bar Cal couldn't see what Daniel was talking about, so he just nodded. He knew better than to question the Marine's senses. Briggs was a man of few words, so when he talked you listened. Not to mention he had an uncanny sixth sense when it came to danger. The man could sniff it out like a hound dog.

"So what's our play?" Cal asked.

"Let's just see what happens. Maybe I'm wrong."

Cal smiled and nodded.

Their drinks were served a minute later. Cal took a long pull from his large mug and savored the bitter goodness of the local beer. He'd have to ask what brand it was.

"Any movement from our friends at the bar?"

Briggs shook his head.

"You think we're good to order?"

"Yeah. Let's keep it casual. If I'm right about these guys, I don't want to tip them off," Daniel instructed.

They ordered their food and made random small talk as they ate. Cal had hoped to use the time to plan their search for Neil, but it looked like that would have to wait until later.

Finishing quickly, they asked for the check and paid. The two men at the bar were still downing their second drinks as Cal and Daniel made their way to the exit. There wasn't even a glimpse in their direction by bird nose and his companion.

Briggs hoped the warning was just in his mind. It would make their search for Patel a lot harder if they already had a tail.

"Let's take a little walk around the village and digest some of those ribs we just ate," Briggs suggested.

They headed uphill toward the large ski lift that was running the last tourists off the mountain. Both men were in excellent shape but could still feel the effects of the elevation. During their time in the Marine Corps, they'd each trained at the Mountain Warfare Training Center in Bridgeport, California. They knew it would take a couple days to acclimate to the decreased oxygen. Hopefully they wouldn't have to test their sea level legs quite yet.

After thirty minutes of walking through the modern ski village, and ducking into most of the little shops, Briggs led the way back towards the hotel. He hadn't spotted the two men from the restaurant. It didn't really surprise him. Teton Village wasn't big. It would be easy to be observed and not even know it. It would be easier to lose a tail once night fell. Darkness was already imminent.

Daniel took a right turn past a small playground, heading toward the hotel's front desk. Instead of walking into the hotel, he continued past. The darkness was almost complete as they walked by the little sushi restaurant and headed up the street toward the mountain. Briggs wanted a little free space to see if anyone was following.

Just as they rounded the corner past the last neighborhood, a set of high beams switched on and blinded the companions. They heard an old truck door open and saw a man get out and walk toward them.

"You two weren't planning on going up the mountain were you?"

Briggs could now make out the man's shape. He was wearing a Park Ranger's uniform.

Cal answered first. "No, sir. Just taking a little walk after dinner."

The young man came closer. "Just wanted to make sure. We've had a lot of bear activity up that way." He pointed up the mountain. "Bears are hungrier than usual what with the lack of berries this year."

"Lack of berries?" Cal repeated.

"Yep. This is my first year, so I don't really know the details, but the old-timers are saying the weather kept the wild berry bushes from growing enough fruit. We've even had one grizzly break into a house looking for food. Luckily the family was out of town at the time."

"Thanks for the heads-up. I think we were gonna turn around soon anyway."

They said their thanks and headed back down to the hotel. Once they were out of earshot, Cal coughed a laugh. "I almost pulled my pistol out when those lights came on."

Briggs chuckled too. "I don't think that kid knows how close he came to having his truck shot up."

Now that the tension was broken, they enjoyed the cool night air as they strolled down the hill. It was the last night of calm they'd have for the rest of the trip.

―――

"We got eyes on the two guys. You want us to hang out?" the man with the beak nose asked his employer on the phone.

"Yeah. Get a room at Terra, and be up early so you can stick close. They'll probably start asking around about their friend. Just make sure you don't lose them," Nick Ponder instructed.

"You got it, boss."

"And, Trapper..."

"Yeah, boss?"

"Don't do anything to them until I give the okay."

The skinny man known simply as Trapper licked his lips as he thought about the coming confrontation. "I know, boss. You just let me know when."

Ponder terminated the call and sighed. He wanted to make sure his team kept tabs on all the guys SSI sent to his backyard. If he knew where they all were it would be easier to take care of them when the time came.

He'd be paying his boys overtime for around-the-clock surveillance, but it didn't matter. That would be chump change soon enough.

Ponder dreamt of his coming riches as he watched the live video of his prisoner. Patel was even now trying to hop to the small toilet in the corner of his cell. Ponder chuckled at Neil's discomfort. That leg sure had to hurt. He hoped his buyer wouldn't be too pissed that he'd had to lop the guy's foot off. It just wouldn't do to have a tracking implant around once his buyers showed up, and cutting it off had been easier than trying to dig it out.

Negotiations were still underway for the final payment amount. A small escrow of one million dollars had already been deposited into Ponder's Cayman bank account. That wouldn't even pay his mortgage on his multiple homes. No, he was in it for the big payday. Once he delivered Patel to his buyer, life would be a whole lot sweeter. Maybe it was time to ask for more money.

Nick Ponder grinned as he thought about not only the cash, but also the sweet revenge he was about to drop on Col. Stokes's company. The old man would probably roll over in his grave.

HOTEL TERRA, TETON VILLAGE, JACKSON HOLE, WYOMING

7:17AM, SEPTEMBER 27TH

Cal and Briggs had both been up since five am, ready to start the search for their friend. After a quick workout in the hotel gym, they walked over to one of the small cafes lining the village square. Cal paid for the chocolate croissants and coffee as Briggs scanned the area for prying eyes. There were none that he could see.

"Let's eat while we walk and then get ready for the rest of the boys to get here," Cal said through a huge bite of pastry.

Returning to their room without incident, they took turns showering, and Cal checked his email. No updates from Travis.

Marine Master Sergeant Willy Trent would be arriving via private jet in the next twenty minutes. Another three SSI employees were accompanying him, including former Navy Corpsman, Brian Ramirez. Along with the four SSI operators, the Learjet was also carrying most of the gear they would need if they had to go exploring in the wild. This time of year you never really knew what kind of weather you might get. It could be bright and sunny with a high of seventy, or cold and blustery with heavy snow. Better to be prepared.

Cal had hand selected sixteen men to come along for the search.

He based the selection on their prior experience with him (Trent, Briggs and Ramirez were all veterans of at least one of Cal's covert ops), and their training in mountain warfare. Cal wasn't taking any chances this time around. He also had two more teams of sixteen standing by at SSI's Tennessee headquarters if the need arose for more firepower.

Briggs walked out of the bathroom, drying his hair with a towel. "Any word from Mr. Haden?"

"Dude, I told you four times already, his name is Travis," scolded Cal.

"I know, I know. Old habits die hard, Cal. He is the CEO of our company."

"So how come you don't call me Mr. Stokes?"

"'Cause you're just a dumb grunt like me." Daniel smirked.

"Whatever," Cal returned mockingly. "No update from Trav. We're kinda dealing with a needle in the proverbial haystack."

Briggs didn't say anything as he threw the towel back in the bathroom and got dressed. "I've got an idea I wanted to run by you."

Cal looked up from his laptop. "What's that?"

"Call me crazy, but I still think those two guys from the bar last night were keeping tabs on us. I was thinking about finding them first and seeing if we couldn't...extract some information out of them."

Stokes thought about it for a minute. While he didn't doubt the sniper's abilities in the least (they called him Snake Eyes for a reason), the tiny cautious part of Cal's subconscious still wasn't sure about making a scene. "So you're sure those guys were following us? I know I don't have to tell you this, but the last thing we need is a mess right in the middle of Poshtown."

Briggs shrugged his shoulders. "You have any better ideas?"

Cal didn't, and he hated it. They were really just waiting for word from Travis before they could do anything. Apart from doing the street cop thing and knocking door-to-door, Stokes didn't really have anything better.

"Okay, tell me what you had in mind."

TRENT DUCKED his near seven foot frame under the Learjet's exit door. He stretched to his full height as he stepped out onto the top platform of the portable steps. MSgt Trent was a black man with the muscular build of an NFL linebacker. Not only was he a professionally trained chef, Trent was also lead instructor for SSI's hand-to-hand combat training course.

"Enjoying the view, Top?" The question came from behind him.

Trent turned around to face Brian Ramirez. "Sure thing, Doc. That, and I'm trying to get the kinks out. My big ass gets a little cramped even in the nicest jets Cal puts me in."

Ramirez laughed as he and the two other SSI operators followed Trent down the stairs. In comparison, his five foot nine body fit comfortably in the luxury jet they'd just spent close to four hours on.

"I'll bet you loved spending time in AAVs," ribbed Ramirez.

"Hell no! I prefer humping to wherever I need to go, Doc."

The four SSI men gathered the gear that the airport staff was now unloading off the back of the plane. As requested, there were also four pushcarts already standing by for them to pile everything on. Within minutes, the bags and boxes were stacked neatly on their respective carts and the small team headed for the terminal.

They passed under an arch of antlers and Trent pointed up. "What the hell animal do those come from?"

"They're elk antlers. I hear they've got a big elk preserve just down the road. The Boy Scouts and some other groups go out there and pick up the antlers and give them to local craftsman. In that book I was reading about Jackson Hole they had some pictures of downtown Jackson where they've got four huge arches made out of the damn things. Pretty cool."

Trent whistled in admiration. "Can't imagine how much the things weigh." He shook his head as they continued on into the single story terminal building.

Fifteen minutes later they'd loaded all the gear into the two rented SUVs. It was a tight fit, but they'd manage to cram it all in. Trent picked up his phone and dialed Cal.

"You guys on the ground?" Cal asked.

"Yeah. We're loaded into the vehicles and headed your way. Any updates on Neil?"

"None. Travis still has the tech boys doing background checks on the people at the conference. We're trying not to alert anyone that he's missing yet."

"Good idea. I'd rather catch whoever's behind this by surprise," Trent growled. He and Neil had become close over the years. Although their backgrounds were completely different (Neil came from a rich Indian family and Willy came from the streets of Atlanta), they both respected the other's talents and often spent their time off together. Trent couldn't wait to get his big hands on whoever was behind Neil's disappearance.

"Slight change of plans. Briggs caught a couple locals tailing us. Just to be safe, we rented a house next to Teton Village to stage everything. It'll be a little cramped with all our boys, but at least we can secure it."

It sounded like a good plan to Trent. "I call dibs on one of the real beds."

Cal was always glad to have the crusty Master Sergeant around on ops like this. He had a way of keeping things light even in the face of imminent danger.

"You got it. The new place has six bedrooms, so you can take your pick when you get here."

Cal gave him the new address, and Trent relayed the information to Ramirez to plug into the vehicle's GPS.

"See you in thirty, Cal."

JUST UNDER THIRTY minutes later the two SUVs pulled into the driveway of the vacation home.

"Cal sure likes to travel in style," Brian commented as he looked up at the huge single-family home.

"I think he finally realized that not spending his money wasn't an option. Besides, you know he likes to take care of his troops."

The former Corpsman nodded. It was one of the main reasons he'd accepted the invitation to join SSI. The place was like home. SSI was a group of warriors that took care of each other no matter what. That philosophy came from the very top starting with Travis Haden and Cal Stokes. They would die before seeing one of their men suffer. Their approach ensured absolute loyalty amongst SSI employees. Staff and operators were taken care of and expected to perform at the highest levels. They were an elite team dedicated to making America safer while at the same time taking care of their brothers on their left and right.

Cal lived frugally by habit. His father had done the same. Both Marines spent their time and money ensuring the well-being of their troops. One of the perks of having a highly profitable company was that Cal could fly his people first-class when appropriate and put them up in the nicest accommodations. He figured it was a very small price to pay for men who'd put their lives on the line for years and continued to do so. He could finally give back to the men who meant so much to him.

As they piled out of the vehicles, Stokes and Briggs walked out onto the second story patio.

"You guys need a hand?" Cal asked.

"You kidding? Did you not see all the shit you requested?" Trent answered in mock indignation.

Stokes grinned and headed down to the first floor to help their second group of guests unload the cold weather, hiking and mountaineering gear he'd ordered from SSI's logistics division. There wasn't much a grunt liked more than a new piece of gear.

GRAND TETON MOUNTAIN RANGE, WYOMING

11:55AM, SEPTEMBER 27TH

Nick Ponder had yet to visit his prized guest. There was too much else to do. Coordinating his buyer's arrival had been a real pain. His contact was starting to get a little attitude about the pending acquisition. They were starting to balk at the rising purchase price. During their last conversation he'd stretched the truth by telling the guy that he had two more buyers waiting with offers. It wasn't true, but after thinking about it for a while Ponder was starting to realize the possibilities. What communist country or terror organization didn't want the brilliant mind of a resource like Neil Patel?

As he continued to mull over his options, he pulled up the latest weather report on his desktop. Shit. The updated report was calling for a huge snowstorm. He'd only been in the area for one other early winter, and it'd made the normally unflappable mercenary more than a bit uncomfortable. The remoteness of his property had its advantages, but a heavy snowfall could easily hinder his plans. If he didn't get the buyer in and out in the next day or two, they might have to wait another week. He needed to buy some time. Luckily, he had a couple contingency plans.

He logged into one of his many email accounts and composed a message that would remain waiting in the drafts folder for the only other person who knew of the account's existence.

―――――

TERRENCE ZHENG TOOK another gulp from his Diet Red Bull. The higher ups at SSI had him doing triple work since Neil's disappearance. He had barely stopped for the last two days.

Taking a quick break from the background check he knew would be fruitless, Zheng got up from his chair and walked to the restroom. He stepped into the large handicap stall, sat down on the toilet and pulled out his smart phone. Tapping on the appropriate application, he opened the browser and clicked on a bookmark labeled 'Vacation.' The email provider's website popped up a second later and he logged in.

There was a message waiting for him in the Draft folder.

TETON VILLAGE, JACKSON HOLE, WYOMING

12:17PM, SEPTEMBER 27TH

They now had three quarters of their sixteen-man team sitting around the large dining room table. Cal had ordered pizza and everyone was eating their fill. Briggs had just run them through the plan he'd devised to flush out the bad guys.

The last team arriving was led by one of Cal's new go-to guys. He was a short Hispanic who everyone called Gaucho. Eccentric in his own way, the small Mexican-American wore a braided goatee and commanded his men with flair and daring. As a former Delta commando, Gaucho was no novice to covert operations. He was the first man to volunteer to accompany the expedition despite his dislike of the cold environment.

Gaucho's group of four was even now pulling into the quiet ski village. They'd be at the rental house any minute.

"Hey, Cal, make sure we save a couple pieces of that jalapeño pizza for Gaucho. You know what'll happen if you don't," MSgt Trent joked to the room. The men laughed because they knew it was true. Gaucho was the first one to make fun of himself and his ancestry, but beware to the person that got in the way of him and spicy food. Despite the gravity of the situation, Stokes always enjoyed being with these men. There wasn't a guy present that wouldn't give his life for another. It was a hard thing to find outside of the military.

"So, is everyone good with Daniel's plan?" Cal asked.

Everyone nodded. Briggs knew what he was doing. Besides, the plan only entailed finding and possibly capturing two guys. It was a stroll in the park for these operators.

GAUCHO and the last three team members pulled into the long driveway twenty minutes later. It didn't take Cal long to brief the newcomers and get them something to eat.

"Thanks for saving me some jalapeños, Boss," Gaucho said through a mouthful of greasy pizza.

"You're just lucky I didn't put Top in charge of the pizza," Cal quipped.

"You messin' with my pizza, Willy?"

Trent waved his hands in mock fright. "No way, hombre! You know I wouldn't get in between a Mexican and his hot peppers."

"Very funny, Top. I could say the same thing about you and some fried chicken," the small Hispanic smiled.

"Now don't be talkin' about Mama's fried chicken. Besides, I don't just eat fried chicken, I eat HOT chicken," Trent added, rubbing his six pack abs.

"That's right I forgot about that. Some spicy shit, right? You sure you don't have some Mexican in you, Top?"

"Not that I know of, brother. But who knows, maybe you're a brother from another mother." Trent smiled wide, walked over to Gaucho and gave him a big bear hug.

The tough little Hispanic wiggled out of the giant's arms and just managed to save his slice of pizza from falling on the ground. "Okay, Willy. I know how you boys in the Marine Corps like to hug but save that for Doc over there."

Looking up from his bag, Brian Ramirez gave Gaucho the finger.

"Whoa, whoa, watch where you stick that thing, Doc. I'm here for business not a medical exam." Gaucho was now snickering along with some of the other men.

"All right, ladies," Cal raised his hands in surrender. "As much as I'd love to see where this thing ends up, let's get all the gear staged. I just got a weather update from HQ and it looks like we've got a big snowstorm moving in. The cold weather gear we brought along might be coming in handy sooner than we thought."

Gaucho groaned. "You're kidding me right, Boss? You know how much us Mexicans hate the cold."

"Really? Why don't you just hitch a ride on Top's back? I'm sure he can keep you warm," Cal offered innocently.

The remark elicited a middle-fingered salute from the former Delta man and MSgt Trent.

"What have you got for me?" Nick Ponder asked Trapper.

"They haven't left the hotel. I'm thinking they gave us the slip."

Ponder's temper flared. The last thing he needed right now was an enemy force snooping around in his territory.

"So what are you doing to find them?"

"We got their room number from our contact at the hotel. We're about to go take a look inside."

"Call me as soon as you know."

Ponder slammed the phone down. He was losing precious time. The snowstorm was really constricting his timeline. Pretty soon he'd have to recall his men. He only had a handful of contractors working security at his home base. He'd need the full contingent for the buyer's arrival and to deal with any possible incursion from the SSI team. Maybe it was time to trigger his back-up plan.

After consulting his small journal, he picked up the secure phone again and dialed a number. It connected after one ring.

"Yeah?"

"Jack, I need a favor."

CAMP SPARTAN, ARRINGTON, TN

3:46PM CST, SEPTEMBER 27TH

Travis Haden was on the phone when Marjorie "The Hammer" Haines, SSI's lead attorney, walked into his office. Wearing her usual form-fitting office attire, Haines was always impeccably dressed in clothing that enhanced her already attractive form. Most people underestimated the beautiful brunette. Not only was she a lion in the courtroom, The Hammer was also an accomplished martial artist. She'd bested many of the toughest of SSI's operators in practice sessions or wager-inspired sparring.

She motioned for him to end the call. After apologizing to the caller, he hung up the phone.

"What's up?" Haden asked with concern. It wasn't often that Haines came into his office unannounced.

"We've got a little...situation. I just got a call from my source at the FBI. It looks like they're about to conduct a little *unofficial* investigation on us."

Travis frowned. It's wasn't that he'd never expected the request. Hell, after the Black Knight affair a few years ago most of the security contracting companies had been investigated in some form or fashion.

SSI had thus far avoided the FBI's scrutiny by maintaining the proper transparency and cultivating the relationships needed to keep the company out of hot water.

What concerned Travis was SSI's covert wing. They'd operated outside the laws for years, protecting a country that still seemed unaware of their presence. Living and breathing their founder's concept of *Corps Justice*, SSI quietly intercepted threats that normal law enforcement couldn't handle. Each operation could only be sanctioned by Travis or Cal. Secrecy was key.

Had someone tipped-off the FBI? Cal had only recently saved the President's life in an operation in Las Vegas. They'd worked directly with the President and the Secret Service to keep the entire affair quiet but that didn't mean anything. Somehow secrets always got out. It was directly proportional to how many people actually knew the secret. The Vegas incident was still fresh. Did the President have a turn of conscience?

"Do you have any details?"

Haines shook her head. "Nothing yet. My contact says we should be getting the subpoena within the hour."

"Shit. This couldn't have happened at a worse time. Where will they start?"

"From what I heard from some friends, they'll start digging into finances and operations. They want to make sure income and expenses match."

"Is there any way they can trace us back to any of our clandestine ops?"

"I don't think so...at least not on paper." The look on Haines' face told Travis she was holding something back. He gave her a 'give it to me' hand gesture.

"I didn't want to say anything until I had a chance to think about it more, but I'm concerned that we've got a mole." She let the comment sink in. Marge could see by the look on Haden's face that he found the idea pretty far-fetched.

"You're kidding, right?"

"Think about it, Travis. Neil gets kidnapped then not days later we have the FBI breathing down our necks. That can't just be coincidence."

Travis didn't know what to think. Ninety plus percent of the employees at SSI were former Military personnel. They'd each been exhaustively vetted mentally, physically, financially and through intense background checks.

"Okay. Let's assume you're right. What do we do now?"

"While I deal with the FBI, have Higgins and Dunn start doing an internal search."

Dr. Alvin Higgins was a former CIA employee and psychologist. Despite his chubby appearance and jolly charisma, the good doctor was a master interrogator. He'd revolutionized the techniques used by American personnel (both physical and chemical) that now produced tomes of vital intelligence for the American government. Although he abhorred most physical violence, Higgins marveled at the capacity and the inner workings of the human mind. If there was a man that could extract information without laying a finger on a captive, it was Dr. Higgins.

Todd Dunn was SSI's head of security. Where Higgins was outgoing and genial, Dunn was introspective and serious. A former Army Ranger, Dunn was all about business and always vigilant.

Travis nodded. If anyone knew how to be discrete it was Higgins. Tag teaming with the burly Dunn, the two would find the mole soon. "What are you gonna tell the FBI about where Neil, Cal and the rest of his team are?"

Haines shrugged and smiled. "I'll let you know as soon as I know."

WITHIN TWENTY MINUTES Dr. Higgins was executing his plan. They'd talked about the possibility of having a traitor in their midst before. Luckily, thanks to Higgins's experience in the federal government where mole hunts seemed all too common, SSI had a plan in place for just such a scenario.

"I'll take care of it, Travis," Higgins said in his fatherly tone.

"You'll let me know what you find out right, Doc?"

"Certainly, my boy. Just give me little bit of time. These things have a way of working themselves out."

Travis wasn't too sure. Since his time with the SEALs he'd become accustomed to working in an elite environment. Amongst warriors it was absolutely unspeakable to betray your brother's trust. That gave Haden an idea.

"Hey, Doc, how about you start with the support staff. Most of our operators don't even have a clue about what's going on outside their current mission. Might save us some time and heartache."

Even though he'd already come to the same conclusion, Dr. Higgins was never one to take credit or condescend. "Good idea, Travis. I'll start there."

As Travis left the doctor to his craft and went to find Dunn, he could only hope that the internal investigation wouldn't tear his company apart.

TETON VILLAGE, JACKSON HOLE, WYOMING

3:15PM, SEPTEMBER 27TH

Cal walked into the garage where his men were busy staging their equipment. Some checked weapons as others ensured their cold weather gear fit properly.

"Top, you got a minute?"

MSgt Trent looked up from his conversation. By the look on Cal's face he knew another wrinkle had just been added. Trent nodded and followed Stokes upstairs.

Ramirez, Briggs and Gaucho were already seated around the dining room table. Trent took a seat while Cal remained standing.

"I just got a call from Travis. It looks like they're having their own little party back at headquarters. The FBI's about to investigate SSI."

To their credit, the men seated around the table remained silent. They knew it wasn't time for questions.

"Travis and The Hammer aren't sure what they're looking for but I agree with them that it's mighty convenient considering Neil's disappearance. What makes things worse is it also looks like there might be a mole at SSI."

Now the gathered warriors looked shocked. Could it be? Could one of their own actually be conspiring to destroy a company they'd all fought hard to build?

Trent was the first to interject. "How sure are we about this, Cal? I mean, this could be bad for all of us."

"I know. Trav has Higgins and Dunn on it. If anyone can ferret this guy out it's them."

They all nodded solemnly. Each man was well aware of Higgins's expertise.

"So how does this affect what we're doing out here?" Gaucho asked, seeming almost nonplussed about the situation back home.

"As usual we'll have to make sure we stay under the radar. I've also recommended to Travis that he keep all updates I send him to his immediate leadership team. No one else really needs to know about what we're doing," Cal explained.

"What if we need more firepower, Cal?" asked Ramirez.

"I think we need to try and get this done without asking for more people. Besides, if what they're saying about this snowstorm is true, we wouldn't be able to fly anything in anyway."

These men were all used to working on their own. They knew the risks involved. Not having the ability to call in support would not hinder them from seeing the mission through. They would make do.

"Cal, I know we shouldn't be thinking this," Trent started, "but have you considered that maybe Neil isn't even here? I mean, what if they flew him out of here the second they picked him up?"

"I've discussed that with Travis and we're both in agreement that it's the risk we have to take. We don't have anything else to go off of. Besides, if Daniel's right and some unknown group is out there watching us, that probably means it's worth it for them to keep tabs on us. I don't think they'd do that if he was already shipped overseas."

Trent wasn't so sure, but he didn't disagree. They all had to hope that they could reach their friend in time.

NEIL RUBBED his sore leg for maybe the thousandth time. The pain was getting worse, which meant his captors would be bringing him his pain meds soon. He'd kept a mental time clock since waking in the small cell. At regular intervals a large man with a black mask would silently open the door, place a plate of food along with two pills on the floor just inside the room. There was no need to worry about the prisoner attacking the guard. Without the use of his foot he was effectively immobilized.

After the first delivery, Patel had refused to eat the food or take the medicine. An hour later his jailer had returned as Neil lay shivering and pain-wracked on his small cot. The large man forced Neil's mouth open with one hand and shoved the two pills down his throat with the other. It was impossible for Patel to resist.

Within minutes the pain had receded. Neil had learned his lesson. Take the pills or live in excruciating pain.

As he counted down to his next meal, Neil thought about his friends. He knew they'd be out looking for him. Would there be any clues left to find?

Deep down he knew it was his fault. For years Travis and Todd Dunn had hounded him about taking along security when he went into public. They'd said he was too valuable an asset to lose. Cal had one day said he was, in fact, a prime asset. He'd always shrugged off the worry. As fate would have it, his father had once been kidnapped and murdered while travelling on business overseas. Would he endure the same fate? Something told Neil that wasn't the case. They had something in mind for him. Why else would they go through all the trouble of taking care of him?

He wracked his brain thinking of possible ways he could escape, or at least figure out what they wanted from him. Neil knew they would tell him soon. His sixth sense told him it wouldn't be pleasant.

———

Upstairs Nick Ponder went over the latest email from his buyers. They'd accepted his counteroffer with some conditions. The mercenary was ecstatic. Pretty soon he'd be rich and never have to worry about petty little jobs again. But first he had to have a little talk with his prisoner. It looked like the buyers wanted to run a test to see that they were getting what they paid for.

Ponder cracked his knuckles as he thought about the coming session. It would be good to be rich again.

Neil's cell door opened and a huge man with a shaggy black beard and shaved head walked in. Patel knew the boss had arrived.

"You and I need to have a little chat, Mr. Patel," Nick Ponder growled in baritone.

"Is this where you tell me I get to go home now?"

Instead of answering, Ponder walked across the small space, grabbed a handful of Neil's hair with his left hand and clamped his right hand around Patel's neck and started to squeeze. With barely any effort, he lifted the smaller man off the cot and up against the wall.

"Now you listen here, you little shit. I'm someone you don't want to fuck with. If you're looking for God, I'm him. I could squeeze the life out of your pathetic little raghead body right now."

Patel didn't doubt the man. No longer able to breathe, he fought to maintain his consciousness. This guy was incredibly strong.

Without warning, Ponder dropped Neil back on the small cot. Patel screamed as his stump hit the floor. His captor laughed.

"Like I was saying, I am God to you now. Whatever I say, you do. Understand?"

Through gritted teeth and watery eyes Neil nodded. He didn't have much of a choice. Even at full strength he was no match against the large man.

"I'll be back in a couple hours with some things for you to do. Get your mind right, and you might leave here in one piece."

Without another word Ponder left the room. Neil was left to wonder what the sadistic man had in mind.

TETON VILLAGE, JACKSON HOLE, WYOMING

5:15PM, SEPTEMBER 27TH

"Everybody ready to go?" Cal asked the sixteen men. Needing to blend in, they were all attired in varied hiking and casual clothing. Each man carried a small arsenal under his coat. Cal had his trusted double-edged blade strapped to his left wrist along with a pistol in his waistband.

They'd agreed that Cal and Trent would be the bait. The Mangy Moose restaurant had an outdoor seating area where the two Marines would grab a table and have a leisurely dinner. Briggs was certain that the enemy would find them soon in the small ski village.

The small teams set off at staggered intervals. Some left in groups of four, others left in groups of two or three. Briggs was the only man to go out alone. The sniper they called Snake Eyes was already making himself comfortable across the quad on the pool deck at Hotel Terra. It afforded a full view of the common area. All the other teams would take up positions at various points in and around the Mangy Moose. The only thing left to do now was wait.

TRAPPER and his partner sat at the outdoor restaurant attached to the large ski lift. They'd searched Cal's hotel room earlier in the day and found it completely empty. Ponder had already recalled the other contractors because of the storm. That left Trapper to coordinate the search in Teton Village.

The wiry man kicked himself for not taking out the two Marines when he'd had the chance. It would've been so easy that first night. Now it seemed that his quarry was on to them. To make matters worse, the rest of the sixteen man team Ponder's guys had already confirmed landing at the Jackson Hole airport had also disappeared. Trapper wished someone had listened to him when he'd suggested putting a couple tails on the arrivals after they left the airport. Ponder was so confident that the SSI men would start the search in Teton Village that he'd ignored the suggestion.

Trapper was a veteran of the Army's military police. He'd gained his nickname by being able to track and trap anyone. There wasn't a man or woman that he couldn't find. The only reason he hadn't stayed in the Army was the 'questionable' methods in which Trapper had used to detain his captives. In the end, there had been allegations of abuse and torture. While Trapper knew they could never prove anything (he was also a master at manipulating evidence and witnesses) he felt the writing was on the wall. Certain senior officers had made it their patriotic duty to see him drummed out of the service.

Instead of going out their way, Trapper decided to take early retirement at sixteen years and head to the civilian world. Not long after he'd contacted his old friend Nick Ponder. They'd partied over booze and drugs, all the while lamenting the Army's decline as a military force. The next morning over Bloody Marys, Ponder offered him a job with what he'd affectionately dubbed 'Ponder's Misfits.' It didn't take Trapper long to find out that the majority of contractors hired by the Ponder Group were indeed misfits. Released from active duty for an assortment of reasons, Ponder snatched them up willingly knowing that they had nowhere else to go. As a result, they were only too happy to do his dirty work.

Trapper glanced at his watch. "Five more minutes, and let's take a walk around."

His partner nodded silently and finished his coffee. Trapper paid the waitress and minutes later the two men were strolling downhill doing a surveillance sweep toward The Mangy Moose.

———

BRIGGS SPOTTED the two men right away. It was hard to forget their mismatched faces. They looked completely nonchalant as they walked down towards Cal and Trent.

Daniel pulled out his cell phone and texted the rest of the team: *2 **TARGETS HEADED TO THE MOOSE**.*

Once he got confirmation from the team leaders, he slipped the phone back in his pocket and stood up. It was time to see who these guys were. He slipped out of the pool deck quietly and headed to the stairwell.

———

TRAPPER SPOTTED Stokes and Trent as soon as The Mangy Moose came into view. He nudged his partner. The man looked up and nodded. At least they'd found them again. Now it was time to take up a position and watch.

The two contractors veered to the right and found a spot on one of the outdoor tables maybe a hundred yards away. Trapper casually pulled out a pack of cigarettes and sat down. While he wished there were more people around, at least the darkness would give them some cover. Stokes, on the other hand, was sitting in a well-lit area that afforded Trapper a perfect view.

He and his partner were so intent on their targets that they never noticed Briggs watching them from behind.

———

DANIEL EXTRACTED the two pistols from his voluminous coat pockets. He'd have to make his shots count. It was something the sniper was used to. Briggs never missed.

As Trapper took another drag off his cigarette, he sensed movement to his left. He turned to look and felt a stabbing pain in his neck. He reached up, grabbed the dart and yanked it out while staggering to his feet. His partner was doing the same. Trapper had just enough time to register that it was Briggs approaching when he fell to the ground. The powerful tranquilizer quickly rendered both men unconscious.

Daniel rushed to check on them and waved for the other team members to come help. Four SSI men materialized out of the darkness and swiftly picked up the two men and carried them to a waiting vehicle.

Briggs was scanning the area to make sure nothing was left behind when an older couple walked up concerned.

"Excuse me, son, but is everything okay with your friends over there?" the old woman asked.

"Yes, Ma'am," Daniel answered politely. "My buddies just had a little too much to drink over at the Moose."

The husband smiled knowingly. "You tell them to take it easy on the booze at this altitude. Had a bad go of it myself a few years ago."

"Yes, sir, I will. You have a nice night."

Briggs walked away and breathed a sigh of relief. His silly little plan had worked. Now it was time to find out what these guys knew.

TETON VILLAGE, JACKSON HOLE, WYOMING

7:02PM, SEPTEMBER 27TH

They'd put the two men in separate rooms. Briggs had recommended they start with the big guy first.

Cal had disagreed. "I really think we should start with the guy with the beak nose, Daniel."

"Don't ask me why, but I get the feeling that he's gonna be a hard nut to crack. It's something in the guy's eyes."

Cal knew better than to question the sniper's judgment. In the short time he'd known Briggs, the Marine had never been wrong. "Okay, let's do it your way. What did you have in mind?"

LANCE UPSHAW WASN'T a bad man. He just wasn't the brightest guy that ever walked the Earth. What he lacked in mental ability he more than made up for in strength and skill. Since his first day in the Marine Corps even his drill instructors had taken to calling him 'The Swede' after the character in Clint Eastwood classic *Heartbreak Ridge*. Upshaw had excelled in all physical aspects of boot camp. He'd continued his growth training in the fleet. His large athletic frame, honed from years on the football and baseball field was perfect for the Marine Corps. It was his ability to be manipulated that became his final downfall.

They'd given him an Other Than Honorable discharge from the Marine Corps because of a certain hazing incident he'd been convinced to participate in. Upshaw's fire team leader, a skinny sadist named Cpl. Kliner, had taken offense to the 'tone' of one of his new PFCs. The kid was a college drop-out who'd instantly incurred Kliner's wrath. After a few drinks at the Enlisted Club on Camp Pendleton, and under Kliner's direction, Upshaw methodically beat the young 'college boy' within an inch of his life.

Something in Upshaw knew that what he'd done was wrong, but it had been an order from his fire team leader. Wasn't he supposed to follow orders? That's what his DIs had said at Parris Island.

Upshaw remembered sitting in the courtroom in complete shock as the officer read his sentence. How could the Marine Corps send him away for following orders? He loved the Corps.

Sitting in his cell months later, he'd welcomed the visit from Nick Ponder. The man understood his situation and even admitted going through a similar episode years ago. Once Lance served his year in the brig, he happily took a position with The Ponder Group. After all, they knew what it was like to be misunderstood.

Lance Upshaw shook his head as he regained consciousness. He didn't remember how he'd ended up in the room. *Where the hell am I?* His arms and legs were hogtied behind the wooden chair someone had strapped him to. He couldn't feel his hands and feet.

As his vision cleared, he finally made out a figure standing in front of him. The man was around six feet in height with a blonde ponytail. Lance thought that he had kind eyes. Despite his lack of brainpower, Lance knew the difference. He'd seen evil in many of the men he'd met in jail.

Daniel pulled up a chair and sat down in front of the large captive. "What's your name?"

Upshaw wasn't sure he should respond. He remembered something from boot camp about only giving out your name, rank and serial number. "Upshaw, Lance. Seven, three, three, two, nine, eight, one, two, one."

"So you were in the Army?" Briggs asked kindly.

Upshaw made an almost disgusted face. "Marine Corps."

Briggs smiled. "Me too."

Upshaw didn't say anything. He'd learned to keep his mouth shut. Daniel let the silence linger. This guy looked liked a perfect candidate to handle a medium machine gun but would never be found planning a raid. He had the hard look of an abused animal.

"Look, I'm a little short on time so I'm just gonna get to it. That cool?" Daniel asked.

Upshaw still didn't know what to say. The last thing he remembered was sitting next to Trapper and watching the guys Ponder had sent them after. He was just the muscle sent along to help his partner with any heavy lifting. He'd always been told to not saying anything in the event he was captured or questioned.

"I'm not gonna hurt you, Lance, but I need to know what you and your pal were doing following us."

Options swirled in Lance's head. He knew Trapper and Ponder would kill him if he said anything.

"I'm not supposed to say."

Daniel wasn't surprised by the response but happy that he'd at least validated his initial impression. These guys were on SSI's tail. Without saying another word, he got up from his chair and went to find Cal.

———

NICK PONDER WAS STARTING to think it'd been a bad idea to send his guys to watch the crew from SSI. He'd known there was always the chance they might be spotted. That's why he'd sent Trapper. The guy was a one-man surveillance machine and mean as a snake. He was Ponder's kind of guy.

He tried calling Trapper's cell phone for a fourth time. Sometimes the signal was crappy up in the mountains. He figured the gathering storm wouldn't help much either.

For the fourth time Ponder got the error message trying to connect to Trapper's phone.

"Shit," he grumbled.

Half of his men were already back. He'd need to bring the rest home soon. The helo wouldn't be able to fly in the coming blizzard.

Where the hell were Trapper and Upshaw?

TRAPPER REGAINED CONSCIOUSNESS SLOWLY. He looked around the room then tested his arms and legs. They were bound behind the dining room chair he was sitting on. The former military policeman was pretty sure he could get out of the restraints as long as he could force some blood flow back into his limbs. There were benefits to being somewhat of a contortionist. The problem was he didn't know what he was up against. He was sure his captors would make an appearance soon enough. Meanwhile, he'd bide his time, work his arms and legs, and figure a way out.

"THIS GUY'S NOT the smartest is he?" Cal asked Daniel as he continued to watch the live video feed from both holding rooms.

Daniel shrugged. "He's smart enough to keep his trap shut. At least we know they were keeping an eye on us. You okay with me laying into him a little more?"

Cal looked up from the video screen. "If it gets us closer to Neil, do it. I'd prefer not leaving any marks on these guys..."

"I don't think it'll come to that. I'll be subtle."

"Do what you need to."

Daniel nodded and headed back in to talk to Upshaw.

DANIEL TOOK his seat in front of Upshaw and stared at the man for a minute. To his credit, Upshaw returned the stare without flinching.

"Where are you from, Lance?"

Upshaw hesitated. He didn't remember anything about not talking about his personal life. There couldn't be anything wrong with that, right?

"I'm, uh, from Dallas."

"You play football down there?"

Upshaw's eyes lit up at once. "I did," he said with pride and almost puffed out his chest before remembering that he was tied to a chair.

"Thought so. I'll bet you tore it up on the field. Linebacker?"

"Running back," Upshaw said with a grin.

"Really? You're a pretty big dude to be dodging tackles."

"I'm fast, and I can run over most guys."

Briggs whistled in admiration. He would honestly love to see the man in action.

"You play college ball?" Daniel asked, already knowing the answer.

"Nah. Didn't have the grades."

"So you went in the Corps instead."

Upshaw nodded his head. Although it'd taken some studying with his recruiter, he'd finally passed the military aptitude test and was allowed to go to Parris Island.

"So when did you get out of the Corps?"

Lance scrunched his face thinking. Numbers and timelines sometimes got jumbled in his head. His mother always said that God could only give a person so many gifts and that Lance had gotten a lion's share of physical ability. In exchange, God couldn't give him as much intelligence as other kids his age.

"I think a couple years ago."

"What did you do after you got out?" Daniel asked.

Upshaw hesitated again. His mind tried to process whether answering would be right or wrong. It was hard to keep it straight.

"Went home for a little bit."

"Just hung out with your family?"

"My ma raised me as a single mom. I hadn't seen her in, like, a year. Stayed with her for a while."

Briggs could feel the walls coming down. "Did you get a job down in Dallas?"

Upshaw shook his head. "No. I just helped Ma and some of her friends. Got free food and a place to sleep."

Daniel nodded thoughtfully. He didn't want to have the guy clam up again. It was important to get him to keep answering questions. Briggs said a silent prayer that God would guide him to the answer.

"Your mom still live down in Dallas?"

"Yeah."

"You still see her?"

"I fly down one or two times every year."

"She pay for your flight?"

It was another one of those funny questions Lance wasn't sure about. Why was he asking?

"Um...no. I pay for my tickets."

"Oh! So do you have a job up here?"

"Yeah."

Briggs noticed the drop in Upshaw's demeanor. He had to keep it light.

"Cool. It must be pretty awesome living up here. It's beautiful."

Lance nodded as enthusiastically as a little kid. "You should see it when the leaves change. It's really pretty. All the moose and bears come out too. I like the bears."

"You ever see one?" Briggs asked with eyes wide open.

"All the time! Right now they're really coming out. People are saying they're more hungry than other years."

"That's what I heard too. You ever get charged by a bear?"

Upshaw was suddenly serious. Briggs thought that maybe he'd gone too far and delved into a memory that would end the man's cooperation.

"Just one time. Damn grizzly was huge. We were hiking back down to Phelps Lake and all of a sudden this bear was just sitting in the middle of the path soaking up some rays. I tried to scare it away, but it got up and roared at us. Before we knew it the thing was charging."

"Holy crap! Was your buddy in the next room with you?"

"Nah. Trapper was back at HQ. I was with some of the other guys."

"So what did you guys do?"

"The only thing we could do. We shot the fucking thing!"

Daniel whistled again. "Wow. Did you kill it?"

"Damn right. It was him or us."

"Can't you get in trouble for killing a grizzly around here?"

"Yeah, but we didn't stick around. Would've moved it but those things weigh a ton."

"I'll bet. So you work with some other guys at one of the ranches around here?"

"Yeah, sort of," Lance answered quietly.

"So you do guided hikes, trail rides, that sort of thing?"

Upshaw hesitated again. He'd already made one decision in his mind: that this guy asking him questions was actually a nice guy. Lance didn't think he'd tell his boss if he said anything.

"No, we do some security work."

"Really, that's cool. I kinda do the same thing. Who'd you say you worked for?"

"I…uh…didn't."

"Yeah, but wouldn't it be easier if I talked to your boss about all this instead of bugging you? The sooner you tell me where you work, the sooner I can give them a call and get this whole thing straightened out. You seem like a good guy, Lance. I don't want you to get in trouble."

Trouble was the last thing that Lance wanted. What could it hurt? As long as they didn't say anything about him telling.

"You promise you won't tell them I told you?"

"I give you my word as a Marine, Lance."

That was good enough for Upshaw. "I work for The Ponder Group."

CAMP SPARTAN, ARRINGTON, TN

8:37PM CST, SEPTEMBER 27TH

Travis hadn't left the office since Neil disappeared. He'd commandeered one of the large suites at The Lodge so he could stay close by. The phone on the bedside table rang just as he dozed off for a quick nap.

"Haden."

"Sir, I have a call for you from Mr. Stokes," the operator said.

"Patch him through, please."

Luckily, all the phones at The Lodge were highly encrypted and therefore highly secure. With the number of VIPs SSI courted, it was important to have a way for guests to communicate with their offices while away. It was one of the many improvements Neil Patel had instituted over the years.

"You there, Trav?"

"Yeah. What's going on?"

"You ever heard of some company called The Ponder Group?"

Haden sat up in bed. "Yeah, why?"

"We've had a tail since we got here, and we just found out that they work for this Ponder Group."

"How do you know?"

Cal hesitated. Even though the line was supposedly secure, he still wanted to be careful just in case someone was listening.

"Let's just say we have two more guests at the house."

"Invited or uninvited?" Travis asked.

"They were...invited. Daniel made it a...personal invitation."

Travis correctly deduced that they'd somehow apprehended the men.

"Tell me you've used kid gloves on the guys."

"You know me, cuz, always trying to do things the right way."

"I'm not messing around here, Cal. Tell me you didn't put the screws to these guys."

Cal laughed at his cousin's unease. "Of course not. Briggs just had a little chat with one of our new buddies. So you wanna tell me who this Ponder Group is?"

Travis swept his hand back through his dirty blonde hair. Where to start?

"SSI has a little history with The Ponder Group," Travis started disgustedly.

"What kind of history?"

"The CEO of The Ponder Group is a prick named Nick Ponder. The guy is former Army. Mean son-of-a-bitch. He's as crooked as they come. So anyway, back in the nineties, he and your dad..."

Travis told Cal the story of the conflict between Cal Sr. and Nick Ponder.

"How come you never told me about this?" Cal asked indignantly.

"There was never a need to. It happened a long time ago. I've heard rumors about him over the years, but he knows to stay clear of us."

"Looks like that's not the case anymore."

"Yeah. The only good thing I can think of in this whole situation is that Ponder is just a thug. He likes money and inflicting pain and not much else."

Cal was fuming. He didn't know how his cousin could stay so calm. "I'm having a hard time understanding what in the hell you're talking about. While we're sitting here chatting about this asshole, he's probably torturing or even killing Neil!"

Travis took a slow breath. "Look, now that we know WHO has Neil, we can actually do something."

Cal knew his cousin was right. A couple hours ago they had nothing. Now they had a name.

"How can we find out where this guy lives?" Cal asked.

"Let me call you back. With a possible leak here at home I'd rather take care of this myself. I'll do some digging and get you the details in a few minutes."

It wasn't good enough for Cal, but he wisely held his tongue. Venting his frustration on Travis wouldn't accomplish a thing. He needed to focus on one thing: Nick Ponder.

TRAVIS HUNG up the phone and stared at the wall. Where to start? He hesitated using any of the computer guys until he knew where the leak was. There was always the Council of Patriots, an ultra-secret group of retired (and one active) politicians. Typically, the Council came to SSI for help in going operational on intel. This was a different story. Travis had never contacted the Council for help. He'd put that on hold for now.

He picked up his cell phone and speed-dialed his head of security, Todd Dunn.

"Dunn," answered the former Ranger in his gruff tone.

"Todd, I need to talk to you in person."

Travis could hear Dunn getting up from whatever chair he'd just been sitting in. Once set in motion, Todd Dunn was never moved off track.

"What's up?"

"Cal just found out that Neil might have been taken by an old friend."

"Who?"

"Nick Ponder."

"I'll be right up."

Travis placed his phone back on the bed and looked up at the ceiling. It was going to be a very long night.

TETON VILLAGE, JACKSON HOLE, WYOMING

9:55PM, SEPTEMBER 27TH

Daniel hadn't gotten anything else out of Lance. It had probably finally sunk in the large man's brain that he'd divulged a little too much information.

"You want me to go talk to the other guy?" Briggs asked Cal.

Cal had already told the rest of the team to get some rest. They might have to leave soon, and he wanted them to get any sleep they could. It was one of the many things he'd learned in the Marine Corps: sleep whenever and wherever you can.

"Let me go see if I can get anything out of him. I'm starting to think you were right, though. Looks like a tough nut. Wish we had Doctor Higgins with us. He can make anyone talk."

"Just be careful, Cal. He's tied up pretty good but don't take any chances. You want me to come in with you?"

"Nah. Why don't you just watch the monitor. If anything happens, you can come to my rescue." It was meant as a joke, but neither man was laughing. As men of action, they felt stifled. Better to be moving than to remain static. Without the information on Ponder's whereabouts, they couldn't do a damn thing.

Daniel took a seat in front of the video display and settled in to watch.

CAL STEPPED into the second holding room and closed the door. He looked at his captive. The man looked bored.

Ignoring the look, Cal grabbed a chair, positioned it six feet from his prisoner and sat down.

"So, Trapper, you wanna tell me what your deal is?"

Trapper seethed inside. Apparently Lance had opened his big fucking mouth. He'd have a little talk with the dumb shit soon.

Instead of answering the question, Trapper started laughing. It started off as a chuckle and escalated from there. Soon, the man was almost convulsing with laughter.

This guy's a lunatic, Cal thought. He glanced up to the camera and shrugged at Briggs.

Soon, Trapper settled down and sat taking in brief breaths of air between giggles.

"What's so funny, Trapper?" Cal asked, not amused.

"Ha...ha...ha!...You...you're...funny..." Trapper spit out in the middle of girlish snickering.

His patience already thin, Cal stood up from his chair. "How about you shut your fucking mouth before I shut it for you," he growled.

The order fell on deaf ears. Trapper went back to howling like a madman. Cal just stood and watched. He couldn't do anything with this guy. Hopefully Travis would call back soon with something they could act on.

"Have it your way, buddy. Laugh all you want. You've got two choices: either help us out or get thrown in a deep dark cell somewhere."

This caused another riotous uproar from the beak-nosed man.

Cal shook his head and turned to leave.

"Wait...wait...I want to...tell you something," Trapper just managed to get out.

Cal turned back. "What do you want to tell me?"

"A...a secret."

Wary, Cal stepped closer to the man but still kept his distance. He would've felt better with a baseball bat in his hand. "What is it?"

"Come...closer...hee hee," Trapper coughed as he threw his head back again.

"No way. Tell me your secret."

Trapper's head snapped down and his gaze steadied on Cal.

"There's a third option," Trapper responded clearly.

Cal's blood froze and the hairs on the back of his neck stood up. Just as he reached for his pistol, Trapper somehow, impossibly, spread his legs that were no longer tied, and hoisted the chair over his head. Cal went to block the coming swing but instead of hitting him, Trapper continued his swing and launched the heavy chair at the oversized bedroom window. The skinny man followed the chair's trajectory. With hands and feet now free, he ran the short distance to the window and jumped.

Instead of shooting with his drawn pistol, Cal stood shocked. He didn't really want to fire his pistol in the small residential community. The cops would come running. A split second later, Cal was jumping out the window too.

DANIEL HAD BEEN WATCHING the interaction closely. He knew something was up Trapper's sleeve, but the man hid it well. Almost the same instant that the crafty captive stood up from his chair, Daniel was doing the same thing. With his pistol extended, he bolted for the bedroom door.

TRAPPER HIT the yard with his feet and immediately went into a roll to lessen the impact. His teeth still rattled as he sprang up and sprinted away from the house. He needed to get in touch with Nick Ponder.

CAL LANDED LESS GRACEFULLY than his quarry. He thudded painfully and fell forward. Luckily they'd jumped onto the grassy yard instead of the concrete driveway barely four feet away.

Only steps ahead, Trapper was moving in high gear as Cal struggled to regain his balance. The guy was moving incredibly fast. Cal chided himself for not checking the man's restraints. It was a basic rule in handling prisoners.

Pocketing his pistol in case they encountered neighbors, Cal ran after Trapper.

———

DANIEL SKIDDED to a halt at the bedroom window and stuck his head out. He could see Cal running into the darkness. Without another thought, Daniel avoided the broken glass, climbed onto the window frame and jumped. Hitting the grass, he rolled out gracefully and hopped into a sprint. He took off after the two men hoping he wouldn't be too late.

———

THERE WEREN'T many places for Trapper to go. The terrain was pretty open. Luckily it was pitch black out. He was free, but for how long? He'd chased countless criminals on foot so he knew the pursuit was all about tenacity and the wits of the man being chased. His mind processed the landscape and alternative routes. The neighborhood would end soon.

Trapper turned left on McCollister Drive, running up the incline. The only chance he had was using the clumps of trees on the slopes as cover. He knew exactly where to go.

———

CAL WAS LAGGING BEHIND. Not a bad athlete in his own right, Cal was no match for Trapper's speed. The only reason he could still see his former detainee was because the guy had stayed on the well lit road.

Cal was sure that wouldn't last long. He'd glimpsed Daniel coming up from behind but couldn't wait for his friend.

He pushed his legs and lungs to their limit. Neil's life depended on it.

Trapper hit the tree line and smiled. Unless his pursuer had somehow managed to grab a set of night vision goggles or a hound dog to sniff him out, there was no way he was getting caught.

Trapper looked back once, then disappeared into the woods.

Cal saw Trapper glance back just as Daniel caught up. Both men extracted their pistols and rushed forward. They ran in silence knowing that their chances of catching the man had just decreased exponentially.

Daniel stopped Cal as they approached the tree line. "Let me go first," the sniper ordered.

Cal would've ignored most other men but knew Daniel's skills outweighed his own when it came to the cat and mouse game they were playing with Trapper.

Without waiting for his employer to reply, Daniel melted into the wooded area.

After thirty minutes of looking, the two Marines emerged. The only thing Cal had to mark the occasion was a slightly sprained ankle and a variety of scrapes on his face. Daniel, on the other hand, looked clean and composed. How was it that he never seemed to get scathed?

"Thanks for coming after me," Cal offered.

"Sorry we didn't get the guy."

"It's my fault. I should've checked him," grumbled Cal.

"I'll bet if we look back at the video we won't even see how he got out of those restraints. That guy's a real pro."

Cal simply nodded. Just when he thought things might be going their way, it had gotten worse.

"Shit."

Daniel looked at Cal with serene confidence. "We'll get Neil back. Don't worry." He patted Stokes on the shoulder twice and started walking.

Cal stared back at his friend. For some reason he believed him. There was something in Daniel that inspired trust and calm. He'd talked about it with Trent a couple days before. MSgt Trent, being a much more spiritual man than Cal, thought that Daniel had some kind of God-given gift. He tried explaining it to Cal.

"I knew a preacher when I was a kid. Momma always said he was blessed by Jesus. This dude would walk into crack houses and gang hangouts and somehow come out untouched. He had this calming presence that good people flocked to and that bad people respected and were scared of. It's hard to explain other than to say that your boy Daniel has the same thing. Have you ever seen the kid get hurt or angry?"

Cal had not. He remembered the story Daniel had told him about his last time in Afghanistan. After the SEAL team they'd accompanied got killed by a large insurgent group, a building collapsed on him and his spotter. His spotter died and Daniel walked away unscathed except for the mental scars. After leaving the Marine Corps and wandering aimlessly through alcohol and bad dreams, Briggs found God. He never talked about it, but you could almost feel the invisible bond the former sniper held with the Almighty.

He looked over at Daniel as they walked back to their house. Briggs walked with an air of confidence that most men wished for. Cal hoped that Daniel's gift would help them find and rescue their lost friend.

TETON VILLAGE, JACKSON HOLE, WYOMING

11:34PM, SEPTEMBER 27TH

It hadn't been hard to lose his pursuers. Trapper knew the area well, and the dark night further aided his escape. He paused again to catch his breath and listen for sounds of pursuit. Nothing.

The safe house wasn't far. Just another ten minutes of jogging and he'd be there. Trapper took off down the dirt path. There was a storm looming on the horizon, and it had nothing to do with the weather. The killer's mind imagined the retribution he'd soon levy against Cal Stokes and his men.

Cal and Daniel returned to the house and awakened the team. Two men were posted to guard their remaining prisoner. They wouldn't lose this one.

After reviewing the taped interrogation two more times, they agreed that it was very likely that The Ponder Group had at least a base of operations if not a headquarters in the area. The assumption was confirmed minutes later by a call from Todd Dunn.

Cal had a pen and paper out, ready to take notes as he talked to SSI's security head.

"I've confirmed that Ponder registered his corporation in Wyoming. He's got a P.O. Box listed in the public record along with his attorney's address. The lawyer's office is in Wilson, which is just around the corner from Teton Village. I'm still working on locating his physical address."

"Sure would be nice to have Neil around right now," Cal noted ruefully.

"Yeah, he would've found Ponder in a couple minutes."

"Any progress on finding out who the leak is?"

"I think we're getting close. Me and Higgins narrowed it down to five guys in the R&D department. Neil hired them all. Looks like they didn't get as thorough a check as most new hires do."

"How did that happen?" Cal was confused about the security lapse by the otherwise overly cautious Dunn.

Dunn exhaled. "I won't blame it on Neil, but I'll probably have to have a little talk with him if we get him back."

"WHEN we get him back," Cal corrected.

"Right. WHEN we get him back, Neil needs to have a little class on security. We all know he's prone to seeing the good in people. Looks like this time it's really coming back to bite him in the ass."

"That seems a little harsh, Todd."

"I know it might, but we wouldn't be in this mess if it weren't for Neil. Shit, Cal, you know I love him as much as you and Travis do, but Neil really messed up on this one. First he denies the personal security and now we're finding out that he probably hired a rat. I think it's time for a little wakeup call for Mr. Patel."

Cal knew Dunn was right. He could only imagine how bad Neil's wakeup call was going.

NEIL WAS in the process of learning another lesson at the moment. He'd refused to do the 'test' Ponder had demanded. Now, for the third time, Neil was stripped naked and tied to a post outside the compound. The first time had been a warning. The second time lasted longer. This time Neil was sure he was almost hypothermic.

The temperature had to be in the low thirties. To make matters worse, every five minutes Ponder would walk outside with a bucket of cold water and dump it on the shivering Patel. Neil would cower and try to make himself as small as possible. He had no idea how long this time would last.

He kept himself going by thinking about his friends: Cal, Trent and Brian. Neil knew they wouldn't back down. He'd seen the after effects when they'd finally rescued Cal from the gangster Dante West. His friend came out beaten and bloody but in good spirits and, more importantly, alive.

Neil vaguely remembered MSgt Trent telling him that it was all about toughness and humor in the beginning. First get pissed off, then make it funny. *Didn't Senator McCain say the same thing?*

Neil knew that eventually all men broke under torture. He had to hold out as long as possible. The alternative was simply too terrifying to think about. If he used his talents to do what his captor wanted, he knew where it would lead. They were testing him. Patel was simply a tool to be used.

Despite his time with the company, he never truly understood the dangers their elite warriors faced. He'd heard the stories from the sidelines of the action, but being in the thick of it was something else entirely.

The front door of the low building opened and light spilled out into the darkness. Ponder's form appeared with his now familiar metal bucket.

"You ready to take your test or do you want to take another bath?" Ponder asked.

From his position on the ground Neil thought once more about his friends. *What would Trent say?* Between chattering teeth he answered. "I thought you'd...never ask. I was getting...hot out...here."

Ponder walked faster and threw the water right in Neil's face. It jolted him and took his breath away. Whatever reprieve Neil expected disappeared a second later when Ponder bent down and put his face right in front of Patel's.

"Now you listen here. I can do this shit all night. You'll feel like you're about to die and then we'll bring you back to life."

He reached down and grabbed Neil's bandaged stump. Neil clenched his teeth as Ponder began to squeeze.

"Come on, you pussy. You know you want to scream. Go ahead, no one can hear you anyway." Ponder squeezed harder and harder as Neil struggled to stay lucid. Tears streamed down his face as he turned to his aggressor.

"You're...the....pussy."

Ponder yelled in his face and followed it up with a quick head butt. Neil crumpled into unconsciousness.

"Shit," muttered Ponder. He hadn't meant to knock the kid out. Time was running out and so was his patience. The buyers were hounding him about providing proof that Patel was the real deal. Add the snowstorm blowing in and Ponder was scrambling to keep the transaction together.

He fished out a walkie talkie from his coat pocket. "Come out here and get him."

Thirty seconds later, the hooded jailer walked out, unlocked Neil from the pole, and picked him up gently.

"Put him back in his cell and warm him up. We'll try again in the morning," Ponder ordered.

The jailer nodded and carried his package back into the building.

Ponder stood outside, marveling at the stars. The view was crystal clear. It would be gone tomorrow when the clouds rolled in. He hoped it wasn't a sign of things to come. There was too much riding on the sale.

NEIL REGAINED consciousness just as he was being laid back down on his cot. He pretended to still be unconscious as the guard covered him with a blanket and left to fetch the large electric heater they used to bring Neil's body temperature back to normal.

Shivering under the wool blanket, Neil had one more thought as he drifted off into a fitful sleep. *I won this round, asshole.*

CAMP SPARTAN, ARRINGTON, TN

12:40AM CST, SEPTEMBER 28TH

Dr. Higgins and Todd Dunn were looking over the files of the five suspects. All five were relatively recent hires. Only one had been at the company for longer than a year. They were similar in that they all had some kind of computer science background. Under Neil Patel's leadership, SSI's R&D division had grown quickly over the preceding years. Cyber attacks were becoming more and more frequent around the globe, and Neil wanted to be part of the force fighting it.

The year before, the U.S. military's new Cyber Command had enlisted SSI's aid in building a more secure infrastructure. They now had SSI on retainer for future consultation with the caveat that Neil Patel be the lead troubleshooter.

"Do we still have all of these men on the premises?" asked Higgins.

"Yep. I gave the whole division orders to stay close a couple days ago. They're effectively on lockdown working around the clock."

"Good. They're probably nearing exhaustion. That should help our interrogation."

"What do you want me to do, Doc?" Dunn knew a thing or two

about questioning suspects, but he also understood that Dr. Higgins's skills were on a whole other level. The pudgy professor was the most effective interrogator Dunn had ever witnessed. You don't get to be the CIA leading expert on interrogation techniques without having a lot of success. Higgins had paid his dues around the globe countless times.

"I'd like for you to be with me for the questioning. Do you think you can play bad cop?"

Dunn offered a rare smile. "No problem, Doc."

Higgins went back to the files.

"I know I don't have to tell you this, Doc, but we need to find the leak fast and have time to assess the full extent of the damage. Marge says the federal investigators are coming tomorrow."

Higgins looked up from his scanning. "Then I guess we better get to work then."

Dunn shook his head in amusement. Leave it to Higgins to state the obvious.

THIRTY MINUTES later they'd devised their plan. Dunn picked up the office phone and dialed his deputy's number.

"I need four guards to meet me at the Batcave now. Tell them to come loaded." The Batcave was what everyone called Patel's underground research and IT facility. It not only held multiple office suites full of computers, but it also housed a large warehouse area that the teams used to test new technology. As a joke, someone had even plastered a few *Batman* movie posters on the door leading into the cavernous main room.

He hung up the phone and looked at Higgins. "You ready to go?"

"After you, Todd."

FIVE MINUTES LATER, Dunn and Higgins linked up with the four-man team waiting at the security desk outside the R&D labs. Each man wore all black combat suits and carried an H&K G36C automatic carbine. The fire team leader nodded to Dunn, who motioned for the men to follow.

The six men walked quickly down the long hallway leading to the entrance of the Batcave. Dunn put his hand on the entry scanner, and a second later the heavy magnetic lock clicked open.

Grabbing the door handle, Dunn turned to the fire-team leader. "Take Dr. Higgins down to the interrogation rooms. Help him setup whatever he needs. I'll be down in ten minutes."

SSI kept 'mock' interrogation rooms in the depths of its Tennessee campus. Used mostly for training, the rooms were now being utilized for the first time ever on SSI's own employees. It still shocked Dunn that a breach of this magnitude happened on his watch. He promised himself that it would never happen again.

As the four operators escorted Higgins to the lower level, Dunn headed to the common computing room that most of the geeks occupied after hours. He'd already confirmed with security that the five men he wanted to question were still there.

He walked into the large common room and looked around. Even though he'd never been to the headquarters of Google or Facebook, this is what he imagined it probably looked like. The room was huge and wide open. There were dartboards and a ping-pong table in one corner and a full array of video game systems in another. The center of the space housed modern tables of varying shapes and sizes. Twenty some odd programmers and technicians were scattered around the room engaged in both work and play. Dunn understood the necessity to blow off steam, especially if you spent all hours underground. The guys worked hard and deserved the added amenities.

Scanning the large room, he quickly found the group he was looking for. They were clicking away on mini laptops. Everyone was so engaged that they didn't even turn as Dunn moved closer. One young man finally looked up. "Can I help you, Mr. Dunn?" The caution was evident in his tone. Todd Dunn was known throughout SSI for his no B.S. attitude. If he came calling, you stood at attention. The rest of the small gaggle took the hint and stopped what they were doing.

"I need to see some of you." Dunn read off the names. "If you can close up whatever you're working on and meet me in the next room in five minutes, I'd appreciate it."

Without another word, Dunn turned around and left the room.

"I wonder what that's all about," commented one of the programmers.

No one bothered to answer the statement. The five employees called out by Dunn quickly packed up their gear.

Terrence Zheng tried to hide his discomfort. He'd been one of the five Dunn had requested. Zheng tried to act casual as his nerves rattled inside. The last thing he wanted to do was spend time with Dunn. He'd thought that the FBI investigation would've given him the opportunity to leave the campus unnoticed, but there hadn't been a chance to yet. Not only was his division being worked overtime, it had also been discretely recommended that they all remain on the headquarters' grounds.

Terrence had to somehow get word to Ponder that they were starting to question employees. Maybe his newest benefactor could get him out of it.

As the five men stepped out in the corridor Zheng spoke up.

"Hey, can you tell Dunn that I'll be there in a minute? I've gotta hit the bathroom. Too many Red Bulls," Zheng offered embarrassedly.

"You better hurry up," answered a small Vietnamese named Tony. "I heard the last time someone kept Dunn waiting he made him strip down and do push-ups in the cafeteria cooler."

Zheng gave Tony an exasperated look as the others laughed. "I'll be there in a second."

He walked quickly to the restroom and headed for the nearest stall. Sitting down to relieve himself, Zheng pulled out his cell phone and logged in to the remote email server. He wrote a quick note and left it in the drafts folder. Flushing the toilet, he hoped the entire ordeal would be over soon. He looked forward to a much-needed vacation on a beautiful island.

CAMP SPARTAN, ARRINGTON, TN

1:25AM CST, SEPTEMBER 28TH

Terrence Zheng left the restroom and joined the others.

"Sorry about that, Mr. Dunn. Figured I should take a piss before we got started," Zheng offered.

Todd Dunn nodded. "We're headed downstairs. There've been some developments in Neil's disappearance but we need your help. It shouldn't take long."

They all looked at Dunn in confusion. Usually they were allowed to work independently. Initial guidance was given followed by the occasional check-in. Then again, the current situation was unique. They all knew Neil well as he'd hired each one of them. The overtime they'd logged wasn't just mandatory, every man had volunteered to stay and work.

Zheng played along because everyone else had. He couldn't wait to walk out that door and never look back.

Dunn continued, "We're trying to nail down details so we can find out what happened. I know you've probably already answered some of this stuff but me and Doc Higgins wanted to hear it personally."

Two of the men groaned. What had already looked like a long night just got longer.

Dunn ignored the frustrated sighs, then turned and headed to the stairwell. As he walked, he was already running the interrogation through his mind. He'd already chosen his first target: Terrence Zheng.

THE MOOD WENT SOUTH AS SOON as they reached their destination. Even though they were used to working in the subterranean facility, this was something else. The main waiting area held stadium seating similar to what you might find in a university or outside an operating room in a teaching hospital. Everything had the sterile feel of a medical facility too. There were no decorations or even the slightest attempt to warm the place up. It was what it was, an interrogation facility.

The seating overlooked ten rooms, each about twelve by twelve with a metal table and two sets of chairs. Although the lighting was comfortable in the gallery, the interrogation rooms looked like they were lit by prison spot lights.

None of the five had ever been to the interrogation pod. There were only a handful of SSI employees that had the security access to come this far underground.

SSI's head of security didn't try to lighten the mood. This was exactly what he wanted. He needed them to be on edge. They were visibly uncomfortable. Dunn directed the suspects to leave their belongings on a table in the middle of the room. They were then searched from head to toe by one of the guards and escorted to separate rooms.

As the five men entered their respective space, Dunn stepped into a side room that housed the control room. One wall was comprised of flat panel screens displaying video of each of the ten rooms. Dr. Higgins was sitting in one of the comfortable leather couches, reviewing his files one last time. He looked up as Dunn walked in.

"Everything go well with the roundup?" he asked cheerfully.

Dunn nodded. "They didn't freak out until we walked into the gallery."

"That's to be expected. I can only imagine what is going through their heads at this very moment."

"I think I know who we should start with. This Zheng kid." Dunn pointed at the screen broadcasting Terrence Zheng in high definition. "Something doesn't feel right about him."

"Anything tangible?"

"Not that I can put my finger on, but there's something in his eyes. It just looks like he's hiding something."

Higgins pulled out Zheng's file.

"Let's see. Terrence Zheng, born April 3rd, 1989 in Burbank, California. Parents are from Beijing, China. He attended the University of California at Berkeley for undergrad. Graduated with honors in three years and double-majored in Computer Science and Electrical Engineering. Went to MIT for graduate school. Dropped out after his first year to run a start-up. Won a spot in SSI's business mentoring program. His company was sold last year for a tidy sum, and Zheng was then hired by SSI. He is now part of our cyber-security team and is tasked with monitoring our network and preventing intrusion.

"I must say, Todd, if this is our man, we might have quite a predicament on our hands."

Dunn sighed. All but one of the five suspects worked in some critical capacity at SSI. He didn't even want to think about the possible calamity should SSI's network be laid bare.

"You have any problem with me playing the bad cop?" Dunn asked.

"I was rather hoping you would."

ZHENG LOOKED up at the mirrored observation window. It was even brighter in the room than it had seemed from the observation deck. He was uncomfortable but tried to act calm as he waited for someone to begin the questioning.

Todd Dunn and Dr. Higgins entered. Higgins took a seat while Dunn leaned against the opposite wall. The muscular man's calm demeanor was gone. It felt like Dunn was staring a hole right through him. Despite his thought to do otherwise, Zheng began to sweat.

Dr. Higgins started. "Hello, Terrence, my name is Dr. Higgins." He reached across and shook Zheng's hand warmly. "I'm sorry we've taken you away from your work but we had some pressing questions to ask you and your colleagues."

"Anything I can do to help, Doctor," Zheng offered as cheerfully as he could.

Higgins smiled. He could feel the nervousness rolling off of the young man. It wasn't unusual even for innocent men to feel uncomfortable in such surroundings. Through the years Dr. Higgins had developed a highly accurate barometer for judging people's innocence. It usually only took a little friendly banter for Higgins to deduce whether a suspect was, in fact, hiding something. Getting the person to divulge the information was something else entirely.

"I appreciate your help, Terrence. Now, as you know, we've lost one of our most important assets, Neil Patel. We'd like to ask you some questions to see if we've possibly missed something. Sometimes in these investigations it's the smallest, most mundane detail that solves the case."

Zheng nodded gravely.

"How long have you known Neil?"

"Uhh, I'd say a little over two years."

"You were one of the recipients of our start-up funding, were you not?" Higgins asked.

"Yes. I started a company called PlanBot. It was essentially cloud-based planning software."

Higgins glanced down at the file. "Ah yes, and it says here that you later sold the company."

"That's right. With SSI's help we found a larger company that wanted our technology."

"Fantastic! You must have been very excited." Higgins smiled.

"It was a lot of fun. I couldn't have done it without you guys, and Neil, of course."

Higgins paused again and pretended to go through the file. He had already memorized the key points and merely used the time to form his next line of questioning.

"So after you sold your company, you decided to come work at SSI. Was there a reason you didn't go into, what do they call it nowadays... early retirement?"

"Honestly, I considered it. I made enough money that it would've been easy to find a place and settle down."

"So what made you come to work here?"

"I really enjoyed working with the guys when I was in the start-up pipeline. There was always the opportunity to start something new again but this seemed like a good challenge. After a couple conversations with Neil, he offered me a job."

Higgins knew he was being told the truth. Not only did he sense it, he'd taken a similar path after working with SSI on a particularly challenging assignment during his tenure with the CIA. The caliber of individual and the high degree of integrity impressed Higgins immensely and ultimately led to his retirement from government service. He'd never looked back. It was a common story amongst SSI employees. Here they were valued.

"How do you like it now that you've been here for a bit?"

Zheng hesitated. He knew this was where he had to be careful. "It's been good."

Higgins caught the hesitation. Was it simply a matter of an employee being unsatisfied with his work or was there more?

"Let me rephrase the question. Do you feel like you've been challenged professionally since you've been here?"

After a brief pause, Zheng answered. "At first I don't think Neil knew where to put me. To be honest, some of the stuff he had me working on was pretty basic. Once he had a better idea of my capabilities he started giving me more and more."

It sounded reasonable. After all, Zheng was used to running his own company. Former business owners didn't always turn out to be the best employees. Going from a world where you make all the decisions to having someone else telling you what to do wasn't always easy.

"And how is your relationship with Neil?"

"I think it's pretty good. He doesn't really micromanage so I mainly just see him in staff meetings."

"Did you know about the conference Neil was attending in Wyoming?"

Zheng hesitated for the briefest of moments. *Here it comes*, he thought. It didn't matter. They couldn't trace a thing to him unless Ponder gave him up. He knew that would never happen. Plus, he'd covered his tracks like a true professional.

"Sure. We all knew he was going out there. I think someone even bought him a cowboy hat as a joke."

Higgins chuckled. "I think I heard about that. Did you know what the conference was for?"

"I'm not sure. Neil mentioned it was some VIP thing. I did hear that he was giving a class or maybe a lecture."

Zheng began to relax. Maybe they really were just ironing out the details. Deep down he enjoyed this game of cat and mouse. He'd played it for years online. There'd been a few close calls in his early days of hacking, but he hadn't come close to being caught in a while. This was the first time he'd experienced the adrenaline rush of a face-to-face confrontation. The excitement played through his body as he secretly savored the moment. He was better than them.

"Did he mention where he was staying in Wyoming?" Higgins asked.

"I'm not sure. I know he was in Jackson Hole, but I didn't have the details." In truth, Terrence Zheng knew all the details. Neil was never very careful about hiding anything from his staff. Zheng had Neil's entire itinerary memorized. He'd even pulled up the Google Earth image of Hotel Terra during the time he knew Neil was being kidnapped. What he wouldn't have paid to see the look on the cocky bastard's face.

"Did you know that Neil refused to take any personal security on the trip?"

Zheng did. "I think he mentioned something about that. Neil doesn't seem like a big fan of being escorted around."

As the suspect finished his answer, one of the guards walked in and handed something to Dunn. Trying to look nonchalant, Zheng glanced their way. *That's my phone!* For a split second Zheng panicked. He quickly calmed, though, knowing there was no way they could get past the encryption he'd installed. If they tried, the phone would effectively cease to work. He knew how to cover his tracks.

After a few whispered words, the guard left and Dunn turned his attention back to the questioning. Higgins twisted around in his chair and looked at Dunn. "Any updates?"

Dunn nodded, walked to the table and raised Zheng's phone. "You wanna tell me what you were doing with your phone in the bathroom?"

"I was just checking my email."

"Anything interesting?" Dunn asked with a raised eyebrow.

"Not really."

"Let's cut the crap, Terrence. Tell me what you were doing with your phone," Dunn ordered.

Zheng stood his ground. "I told you, I had to take a leak and out of habit I checked my email. I might've gone on Facebook too, I don't know."

Dunn looked his suspect right in the eye. "Tell me how you know Nick Ponder."

Zheng's eyes dilated rapidly, but he caught himself before panicking. "I don't know…"

There wasn't time to finish. Faster than Zheng thought possible, Dunn came around the table, grabbed him by the neck and pinned him against the wall.

The smaller man struggled. He didn't know how to respond. Unaccustomed to physical violence, Zheng pissed his pants as Dunn squeezed harder.

"I'll ask you again, how do you know Nick Ponder?" he loosened his grasp just enough for Zheng to croak back.

"I…don't…"

"Wrong answer, asshole." Without warning, Dunn smacked him across the face. "Now tell me how you know Nick Ponder!"

Zheng looked to Dr. Higgins for help. To his surprise, the jolly doctor sat placidly. He actually looked like he was enjoying the exchange.

"You…can't…do…"

Dunn answered with another slap that brought tears to Zheng's eyes. "I can do whatever I want, you little traitor. Now you listen to me. What I'm doing right now is child's play compared to what the Doc over there can do to you. You either answer me now or I let him have you."

Zheng's mind couldn't comprehend what was happening. There were laws. He had rights. They couldn't torture him, could they? His mind was clouding and he didn't know how to respond. He wasn't prepared for this.

"But...I don't..."

Dunn answered the unfinished statement by slamming his forehead into Zheng's nose. Bone and cartilage cracked as the small man crumpled to the ground and fell into unconsciousness.

———

PONDER WAS STILL awake monitoring the deteriorating weather and hoping he wouldn't get another message from his buyer. He'd have to get more creative with Patel. There was just too much riding on the transaction.

He opened up another tab on his internet browser and logged in to the email account he shared with Terrence Zheng. The last he'd heard from Zheng was that SSI was preparing for the FBI audit by working them overtime. Ponder didn't care about how much the little Asian worked. He wanted to make sure they weren't on his trail yet. After selling Neil, he didn't give a shit who knew. Ponder would be long gone by then. Until that happened he might have to tie up some loose ends, like Terrence Zheng. The kid had been useful in getting Patel's travel itinerary and giving him a heads-up about the teams that followed, but ultimately he was a liability. Ponder figured he'd probably have Zheng killed as a precaution. He'd done it before. The thought of killing another human was more a necessity for Ponder than a crime.

His internet connection was slow, so he waited impatiently for the email server to load. Finally coming up on his screen, Ponder clicked on the Drafts folder. There was a message from Zheng.

My presence requested with four others by Dunn. I'll let you know when I'm finished.

Ponder froze. The message was casual only because the little shit didn't know who he was dealing with. Ponder knew Todd Dunn only by reputation. The former Ranger was regarded throughout the industry as a thorough operator. Dunn never cracked under pressure. He was as solid as they came.

Maybe there was a chance that they were still safe. Ponder quickly discarded the thought. He had to plan for the worst. Just as he was mulling over his options, his cell phone rang. He didn't recognize the number but only a limited number of people knew where to reach him.

"Hello?"

"It's me."

Trapper!

"Where the hell have you been?"

"I'm at our house in the village."

Ponder knew that meant Trapper was at their little safe house in Teton Village.

"What are you doing there?"

"We ran into a little distraction," Trapper answered cryptically, always cautious about using even secure phones.

The hairs on the back of Ponder's neck rose. "What kind of distraction?"

"Those friends we were looking out for invited us in for a little talk. I had to leave Lance so I could let you know."

"How bad is it?" he asked.

"I think you're about to have company."

He gripped his cell phone to the point of breaking it. Nothing was going according to plan. It was time to salvage the situation.

"Can you get back here?"

"Not quickly."

"What if I arrange a helo?"

"Sure."

"Okay. I'll call you back."

Ponder ended the call and looked at Neil Patel's sleeping form in the small video window of his computer screen. "Your friends aren't gonna fuck this up for me."

He picked up another phone and dialed the afterhours line for a helicopter pilot that owed him a few favors. Ponder had saved the guy's helicopter company from creditors. In exchange, The Ponder Group had free use of the company's helo.

After four rings the man picked up in a groggy voice. "Yeah?"

"It's Ponder. I need you to fly one of my guys from Teton Village over to my place."

"Can't this wait until tomorrow?"

"No, it can't. Now get your ass out of bed. My guy will be calling in a few minutes."

Ponder slammed the phone down, picked up his cell phone and dialed the number Trapper had called from. He quickly gave his employee the phone number for the company owner and told him to get back as soon as possible. He'd need all the manpower he could get.

"Hey, boss, why don't we just bug out for a while? We can take your new friend and get out of town."

"I'm not running away. We'll deal with these guys once and for all."

Trapper knew better than to try to dissuade him. Once he made his mind up, that was it.

"Just don't do anything until I get there, okay?" Trapper requested.

"Then hurry your ass up!"

Ponder threw his phone across the room where it crashed into the far wall and smashed into a hundred pieces. He calmed enough to think about the looming conflict. Part of him wanted to get the sale over with and leave. The fighter in him wanted to stick around and deal with the SSI problem. Maybe he could do both.

Grabbing another thick cigar, Ponder mentally ran through his options. He'd often dreamt about defending his castle against invading hordes. It looked like this might be his chance.

CAMP SPARTAN, ARRINGTON, TN

2:36AM CST, SEPTEMBER 28TH

When Terrence Zheng finally awoke, he found himself strapped to a hospital gurney. His arms and legs were secured with Velcro restraints. He tried to lift his head and almost screamed in pain. His face throbbed from the vicious head butt administered by Todd Dunn. Zheng took a couple steadying breaths and looked up slowly.

They'd moved him into another room. It was similar to the first but as he looked around, Zheng saw a variety of medical equipment neatly arranged on two wheeled tables. Next to the tables were three IV stands.

"I see you're awake, Terrence," Dr. Higgins's voice came over the speaker system. "I'll be right in."

Part of Zheng hoped it was all a bad dream. Maybe the FBI or even Nick Ponder would come running through the door and rescue him. He let his mind wander until Higgins entered through the room's only door. He was attired in black scrubs and almost looked like a contestant on *Top Chef* except for the face shield he had propped on the top of his head.

"I'm sorry about Mr. Dunn's little transgression. I got you cleaned up as best I could."

"That man is a lunatic! When I get out of here..."

"Shhh," Higgins ordered with a finger to his lips. "You might want to watch what you say. Mr. Dunn is still listening." He pointed to the one-way window.

"But I haven't done anything wrong!"

Higgins shook his head as if disappointed.

"We both know that's not true, Terrence."

"You don't know..."

"Oh but I will, Terrence," Higgins replied with an almost embarrassed shrug. "Do you know what I do at SSI, Terrence?"

"You...uh...you're a shrink or something."

"That's partially true. While my job does require me to attend to the mental well-being of SSI employees, my background is actually in interrogation."

Zheng strained to look back at the doctor.

"Oh, I'm sorry. How rude of me." Dr. Higgins moved to the side of the gurney and reached underneath. Something clicked and Zheng flinched as he heard the electric hum. The stretcher slowly tilted forward so that he was no longer lying flat.

"Is that better?" Higgins asked.

Zheng nodded through fear-filled eyes.

"So, as I was saying, my background is in interrogation. I rather hate the word but it is quite accurate." Dr. Higgins adjusted his glasses as he walked over to one of the IV stands.

"You see, I spent the first part of my career with the Central Intelligence Agency. When they wanted someone to talk, they flew me in. You can't imagine how many countries I've been to. Now, I only tell you this so that we might save time."

"What...what do you mean?"

"One way or another you will tell us what we want to know. Most people think they can resist divulging the truth. I think it's because they watch too many movies. Well, that's simply not true. Everyone talks. It's just a matter of when."

Zheng couldn't believe what he was hearing. He'd seen the chubby doctor around the campus on many occasions. Higgins looked more like a jolly uncle than what he'd just described. He was always chatting with SSI employees and telling the latest jokes he'd heard. Zheng just couldn't get it through his head that there could be any other reality.

"Doctor, I really don't know what I'm doing here. I work on the computer systems and that's it. I'm not even..."

He realized Higgins wasn't listening. Instead, he was preparing the various IVs and instruments, and moving them closer to the gurney. Dr. Higgins finally turned back to Zheng.

"I've been working on a very special recipe. I haven't had a chance to try it out on a human subject, so this will be perfect timing."

Zheng's eyes went wide as Higgins swabbed his arm and inserted the IV needle. "Now, this won't hurt as long as you don't struggle. Allow the drugs to work their way into your system." He turned the dial on the IV, and Zheng felt the cold flow of liquid entering his blood stream.

"I'll let that run for a few minutes, and then I'll be back in to talk to you."

"Don't leave me in here!" Zheng screamed in panic.

Higgins ignored the outburst and left the room to consult with Dunn. He was sure they'd have their answers soon.

―――

"Have you found anything on his phone?" Dr. Higgins asked Dunn.

"No. I've got one of the other computer guys taking a look at it now. Looks like Mr. Zheng might have loaded it with some extra security features."

Higgins had expected as much. This new breed of youth was comfortable manipulating technology. Besides, he wasn't sure they'd get any more out of the phone than through the interrogation.

"I'll give him ten minutes and the solution should be fully in his system. Is there anything else you'd like me to ask?"

"Just what we discussed before. I need to get Cal as much intel as I can. There's a big snowstorm about to blow into Wyoming, so we need to work fast."

"I always do, my boy."

"We do need to figure out what to do with the kid once we're done questioning him."

SSI had never had to put away any of its own employees before. It wasn't possible to just dump him on the local police department. Zheng knew too much. Dunn also didn't want to kill the guy. They weren't murderers.

"Let me see if I can make a call to some of my old friends at the Agency. I'm sure they can find a space for our friend in one of their maximum security cells."

Dunn liked the idea. If they could pull a few strings, Zheng would never see the light of day again. It's what he deserved for selling out Neil and the company.

"Go ahead and do that. In the meantime, we'll hold him here until this whole thing with Neil gets resolved."

Higgins agreed and left the room to make the phone call. Dunn looked into Zheng's holding room. *We better get some answers soon.*

DR. HIGGINS STROLLED BACK into Zheng's room, this time with the face shield down. You never knew when someone might like to spit in your face.

"How are you feeling, Terrence?"

Zheng couldn't respond for a moment. He'd been surprised to find that no pain accompanied the IV's injection. In fact, instead of feeling worse, he almost felt euphoric.

"I'm feeling pretty damn good, Doctor!"

Higgins smiled warmly. He never knew why some interrogators insisted on administering pain to make suspects talk. Through the miracle of modern medicine, there were now easier ways. Over the years, Higgins had learned to manipulate men with the use of a variety of intoxicating tools. He'd learned to vary his doses based on not only the physical characteristics of the subject, but also their temperament. Like an expert anesthesia practitioner, Higgins knew exactly how to manipulate the body to get a desired effect. He felt it was better to have a compliant and happy subject, and mixed his drugs accordingly. Let them gnash and scream later. His job was to find the answer in the quickest and most humane way possible.

"I'm glad you're feeling better, Terrence. Now, are you ready to answer some of my questions?"

A small part of Zheng screamed alarm, but the thought was swiftly pushed aside by the swirl of the potent drug. "I'm happy to help in any way I can," he answered.

"Good. Let's start with some easy questions, shall we?"

Zheng nodded eagerly. For some reason he had an overwhelming urge to help. He wanted to tell the truth. The real story of his life felt like it was going to burst out of his lungs. Why had he been so defensive earlier? Dr. Higgins only wanted to help him, right?

"First, your name is Terrence Zheng, correct?"

"Yes, but my friends call me Z."

"Ah. You don't mind if I still call you Terrence, do you?"

"Nope."

"How long have you worked for SSI, Terrence?"

"I think for about a year."

"And what is it you do at SSI?"

"I help maintain the company's network security."

"Do you do any work for our clients?"

"I've done some consulting with the Department of Defense."

"And what was the nature of the consulting?"

"They're trying to beef up their new Cyber Command. If you ask me, they're way behind the power curve."

"What do you mean, Terrence?"

Zheng laughed out loud. "I could out-hack any of those guys."

"So you're a hacker, Terrence?"

"Yeah, I've been breaking into stuff since I was a kid."

"I assume it always came easy for you?"

"Yeah. I think the first time I hacked into someone's computer was when I was, like, eight years old. My dad wouldn't let me play games on his PC, so I learned how to break in."

"How would you rate your skills as compared to your peers?"

Zheng thought about his answer. He wanted to be as precise as he could for the kind doctor. "I'm not saying I'm the best in the world. The best guys spend all their time hacking. I'm more of a part-timer."

Higgins had a hunch he wanted to work out. "How would you say your skills compare to say…Neil Patel?"

Zheng's face scrunched up, and then he smiled proudly. "I'm better."

Higgins wasn't so sure. He'd heard from numerous friends that Patel could possibly be one of the world's elite computer geniuses. He hadn't heard of a single system Neil couldn't break into. Higgins was starting to feel that Zheng had a highly inflated opinion of himself. Was that a possible motive? He'd be testing the potency of his drug mixture, but Higgins was all about experimentation.

"Why do you feel you're better than Neil?"

"I'm younger and I know the newest ways to get around things," Zheng stated.

"So you feel that you could do Neil's job better than he does?"

Warning bells once again sounded in the recesses of Zheng's mind. Was he supposed to answer that question? As before, the drugs swept away any doubt.

"I definitely think I can do the job better."

It was time to ask the most damning question. Higgins was now sure that the young man would answer truthfully. Although he wanted the answer, he still dreaded it.

"Is that why you helped Nick Ponder kidnap Neil?"

Zheng answered without hesitating. "Yes."

CAMP SPARTAN, ARRINGTON, TN

3:56AM CST, SEPTEMBER 28TH

After almost an hour of questioning, Dunn and Higgins felt like they had everything they needed. Zheng's motive had been power. He didn't really need the money. Even though Zheng was set to make a pretty penny from Ponder, it was the possibility of taking down a man like Neil that had truly motivated him. For him it was a challenge similar to breaking into his father's computer the first time.

Dunn cursed the young upstart for his stupidity.

"How long will he be doped up like that, Doc?" Dunn asked.

"He should be coming out of it soon. Do you think what we learned will help get Neil back?"

"The biggest thing we needed was to confirm that Ponder was behind it. That guy is a real piece of work. If the FBI wasn't coming tomorrow, I'd be going out there myself. As it is, we won't be able to send Cal any more help what with the storm and the FBI audit."

"Don't you mean today?"

"What?"

"The FBI is coming TODAY, Todd."

Dunn looked at his watch and groaned. "Shit. I've gotta go. Can you take care of our young friend there?"

"Consider it handled. Please let me know if there's anything I can do to assist with the investigation."

"You've already done more than you know, Doc. Thanks again."

Dunn left in a hurry. The first person he had to call was Cal. He'd love to know that their target was confirmed. Dunn placed the call as he rushed to the stairwell.

"Stokes."

"Cal, we just confirmed the kidnapper's identity."

"Is it who we thought?"

"Yes."

"Good, thanks."

"Hey, Cal?"

"Yeah."

"What's your next move?"

Dunn could hear the fierce determination in the Marine's voice. "I'm going to get Neil back."

TETON VILLAGE, JACKSON HOLE, WYOMING

3:13AM, SEPTEMBER 28TH

Cal gathered his men in the living room. Although most had just been awakened, he could feel the charged energy in the air. It was almost time to move. They waited expectantly for their young leader to speak.

"I just got confirmation from Dunn. The guy behind the kidnapping is a former soldier named Nick Ponder."

There were murmurs around the room. Apparently some of the men knew who Ponder was, and by the sound of the comments, their opinions were not favorable.

"According to Travis, this asshole is a real piece of work. He's also downright deadly. Ponder has a habit of being connected with the wrong crowd. The two guys we brought in last night work for The Ponder Group. Unfortunately one of them got away, but that shouldn't matter."

Cal paused and looked around the room at his highly trained warriors. "Now, you know I'd never ask any one of you to do something that I wouldn't do myself...so I'll tell it to you straight. Once we find out where this Ponder guy lives, I'm going in there and taking him out. From what I've heard of the fucker, it probably should've been done a long time ago."

He searched his men for any sense of unease, but all he saw was seething anger. "So here's your chance. If you want out, tell me now. If you want in, pack your snow gear because we're headed into the mountains."

No one made a sound. The silence lingered until MSgt Trent spoke.

"Well, if Gaucho's going, I'm going."

"What are you talking about, Top?" asked Gaucho, confused about being called out.

"Hombre, I've been waitin' to see you freeze your cojones off for years!" The men snickered at the comment. Once again the large Marine succeeded in keeping the mood light. Cal loved him for it.

"Fuck you, Top," Gaucho replied with a grin.

THIRTY MINUTES later they were putting the finishing touches on their plan. The biggest problem was figuring out what to do with their prisoner.

"Let's bring him along," suggested Brian.

Cal didn't like the idea. They'd have enough to worry about. Babysitting the overgrown child wasn't exactly what he had in mind.

"I'll take care of him, Cal." Everyone looked at Daniel in surprise. "I don't think he's a bad guy and I don't think he'll give us any trouble."

"I agree with Snake Eyes," offered Gaucho. "If we leave him here we'll have to leave two of our guys back too. Without any extra men coming from HQ, I think we need everybody we've got."

Cal wasn't sure. It wasn't that he didn't trust Daniel's judgment or skills. He knew the sniper could handle most men, but he would rather have the deadly warrior's eyes looking for coming threats.

"If you think you can handle it…okay. But you make sure he knows that if he slows us down even a bit, I'll tie his ass up and leave him on the mountain."

Daniel knew his boss wasn't that cruel, but he also knew Cal was deadly serious. He wouldn't stop until Neil was rescued. Daniel needed to have a good talk with Lance.

CAMP SPARTAN, ARRINGTON, TN

5:35AM CST, SEPTEMBER 28TH

Travis Haden walked into the conference room. Dunn, Haines and Dr. Higgins looked up from their discussion.

"I just got word from Cal. They're heading into the mountains soon." He walked over to the coffee pot to fill his mug.

"What are they doing with their prisoner?" asked Dunn.

"He's going along for the ride. Cal doesn't think the guy will give them any trouble."

"Do you really think that's a good idea?" asked Haines.

Travis shrugged. "It's Cal's operation, and I won't stand in his way. The good news is that by taking him the whole team will be together." Travis took a sip of his coffee. "Do we know when the FBI investigators are arriving?"

As the point person for the audit, Haines answered. "They should be here at seven."

Travis looked down at his watch. "That gives us just under two hours. I'm not worried about them finding anything with our contracts. Have we taken care of our little leak?"

"He's on his way to his very own private cell in the middle of nowhere, Skipper," responded Dunn. "Doc Higgins made a call and thirty minutes later a delivery van showed up at the gate and took the little shit out of here."

"Are we covered in case the Bureau asks questions about Mr. Zheng's whereabouts?"

"We've got the story all ironed out. He's taken a leave of absence due to mental instability," smirked Dunn, clearly not worried about the possibility of the story being dissected by the FBI.

"Good. Marge, who's running the show for the FBI?"

"A man named Jack Malone. I've checked with my contacts and he's got a good reputation within the Bureau. He's a thorough investigator but well-liked by his peers. Agent Malone's moved up the ladder swiftly over the last ten years. We're not the first security contractor he's audited. I don't think he'll be a problem."

Travis was still worried. Why had the FBI chosen this very moment to investigate SSI?

"Have they given you any indication as to why we're under the microscope?"

Haines shook her head. "Malone made it sound pretty routine. He even told me not to worry about it, that it's just our turn."

Something was wrong. Travis could feel it in his bones. "I want you to have their entire team monitored. Cell phones included."

Dunn looked at his boss cautiously. "You sure that's smart? What if they find out?"

"I'm not taking any chances right now, Todd. If they catch wind of it, tell them we monitor all non-SSI personnel. If they really press it, have them talk to me. Something stinks about this whole thing, and I'll be damned if I let another rat into our house."

It was a risky move, but they all knew he was right. The sooner the FBI left the better.

TETON VILLAGE, JACKSON HOLE, WY

5:08AM, SEPTEMBER 28TH

Cal's team loaded into the SUVs. They were taking enough cold weather gear and rations to last at least a week. Cal hoped they wouldn't have to test the duration.

The team would drive twenty minutes to the trailhead for Phelps Lake. To casual observers, the warriors would look like a group of hunters taking an extended trip into the Tetons. It wasn't one of the normal routes for gamesmen to take but not completely out of the ordinary.

Lance Upshaw was equally fitted with gear. Luckily, SSI's supply chief had sent some extra, just in case. Each man would carry a large mountaineering backpack with skis and snowshoes strapped to the outside. Due to the possibility of running into park rangers, they'd elected to bring along a mix of civilian hunting rifles and side arms. Each man also carried a collapsed H&K submachine gun in their packs. It wouldn't be the best thing if they were ambushed, but they'd have to make do.

Every man would be carrying around one hundred pounds on his back. It wouldn't be the easiest trek, but no one would complain. They'd all been through worse.

TWENTY MINUTES LATER, the caravan pulled into the dirt parking lot at the trailhead. The sun was starting to peek out over the mountain range. It was the last sunlight they'd probably see for days. On Cal's last weather check it looked like the snowstorm would blow in around nine in the morning. It was imperative to make as much progress as possible before it hit.

The limited visibility would hamper their ability to travel and watch their flanks. It would've been a lot easier to take a helicopter, but every pilot they'd contacted had already grounded their aircraft because of the storm. Their only option was to hike in. It wouldn't be an easy journey, but they'd all endured far worse. Ponder's mountaintop headquarters was perfectly situated for its seclusion. Cal worried that the hideout was also an ideal stronghold.

They'd be humping up through the aptly named Death Canyon, then make their way toward Battleship Mountain. From the information headquarters had provided, it looked like Ponder's place was situated at the base of the northern side of Battleship Mountain.

It took five minutes for the men to strap on their packs, inspect their teammates and move out. Gaucho took point against Cal's request to be up front.

"We can do this without you, Boss. Let me get shot at first," the squat Hispanic said with a wink.

As they stepped off toward their destination, Cal could only hope that they wouldn't be too late.

AT ALMOST THE SAME MOMENT, the buyers' representatives were starting a similar journey from the west side of the mountain range. They'd prepped for the journey at the small Best Western in Driggs,

Idaho the night before. None had slept. The small group of men was used to operating without sleep. Even their leader was a former commando and well-trained in cold weather warfare. Their country had fought for years in high altitudes. These men were the representatives sent by their homeland to deliver a new weapon that would transform their battle on a global front. Handpicked by their leader, each man was ready to die for their cause. Preparations had already been made in case they should perish.

The five operatives parked their two rented vehicles at the Teton Canyon Trail Head. Three minutes later they departed on foot toward Battleship Mountain.

NICK PONDER and Trapper were huddled over a topographic map of the area when the phone rang. Ponder answered with a grunt, listened, and then replaced the receiver.

"That was our buyers. They're on their way," Ponder muttered, deep in thought.

"You know when they'll be here?" asked Trapper.

Ponder shook his head. "They just said they're coming in on foot."

"I don't like it, Boss. It's bad enough that we've got the SSI guys headed our way. We don't have enough men to guard every pass leading into this place."

Ponder slammed his fist on the desk. "I know, goddamit! Just give me a minute to fucking think!"

Trapper held his tongue. He knew better than to press the point when his employer was upset. The man had a legendary temper, and Trapper wasn't in the mood to take a tongue lashing.

"How many men do we have?" Ponder asked for the fifth time.

Trapper stifled the urge to exhale before answering. "We've got twenty two, not including you and me. I figure we should keep at least half of them here at the complex. The rest we can break into two-man teams and post them on the most likely ingress routes."

The two men looked at the map again, and Ponder pointed to the positions he'd already selected in his mind.

"I want a team here, here and here. Make sure they'd got good radio equipment. I want to know as soon as they spot movement."

Over the years Ponder had secretly hoped for an invasion of his mountain lair. He'd prepared cave positions in strategic locations to serve as forward outposts. Ponder had played the scenario over and over again in his dreams. He was pretty sure some of his ancestors had died defending castles from invading armies. It was in his blood.

Ponder was sure that his small army could hold off anything but a full-scale assault by an overwhelming force. Even now his men were mounting heavy machine guns and other defensive weapons around the perimeter of his compound. Tucked into the side of Battleship Mountain, Ponder's headquarters was a perfectly designed fortress. It was well concealed and afforded a perfect view of the large mountain basin to the northeast. The only way to assault the stronghold was from the basin. It was possible to skirt the ledge that ran from northwest to southeast, but it would also be suicidal considering the perfect field of fire possessed by the defenders. Ponder at one point thought it was possible for an invading force to come over Battlefield Mountain and walk down the mountain. That was until two winters before when he'd tried it himself. He'd almost died trying to traverse the steep slope. Knowing that, Ponder had designed a beautiful kill zone right in his front yard. The SSI assault team wouldn't have a chance.

"I want you here with me coordinating everything."

Trapper made a face at his boss's order.

"What is it?" Ponder growled.

"I was kinda hoping you'd let me go find the SSI guys."

"By yourself?" Ponder asked incredulously.

Trapper smiled. "This ain't my first rodeo, Boss."

Ponder knew the man was right. They called him Trapper for a reason. He had a talent for finding and getting rid of people no matter the time or place.

"So you know where they're coming from?"

Trapper nodded with a sly grin.

"Are you gonna tell me?" Ponder solicited.

"Let me make sure, and I'll call it in as soon as I've got eyes-on."

Although Ponder trusted his Lieutenant, his gut was telling him to order Trapper to stay at the compound. He shook the thought off as quickly as it had come. He'd be a lot better off if one man could decimate the SSI band.

"Fine, but make sure you take care of deploying our men before you go."

They finalized their campaign and toasted their victory over a welcomed shot of Jack Daniels.

CAMP SPARTAN, ARRINGTON, TN

7:00AM CST, SEPTEMBER 28TH

The FBI contingent arrived precisely at 7:00am. Four black Chevy Suburbans rolled through Camp Spartan's front gate and headed to the SSI's headquarters.

Travis, Todd and Marge met the investigators in the entryway. An average-looking man in his early forties led the way. His thinning hair and deep bags under his eyes belied his stressful position. He walked right up to Travis and offered his hand.

"Mr. Haden, I'm Jack Malone. Thanks for meeting us."

"Please, call me Travis."

Introductions were made and the group made its way to the large conference room reserved for the occasion. There was coffee and a mixed assortment of breakfast food arranged for their guests.

"Thanks for the food and coffee, Marge," Malone offered. "We don't always get the best reception during our audits."

Haines gave the agent a thin smile. "There's no reason for us not to be cordial. We know that this is just one of the requirements of being in the security business."

Malone smiled and grabbed a glazed donut. "I hope you don't mind if I grab a bite while we talk. I didn't get a chance to eat anything earlier. I'm starving."

He quickly devoured three donuts and washed it down with some coffee. The others took seats around the conference table as they ate.

Still standing, Malone wiped his mouth and addressed the SSI leadership. "Like I told Ms. Haines over the phone, we're here to do a routine audit. Somehow you've avoided the list all these years." He smiled at his joke. "We'll try to make it as painless as possible. Starting with your accounting department, my crew will dig into your operations over the past five to ten years. As long as there aren't any discrepancies, we'll be out of your hair in a day and a half, two tops."

Travis wasn't worried about the FBI uncovering their covert division. There were no files. All their equipment was purchased with cash or handled through one of the many offshore accounts administered by Neil Patel. Haden's only concern was not being able to actively monitor Cal's team out west. Cal was on his own.

"Just let us know what you need to look at and we'll get it to you. I'll be in my office if you need me," Travis said.

"Thanks. Okay then. Let's head over to accounting."

Travis pulled Marge aside as the rest of the entourage filed out of the room.

"Let me know if you hear anything. I'm about to put in a call to one of our friends in D.C."

"Who?"

"Zimmer."

Congressman Brandon Zimmer was a first term representative from Massachusetts. He'd recently been involved in a nasty encounter with a group of Japanese imperialists looking to relive Japan's glory days. Cal's team had helped Zimmer uncover the plot by Zimmer's now deceased father, Senator Richard Zimmer, to claim the Presidency. The younger Zimmer had proved his worth by eliminating his father before the President could be killed. Brandon was now part of a very secretive group of retired politicians known as the Council of Patriots. Only a handful of people in the world knew of the Council's existence.

"Are you sure that's a good idea? Isn't he in the middle of the special election for his father's Senate seat?"

"Marge, you know he owes us big time. Besides, I just want him to see if he can pull some strings and find out why we're being investigated. I don't believe this bullshit about a routine audit."

They agreed to meet again at lunch to discuss any developments. Travis walked to his office and placed the call.

FALLS CHURCH, VA

8:41AM EST, SEPTEMBER 28TH

Brandon Zimmer was enjoying a much-needed morning off from campaigning. The last week had been a whirlwind of hand-shaking, speeches and phone calls. Washington insiders believed that the young Congressman would likely win an overwhelming victory against his opponent. It hadn't hurt that former President Hank Waller made the unexpected move of publicly endorsing Zimmer for the vacated seat. Preliminary polls were showing Brandon with almost seventy-five percent of the likely vote.

He'd learned from experience not to take a lead for granted and pushed his campaign staff hard. Zimmer was in the middle of perusing the college football matchups for the coming weekend when his cell phone rang. He looked at the caller ID and smiled.

"Hey, Trav!"

"Good morning, Congressman...or should I be calling you Senator now?"

"Not yet, and you know you can always call me Brandon."

"I know." Travis paused.

Brandon caught the hesitation. "What's going on?"

"Are you on the cell phone we gave you?"

"Yeah. Why?" Zimmer perked up at the question. Travis typically got right to the point.

Travis quickly outlined the details of Neil's kidnapping and Cal's operation to get him back.

"God, I'm sorry. Do you think he's still alive?"

"To be honest with you, I'm not sure. Then again, I don't know why this guy would go through all the trouble to take Neil just to kill him."

"Do you have a motive?"

"Not yet, but I'm sure we'll find out soon enough."

"How can I help?" Zimmer asked.

"Actually, I called to ask for your help with something else," Travis answered cryptically.

Now Brandon was really confused. "Something else?"

"Yeah. It just so happens that as soon as we got Cal to Wyoming, the FBI says it's time for an audit. They just got here."

Travis didn't have to tell Zimmer that the timing was more than a little coincidental. "So you think it has something to do with what's going on with Neil?"

"I do. If my hands weren't tied with our guests, I'd make some phone calls. I was wondering if you wouldn't mind making some discrete inquiries within your little club."

Brandon knew he was talking about the Council of Patriots. The combined Rolodex of the two former Presidents and the seven former senators and congressmen in the group made for a powerful information-gathering asset. It was, however, important not to drink from the well too often. The Council's secrecy was paramount.

"Let me call our friends and see how they can help."

"I really appreciate it, Brandon. Please call me if you find out anything."

"I will. And, Trav...?"

"Yeah?"

"Call me for help any time."

"Roger."

Zimmer ended the call and sat for a moment. He had a lot of

pressing matters to attend to this afternoon, but this would take priority. He owed Cal and Neil a huge debt. If it weren't for them, he'd probably be in jail and the President would be dead. Brandon would do anything to help his new friends.

He picked up his cell phone again and scrolled through his contact list. After pressing the right record, he held the phone to his ear. The call connected and Zimmer spoke. "Mr. President, I need a moment of your time."

GRAND TETON MOUNTAIN RANGE

7:05AM, SEPTEMBER 28TH

"Rise and shine!" Ponder's bellow was followed by a kick to Neil's wobbly cot. Neil just barely caught himself before he fell off and onto the floor.

He looked up at his captor through bleary eyes. He'd just managed to fall asleep and suspected Ponder had waited for his slumber just to torment him.

"What time is it?" Neil dared to ask.

"I said it's time to rise and shine! Now get cleaned up. We're taking you back to the server room." Ponder stormed out of the cell.

It was the same journey they'd repeatedly forced him to make. He'd resisted their requests but knew his time was running short. Neil had to deliver something or else they'd kill him.

He sat up painfully. Shivering uncontrollably, Neil wrapped the thin blanket around his shrinking body. Although his time in captivity hadn't been long, Neil knew he'd already lost weight. The constant stress led to a complete lack of appetite in the normally fit Indian-American. Somehow he managed to force down several bites of food every time the jailer brought it. He knew it wasn't enough.

Just as he'd fallen asleep, the tech genius was trying to think of a way to alert his friends at SSI. If he had more time with a computer it would've been easy, but every time they set him at the workstation there was someone watching.

The guard arrived and unceremoniously picked Neil up like a baby and carried him out of the cell. A minute later they arrived at the now familiar server room. It wasn't much compared to what Neil was used to, but still impressive for a mountain top retreat.

Ponder stood over his shoulder just as he had done before. "Let's try this again. Are you going to do it or not?"

Neil didn't have the will to say no. What reserves he'd had now lay scattered on the frozen ground outside the complex. "I'll do it."

Ponder was secretly relieved. "Now remember what I told you," Ponder growled as he extracted a large knife from its leg holster, "you try anything funny and I'll take off your other foot personally."

Neil didn't doubt the man's threat. In the short time he'd been a guest at Chateau Winter Wonderland, as Neil now thought of the compound, he'd come to realize that the man in charge was not only ruthless, but probably had a few screws loose upstairs. His ability to pivot from anger to mirth spoke volumes of the grizzled man's mental faculties.

Shifting uncomfortably, Neil moved closer to the computer's keypad. He tried to place his hand on the mouse but his hands kept shaking.

Ponder turned to his sentry and barked, "Get a couple space heaters over here and bring some more blankets too. Have the cook bring down some hot soup and cider."

He looked down at Neil. "Well what are you waiting for? Get back to work!"

Neil whipped his head back around and did his best to grip the mouse and click through the screens.

TRAPPER WAS MAKING good time on the mule he'd saddled. Something told him that the SSI operators would take the Death Canyon entrance. It was well traveled and easy to access from Teton Village. Trapper had already confirmed with the few helicopter companies in the area that no one had booked a flight. That left his enemy with only one option: trek in on foot.

He pushed his mule hard hoping he'd make his destination before the storm hit. If he did, the slaughter would be easy. He'd have a perfect view. The former soldier grinned as he imagined the coming battle.

THE MEN WERE silent as they moved swiftly down the trail. They'd made good time so far and hadn't encountered many hikers. The few people they had seen were going the opposite way, eager to avoid the blizzard. Everyone could feel the weather shift as the storm crept closer. Cal was hiking in the middle of the pack, allowing his mind to drift back to his days in the Marine Corps, hiking countless miles with fellow Marines.

Brian Ramirez pulled up beside him.

"What's going on, Doc? Not enough action in the rear?"

Brian had elected to stay in the back of the group just as he'd done during his time with Marines. It was customary for the Corpsman to tend to the stragglers and injured with the company gunny.

"Was wondering if you'd heard anything else from Camp Spartan."

Cal shook his head. "They're busy handling the FBI guys that someone shoved down their throats. I can't believe I'm saying this, but I'd rather be here than dealing with that right now."

Brian agreed. "So we're really going in as is? No more support from home?"

"It's just us, Doc."

Brian wasn't the only one that couldn't shake the feeling that they were walking into a shitstorm.

"I know what you're thinking, Doc, but our options are limited. We know where they're keeping Neil so we've gotta go get him."

"But how do we know for sure that he's up there?"

Cal was getting tired of the conversation. Brian was one of his best friends, but the last thing he needed right now was to have his judgment questioned.

"It's all we've got to go on. Look, I gave everyone the chance to stay back. If you think it's such a bad idea feel free to turn around now," Cal noticed a couple of the men around them glance back in concern.

"You know I wouldn't do that, Cal. I just want to make sure you've thought this whole thing through. I'm not trying to make waves. I just want to help."

Cal calmed in response to Brian's conciliatory tone. The stress was getting to him. He knew he had to be careful and keep his temper in check. Nothing good came of barking at his team.

"Sorry, Doc. Just forget what I said. I couldn't do this without you."

"Don't worry about it. Is there anything I can do to help?"

"Just make sure you catch Top when he falls out back there," Cal said loudly enough for the huge Marine Master Sergeant to hear.

"I heard that!" Trent boomed as loudly as he dared.

The men around them chuckled quietly.

"Seriously though, Doc, we just need to get up there as soon as we can. I'm afraid of what they're planning for Neil."

"Yeah," Brian said absently.

It was good that they had the winding path to worry about because it was impossible to imagine the fate of their friend. By now they'd all heard the stories about Nick Ponder's exploits. There wasn't a man in the group that didn't want to see the man in jail or dead.

Brian dropped back to the rear of the formation and left Cal to his thoughts.

GRAND TETON MOUNTAIN RANGE

8:17AM, SEPTEMBER 28TH

"Okay, I'm in," announced Neil.

Ponder strained to make sense of the code on the monitor. A second later the screen changed and displayed the control panel of the Shiloh Wind Power Plant in Bird's Landing, California.

"Shut it down," Ponder ordered.

He'd told Neil on their first attempt that the test was to shut down the plant's power for a full minute. Neil knew it would be an easy feat with his computer prowess. Hell, with his own equipment he'd have done it in less than five minutes. In Ponder's lair he'd had to build a hacking system from scratch. Although labor intensive, it had allowed Patel to imbed some extra code into the program. He hoped it would be enough to alert his friends to his location.

"I said shut it down!"

Neil did as he was told.

MILES away at the Shiloh Wind Power Plant, Bernice Ormand was monitoring the plant's computer systems. She'd been in the control room since 6:00am and casually swept her gaze across the assorted meters. Bernice still marveled at the newly computerized system. She'd been at the power plant since it opened in 2006. Back then they'd installed a very rudimentary monitoring system just to get the plant built under budget. It wasn't until the new President was elected in 2008, and his green energy funding went into effect, that the Shiloh Wind Power Plant installed a completely computer driven monitoring system.

Bernice sipped her second green tea of the morning as she jotted down some notes in the plant's logbook. As she went to complete her entry, all the screens on the panel went dark.

"What in the world?" Bernice said.

She grabbed the phone and dialed the station manager.

"Stan, it's Bernice. The monitoring system just went down."

"I'm checking one of the turbines right now. I'll be up in five minutes."

Stan seemed unconcerned and his attitude served to calm Bernice's nerves. She'd never seen this happen before. They'd had intermittent issues with malfunctioning turbines in the past, but the monitoring systems had always performed flawlessly. By the time she'd collected her thoughts enough to grab the logbook the computer screens flickered back to life.

Huh. I better call Stan back, she thought. Bernice picked up the phone and dialed the manager's number again.

"The computers are back online, Stan."

"Good. Let me know if it happens again. Thanks, Bernice."

She hung up the phone, entered the incident into the logbook, then grabbed her Sudoku puzzle book and dove into her unfinished brainteaser.

"THE SYSTEM IS BACK ONLINE," Neil declared somberly.

"Well I'll be damned!" Ponder exulted. "Get him back to his cell so I can make a phone call," he told his employee.

As the jailer took Patel back to his room, Ponder pulled out his cell phone and dialed his contact's number.

"Yeah, it's me. Are you happy now?" Ponder asked.

"We have received confirmation of the test results. One half of the purchase price will be deposited into escrow. I will email you the deposit receipt momentarily." The line went dead.

Ponder almost drooled at the thought. He was so close to wrapping up the deal. Now he could focus on tying up some loose ends. With barely concealed glee he placed another call.

"Are you there yet?" he asked his right hand man.

"Almost," Trapper said breathlessly. Ponder could hear the man being jostled as he rode.

"Good. We just passed our test so the buy is a go."

"Congrats, Boss. How about I take care of our friends and then you buy the first round in Bora Bora?"

"You got it," Ponder responded, almost cheerfully.

He replaced the phone in his pocket and allowed himself a second to take in the moment. In a matter of hours he would be a very rich man.

THE BUYER'S agent answered the silent ringing.

"Yes?"

"You have authorization to proceed."

"Understood." The man ended the call and scanned the surrounding area. His men were ready for a fight. They moved silently through the mountainous terrain, ever vigilant through years of hard training. He wondered if the seller even suspected what would soon happen. Doubtful. The arrogant Americans never suspected treachery when a payday was close at hand. They were greedy and short-sighted. It was all the more reason to crush them. The foreign emissary relished the thought and plodded along with his assassins.

CAMP SPARTAN, ARRINGTON, TN

11:20AM CST, SEPTEMBER 28TH

True to Jack Malone's word, the investigation progressed swiftly. SSI employees were accommodating and the FBI agents were courteous in their questioning. Marjorie Haines was hopeful that it would all end soon. She had more important things to do than monitor their visitors.

Her phone rang and she answered. "Haines."

"Marge, it's Dunn. I've got something you need to see right now."

"Where are you?"

"In the Batcave."

Haines looked at her watch then over at the FBI teams going through paperwork. Jack Malone had left earlier to take a tour of the campus.

"Give me a minute to excuse myself and I'll be right down, Todd."

Marge checked to make sure that the investigators didn't need her for a few minutes, and then headed to meet up with SSI security chief.

DUNN WAS STARING at a computer screen when Marge entered the Batcave. He had two of Neil's computer techs assisting. They were watching a video. As she got closer, she realized the recording was of Agent Malone.

"What's going on, Todd?"

Dunn turned around, surprised by the interruption. "Oh hey, that was fast."

"It sounded important so I got over here as quickly as I could."

"It is. Come take a look."

The two techs made room as Haines squeezed in to get a better view.

"Tell me what I'm looking at."

The tech with a head full of unruly red hair spoke up first. "Well, Ms. Haines, Mr. Dunn told us to keep tabs on all the FBI guys. It was pretty easy until this guy…"

"Agent Malone," Haines furnished.

"Yeah, until Agent Malone went on a tour of the campus with Kendall from operations."

Haines was confused. "What do you mean *until?*"

The tech scratched his scraggly beard, unfazed by Marge's tone. "Well, as long as he was in one of our buildings it was easy to jump from one camera to the next and follow him. It was when he went outside that we had a problem."

"How so?" Haines asked impatiently.

"We have a limited number of cameras in the outdoor areas. They're mostly at the front gate and around the perimeter. There's usually no need to have them. So that posed a slight problem. How could we watch and listen in on what he was doing?"

"I'm sorry…"

"Bowser."

"Your name is Bowser?"

"Actually my name's Patrick but everybody calls me Bowser."

"Okay, Bowser, tell me what you did to fix the problem."

"You know that Neil built his Baby Birds a while back…"

Baby Bird was the nickname the SSI operators had given to Neil's tiny surveillance drone. The thing looked like a helicopter, fit in the palm of your hand and could be controlled hands-free with a special pair of sunglasses similar to the eye control systems used by Apache pilots.

"...and we've outfitted a couple of them with long range microphones. We launched two of them to follow Agent Malone while he was outside."

"Bowser, this is all very fascinating, but would you please mind getting to the point?" Haines requested as politely as she could muster.

"Sorry, Ms. Haines. Anyway, long story short, once they got near the chow hall Agent Malone asks if he can use one of the Porta-Johns the construction crews are using. He said he had too much coffee and really had to take a leak."

Haines rolled her eyes and motioned for the young tech to hurry up with his explanation.

"So he walks over to the Porta-John and, once he's out of earshot from Kendall, he pulls out his cell phone."

Dunn interrupted, "So that's where we'll start the video for you."

Bowser took the cue and started the video. It showed Agent Malone walking to the blue porta-potty. He paused just as someone would do if their phone rang in their pocket. Malone extracted his cell phone, pressed a button, then held it to his ear.

"Hey, I'm in." The recording was scratchy, but Haines could make out every word.

Malone listened to the person on the other end of the call.

"Yeah. After I take this little tour and let them soften up a bit I'll ask for your little buddy Zheng. Once I get my hands on him, I'll order him to start opening up all the locked doors in this place."

He listened again and nodded.

"Don't worry, I'll get him out of here, but it's gonna cost you extra."

Malone paused to listen and then chuckled. "Sure, I'm ready for a little vacation too. Let's wrap this up and then I'll use some of my accrued leave. At least the Bureau gives me that much. I'll call you in a couple hours."

Haines's normally calm face raged red. "Do we know who he talked to?"

"Bowser tracked it to a tower in the Jackson Hole area," Dunn answered, dead serious. "You want me to take care of this?"

Haines thought for a moment. What they should do is turn the piece-of-shit-Malone in to his superiors. But Haines came from a warrior background. Her father was a former Special Forces soldier who'd fought in Vietnam. She probably would have tried to become an infantry officer if the military allowed it.

"I'll take care of Agent Malone. Bowser, can you email that video to me?" Bowser nodded. "Todd, would you mind setting up one of your interrogation rooms?"

The two techs looked at Haines in awe. They'd heard rumors of her physical prowess, and she was undoubtedly beautiful, but seeing the lioness come out right before their eyes was astonishing.

Dunn and Haines went to leave, but Bowser had one more question.

"Hey, Ms. Haines, what's Z...uh, I mean what's Terrence Zheng got to do with all this?"

Haines stopped and turned around. "Loose lips sink ships, gentlemen. You won't be seeing Mr. Zheng any time soon."

Without another word, she turned away and left the room, Dunn in tow.

Bowser looked at his companion in wide-eyed wonder. "I call dibs on Zheng's Xbox profile!"

DUNN SPLIT off as Haines walked swiftly to the security desk. "Can you please ask Agent Malone to join me in the lower level observation deck?" she asked the large sentry.

"Yes, Ms. Haines. I'll escort him down personally."

"Thank you."

Haines headed back toward the Batcave. As an afterthought, she pulled out her phone as she walked.

"Travis, I think we've found the connection."

FIFTEEN MINUTES LATER, Malone, escorted by the guard, entered the gallery overlooking the interrogation rooms. With a nod from Dunn, the guard left and Malone joined him and Haines.

"So what's up?" Malone asked conspiratorially. "Is this where you do your secret interrogations?"

Haines answered with a dry laugh. "I just thought you might like to see this and get a quick tour. It's state of the art and where we do all our training for new SSI personnel going into the field."

"Nice," Malone admired as he gazed down at the brightly lit rooms. "Lead on, Ms. Haines!"

Dunn made no move to follow. "You're not coming with us, Dunn?" Agent Malone asked.

"I've got some things to take care of upstairs. We'll have lunch waiting for you when you're finished here." Dunn headed to the stairwell and disappeared.

Haines led Malone to the control room first. He gave it a cursory examination and, once satisfied, indicated they should move on to the lower rooms.

They stepped down the side staircase and entered the first room they encountered.

"As you can see, we have cameras installed there and there," Haines pointed to the locations of the observation equipment. "And anyone in the gallery can watch through the one-way window."

Agent Malone traced his hand along the edge of the metal table in the center of the room. He stared at Haines lasciviously. "You want to tell me why you really wanted to get me down here…alone?"

"I don't know what you're talking about, Jack," Haines answered in feigned surprise.

"You could've gotten anyone to show me this place. Why did you want to bring me down here?"

Haines looked back at Malone with an embarrassed shrug. "Am I that obvious?" she asked innocently.

Agent Malone's eyes lit up as he moved closer to the attractive attorney. "Well, I can't say that I'm surprised."

"Oh?"

"You're surrounded by these meatheads all day long. I'm not surprised you're more attracted to the polished type."

"And you're saying you're the polished type?" Haines purred.

"I am."

"So what should we do now?"

Malone glanced up to the invisible cameras. "What about witnesses?" he asked.

"I turned those off when we were in the control room."

"And what about someone seeing us from the gallery?"

Haines smiled mischievously. "I told Dunn to give us some time alone. We should have plenty of time." She slinked up to Malone and placed a hand on his chest. Suddenly, he seemed nervous and uncertain.

"Would you feel more comfortable if I turned off the lights?" Haines asked.

Malone could only nod through parched lips and slowed brain function. *Is this really happening?*

Haines walked to the door and turned off the lights. The room was thrust into darkness except for the small amount of light seeping in through the one-way mirror.

"Where are you, Jack?"

"Over here," Malone responded hoarsely. He started to loosen his tie so he could breathe.

Seconds later, Haines's hands were back on his chest and he could feel her hot breath on his neck.

"So how do you want to do this?" he asked.

"I thought we'd get to know each other a little bit first," she teased, yanking down playfully on his tie.

"Uh, sure. What would you like to know?"

"Oh, I just have one question for you, Jack." She grazed her nose along his jaw line, and he shuddered in anticipation.

"Okay. What's your question, Ms. Haines?"

She took his head in her hands and brought his ear down to her mouth. "I just want to know one thing. How long did it take before you turned traitor?"

Before Malone had time to respond, Haines blasted her knee into his groin. As he doubled over in pain, she bent down and whispered in his ear one last time. "Now you know why they call me The Hammer, you piece of shit."

Grabbing his head again, she slammed her knee into his temple and let him drop unconscious onto the floor. Marge checked to see that he had a pulse, then grabbed the handcuffs from Malone's belt and strapped his two hands behind his back. After relieving the crooked agent of his sidearm, Haines left the room to fetch Dr. Higgins.

———

AGENT JACK MALONE kicked and screamed as Dr. Higgins wheeled in his tools. The guards had strapped him to a gurney as he lay unconscious.

"I don't know what that bitch told you, but you guys are in some deep shit. I am an FBI agent!"

Higgins ignored the man and continued to set up his supplies.

"Talk to me!" yelled Malone.

The expert interrogator continued to pay him no heed. Higgins liked to get a first impression of his subjects. It allowed him to assess the person's demeanor in order to administer the correct dosage of his truth serum. Agent Malone might be a challenge, but the wizened doctor relished the test.

Higgins finally turned to face Malone. "Mr. Malone, I am here to ask you some very specific questions. I will tell you that it's pointless trying to resist. Either tell me the truth or we'll extract it in other ways."

Malone's eyes bulged in anger. "You fucking quack! I'm gonna have your ass for this! You know how illegal...!"

Instead of listening further, Dr. Higgins adjusted the mechanical gurney to give him better access to the apparatus. Malone silenced as soon as he saw the needles. "What...what's that for?"

"I told you, Mr. Malone, if you don't want to cooperate, we'll coax you into cooperating."

"What are you talking about? I'm here to investigate YOU!"

"I guess you could say the shoe is on the other foot now, wouldn't you?" Higgins asked.

Malone kept screaming obscenities until Dr. Higgins inserted the IV needle into his arm. Higgins waited five minutes for the drug to fully take hold. He could see that Malone was completely relaxed.

"There, now that's better. How are you feeling, Mr. Malone?"

"I'm...nice." Malone's face was calm. It looked like the drug had performed as planned.

"Is it okay if I ask you some questions now, Mr. Malone?"

"Sure," answered the suspect dreamily.

Like Zheng before, Agent Malone was more than happy to answer any and all questions. Malone described his relationship with Nick Ponder. They'd met while serving in the Army and reconnected six years earlier when Agent Malone had been part of the team that audited The Ponder Group. They shared a love of fast women and money. Over the years, Malone had come to Ponder's rescue, for a price. Files were misplaced and agents were reassigned from ongoing investigations. Malone knew how to manipulate people and the system. They'd both become wealthy through the mutually beneficial relationship.

"How is it that you came to investigate SSI?" Higgins asked, knowing that Dunn and Haines were digesting every word in the control room.

"I got a call from Nick. He said he needed SSI out of his hair for a while. Told me it would be helpful if we could run a little investigation. Nick said he had a guy on the inside that was feeding him intel and that there might just be some juicy stuff in it for me."

"So you were tasked with keeping us busy?"

"Yeah, but the silver lining for me was finding something that could shut down your whole operation."

"Did Mr. Ponder give you any specifics on what you might find?"

"Not really, but this Zheng kid was supposed to start the digging. Hey, where is Zheng anyway?"

"Mr. Zheng is no longer your concern, Mr. Malone."

Malone shrugged nonchalantly.

Higgins had all the information they would need. A condensed version of the recording would be delivered to one of their contacts in the Hoover Building. Jack Malone would be quietly put away in a maximum-security federal prison. The FBI didn't like traitors and dealt with them swiftly.

"It was a pleasure speaking with you, Mr. Malone. Best of luck in the future."

Higgins gathered his gear and headed for the door.

Dr. Higgins joined Marge Haines and Todd Dunn in the gallery.

"I've gotta say, Doc, you are an artist when it comes to making people talk," Dunn offered, impressed yet again by the doctor's skill.

"Lots and lots of practice, Todd. Although I must say that with a man like Mr. Malone, sometimes I wish I could deliver some damage like Marjorie."

It was hard to get Haines to blush and yet she did. She held Dr. Higgins in high esteem and sought his insight often. "I'll start giving you classes in the gym whenever you're ready, Doctor."

Higgins chuckled warmly. "That's quite all right. I'll leave the tough stuff to you and the boys."

"On to a more serious topic," Dunn interrupted, "I've already emailed the edited transcript to a buddy of mine at the Bureau. I'm thinking this audit will be over before we know it."

Haines and Higgins nodded. Once the FBI found out that one of their investigative teams had been tasked under false pretenses, they would likely do everything they could to extract their people as soon as possible.

"Is there anything else you'd like me to do?" Dr. Higgins asked his colleagues.

Dunn shook his head. "As long as we don't have any other traitors in our midst, I think we're good."

"Any word from Cal?"

"The last we heard they were a couple hours into their insertion." Dunn looked at his watch. "They should be getting a good dose of the storm right about now."

GRAND TETON MOUNTAIN RANGE, WYOMING

10:36AM, SEPTEMBER 28TH

As soon as the storm hit, they couldn't see five feet in front of them. Although it definitely slowed their forward progress, it also gave them cover should anyone be tracking from a higher elevation.

Cal's team had donned all white coveralls as the snow started to fall. The white camouflage would further conceal them from enemy eyes.

They were still walking through the middle of Death Canyon, but wouldn't for much longer. It had been a gamble to take the well used path in order to speed their progress. Cal glanced at his GPS. They were nearing their scheduled checkpoint. After a short rest, the group would break into two teams. They'd approach the objective from two directions.

Cal and Daniel would accompany Gaucho. Lance Upshaw, the helpful prisoner, would also be with Cal's group.

MSgt Trent and Brian Ramirez would go with the other team.

The halt signal was passed back through the dispersed formation.

Cal made his way to the front. Gaucho was rooting through a pack of cold weather rations as Cal moved up next to him.

"How are you liking the weather, Gaucho?"

The Hispanic warrior made a comical face. With the snow already starting to stick to his braided beard, Cal thought his team leader was starting to look more and more like a mountain dwarf from the *Lord of the Rings*.

"I'm gonna freeze my nuts off tonight!"

Cal laughed. "That's only if we stop moving. How much longer do you think we have?"

Gaucho pulled out his map and pointed to their current location. "As long as we keep making good time I think we'll get there just after midnight."

Cal looked up at the obscured sky. The snowfall was picking up and already starting to accumulate. He guessed that there was already a good three inches on the ground.

"I'll tell you that I'm not looking forward to putting these damn skis on, Boss." Gaucho looked back at the cross-country skis strapped to his pack.

Cal could only image what the short Mexican would look like on skis.

"At least we'll have skins for when we're going uphill. You ever tried to go up a slope without them?"

Gaucho nodded sadly. "I think the Army played a trick on me when they sent me to your Marine Mountain Warfare Training Center in Bridgeport."

Cal snorted at the thought. He'd spent six weeks at the remote training center with his battalion as a young corporal. Fully half of the Marines in his unit ended up not finishing the training mostly from injury or illness. Some just couldn't take the altitude and the cold. He remembered being in shock when some of the toughest Marines in his company had refused to go back up the mountain. Cold weather separated the men from the boys even amongst Marines.

"That big kid giving Snake Eyes any trouble?" Gaucho asked.

"He's kept pretty quiet. Hasn't complained once. Daniel even said he offered to carry more gear before we stepped off."

"No shit?"

Cal nodded. "I think he's getting it through his head that we're not the bad guys. He might even come in handy when we get close to Ponder's place."

Lance Upshaw had come to the realization that he'd probably been playing for the wrong team since joining The Ponder Group. There'd been warning signs, like when a couple of new guys had disappeared on an overseas op. Ponder had merely shrugged and noted that it was the price of doing business in a dangerous world. There were no memorials and no letters of condolence.

Then there were the actual men that Ponder hired. Most had washed out of the military for one reason or another. At first Lance thought it was a blessing that a man like Nick Ponder would lend a helping hand to men who needed a second chance. It didn't take Lance long to see that most of Ponder's contractors didn't deserve a second chance. They were bullies and criminals. In his third month of employment, Lance had to fight off three separate challengers until the rest had realized that he was more than a match for them. Now they mostly left him alone.

And that's how he'd felt for most of the past year. Luckily Trapper had recognized Lance's work ethic and took him along when he needed some muscle. It wasn't bad work but Lance still felt unsatisfied. There had to be more to life.

Since being captured by the SSI guys, he'd quietly observed their interactions. It was obvious they all respected one another. Also, despite the fact that he was the enemy, they still treated him with respect. Not once had any of the men degraded him, and it all started with Daniel Briggs. In Briggs, Lance saw the Marine he wished he himself had become. Silent in his approach, the man the others called Snake Eyes was obviously a highly valued part of the team. And he did it all without yelling or cussing. In fact, Lance could have sworn that he'd once seen Briggs say a prayer and then finish with the sign of the cross.

It all gave the disgraced Marine a lot to think about. These men were walking into almost certain danger, all for the love of a friend. *Would Nick Ponder do the same thing?* Lance didn't think so.

FAR ABOVE, Trapper rubbed his hands to ward off the cold. Although he couldn't see the troops moving into his territory, he had laid small pressure plates along the trail to alert him of their passing. He silently congratulated himself for choosing the right route. Now all he needed to do was track and take them out once the time was right.

BATTLESHIP MOUNTAIN, GRAND TETON MOUNTAIN RANGE, WYOMING

11:19AM, SEPTEMBER 28TH

Ponder paced back and forth on the hardwood floor. The pieces were coming together, but he still had some concerns. Most importantly, he hadn't heard from either Terrence Zheng or Jack Malone. His greedy mind hoped they were too busy to call because they were torpedoing SSI.

Ponder figured that it was impossible for a security contractor not to be into some kind of illegal activity. Hell, he'd skirted the law for years. Jack Malone knew how to find things and would be even more effective with Zheng's help.

Still, he couldn't shake the thought that something was wrong. He moved to his laptop and checked the email account he shared with Zheng. Nothing. Next he scrolled through his other email accounts for word from Jack. Nothing again.

Ponder allowed himself to think about the worst case scenario. If the assholes at SSI had figured out not only his involvement, but also the actions of Zheng and Malone, his path was less certain. The thing he had to focus on was the money that would soon be in his bank accounts. He'd scatter the funds to the four corners of the globe through transfers he'd already arranged with his international brokers. Ponder would be paying some hefty fees, but it would be worth it. With his money safely stashed he could make a new home anywhere.

Cracking his knuckles, he imagined Trapper silently stalking his quarry. If he survived, fine. If not, there would be one less person to pay from his treasure chest. Ponder smiled despite his nerves. Maybe a new house in Costa Rica was just what he needed.

CAMP SPARTAN, ARRINGTON, TN

12:35PM CST, SEPTEMBER 28TH

"Are they all gone?" Travis asked Dunn, who'd just stepped into his office.

"Yeah. The last SUV just rolled out with Agent Jack Malone hog-tied in the back."

"Did you get everything squared away with the Bureau?"

Dunn nodded. "We shouldn't have another audit for a while. They even apologized and thanked me for helping with Malone."

"Good. Let's get some more personnel out to Cal."

"Isn't the weather turning to shit out there, Skipper?"

Travis's eyes went cold. "I don't care. If they can't fly onto that fucking mountain, get them as close as we can."

"I'll go with them and make sure it's done."

"I can't spare you right now, Todd. We've got to…"

"I'm going, Skipper," Dunn interrupted curtly.

Travis looked at his friend in surprise. He couldn't remember the last time Dunn had put his foot down. The fact was he'd gotten used to having Dunn around. With his own time in the field effectively at an end, he'd kept his head of security with him. Although barely in their forties, but still fit enough to be in any Special Forces unit, they'd both become consumed with the day-to-day running of SSI. There were times Travis longed to be on the battlefield again. His position as CEO pretty much negated that option.

"I guess it would be wasted breath trying to persuade you to stay?"

"It would."

"Why now?"

"Honestly?"

"Honestly," Travis answered.

"Two reasons. First, it's been a while since I've been out with the boys. No disrespect, Skipper, but sticking close to the office can wear on a guy."

Travis smiled and motioned for Dunn to go on.

"Second, I've got a really bad feeling on this one. I think Cal's gonna need every man he can get."

"Then let's get our things packed," suggested Travis, already heading to the locker room.

"Wait...but you can't go!"

Travis swiveled around and flashed Dunn a sly grin. "Why not? I'm the boss. I think you're right. Cal needs every man we can spare."

Dunn's mouth was hanging open. He couldn't order his boss to stay behind.

"But what about...?"

Travis stopped the question with a raised hand. "Come on, Todd. If things blow up in our face it's not gonna be because I jumped on a plane to rescue my cousin."

Dunn knew he was right. They were both warriors and felt compelled to run to the sound of battle.

"Okay. You let Haines know what we're doing - she's gonna shit by the way - and I'll mobilize the men and book the flight."

"Make sure you get the craziest SOB pilot you can find. We'll need one to fly into that snowstorm."

Dunn returned his boss's smile and said, "I think I know just where to find one."

Thirty minutes later, Travis, Dunn and twenty four fully loaded SSI warriors climbed into three separate helicopters. They'd make the quick hop to Nashville International Airport and then catch a special flight out to Wyoming.

Travis put on a headset so he could talk to Dunn.

"Who are we meeting at the airport?"

Dunn smirked at the question. "It's a little surprise, Skipper."

"You know how much I hate surprises, Mr. Dunn."

"I think you'll like this one."

With no explanation forthcoming, Travis turned back to his phone and texted Cal again. None of his previous attempts had gone through. *Must be the weather out there.*

The flight didn't take long, and Travis peered out the window as they neared the airport. Instead of heading to the helicopter pad Travis was accustomed to, the pilot veered the aircraft to the south. He turned to Dunn.

"You want to tell me where the hell we're going NOW?"

Dunn could see he'd maxed out his boss's patience. "We're getting a lift from the 118th Air Wing."

"The Air National Guard?" Travis couldn't remember ever having any interaction with the unit. Their base sat right next to Nashville's airport.

"Yeah. I've got a buddy I served with in the Army. He left the Army and re-enlisted as a First Sergeant in the Air National Guard. I gave him a call and asked if they were looking to run any practice drops. He said yes and the deal was done."

"Did you say practice drop?"

"Oh, yeah. Didn't I mention that we're gonna parachute in?" Dunn's smile reminded Travis of a certain overly-chipper instructor he'd had at BUDS. The damn guy always seemed so cheery about making the SEAL candidates do anything dangerous.

"You've got to be shitting me, Todd."

"Now why would I do that, Skipper?" Dunn asked innocently, the bright smile still plastered on his normally serious face.

TO EXPEDITE THE PROCESS, the helicopters landed just yards from the waiting C-130 Hercules. Dunn's friend made the quick introductions and had a crew waiting to help load gear.

"You sure this is just gonna be a one way trip, Todd?" the grizzled First Sergeant asked.

"That's all we need. Thanks again for the last minute lift."

"Don't thank me yet. Your pilot, Captain Jeffries, is known as a little bit of a cowboy around here. In fact, his call sign is Cowboy. Might make for a fun ride." He patted Todd on the back and moved to help his men finish loading the packs.

Dunn looked at his friend in confusion then stepped in line to board the aircraft. By the time he got onboard, Travis was chatting with the pilot. Capt. Jeffries looked to be about sixteen years old. Despite his youthful appearance, he sported a very blond and very waxed handlebar mustache. A pair of aviator sunglasses was perched on his head, and he leaned his small frame casually against the plane's bulkhead.

Travis turned as Dunn approached. "Todd Dunn, meet Captain Jeffries."

Jeffries smiled and shook Dunn's hand firmly. "Call me Cowboy." He pointed to the patch on his flight suit that sported his moniker.

"Good to meet you, sir," Dunn offered carefully. He never knew how to handle these non-military-looking pilots. "Thanks for giving us a ride."

"Not a problem, buddy. Thanks to you guys I won't have to fly a thousand circles over Nashville today. Gets boring after the first two turns. Besides, I've always wanted to fly into a snowstorm. Should be fun!" Jeffries really did look like a kid on Christmas day when he smiled.

Travis was enjoying Dunn's unease. He decided to push it a little farther. "Hey, Cowboy, I know Mr. Dunn was just dying to ask you about your mustache."

Cowboy beamed and carefully stroked both ends of the impressive formation. "I know it's not really within military regs, but my boss lets me keep it because of all the trips I take to Afghanistan. It wouldn't be right if I crashed and got captured with my baby face. At least this way the terrorist that gets his hands on me might be impressed by my studly 'stache and keep me in the land of the living."

Dunn didn't know how to respond. Travis just chuckled and moved to find a seat. It would be an interesting flight to Wyoming.

GRAND TETON MOUNTAIN RANGE, WYOMING

11:58AM, SEPTEMBER 28TH

Visibility had turned to shit. In order to avoid being split up, Cal's team had opted to close the gaps between men. It wasn't the best tactical decision based on proper troop dispersion, but it was a practical call made out of necessity.

They'd just entered another gully that had only recently been a stream full of running water when an explosion knocked Cal from his feet. As he settled in the snow, he looked around. He could see a couple of the men struggling to get up and find cover. One man had a hand pressed to his bloody face. *Where the hell did that explosion come from?* Cal thought as he crawled over to a rock outcropping and made himself as small as possible. A minute later Gaucho was next to him, his white trouser leg covered in blood.

"You okay?" Cal asked, concerned.

"No problem, boss. Just a scratch."

Gaucho had already applied a hasty bandage to the shrapnel wound.

"Have any idea where that came from?" Cal said as he tried in vain to see anything through the incessant snowfall.

"I'm pretty fucking sure nobody shot at us. I think it was a triggered IED."

"Anybody hurt?"

"Just some minor cuts and bruises. We got lucky because of the snow, I think. I'll bet that damn thing was on a delay or I would've been smoked. We've gotta get off this trail."

Cal nodded. The terrain wouldn't open up for a while. Staying on the narrow trail had been a gamble they'd just been called on. They were sitting ducks despite the snow cover. It would be easy for their enemy to rig traps all along the winding path. Taking to the higher trails would slow their journey considerably, but was necessary considering the alternative.

"Okay. Why don't you run point on the left side of the canyon and I'll take the right. As long as we keep going uphill and don't shoot straight across the ravine, we should be all right."

Gaucho didn't look pleased with the idea of splitting his team further, but he trusted Cal's judgment. The Marine was a formidable warrior in his own right and could handle himself.

"Just promise me one thing, boss."

"What's that?"

"Wait for me to catch up before you take out all the bad guys."

Cal grinned and crawled off to find Daniel.

TRAPPER PEERED through his thermal scope. He could only pick up faint blurs because of the blizzard, but he could see that his plan had worked. The small IED wasn't meant to kill anyone, although the ruthless mercenary wouldn't have minded. His goal was to get them to do exactly what they were now doing: separating.

Ponder's second-in-command loved a challenge. Trapper knew that if his boss was with him he would've wanted the attackers killed quickly. "Kill those fuckers right now," he would've said. That wasn't Trapper's style. He liked to take out enemies slowly and methodically.

Trapper loved the hunt almost as much as the final kill.

Cal found Daniel and Lance behind a pile of fallen trees. The men were deep in conversation.

"What's going on, Daniel?" Cal asked over the howling wind.

"Lance thinks the explosion was from his friend Trapper."

"The guy that got away?"

Briggs nodded. "He's some kind of tracker. Lance says he's really good. Tell him, Lance."

Lance looked at Cal uncertainly. "Yeah. Trapper likes the hunt. I think he was an MP in the Army. He gets off on seeing other people in pain."

Cal didn't know what to believe. While he trusted Daniel's judgment regarding their prisoner, he couldn't bring himself to believe in Trapper's former partner. "So where do you think he is?"

Lance pointed up to the ridgeline. "Up there somewhere. He used to bring me over here to scope out the area and check on his hides. He liked to shadow hikers. Trapper said it kept his skills sharp."

"Did you say he has hides up there?" Cal asked incredulously. "Why didn't you tell us about that before?"

Lance looked to Daniel for support. Daniel answered for him, "I asked him the same thing, Cal. He figured Ponder would probably keep Trapper close to home. They don't have a ton of guys to guard the place. I believe him."

Cal knew it was a moot point. "You think you can show us where the hides are?"

Lance nodded. "It might be a little harder with the snow, but I've been here a few times, and I'm pretty good at land nav. I think I can find them."

"Good. The three of us will go together. Daniel, go find Gaucho and tell him what we're doing. I want to have a little talk with Lance."

Daniel stared at Cal for an extended moment then left to brief Gaucho. Cal knew what Daniel's look meant. *Keep your temper in check, Cal.*

Cal turned back to Lance. "I want to make sure we're on the same page here, Lance."

The blonde giant gazed back in confusion. "What...what do you mean, Mr. Stokes?" Lance had seen how the other men respected the young leader. He looked uncomfortable under the Marine's scrutiny.

Cal's eyes went cold. "I appreciate you helping us this far and not giving us any trouble. But I want to tell you that if you so much as think about betraying us, I will take care of you personally."

Lance's face turned serious. "Mr. Stokes, I know what you're saying, but let me tell you something. You guys have treated me nothing but decent. I mean to repay that favor by helping you find Trapper and Mr. Ponder. I won't let you down, sir."

It wasn't the reply Cal had expected. Up to this point, Lance hadn't said a word to Cal.

"Okay. I'll make you a deal. When we get out of this thing alive, I'll put in a good word for you when you look for a new job."

Lance knew it was more than he deserved. He was grateful for the chance. The disgraced former Marine knew that Ponder wouldn't give him the same chance.

"Thank you, Mr. Stokes." Lance reached out to shake Cal's hand.

Cal grabbed his hand and shook it firmly. "Just one thing. Stop calling me Mr. Stokes. It's Cal."

FIVE MINUTES LATER, Lance was leading the way up the steep slope. He'd told Cal and Daniel that Trapper had as many as twenty observation points in the area, but that of those, only two or three were in the immediate vicinity.

The rest of the team was fanning out in pairs, keeping as much dispersion as possible considering the heavy snowfall. Over Gaucho's objections, Cal had ordered the rest of the men to proceed toward Ponder's hideout. He knew they were running out of time. Daniel and Cal would take care of Trapper.

GRAND TETON MOUNTAIN RANGE, WYOMING

1:36PM, SEPTEMBER 28TH

"Have you heard from Cal? Everybody okay after that IED?" Brian Ramirez asked MSgt Trent as they both stopped for a quick sip of water. The going had gotten a lot tougher since they'd left the trail. They had to resort to taking quick breaks both to recharge a bit and to check in with the other teams that were somewhere out in the invisible terrain. Their small radios were struggling to transmit in the storm.

"Last time I had a signal, they were breaking into smaller groups too. Cal said he and Briggs were gonna find that guy that escaped."

"The guy with the nose?"

Trent nodded as he stuffed a whole Power Bar into his mouth. "Cal says the Upshaw kid might know where he is."

"I don't know if we should be trusting him."

Trent just shrugged. "If Snake Eyes thinks he's cool, that's good enough for me. Besides, if Cal takes out Ponder's number two guy, we'll be doing a lot better than we are now, Doc."

Brian had a hard time agreeing. From the start, the whole operation felt like they were three steps behind. It wasn't anyone's fault, least of all Cal's, but Brian couldn't shake the feeling that they were walking into a trap.

After checking in with the rest of their team, Brian and Trent continued up the mountain.

THE FIRST HIDE they found was empty. Lance told them that normally there was a stash of survival goods hidden in a small depression in the back of each small cave. They didn't see any signs of recent passing.

Cal looked down at his watch. They were losing a lot of time looking for someone that might not even be there. "I think we need to split up. The next two hides aren't too far apart. Maybe we can save some time if I take one and you and Lance take the other."

By the look on his face, Daniel didn't like the idea. "We're already spread thin, Cal. It won't take much longer for all three of us to check the other two hides. We might need all the firepower we can get."

Cal knew the sniper was right, but he'd already made up his mind. "Let's split up and then meet at the next checkpoint. If one of us doesn't show an hour after that, we can go looking for each other."

Daniel knew he couldn't change Cal's mind. They reviewed their maps one last time and went their separate ways. Daniel watched as Cal disappeared into the squall. He could only trust that he would see his friend again soon.

CAL FELT ALIVE. Being alone in the wintery wilderness, he suddenly remembered what he loved most about being a Marine. He loved the thrill of coming to a brother's aid, even in the face of almost certain death. Cal didn't want to die, but he wasn't afraid of it. Like many other warriors, he'd always hoped that his life would come to a swift end. He'd seen fellow Marines suffer and fight through horrendous injuries only to succumb in the end. No, Cal preferred a sniper round to the head. Instant. No pain.

He shook the macabre thoughts from his head. It wasn't his time to die. He had to save Neil and get his men out alive.

Ten minutes later, Cal knew he was getting close. He stopped to consult his map and study the terrain. Despite having an ultra-reliable GPS, Cal still liked to fall back on his land navigation skills. As long as he had a map and a compass, Cal could find his way.

Confident that he was exactly where the GPS indicated, Cal moved cautiously toward his objective. He didn't want to approach the hide from the most obvious route. It would take him a few more minutes to traverse up and over the objective, but Cal didn't want to leave anything to chance.

Just as he neared the point where he'd decided to stage his pack, he caught movement out of the corner of his eye. He looked around. There wasn't anything in his field of view. Turning back to his pack, he took off his skis and arranged them in a standing X over his gear so he could find it again after clearing the objective. It wouldn't help one bit if he lost all his equipment.

As he stuffed his last spare magazine into one of his large cargo pockets, he heard what sounded like an animal roar. *What the hell?*

Weapon out, he spun in a quick three-sixty. Nothing. *What the hell was that sound?* His breathing picked up as he tried to scan through the snow. He'd have to get back at MSgt Trent for putting the idea of bears in his head. Almost since they landed, Trent had talked about wanting to see a grizzly bear. He even kidded about the bears being hungrier than usual. "If they're so hungry, I'll bet one of those grizzlies would love to catch them some Mexican meat, Gaucho," Trent had joked.

Maybe my mind's just playing tricks on me, Cal thought.

Cal did one last check of the area and picked up the small day pack that had been clipped to his larger hiking pack. It had some emergency rations and a first aid kit. The smaller pack came in handy. At least he didn't have to lug the larger one around for a few minutes.

Stepping toward the steep drop, Cal looked over. He couldn't see more than ten feet down. *Damn all this snow.* Cal tested his footing and crept along the ledge that would take him to a small game path up ahead. He found the passage and did a quick look around to make sure he wasn't being followed. Looking back the way he came, he squinted.

Holy Shit! He saw a huge form running toward the ledge. An enormous grizzly bear was charging straight at him.

Without a moment to think, Cal turned and sprinted as fast as he could down the game trail. The angry bear wasn't far behind.

DANIEL HAD ALREADY FOUND three claymore mines on their approach. Rather than take the time to disable the booby traps, the expert sniper bypassed them altogether. Trapper was watching his back and using some heavy firepower to do it.

Just like Cal, Daniel and Lance staged their gear as they neared their destination. Briggs grabbed his sniper rifle and handed the smaller H&K submachine gun to Lance.

"You know how to shoot one of these?" Daniel asked.

Lance nodded.

"Good. Hopefully you won't have to use it, but here are two extra mags just in case." Daniel handed the ammunition to Lance. As Lance checked their gear one last time, Daniel pulled out the small radio and tried to reach Cal. All he got was static. He couldn't pick up any of the other teams either. As long as they made their rendezvous, they'd be fine.

Daniel closed his eyes and tapped into his heightened awareness. He said a silent prayer and then motioned to Lance that it was time to leave. They moved off quietly, both wondering if this would be the right place.

CAL'S LUNGS burned as he ran. He could hear the bear getting closer and closer. The path was getting narrower as he moved. He had to be careful not to get too close to the edge.

Ducking under an overhanging tree branch, Cal stopped suddenly. Two inches from his face was a thin wire. Cal traced it to its origin on the rock wall and found a claymore mine carefully concealed behind debris. He'd come within inches of having his head blown off.

The grizzly was closing in despite the size of the path. *Maybe I can use this*, Cal thought. He eased his way under the tripwire. Although he hated to do it, Cal unslung his pack and placed it under the deadly trap. Cal quickly opened the main pouch, took out his small emergency kit and stuffed it in his cargo pocket. Next, he extracted one of the compact bags of cold weather rations and tore it open. He ripped each small food packet open and threw it on the ground. *Maybe that'll give me a couple extra seconds.*

Not waiting to see if his trap would work, Cal turned and moved away from the roars of the angry bear.

DANIEL WAS the first one to see the small hide. It was obvious that someone had been there recently. Despite the heavy snowfall, he could see boot prints. The sniper slowly stalked toward his objective, checking for tripwires as he went.

"Move another inch and I'll blow your fucking head off," came a voice above the cave. Daniel halted and looked up. He could just make out a white form sitting on the branch of a large pine tree. Daniel couldn't see the man's face but he knew it was Trapper. "Put your rifle on the ground and put your hands up," Trapper yelled over the howling wind.

Daniel did as ordered. He couldn't believe he'd walked right into the trap. The only consolation was that apparently Trapper hadn't seen Lance yet. As his enemy climbed down from his perch, Daniel hoped Lance would have the sense to stay out of sight.

AS LUCK WOULD HAVE IT, Lance had just bent down to examine something on the ground when he heard Trapper's voice. Lance froze as he strained to take in the unfolding scene. He couldn't see his former co-worker, but Lance could just barely observe Daniel putting his weapon on the ground carefully and placing his gloved hands on his head.

Lance flattened himself on the ground and started to crawl toward the hide. He stopped again as another figure walked into view. Trapper had his weapon trained on the Marine sniper. Lance didn't know what to do. He wasn't smart enough to come up with some elaborate play to help his friend. Lance decided it was better to sit back and wait. Maybe an opportunity would present itself.

Daniel breathed a quiet sigh of relief as Trapper kept his submachine gun pointed at him. Obviously the man hadn't seen Lance yet. Daniel prayed for guidance.

"Where's the rest of your team?" Trapper asked.

Daniel stood silently.

"I said, where's the rest of your team?"

Daniel smiled. Trapper responded by adjusting his aim and firing a round into the snow next to Daniel's left foot. The sniper didn't even flinch.

"I can't wait to beat that smile off your face, Marine," Trapper said. "Now move."

Trapper motioned toward what Daniel correctly assumed was the hide that he and Lance had been looking for. Like all the others, the observation point was situated along a small path overlooking the ravine.

Daniel ducked his head and entered the alcove. He saw a radio, extra ammunition and claymores lying on the far side of the depression. There was room for almost twenty men to stand comfortably. Daniel was surprised by the size.

"Turn around," Trapper ordered.

Daniel turned and faced his enemy.

Trapper moved into the hide. "Last chance. Tell me where the rest of your men are."

Daniel didn't see the harm in telling the man 'most' of the truth.

"We split up. Some of them are on the other side of the ravine. The rest are probably a mile behind me."

"Why are you by yourself?"

"I'm a sniper. I'm used to being on my own."

Trapper took a few seconds to respond. He'd thought the blonde Marine would have resisted more.

"What did you do with Lance?"

"He's still tied up at the house," Daniel lied.

Not that Trapper necessarily cared about Lance's well-being, but he had been curious about his former colleague's whereabouts.

"So here's what's going to happen. I've gotta go find the rest of your friends and kill them. Since I can't drag you along, you're going to kneel down right there and I'm gonna put a bullet in your head."

If Daniel was frightened, he didn't show it. He knew that when his time came, he would be prepared to meet The Almighty. But something told him that it wasn't his time to go. It might have had something to do with the flicker of movement he saw behind Trapper. Daniel smiled again and kneeled down on the ground.

Lance had silently followed Trapper and Daniel. He'd overheard snippets of their conversation. Lance knew he had to save Daniel, but he didn't know how. His mind worked desperately to come up with a plan. His lack of brainpower and the uncertainty he felt toward harming Trapper kept Lance from making a decision. He knew deep down that Trapper would shoot Daniel.

Stepping up to the alcove's entrance, Lance took a quick peek into the space. Daniel was slowly kneeling onto the floor. Lance knew he had to move fast or his new friend would die. Knowing it would slow him down, he placed his weapon against the rock wall. Lance paused to steady himself and then ran into the cave.

Trapper sensed the movement coming from behind. Moving to his left, he pivoted away from the cave's entrance. He stood in shock for a protracted second as he recognized Lance barreling into the room. His surprise didn't last long as he quickly depressed the trigger and rounds reached out at his target.

DANIEL DIDN'T HAVE time to watch. He extracted the blade strapped to his left wrist. Daniel silently thanked Cal for the welcome gift he'd gotten when he joined SSI. Cal had an identical blade that had been put to good use in the past.

The sniper gracefully hopped to his feet and moved toward Trapper.

LANCE GRUNTED AWAY the shock as he felt the rounds tear into his body. The room seemed to move in slow motion as he kept his focus on the wild-eyed Trapper. It seemed like a never-ending stream of bullets coming his way, violating his muscular body. Lance pressed forward through the pain.

TRAPPER KNEW he'd hit Lance with at least ten rounds, but the man kept coming. It was too late when he finally remembered the other man in the room. Turning back to where Daniel had been, Trapper's eyes went wide. He struggled to swivel his aim as Daniel closed the remaining distance, blade leading.

HIS HEARTBEAT BARELY ELEVATED, Daniel silently slid his blade under Trapper's chin to the hilt and twisted. Trapper dropped his weapon as he moved his hands to stop the blade. While the two men locked eyes, Lance barreled in, knocking all three to the floor in a bloody heap.

GRAND TETON MOUNTAIN RANGE, WYOMING

3:56PM, SEPTEMBER 28TH

The bear had stopped its bellowing. *He must have found the pack,* Cal thought as he inched his way forward. The satisfying boom he was waiting for never came as he sat and listened again. *Maybe it was a dud.*

The Marine hadn't found any other tripwires so far, but he wasn't taking any chances. He had to be careful. The thin path was too easy to booby trap.

Just as he started forward again, he heard a loud explosion followed by a frightening scream from the injured grizzly. Cal didn't like killing innocent animals, but if it came down to a fight, he sure as hell was going to do his damnedest to win, even if it meant killing the bear. Cal closed his eyes, waiting for the grizzly's screams to subside. Instead of stopping, they became angry roars and seemed to be getting closer.

Cal hurried to try to close the remaining distance to the hidden alcove. He glanced back and saw the bear moving effortlessly along the ledge. Cal had no choice but to turn back and defend himself.

His submachine gun felt pathetically small as he looked up at the gigantic bear that had now reared up on its hind legs. Cal fired his

9mm rounds into the grizzly's body. The bullets didn't even seem to slow the bear. With lightning speed, it swatted the weapon out of Cal's hands. The gun fell into the whiteness of the deep ravine.

The bear looked at Cal as if to say, *you have two seconds to run.* Cal took the hint, turned and ran. The grizzly paused for a moment to lick its bloody paw, roared, and then followed. It seemed to recognize that its quarry was cornered. The large male knew every inch of its territory. The path ended soon and Cal would have nowhere to go.

DANIEL CHECKED Trapper to make sure the man was dead. The beaknosed mercenary's eyes stared into nothingness.

Lance was struggling to sit up. As Daniel moved to help him, he saw blood seeping out of the big man's mouth. It didn't look good for his new friend.

"Where are you hit?" Daniel asked in concern.

Lance tried to answer but couldn't speak. He looked down at his torso as Daniel ripped the man's coat open. There were too many entry wounds to count. Trapper had done the job.

Daniel reached into one of his cargo pouches and pulled out a small first aid kit. Knowing the dangers of the battlefield, he'd packed it himself long ago. He extracted a small syringe and looked at Lance.

"This will help with the pain."

Lance looked at Daniel with pleading eyes. He knew he was going to die.

Daniel carefully grasped the larger man's arm and injected the powerful drug. The effects were almost instantaneous. It was a special concoction he'd come across while serving in Afghanistan. The Corpsmen and their Marines called it 'sleep juice.' It was used for the worst cases and only as a last resort. There were some times when you just knew an injured warrior was going to die. Better to let a man die in peace. The drug wasn't officially sanctioned by any of the military branches because of its potency and the obvious ethical issues. After losing his spotter in Afghanistan, Daniel had made himself a promise that he would never let anyone suffer the way Grant had. Better to let a man die in peace.

Lance's features softened as the drug took effect.

"Don't worry, I'll get you out of here," Daniel said softly.

Lance shook his head already knowing what would happen. He would die in the cave. With great effort he grabbed Daniel's arm and spoke through gurgled blood, "I'm...a...Marine."

Daniel nodded solemnly and smiled at the dying man. "You won your honor back, brother. I'll make sure everyone knows you died as a Marine."

Lance's smile filled the room. Daniel would never forget the look of pure joy on the dying man's face.

"Close your eyes, Lance. It won't be long now."

The big man nodded and closed his eyes for the last time.

"God be with you, my friend," Daniel whispered, as Lance exhaled his last breath.

The sniper silently asked God to watch over Lance. Then he stood up, gathered a few items, and left in search of Cal.

CAL REACHED the end of the trail and cursed. He was trapped. As he went to brace himself on the steep rock wall, his hand slipped. Cal barely caught himself before he slammed his head. He hadn't noticed it as he approached, but there was an opening. Looking closer, Cal saw that there was a hole about three feet in diameter. *This must be the hide.*

Hoping that there was something inside he could use, he went head first into the alcove. The space was small. Cal figured that it might be possible to fit two men in the tiny cave. Luckily, there weren't any traps awaiting his arrival. He felt around in the dark for anything he could use as a weapon. His hands finally found a stout stick. Cal picked it up and felt along its length. It was barely two feet long with blunt ends. Cal guessed that someone had probably once used it as a fire poker.

The thought gave him an idea. He reached into one of his pockets and felt the butane lighter he always kept there. His hope somewhat restored by the feel of the lighter, he unzipped the parka and started to tear strips off the bottom of his polypropylene undershirt. Cal wrapped the thin strips around one of the ends of the stick. Just as he went to light the improvised torch, the space went completely dark. The bear had reached the cave's entrance.

AFTER RETRIEVING his gear from where he and Lance had staged it, Daniel took off for the rendezvous point. Daniel was glad that Cal wouldn't have to deal with Trapper. Maybe the rest of the insertion would go smoothly.

GRAND TETON MOUNTAIN RANGE, WYOMING

5:22PM, SEPTEMBER 28TH

Daniel made good time getting to the rendezvous point. He'd waited impatiently as the minutes ticked away and still no Cal. Finally, Daniel made the decision to find his friend. It wasn't far, and he figured out a route that would ensure the two Marines wouldn't miss each other.

The sniper staged his gear and put on his skis. He tried to raise Cal on the radio. There was no answer, so Daniel got his bearings and took off in Cal's direction.

Cal had managed to light his makeshift torch and look around the small cave. There wasn't anything else he could use as a weapon. The bear had at first searched the trail thinking that Cal had jumped off the side. It didn't take the grizzly long to figure out that his target was right behind him in the little recess.

Man and beast had traded swings and shouts of anger. The huge animal couldn't fit in the hole and Cal couldn't deliver any damage with his measly torch. *Whoever said bears are afraid of fire was full of shit*, Cal pondered angrily as he took another ineffective swipe at his opponent.

Despite the claymore mine explosion and being riddled by Cal's rounds, the bear didn't seem to be slowing down. Occasionally he would step back and lick his wounds, only to come back at Cal's hideout with renewed vigor. Cal knew it was only a matter of time before a claw came far enough in to deal a deadly blow.

DANIEL HEARD the bear long before he saw it. He could only hope that Cal was on the delivering end of the wrath in the beast's tone. It sounded like something from the pits of hell.

Following the bear's cries, Daniel made his way along the ridge.

THE BEAR SMELLED something in the wind. It paused briefly and cocked its ear, straining against the howling storm to hear anything out of the ordinary. Nothing. The creature stood back on its hind legs and sniffed the air. The smell was gone.

It turned back to the cave and gave in to its primal instinct. The mighty mammal roared deafeningly as it knew it would soon have its prize.

DANIEL HAD EASED himself down onto the narrow path. It wasn't hard to pinpoint the location of the bear from all the noise it was making. Gazing through the white downfall, Daniel finally saw the brute. It alternated sticking each arm into the hole almost like it had found a gigantic bee hive filled with honey.

Daniel knew at once that it was Cal the bear was after. He could even see a flicker of what he assumed was a torch coming from the small entry. Daniel couldn't understand why Cal hadn't just killed the grizzly.

The sniper couldn't get a good shot from his precarious position, so he went with another option. He started yelling.

It took the enraged bear a second to hear him over the blizzard. Even when he did turn around, he couldn't pinpoint Daniel's location. The beast sniffed the air again trying to find what had now claimed his interest twice.

Daniel watched quietly as the bear searched. He yelled again and locked eyes with the mighty animal. It seemed confused as to what it should do. *Go after the new human or stay with the one cornered in the hole?* While it was deciding, Daniel watched in amazement as Cal climbed out of the hole, took the quick steps to the edge of the ravine, jumped into the swirling wind and disappeared below.

The bear turned just in time to see Cal jump. Much as a child quickly loses interest in a toy, the bear forgot about its first prey and set its angry gaze on Daniel. Daniel watched in amazement as the gigantic fiend deftly maneuvered its way along the narrow path. The Marine turned and ran back up the trail. He could only hope that Cal was still alive. Right now he had to deal with the enormous grizzly.

CAL TRIED to keep his descent as close to the ravine wall as possible. He had no idea how far the fall would be, so he kept trying to grab hold of something. The descent was painful as he hit branch after branch and then twisted his knee slamming into a rock only to be thrown down the wall farther. Cal worried that the drop would never end. As soon as he thought it, the ground greeted him with a painful thud. He lay there for a full minute, listening for the bear that he was almost sure had jumped after him. The animal never came.

Cal rolled over onto his stomach and pushed himself into a sitting position. He tested his limbs, amazed that, despite a few bumps and bruises, nothing appeared to be drastically wrong with him. *I think I just used up another one of my nine lives.*

He got to his feet and steadied himself against a large boulder that he'd just missed coming down on. Cal knew he couldn't climb back up, so the only way to go was through the ravine. *Hopefully Daniel took care of Trapper*, Cal thought as he started walking. *This is gonna be a real pain in the ass without my skis.*

———

DANIEL GLIDED along the path until he came to a small section that looked just big enough for him to lie on. He skidded to a stop and moved into a prone position on the snow-covered ledge. It would give him the best stability to fire his rifle if he was lying on the ground. The bear wasn't far behind. Daniel knew he would only have time to fire one shot. With minimal visibility, the window of opportunity was finite. He could only see ten feet down the path.

He settled his breathing and searched for the bear through the rifle site. The mammoth beast broke through the blinding snow not twelve feet from the prostrate Marine. Daniel aimed at the animal's head and fired.

GRAND TETON MOUNTAIN RANGE, WYOMING

7:35PM, SEPTEMBER 28TH

"They should be here by now, Top," Brian commented.

MSgt Trent tried his radio again. They hadn't been able to establish contact with Cal or Daniel for hours. He'd found out from Gaucho that the two men had gone off to find Trapper. The normally optimistic Trent was starting to fear the worst.

"I don't know if there's much else we can do but wait, Doc. I'll bet they just got distracted catching snowflakes or something."

Trent's attempt at humor fell flat against Brian's anxiety. It wasn't like the two Marines to be late for anything. Brian was usually the one catching flack for not showing up fifteen minutes early.

"Anything from Gaucho?" he asked.

"I just talked to him. He and his boys are waiting for us at the next checkpoint. Says they haven't encountered any bad guys."

Brian nodded and looked back down the ravine. "Where are you guys?"

CAL WAS SLOWLY MAKING his way up the ravine. Not wanting to walk on the possibly booby-trapped trail, Cal's travel was further hindered by frequent holes, rocks and bushes hidden beneath the winter snow. If he had his skis, he would have glided right over them. But with only the boots on his feet, the going was slow and painful. He'd aggravated his knee worse than he'd thought in the fall. Each step brought a shooting pain up his right leg.

At least he still had his map and compass in his pocket. For some reason, that thought made him push harder. He knew where he was going. Now all he had to do was get there. Cal strained his way up the mountain, thinking of Neil as he went.

THE BUYERS HAD JUST ARRIVED at Ponder's compound below the peak of Battleship Mountain. They were escorted in by a cadre of Ponder's most loyal soldiers. He waited impatiently behind his desk, sipping from a large glass of Jack Daniels. He already had a few lines of coke earlier to keep his energy levels up. It had been a long couple of days. Ponder hoped the wait would soon be over.

The head buyer was shown into Ponder's office. He was a man of average height and build. Ponder knew the man was from somewhere in the Middle East as evidenced by his complexion and facial features. He hated dealing with Arabs or Muslims or whatever they called themselves. They were all beggars or thieves in his opinion, but in this case they were his meal ticket.

Nick Ponder extracted himself from his chair and moved to greet the emissary. "Welcome to Wyoming!"

The smaller man bowed slightly and smiled. "Thank you, Mr. Ponder. My name is Benjamin," he said with a slight British accent.

Ponder knew it couldn't possibly be the man's real name, but he didn't care. The two men shook hands and took a seat on opposite sides of the desk. Ponder waved for his guards to leave the room. He waited until the door was closed before speaking.

"Did you bring the money?" Ponder asked, trying not to sound too anxious.

Benjamin raised a black case and set it on the desk. "Cash denominations in Dollars and Euros, along with gold and diamonds, as per your instructions. The balance of the purchase price will be deposited into your overseas accounts once we have confirmed delivery with my superiors."

Ponder nodded and inspected the contents of the briefcase. It was only a small fraction of his fee, but still tantalizing. He fought the urge to drool as he fingered the small bag of diamonds.

"When may we see Mr. Patel?" asked Benjamin.

Ponder looked up from his small horde. "I thought we'd have a little lunch and then head down to see your new pet."

Benjamin smiled amiably. "That is much appreciated, Mr. Ponder, but would it be possible to get our lunch while we administer another test on Mr. Patel?"

Ponder gritted his teeth. "I thought we already got past all this."

Benjamin waved a hand in apology. "It's actually not a test to verify the purchase, Mr. Ponder."

"Then what the hell is it for?" Ponder growled impatiently.

"My superiors merely want to initiate a certain operation prior to our departure. Please be assured that as soon as I see Mr. Patel, your money will be wired to your account."

The comment seemed to calm Ponder. The man known as Benjamin knew the next hour would be the most delicate of his operation. It was important to keep Ponder happy. His superiors had sent Benjamin not only because he was one of his country's deadliest assassins, but because he had the rare dual talents of diplomacy and patience. Benjamin felt just as at home with the Prince of Wales as he did with a common street beggar. Upon laying eyes on Nick Ponder, he knew the man would be easily manipulated by greed.

Benjamin smiled again. "Shall we meet with Mr. Patel?"

NEIL WAS LYING down on his cot trying to rest. He'd heard the commotion almost an hour before. His time had come. Neil was scared. Never before had he felt so alone. That wasn't completely true.

After the death of his mother and father at the hands of Pakistani terrorists, Neil went into a drug-induced nosedive. It was only through the intervention of Cal and his dad that he had come to terms with the murder of his parents. Neil could still hear Cal Sr.'s words: *"I can't tell you that the pain will ever go away, Neil. What I can tell you is that you'll learn to deal with it and get to living again."* The man had been a second father to the young college student.

The doorway at the top of the staircase opened with a loud groan. Neil sat up and waited for the footsteps to come down the concrete stairs. Nick Ponder was the first to come to his cell door.

"I've got a visitor for you, Neil," Ponder said with a wicked grin.

A tiny light of hope flared within Neil. Could it be his friends?

A man stepped in front of Ponder and peered into the room. "Hello, Mr. Patel."

Neil's eyes went wide with terror. He knew this man. It felt like all the oxygen was sucked out of the room and replaced with unbearable cold. Benjamin smiled evilly and nodded. He turned back to Ponder. "I am satisfied, Mr. Ponder. Let us finalize our transaction in your office."

Ignoring Neil, they both headed back up the stairs. Neil stayed in his cell. The shock of seeing the man he thought to be dead shook Neil to his core. All hope was lost.

GRAND TETON MOUNTAIN RANGE, WYOMING

9:05PM, SEPTEMBER 28TH

It was getting harder and harder for Cal to put one foot in front of the other. *What I wouldn't give for some food right now.* He'd been dehydrated before and recognized the signs that his body was giving. He needed water soon, but stopping wasn't an option. Occasionally he would scoop up a handful of snow, stick it in his mouth and suck on it. Contrary to what most people think, eating snow can actually dehydrate you. Cal knew the only way to get water out of snow was to melt it. He didn't have time for that. It was already way past the time he should have met up with the rest of the team.

Cal reached down for another scoop of snow and took a bite.

"Didn't your platoon sergeant tell you never to eat yellow snow, Boss?"

Cal whirled around at the sound of the voice. A red flashlight flicked on. Rising up from the snow and darkness was Gaucho. Cal exhaled in relief.

"Please tell me Daniel and Lance made it too."

Gaucho's smile faded. "Snake Eyes is here, but Lance is gone."

"What happened?" Cal asked.

Gaucho didn't have a chance to explain. Daniel walked up and put a hand on Cal's shoulder. "I can't tell you how glad I am to see you, Cal. What the hell possessed you to jump into the canyon?"

Cal looked at his friend in confusion. "How did you know...?" His tired mind struggled to put the pieces together. "You distracted the bear."

"I was about to shoot the damn thing when you jumped. I thought you were dead. We were giving you until 2200 and then heading out."

"What can I say? I guess some of your good luck must be rubbing off on me," Cal smiled. "Wait. What happened to the bear?"

Gaucho stepped closer and answered for Daniel. "Wouldn't you know it, this crazy Gringo shot that fucker at point blank range. One shot one kill, right, Snake Eyes?"

Daniel shrugged at the compliment. "It was dead before it hit the ground...the ground that I was lying on. The grizzly's momentum almost got me. I just barely got out of the way as it came crashing down."

Cal shook his head in amazement. Was there anything the Marine sniper couldn't do?

"What happened to Lance?"

"He died saving me," Daniel answered solemnly.

"How?"

"Trapper was about to shoot me when Lance came running in and distracted him. The poor guy didn't stand a chance and he knew it. Trapper shot point blank. He died in my arms."

Cal recognized the grief in Daniel's voice. It pained him to see the sniper lose yet another of his men.

"And Trapper?"

"I took care of him."

Cal nodded.

"Please tell me one of you has some water," Cal almost pleaded.

Daniel pulled a Nalgene bottle out of his coat and handed it to him. Cal had to remind himself not to drink too fast, but his overwhelming thirst won out. He downed the entire bottle in seconds.

"Where are the rest of the guys?" Cal asked once he was partially satiated.

Gaucho pointed up the hill.

"Let's go see about finishing this fucking hike," Cal suggested.

The three men headed up the hill, each rejuvenated by the sight of the other.

THE REST of the team was overjoyed to have Cal back. After hearing the story of Cal's suicidal jump from Daniel, no one had held much hope for his survival.

Under the cover of darkness, the SSI warriors prepped for their final journey around Battleship Mountain. They would stick together for the last leg of the movement.

Brian, MSgt Trent, Gaucho, Daniel and Cal huddled together over a map to finalize the plan.

"We'll stay in a column until we get right here." Cal pointed to the map. "At that point, we'll split up and approach Ponder's compound from here and here."

The men nodded. It wouldn't be easy, but it would maximize their chances of closing in unnoticed.

"Any questions?" Cal asked.

Trent raised his hand. "You get word from Travis?"

"Not yet. This weather is really messing with our comm gear. I can't get a signal with either my cell phone or the satellite phone."

"So we don't even know if Neil's still there," stated Brian evenly. He was all about helping a friend, but his feeling of unease grew as they got closer to their objective.

"What can I say, Doc? It's the last place we know Neil was. Daniel confirmed that with Lance earlier."

Brian wasn't convinced, but said nothing. Cal couldn't ignore the look of doubt on his friend's face.

"If you've got something to say, Doc, spit it out."

There were so many things Brian wanted to say, but he didn't want to dampen the men's spirits. "Just ignore me, guys. Must be the cold messing with my Hispanic roots."

"You got that right, hombre!" Gaucho laughed.

The atmosphere lightened. They made their way back to their gear to get ready to go.

Brian followed Cal. "Hey, Cal?"

"Yeah?"

"I'm sorry about that back there. I just can't shake this...vibe I'm getting."

Cal looked at his friend. "I know how you feel. This whole operation has been one big goat rope from the beginning. Trust me, if I had something better, we'd do it. But right now we need to push forward and find Neil."

"I know."

The two men stared at each other for a moment. Brian broke the silence. "Just avoid jumping off any more cliffs, Staff Sergeant. I'm a good corpsman, but not THAT good."

They both laughed. "Don't worry. I hope I never have to do that again."

Cal patted his friend on the shoulder and moved off to put on the gear the team had managed to piece together for him. As he strapped on his new skis, Cal tried to ignore the nagging sense of dread that threatened to overtake his resolve. Neil and the rest of the men were counting on him.

———

Travis stood in the cockpit looking over Cowboy's shoulder. They'd been waiting for the storm to die down for hours.

"We're gonna need to get a refill soon," Cowboy offered conversationally.

"How long will that take?"

Cowboy consulted his navigation system. "I'd say no more than an hour and half. The ground crew is already expecting us."

"You can land in this stuff?" Travis motioned down to the roiling clouds.

"It's all about trusting your instruments."

Travis wasn't so sure. "I'll be right back."

He walked to the troop hold to find Dunn. Dunn looked up from the conversation he was having with one of the team leaders.

"Cowboy says we need to get some fuel soon," said Travis.

"We can't avoid it?"

Travis shook his head. "I think we're already on fumes."

"How long will it take?"

"Cowboy says it'll take no more than an hour and a half."

Dunn looked down at his watch. "That means we probably won't be over the target again until after midnight."

Travis shrugged. "I don't know what else we can do. Any word from home?"

"The weather's still too bad to see anything. I'm sure that even if we had Neil to hack into the spy satellites, they wouldn't be able to get us a clear picture."

Travis did not like waiting. He hated to think what might happen if they couldn't parachute in.

"Let's play it by ear and keep our fingers crossed that the weather clears after we get some fuel. Who knows, we may get lucky."

"I hope you're right, Skipper, because I'd really like to get out of this aircraft."

GRAND TETON MOUNTAIN RANGE, WYOMING

11:26PM, SEPTEMBER 28TH

After some haggling, the final wire transfer was made to Ponder's account.

"Now that you have your money, Mr. Ponder, would it be okay to use Neil in your server room?" Benjamin asked politely.

"Now that I have my money, you can do whatever you want with that little bastard." Ponder downed the remnants of his drink and slammed the glass onto the table with glee. He could almost smell the money he'd just made. Nick Ponder was finally a wealthy man.

"You sure I can't get you a drink, Benjamin?"

"My religion precludes me from drinking alcohol, Mr. Ponder, but thank you for the offer. Now, can you show me to the server room?"

TWENTY MINUTES LATER, Ponder left Neil with Benjamin and his men in the server room. Neil was sitting at the main computer terminal. Benjamin handed him a piece of paper with handwritten instructions. Neil read over the notes and looked up incredulously.

"Are you kidding me? I won't do this."

"Yes, you will, Mr. Patel." Benjamin extracted a pistol from his trousers and rested the barrel against Neil's cheek. "You now belong to my superiors. These are the first orders you will obey from your new masters."

"I won't do anything for you fucking terrorists!"

Benjamin smiled patiently and nodded to one of his men. The large henchman reached over, grabbed Neil's ear with one hand and pulled out a knife with the other.

"You will do as instructed or my friend here will take your body apart piece by piece. We will only take the parts that won't hinder you in your duties. I would have thought that after losing your foot, you would already understand the gravity of the situation, Mr. Patel."

Neil looked up at the man with absolute hatred. This man had orchestrated the kidnapping and murder of his parents. SSI had later conducted a clandestine operation to find the terrorist cell and eliminate its members. It had supposedly been an overwhelming success. Benjamin was supposed to be dead.

"Ah! I see you are still angered and confused by my appearance." Benjamin replaced his weapon and sat down next to Neil. "You thought I was dead, no?"

Neil nodded.

"As you can see," Benjamin gestured to his body, "I am still alive."

"How?" growled Neil.

Benjamin grinned. "My people are not as stupid or primitive as you believe, Mr. Patel. It is quite common for our leadership to employ doubles to ensure our safety. The man your people killed in retaliation for your parents' death was a perfectly crafted duplicate. I have had to stay concealed until the perfect time. It just so happened that my revenge coincided with the wishes of my superiors. You see, Mr. Patel, you have grown as arrogant as your father."

Neil seethed and tears came to his eyes. "You don't know anything about my father, you murderer!"

"I know much more than you think. Now, shall we get back to your first assignment?"

Neil glared at the man he'd killed over and over again in his dreams.

THIRTY MINUTES LATER, Neil's task was complete.

"Are you happy now?" Neil asked, dejectedly.

"Quite happy, Mr. Patel. The sooner you come to realize the wisdom of complying with orders the first time, the easier your time will be."

Benjamin motioned to his men. One of them picked up Neil and threw him over his shoulder.

As the blood rushed to his head, Neil masked his gloom by sending his mind to a happier place.

GRAND TETON MOUNTAIN RANGE, WYOMING

12:08AM, SEPTEMBER 29TH

Ponder watched as the foreigner prepped the three snowmobiles Ponder had given them. He'd wondered how they would transport the crippled Patel down the mountain, and had asked Benjamin about it.

"We came prepared, Mr. Ponder."

Benjamin waved one of his troops over. The big man walked over with his oversized pack.

"Show Mr. Ponder how we're taking Mr. Patel down the mountain."

The man nodded and unloaded the contents of the backpack. It turned out that the team of buyers had a collapsible sled. Fully constructed, it looked like an elongated cocoon. The sled would be completely enclosed and could be towed behind one of the snowmobiles.

"Aren't you worried about the kid puking inside that thing?" Ponder asked.

The ride down the mountain would be treacherous. Ponder couldn't imagine making the journey inside the sled.

Benjamin smiled. "Mr. Patel will be given sleeping medication prior to our departure."

Not ten minutes later, all of Benjamin's men had their gear stowed on the idling snowmobiles. Ponder walked over to the cocooned sled as Neil was being laid in. He watched curiously as Benjamin administered the anesthetic from a small syringe.

Ponder stood over Neil as the drug took hold. "Have a nice trip, Neil."

Neil looked up at his previous captor. A look of amusement crossed his face. "Watch your back, Ponder."

Ponder's eyebrows furrowed. "What?"

Neil grinned like a drunk. "Oh, you'll see."

Before he could say another word, Benjamin stepped forward and closed and latched the lid.

"What was he talking about?" Ponder asked.

"I believe it was simply the effects of the medication. You never know what a person will say."

Ponder's bullshit radar was blaring in his head. Benjamin looked to be saying the truth, but his instincts were telling him something different. He finally shook the feeling off by thinking about all the money in his bank account.

The bearded mercenary grinned and patted Benjamin on the back, gruffly.

"No problem, buddy. You guys all set to go?"

Benjamin breathed an imperceptible sigh of relief. He'd thought Ponder wanted to press the point. This phase of his operation would be the trickiest. Once he and his men left Ponder's compound he'd feel much better.

"We will be leaving momentarily, Mr. Ponder."

"Well, you guys know how to contact me if you need anything in the future."

"Thank you very much for your work and hospitality."

The two men shook hands and parted.

Benjamin jumped on the lead snowmobile and the vehicles left the compound.

Ponder waited until the large doors closed and then turned to go back to the main level. Between transferring his newfound fortune and dealing with the remnants of the SSI team, he still had a lot of work to do.

Benjamin grinned under his mask as his small convoy made its way off Battleship Mountain. It was always fun dealing with greedy Americans. They were so easy to manipulate.

Ponder sat down at his laptop and typed his password. He took another sip of his whiskey as the web browser loaded his bank's homepage. After glancing at a small notebook he'd pulled out of his pocket, Ponder entered his account ID and password. He waited impatiently as the website took him through its various safeguards.

Finally at his dashboard, the large man clicked on his account.

"What the fuck?" he whispered.

The screen showed that his account had a zero balance. Frantically, he refreshed the page. The balance didn't change.

Ponder could feel his blood pressure rising. He wanted to kill someone. Picking up his landline, he dialed his broker's number from memory. The man picked up on the second ring.

"Yeah?"

"It's me," Ponder responded, on the verge of exploding.

"I know who it is, Nick. It's like two in the morning here. What do you need?"

"I need you to get your fucking ass out of bed and find out where my fucking money went!"

There was a commotion on the other end as the broker jumped out of bed, knocking several items off his nightstand in the process.

"What are you talking about, Nick?"

"I told you. My fucking money disappeared!"

Ponder could hear the man clicking away at his own computer.

"Okay, I'm in your account. It says here that the money was wired out less than an hour ago. What am I missing here, Nick?"

"I'm putting you on hold. Don't go anywhere."

Ponder replaced the phone on his desk and ran for the server room. The only thought in his head as he blasted past two stunned guards was, *I'm gonna kill those fucking ragheads!*

HE BERATED himself for not keeping a closer eye on Benjamin. Ponder realized too late that his greed had seriously clouded his judgment.

Logging onto the computer in the server room, he tapped his foot impatiently, waiting for the thing to load.

A new window popped up.

"What the hell?"

Words started appearing in the window as if someone was writing.

Mr. Ponder, We will no longer be needing your services. - Benjamin

Ponder picked up the flat screen monitor and threw it against the wall.

"Motherfucker!"

GRAND TETON MOUNTAIN RANGE, WYOMING

12:30AM, SEPTEMBER 29TH

"Get your asses moving!" Ponder commanded. His men were hurrying to comply with the rushed orders. Some were still scrambling to get their clothes on.

After destroying half of his server room, Ponder had run through his compound rousing the rest of his troops. He'd even radioed all his men posted outside the compound to assemble in the oversized garage they were now prepping in. His only hope of getting his money back was to catch the double-crossing Pakistani.

"Take only what you need. We're not coming back," Ponder ordered.

The mercenaries looked up in confusion. One man had the nerve to question his employer.

"What do you mean we aren't coming back? All my shit's in my room!"

Instead of answering, Ponder stepped up to the man, pulled out his pistol, and shot him in the face. The boom echoed then left the room in silence.

"Anyone else have something smart to say?"

They all looked down at their dead colleague in shock, then went back to the task of preparing the remaining snowmobiles.

Ponder breathed heavily as he held his gun out, ready to fire. Calming somewhat, he knew it hadn't been the smartest thing to thin out his already minimal troop strength. At least his men now knew how serious the situation was.

The Ponder Group's sole owner stomped out of the room, his mind in full crisis mode. He had a few last things to take care before leaving. Nick Ponder was planning on never coming back to his fortress on Battleship Mountain.

CAL'S TEAM had made good time getting around the mountain. They were at their final checkpoint trying to get a look at Ponder's hideout.

"Looks like the weather might be clearing a bit," MSgt Trent observed.

Cal looked up into the darkness with his night vision goggles. He couldn't tell.

"We'll break up into the same groups as last time," said Cal to the group gathered near him. "Remember to keep your eyes out for Ponder's guys. Who knows where he's got them posted."

None of the men commented. They knew their responsibilities and were mentally preparing for the final descent toward the hideout. If the enemy presented itself, their training would take over.

"If there aren't any questions, I'll see you boys on the objective," finished Cal.

They dispersed and Cal caught up to Brian.

"You sure you remember how to fire that thing, Doc?"

Brian looked down at his weapon. "Shouldn't you be worried about making sure you don't get lost again, jarhead?"

The two friends looked at one another. They'd left the tension between them behind. Both warriors knew how dangerous this last part would be. It was entirely possible that they could be walking into a trap.

"Doc, I don't know how to say..."

"I know, Cal. Don't worry. You know I never would have missed this. Every one of us is doing this for Neil. You've done good. Shit, we've been through worse, right? I'll see you down there, okay?"

Cal managed a nod as Brian turned back to his assigned team.

I hope I'm not leading these men to their deaths, Cal thought darkly.

JUST AS HIS team set out, Daniel silently ordered the formation to halt. Through his night vision goggles, Cal could see each man quickly crouch down. He made his way up to the sniper's position.

"What is it?"

Daniel pointed down the mountain. "I think I just saw a bunch of snowmobiles head that way." Daniel motioned to the northeast.

"Could you see how many?" Cal strained to see what Daniel was talking about. He could just make out headlights moving in the direction Daniel had indicated.

"I'm thinking ten to fifteen vehicles."

"Could you make out any of the drivers?"

"No. Visibility is definitely clearing, but it's not that good. I've got a bad feeling about so many leaving at once, Cal."

Cal didn't know what to think. Where were that many vehicles going? *Is it a decoy?* Cal wasn't sure how many men Ponder had. The whole thing was one big guessing game.

"Let's get down there fast, Daniel."

The sniper nodded and motioned for the rest of the men to get up and move out.

Cal did something at that moment that he rarely did. He said a silent prayer. *God, please tell me that Neil is still down there.* When no response came, Cal got back into his position in the moving formation. Time was working against them.

GRAND TETON MOUNTAIN RANGE, WYOMING

1:04AM, SEPTEMBER 29TH

"We're over the objective, Trav," Cowboy announced over the C-130's loudspeaker.

Travis stood up and walked to the cockpit. Keeping his promise, Cowboy's friends on the ground had made quick work of the refueling. Most were combat vets and highly experienced in getting planes back over the battlefield, posthaste.

"How's the visibility?" Travis asked.

"The snow gods must be on our side this morning. Believe it or not, I think it's clearing up."

"That's a relief."

"Now, I'm not saying it's gonna be like a sunny day on the beach, Trav. Your drop is still gonna be hella dangerous."

"You just worry about getting us over the target. We'll let our GPS guide us in."

Cowboy nodded and downed the rest of his third Red Bull. "You wanna stay up here while I get the video feed up?"

"Yeah."

"Give Lieutenant Granes over there a second, and he'll let you take a look."

Cowboy's co-pilot fiddled with his instruments, then looked up.

"I think we've got some tangos down there, Captain."

Travis moved over for a better look. The co-pilot had the aircraft's thermal imaging running.

"Tell me what you see, Mr. Haden," said Lt. Granes.

It took Travis a second to take the picture in.

"That looks like a convoy of some kind. Wait, up on this mountain?"

Lt. Granes nodded. "I make twelve or thirteen small vehicles, or snowmobiles considering the terrain."

"They look like they're going pretty damn fast," Travis observed. "Are they chasing something?" He asked in alarm.

"Let me see." Lt. Granes panned the camera in the direction of the convoy's movement. Seconds later, he zeroed in on a smaller group of three vehicles. "A hundred bucks says that's what the others are after."

"Shit. I wish I knew who the hell they are."

"Who who is?" Todd Dunn asked from over his shoulder. None of the men in the cockpit had realized he'd walked up behind them.

"We've got two groups of snowmobiles down there. It looks like the larger group is chasing the smaller group," said Travis.

"How large and how small?" Dunn asked.

"Thirteen in the big one and three in the smaller."

"Any thoughts?"

"I hope to hell it's Cal in the larger group."

No one answered as they all digested the situation.

Dunn spoke first. "Captain Jennings, do you think you can find a spot ahead of that first group to drop in?"

Cowboy scrolled through his mapping system before replying. "Yeah, I think this'll be as good a spot as any." He tapped the screen to indicate the new drop zone.

"Skipper, have you tried calling Cal again?" Dunn asked.

"Fuck! I completely forgot." Travis hurried to pull the satellite phone out of his cargo pocket. "I've got a signal."

Travis redialed the Cal's phone. Cal picked up on the third ring.

"Trav?" Cal sounded out of breath.

Travis cut right to the chase. "Cal, are you guys on those snowmobiles?"

"Say again? I can barely hear you. My signal sucks down here."

Travis spoke more slowly. "I said, are you on those snowmobiles?"

"No. We just saw them leave from Ponder's place. Ten to fifteen of them, right?"

"So you saw both groups leave?"

"Both groups?"

"Yeah. It looks like the group of thirteen might be trying to catch up with another three," described Travis.

"No. We only saw the one group. Shit, Trav. You don't think they're taking Neil out do you?"

"I don't know, Cuz."

"Wait, are you looking down via satellite?"

"Uh-uh. We're circling overhead in a C-130."

"No shit?"

"No shit."

"Well that changes the game. We're getting close to Ponder's hideout. Do you have enough guys to handle the vehicles while we check out the compound?"

"I think that can be arranged." Travis looked at Dunn who hurried to the troop space to prep their men. "How are you boys doing?"

"I'm a little dinged up but okay."

"You wanna tell me about it now?"

"No. Let me get off the phone so we can start moving. With any luck, Ponder took a few guys with him. Maybe we'll just have to mop things up and leave the real fun to you guys. Are you jumping in?"

"Yeah."

Cal laughed. "You sure your old ass is still up for it? I've been meaning to talk to you about your expanding waistline."

"Fuck you, Cal," Travis said, not without affection. If anything, Travis Haden was more fit than he had been with the SEAL teams. "You call me when you get done, okay?"

"Yes, Dad. Stokes, out."

Travis looked down at the sat phone. Despite the risk, he realized that he'd really missed the fun of being in the field. He turned back to Cowboy. "I'll head back to get suited up." Travis joined his men, a little more swagger in his step than he'd had for years. *To battle.*

CAL WAS NOW able to communicate with Trent and Brian's team. They'd made better time and were even now approaching the main entrance to Ponder's stronghold. Cal was close enough, and the weather had cleared so he could just make out their forms slowly maneuvering into position. He watched the breach team approach the large steel doors.

He was able to raise Brian on his satellite phone.

"The breach team is checking out the front door," Brian described.

"Yeah, I'm watching right now. No bad guys on the way in?"

"Nope. You?"

"No bad guys. I think they're headed down the mountain chasing someone else."

"How do you know that?" Brian asked.

"Trav's playing guardian angel in a C-130 overhead."

"Holy shit!"

"Yep."

"Hey, I think I see you guys. Wave to me."

Cal waved to the other group and Brian waved back. Just as Cal went to sign off from the call, Brian's waving form disappeared in an enormous explosion.

The sound and shockwave swept over his team as Cal screamed for his friends.

"WHAT THE FUCK WAS THAT?" Lt. Granes asked out loud. He'd been monitoring the progress not only of the two groups of snowmobiles but also of Cal's two teams.

"What?" asked Cowboy.

"I think there was just a huge explosion right where the good guys were going."

"Don't just sit there, Granes. Go get Haden!"

Lt. Granes hurried to find Travis.

Seconds later, Travis, fully outfitted for the jump, rushed awkwardly into the cockpit.

"What's going on?" he asked.

"Granes says there was an explosion on your objective. Did your cousin bring a whole lot of C4 with him?"

"No. Let me try to get him on the line. How long until we drop?"

"Under two minutes."

"Okay."

Travis dialed Cal's number. There was no answer. He tried again. Nothing.

"Shit. I can't get him."

"Maybe it's just the weather again," Cowboy offered.

"I hope so."

Travis knew there wasn't anything he could do about Cal's team. He had to focus on stopping the snowmobiles.

GLANCING AT HIS WRISTWATCH, Ponder smiled. One of the precautions he'd taken while building his compound was to rig it with enough explosives to knock down a skyscraper. He'd learned the trick from a drug kingpin in Mexico City. The man had described how each one of his safe houses, warehouses and labs was rigged for complete destruction. When the drug lord told Ponder how much it cost, he was pleasantly surprised and filed it away until his own construction began. He'd done the explosives installation himself with the help of some tips he found online on various demolition how-to sites. The cost was minimal and it gave Ponder an added layer of security should his enemies or the authorities show up.

It'd been an easy choice to set the timer. His cover was blown either way. Nick Ponder would never be coming back to Battleship Mountain. The small pack strapped to his back contained the currency and valuables that Benjamin had given him earlier. It would be enough to help him should the need arise. Ponder grinned again, hoping that some of his enemies had been consumed in the blast. The sadistic mercenary only wished he could've watched.

AT LEAST FOUR of his men were dead including Brian Ramirez. MSgt Trent was badly wounded and unconscious. Gaucho was doing his best to stem the Marine's blood flow. More men were strewn about tending to their wounds.

Cal shook his head in denial as he searched the rubble. The explosion had effectively halved his force and collapsed the entire complex. There was nothing to find. The only reason they'd found anyone was that the blast had blown them all away from the entrance.

TRAVIS WAS SHUFFLING to the open rear end of the C-130 when his phone buzzed. He looked down and saw that Cal was calling. *Shit.* He knew Cal would have to wait. Travis's force had its own mission.

He lowered his night vision goggles and jumped into the darkness.

BENJAMIN HAD TIMED the extraction perfectly. On their journey up, his men had staged additional gear as a precaution. They'd just reached the weapons cache and were taking ambush positions. Their kill zone set, Benjamin waited for Ponder to fall into his trap.

TODD DUNN HAD BEEN the first man out of the aircraft. He and his troops were now floating down through the early morning darkness.

The plan was to land in front of the smaller group of snowmobiles and set up a hasty ambush. Travis hoped that a couple well-placed shots could disable the lead vehicle long enough for them to find out who they were dealing with.

He gazed down through the blackness with his NVGs. *It looks like they've stopped,* Dunn noted. *At least that'll make our timing easier.*

The rest of the SSI operators were cuing off of his descent. It would've been harder to ensure a smooth insertion with moving hostiles. This way they might have a little more time to stage themselves on the ground.

Thank God the damn weather died down, Dunn thought. *The last thing we need is casualties before we fight.*

He watched as the scene unfolded below. It looked like the group was getting off of their vehicles. *What the hell?*

Turning back to the business of insertion, Dunn checked his GPS one last time and prepped for landing.

They'd just rounded a bend when Ponder saw the telltale flash of incoming projectiles. He barely had time to swerve left before a small rocket crashed into the snowmobile next to him. Ponder struggled to stay on his own vehicle but was finally thrown off when he slammed into a large boulder. His body somehow flew over the rock instead of hitting it. The last thing he heard before he slammed into the creek bed was the repeated explosions of more rockets annihilating his forces.

Benjamin smiled grimly as his assassins sent round after round from their shoulder-fired weapons. They'd been a last minute purchase from a Russian arms dealer before leaving Pakistan. Rather than having to rely on accurate aim, the smaller projectiles were, in fact, mini-missiles with heat-seeking capability. The Russian had said that even his dead grandmother could've pulled the trigger and demolished an enemy target. He had not exaggerated. Benjamin made a mental note to thank the Russian and put in a larger order for their next operation.

He signaled for his men to stop firing. Cradling his AK-47, Benjamin approached the wreckage. After quickly dispatching the few wounded survivors, he turned back and ordered his men to get back on their vehicles.

Benjamin took one last look at the carnage and smiled. *Stupid Americans.*

PONDER PEEKED out from his hiding spot. He winced from the pain of his dislocated shoulder. There were no tears shed as Ponder watched Benjamin kill his men, only seething anger. *I don't care how or when, but I'm gonna kill that fucker.*

He slunk back further and waited for his enemy to leave.

GRAND TETON MOUNTAIN RANGE, WYOMING

1:53AM, SEPTEMBER 29TH

Cowboy had readily agreed to stay on-station for as long as he could. His ability to view the battlefield from the air gave the SSI warriors a distinct advantage. He keyed up Travis to give him the latest intel.

"What have you got?" Travis asked.

"Looks like the smaller group just took out the bigger group. Granes said one of the fuckers actually walked around cleaning up the survivors of the ambush. I think we can safely assume that they're bad guys too."

Travis grunted. At least there would be less of an enemy to confront.

"Are they on their way?"

"Yeah. They're heading straight for you."

"Roger, out."

Cowboy shook his head. The last thing he'd expected to see on his training tour was a full-out battle on American soil. *I might have to stick around these SSI boys*, mused the mustachioed pilot.

The snowmobiles were just coming into view.

"Take out the lead vehicle," Travis whispered to the sniper lying next to him.

The expert killer took one last breath and pulled the trigger of his Barrett M107.50 Caliber rifle. Travelling at over 2,800 feet per second, the bullet pierced the lead vehicle's engine and the vehicle sputtered to a stop. A second later, the small convoy stopped right where Travis had wanted. The SSI operators quickly surrounded the three vehicles.

"Drop your weapons!" Dunn commanded.

None of the masked riders complied.

"I said drop your weapons!"

Without warning, one of the snowmobiles gunned its engine and sped off around the others. Travis noted that it was the only one towing some sort of elongated sled. As if on cue, the rest of the riders moved to fire their weapons at Travis's men. The SSI team didn't hesitate. Before the Pakistanis could fire, each man already had an excess of twenty rounds in them.

Travis turned to the sniper who'd stayed next to him in the fray.

"You think you can take out that snowmobile that took off?" asked Travis

"I'll try."

Through his Leupold scope, the sniper tried to find his target in the darkness. In daylight or properly set up, it might've been an easy shot. With darkness limiting his scope's night vision enhanced range, he would be much less accurate. To make matters worse, whoever was driving the thing knew how to maneuver to avoid being shot.

Travis's sniper exhaled and pulled the trigger.

"Hit," he announced, continuing to look through his scope. Despite being hit, the vehicle was still moving. Just as he lined up for another shot, the enemy disappeared into the night.

"What happened?" asked Travis.

"I hit the damn thing, sir, but it's still moving."

"It's okay, O'Brian. We'll have the C-130 keep tabs on it."

Travis went to key his headset when the sniper added, "I think I detached that sled it was pulling, sir."

Travis looked up. "Let's go take a look."

He turned to find that Dunn was approaching. "O'Brian said he might've knocked that sled thing off. You wanna come take a look with me?"

"Sure."

"Can we borrow that last snowmobile?"

"Negative, Skipper. I just checked and it's dead. We must've hit it when we took the bad guys out."

"Then I guess we're huffin' it. Let's grab a couple guys and go."

Dunn nodded and went to fetch some men.

I wonder where the hell Neil is, thought Travis, as he waited.

BENJAMIN CURSED his luck as he pushed the crippled snowmobile to its limit. Not only had he and his men been ambushed themselves, somehow whoever had attacked them had managed to shoot the hitch connecting the vehicle to the sled holding his masters' prize.

There was nothing he could do now. Benjamin put his head down and continued his reckless retreat down the mountain.

THEY APPROACHED the long sled with weapons drawn.

"What do you think's in there?" asked Dunn.

Travis shrugged and stepped up beside it. He examined the exterior and noted that there looked to be some kind of tank strapped to its side. *Oxygen?* he wondered.

Once he determined that the contraption wasn't booby trapped, he unhooked the metal latches holding the metal lid. A hiss escaped as the seal cracked open and warm air whooshed out into the winter cold. Travis carefully lifted the lid and peered in.

"Holy shit! It's Neil!"

GRAND TETON MOUNTAIN RANGE, WYOMING

3:35AM, SEPTEMBER 29TH

Cowboy reported that the only remaining snowmobile had disappeared. With the still unconscious Neil in their possession, Travis had turned his mind back to Cal's team. He'd established variable communication with his cousin and received the news of the team's casualties. Before the connection broke off, Dunn had their men fully ready to head up to Battleship Mountain. They would take turns pulling Neil's sled with a hastily made set of double harnesses. No one complained as they marched through the deep snow.

Upon arriving at Cal's location, Travis took in the devastation. The destruction of Ponder's hideaway was complete.

"How's Trent?"

"He'll live," answered Cal.

Travis could see that his cousin was taking the loss of life hard. He knew the feeling. The former SEAL had lost a lot of friends since 9-11.

"They all knew the danger, Cal." Travis tried to put a comforting hand on his cousin's shoulder, but Cal shrugged it off.

"Did you find Ponder?" asked Cal.

"No. We did a quick search of both groups but he wasn't among the dead."

"So he got away," Cal murmured to the mountain.

"Looks like it."

"Good."

"What are you talking about?" asked Travis.

"That means I can find him...and kill him."

QUETTA, BALOCHISTAN PROVINCE, PAKISTAN

11:49PM, OCTOBER 2ND

Nick Ponder stumbled into his shabby hotel suite, a Chinese hooker under one arm and a half a case of beer under the other. The suite was surprisingly spacious for the price and the location. He closed the door and shoved the beer into the hooker's hands.

"Why don't you go throw those in the cooler I've got in the bedroom. I'm gonna go take a leak, and I'll meet you in there in a minute."

"Any'ting you wan, big man," answered the prostitute in heavily accented English.

He patted her on the rear, then headed for the bathroom. After relieving himself and rinsing off in the shower, he padded toward the bedroom with a towel wrapped around his waist.

Ponder stopped at the doorway. The light was off. He smiled lustily. *Nothing against Chinks, but I'd rather have the lights off anyway*, he thought.

"You in there, honey?" Ponder asked almost sweetly. It had been a while since he'd gotten laid and his member was already rising to the challenge. There was no answer from the bedroom. Maybe this one liked to play games.

He fumbled for the light switch so he wouldn't trip over the mess he'd left in the room. Through his drunken haze, he remembered that the only light in the room came from a lamp on the bedside table.

"Shit," mumbled Ponder, as he tripped over one of his canvas bags on his way to find the lamp. *Sure would've been easier if she'd left it on, dammit.*

Just as he reached under the lamp shade something came crashing down on the back of his head.

Ponder's head was pounding. He struggled to open his eyes through the searing pain. *What the fuck happened?* A moment later, he realized he couldn't move his arms or legs. Panicking, he forced his eyes open. It took a second for his vision to focus.

He was lying on his back looking up at the ceiling. Ponder looked left and right and saw that someone had strapped him to the bed.

Someone dressed in traditional Pakistani robes walked into view. The person's face was covered with material from a black headdress.

"Who the fuck are you?" Ponder croaked.

The robed figure unwrapped the headdress and stared down at him. Ponder looked back in complete shock.

"You were expecting someone else?" Cal asked.

Ponder couldn't find the words to speak. He'd used every ounce of his skill to cover his tracks.

"I'll bet you're wondering how I found you." Cal smiled and turned toward the living room. "Why don't you come in here, Neil?"

Neil Patel walked gingerly on a new prosthetic device. Assisting him was the blond-haired sniper, Daniel Briggs. Nick Ponder's mind screamed. He was in Pakistan tracking down that damn Benjamin. He'd hoped to somehow kill the Pakistani and re-kidnap Patel. It looked like the double-crossing raghead had lost his prisoner too.

"Double surprise, Nick. I'll bet you thought your buyers had Neil hard at work by now," said Cal.

"How?" Ponder managed to ask.

Now it was Neil's turn to grin. "While you had me shutting down that power plant, I planted a program on your server. It not only infected and tracked that computer, but it also sent all the information about everything you hold electronically back to our servers in Tennessee. The minute I had access to my laptop we started tracking you. We've been reading every email you've sent and listening to every phone call you've made."

"Not too bad, huh?" Cal asked. "We figured you might be coming to get your money back from the Pakistanis. It would've been easy to take you at any time, but 'ol Snake Eyes over there," Cal nodded toward Daniel, "thought we should wait and see how your investigation progressed."

When Ponder didn't respond, Cal continued. "Nick, now you're gonna tell us what you found out at your whorehouse meeting."

Ponder felt like a fool. Already disgraced and dead broke, tomorrow was supposed to be his chance for payback. Not even a week before, he'd been so sure of himself. He was supposed to be on some exotic beach drinking all day and screwing all night. Now he didn't know what to say. Ponder shook the helpless feeling away. His confidence returned when he remembered that he was dealing with Goody-Two-Shoes-Stokes' son. They might rough him up a bit, but he'd been through worse.

"You can go fuck yourself, jarhead." Ponder grinned at his comment.

Cal shook his head. "Go get Higgins."

Daniel left the room to make the call to the battered van on the street below. Two minutes later, Dr. Higgins walked into the bedroom with a leather medical bag.

As with the FBI agent and the traitor, Ponder talked soon after the drugs took hold. Cal now had Benjamin's location. He'd instructed Higgins to administer the reversal drug that would bring Ponder back to normal awareness. Dr. Higgins nodded to Cal when he felt Ponder was back to his old self.

"Thanks for your help, Doc."

"Anytime, Calvin. I'll be in the van."

Higgins left, surrounded by four robed SSI security staff.

Cal turned back to his prisoner. "Well, Nick, now that we have what we need, we don't need you anymore."

"What are you gonna do, kill me?" Ponder laughed.

Cal stared back, unblinking. Instead of responding, he pulled out a pistol with a suppressor screwed onto the barrel and stepped up to the bed.

"Come on, man. I'm sure we can work something out," Ponder offered.

"We have Neil, the money, and the buyer's location. Tell me what you might possibly have to offer, Nick."

The comment shook Ponder's bravado.

"You have the money?" he asked.

"Oh, didn't we mention that? Because Benjamin had Neil use your computer, we easily tracked the money and took it. So you see, Nick, we don't need you anymore."

Ponder's eyes went wide, his mind finally comprehending the danger. He'd underestimated the Marine's ruthlessness. Before he could respond, Cal extended the pistol and fired two rounds into Nick Ponder's face.

"That was for Brian."

HANNA LAKE, BALOCHISTAN PROVINCE, PAKISTAN

6:37AM, OCTOBER 2ND

Benjamin relished his early morning rowing on the nearly empty lake. Rowing was a passion he'd picked up while studying at Oxford University nearly twenty years ago. He didn't like much about the Brits, but he appreciated their love of history and sports like cricket and rowing.

After being on the lake for close to an hour, he had worked up a good sweat. In a country where physical fitness was uncommon, Benjamin was a rarity. He never overindulged and, unlike the majority of his countrymen, Benjamin never smoked. His lithe body was a testament to his dedication. There was always the occasional newcomer that would laugh about his workout routine, but that reaction was always their last. The jokester quickly learned that Benjamin's physique was the least of his worries. There was a reason he'd become one of Pakistan's leading terrorists.

This morning's row was especially important because it gave him time to think. His current predicament was aggravating, but did little to unnerve the unflappable assassin. Not only had he lost his entire team, he'd also lost Neil Patel. The only satisfaction he'd received after the berating from his masters was finding out that someone had apparently stolen all the money the Pakistanis had stolen back from Ponder. Luckily, Benjamin had nothing to do with the technological aspect of the operation. Some poor Pakistani geek was probably already dead for failing to protect their masters' funds.

A plan was starting to form in his head as he pulled his racing shell up to the small dock. Standing up, one of his bodyguards handed Benjamin a towel.

"Any phone calls?" asked Benjamin.

"No, sir."

"Good. Pull the car around. I want to go home."

His three bodyguards trotted off down the road while Benjamin finished drying himself with the towel. Throwing on an Adidas windbreaker to ward off the chill, he stretched as he waited, still mulling over his options. The master terrorist still didn't know who had stolen the funds and where Neil Patel had ended up. It bothered Benjamin that a new enemy had somehow ambushed him and probably ended up with Patel. None of the feelers he'd put out had yet to find any of the information he needed.

Benjamin finished his stretches and wondered what was taking his men so long. They'd parked just up the road. He decided to walk down the road and meet them on the way.

After a minute of walking, the car still hadn't come his way. Benjamin cursed himself for not having a weapon. He was getting too lax in his supposedly safe surroundings. Coming around a bend, he spotted the armored black Audi A8 parked on the side of the road. He could hear the smooth engine purring. *What are those fools doing?*

Because the vehicle had blacked out windows, Benjamin couldn't see inside. Moving cautiously around the vehicle, he made his way to the passenger side. *I'll kill these idiots if they're looking at porn again.*

He'd been forced to find new bodyguards after losing his most loyal men days before. Reaching out a hand, Benjamin went to open the rear passenger-side door.

"Hello, Benjamin," said a voice in English.

The Pakistani whipped around, dropping into a protective crouch as he spun. Standing with his hands casually pointing a rifle at him was a man with brown hair and a sly grin. He'd apparently materialized from the tree line next to the road.

"Who are you?" Benjamin asked.

"I'm surprised you don't know, Benjamin."

He stared at the man dubiously.

"I assure you that I have no idea. It seems that you have the upper hand."

The man nodded. "That's true."

"If you know who I am, I can also assume that you know I am a man not to be trifled with. My men will be here any second."

The stranger laughed as if he were the only one privy to a secret joke.

"I'm afraid your men won't be coming to your rescue, Benjamin."

Benjamin's eyes narrowed.

"Go ahead and take a look in the car."

"Are they dead?"

The man shrugged. A chill ran down Benjamin's spine. *How did he get to my men?* This was his territory. He owned every roadblock and soldier in the area.

It would be unfair to say that the terrorist was afraid. He'd been in too many battles to be frightened by death. It would be accurate to say that Benjamin was concerned. No one had ever gotten this close to him in nearly twenty years. He still bore the scars from the interrogation he'd received at the hands of the Pakistani Intelligence Service.

"How did you do it?" asked Benjamin, now casually leaning back against the sedan.

"It turns out the big wigs in your capital don't like you much. Sounds like you've been a thorn in their side for years. They were more than happy to give us safe passage. That, plus a little cash went a long way."

"So you're here to kill me."

"Not me."

"Who then?"

The young man motioned to the tree line behind him. Benjamin looked and saw a figure emerge. His eyes went wide as the second man limped out.

"Surprised to see me, Benjamin?" asked Neil, as he stepped up next to Cal. He stood with obvious discomfort on a new prosthetic. Neil held a pistol in his right hand.

Benjamin shook his head in disbelief. He could not believe that his countrymen would sell him out to the Americans. After all he'd done for them.

"I supposed there is no way out of this," he asked.

Neil took a second to respond. "I can think of one way."

Benjamin couldn't hide his surprise. "And what would that be?"

"Apologize for my parents," growled Neil, tears coming to his eyes as he spoke.

Would it really be that easy? *These Americans are all alike. Weak*, thought Benjamin.

"Very well," Benjamin shrugged. "I apolo..."

Before he could finish the word, Neil raised the suppressed weapon and pulled the trigger twice. The rounds blasted into Benjamin's chest. He slid down the side of the car and ended up on his ass, clutching his wounds.

Neil limped over to the dying terrorist, his pistol never leaving its target. Benjamin looked up at his enemy in pain.

"Apology not accepted," said Neil.

Before Benjamin could utter another word, Neil fired a single round into his head.

THE LODGE, CAMP SPARTAN, ARRINGTON, TN

1:35PM, OCTOBER 5TH

Cal, Neil, Daniel, Travis, Trent, Gaucho and Dunn sat in the weathered leather chairs of the VIP lounge. Each man held a full glass of Tennessee whiskey. They'd just returned from a whirlwind of funerals for their men killed in Wyoming, including Lance. It had been a sobering journey for each of the assembled seven.

MSgt Trent raised his good arm, the other still in a sling, and called a toast. "To the brave men who have gone before us."

Every man raised a glass in silent salute and took a heavy pull from their whiskey.

Cal stared into his glass, thinking about his lost friend Brian Ramirez. He couldn't get the picture of Brian's weeping parents out of his head. They'd hugged him like he was family when, in fact, he'd never met them before.

"Brian told us how much he loved his new friends. He spoke of you often, Cal, and considered you a brother," Mrs. Ramirez had said between sobs. He'd held her and wept, the pain finally pouring out over the loss of his friend.

They'd exacted revenge on Ponder and the Pakistani terrorists.

There was no one left to kill. It was the inner demons that would take time to fade. Like every man in the room, Cal had lost friends before. He knew there was a grieving process. Cal felt that it got harder with age. Maybe it was a finer sense of one's own mortality and an understanding of the fragility of life.

The bartender, a crusty old Marine Sergeant Major, woke Cal from his reverie.

"Can I get you boys another?"

Everyone looked to Cal for a cue. For some reason he couldn't explain that despite the deadly rescue in Wyoming, every man in the room, including Travis and Dunn, now looked to Cal as their commander. It felt strange, but his years in the Marine Corps had showed him that even the lowliest Marine could be elevated in status through his actions on the battlefield. Unbeknownst to him, Cal's swift tracking and killing of Ponder and Benjamin had cemented him as their leader. In their eyes, Cal was his father's son.

"I think I'll finish this and take one for the road, Sergeant Major," answered Cal. The others nodded in agreement and quietly went back to finishing their drinks. They would talk later.

After receiving their refills, the men said their goodbyes and left to get some much-needed rest. Travis followed Cal to the elevators.

"Can I do anything for you, Cal?"

"I'm okay. I think I'll just get some rack time and then get back to work tomorrow."

"Why don't you take a few days off? There's nothing that can't wait."

Cal shook his head. "I need to stay busy right now, Trav. I'll go stir-crazy if I take time off."

Travis understood. He knew the pain his cousin was feeling.

"Fair enough. Why don't we grab breakfast tomorrow morning and then we'll come up with a game plan."

"Sound good."

Cal stepped into the elevator as Travis paused to answer his cell phone. He motioned for Cal to go up without him.

Cal pressed the button for the second level and waited for the doors to close. Just before they slid shut, Travis's hand stuck in and bumped the doors back open. His face had gone serious.

"What's up?" Cal asked.

Travis extended his cell phone to Cal. "It's the President."

I hope you enjoyed these stories.
If you did, please take a moment to write a review <u>on Amazon.</u>
Even the short ones help!

Want to stay in the loop?
Sign Up to be the FIRST to learn about new releases.
Plus get newsletter only bonus content for FREE.
Click here to sign up or visit cg-cooper.com.

Come join my private network at TeamCGCooper.com.

A portion of all profits from the sale of my novels goes to fund OPERATION C4, our nonprofit initiative serving young military officers. For more information visit OperationC4.com.

ALSO BY C. G. COOPER

The Corps Justice Series In Order:

Corps Justice (Originally Titled "Back to War")

Council Of Patriots

Prime Asset

Presidential Shift

National Burden

Lethal Misconduct

Moral Imperative

Disavowed

Chain Of Command

Papal Justice

The Zimmer Doctrine

Sabotage

Liberty Down

Sins Of The Father

A Darker Path

The Man From Belarus

Matters of State

Corps Justice Short Stories:

Chosen

God-Speed

Running

The Daniel Briggs Novels:

Adrift

Fallen

Broken

Tested

The Tom Greer Novels
A Life Worth Taking

Blood of My Kin

Stand Alone Novels
To Live

The Warden's Son

The Interrogators
Higgins

The Spy In Residence Novels
What Lies Hidden

The Alex Knight Novels
Breakout

The Stars & Spies Series:
Backdrop

The Patriot Protocol Series:
The Patriot Protocol

The Chronicles of Benjamin Dragon:
Benjamin Dragon – Awakening

Benjamin Dragon – Legacy

Benjamin Dragon - Genesis

ABOUT THE AUTHOR

C. G. Cooper is the USA TODAY and AMAZON BESTSELLING author of the CORPS JUSTICE novels, several spinoffs and a growing number of stand-alone novels.

One of his novels, CHAIN OF COMMAND, won the 2020 James Webb Award presented by the Marine Heritage Foundation for its portrayal of the United States Marine Corps in fiction. Cooper doesn't chase awards, but this one was special.

Cooper grew up in a Navy family and traveled from one Naval base to another as he fed his love of books and a fledgling desire to write.

Upon graduating from the University of Virginia with a degree in Foreign Affairs, Cooper was commissioned in the United States

Marine Corps and went on to serve six years as an infantry officer. C. G. Cooper's final Marine duty station was in Nashville, Tennessee, where he fell in love with the laid-back lifestyle of Music City.

His first published novel, BACK TO WAR, came out of a need to link back to his time in the Marine Corps. That novel, written as a side project, spawned many follow-on novels, several exciting spinoffs, and catapulted Cooper's career.

Cooper lives just south of Nashville with his wife, three children, and their German shorthaired pointer, Liberty, who's become a popular character in the Corps Justice novels.

When he's not writing or hosting his podcast, Books In 30, Cooper spends time with his family, does his best to improve his golf handicap, and loves to shed light on the ongoing fight of everyday heroes.

Cooper loves hearing from readers and responds to every email personally.
To connect with C. G. Cooper visit
www.cg-cooper.com

FOR YOU

Dear Reader,

Here's something a little different.

I know life isn't perfect. We all get good days and bad. What I've learned from personal experience is that walking through life with friends sure is easier than doing it alone. So...

If you're having a bad day, if life keeps kicking you around, or if you just want a long distance hug, please call me: **615-268-8731**.

If I don't pick up, please leave a message and I promise to call you back. Because no one on Team Cooper should ever feel alone. No one.

Thanks for being an important part of this **wonderful** life.

- C. G. Cooper

Printed in Great Britain
by Amazon